W9-BSV-194

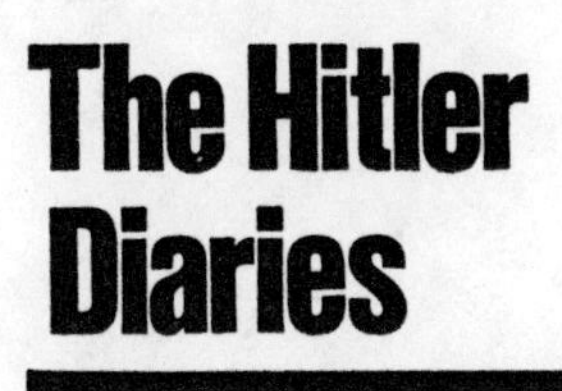
The Hitler
Diaries

The Hitler Diaries

Richard Hugo

WILLIAM MORROW AND COMPANY, INC.
New York / 1983

Originally published in Great Britain in 1982 by Macmillan London Limited.

Library of Congress Cataloging in Publication Data

Hugo, Richard F.
The Hitler diaries.

I. Title.
PS3515.U3H5 1983 813'.54 82-14350
ISBN 0-688-01546-8

Printed in the United States of America

FIRST U.S. EDITION

1 2 3 4 5 6 7 8 9 10

'Frederick the Great too sometimes felt that he must doubt his lucky star, but, as generally happens in history, at the darkest hour a bright star arose and Prussia was saved when he had almost given up all hope. Why should not we also hope for a similar wonderful turn of fortune?'

Dr Josef Goebbels, 23 March 1945

'If you want to live and thrive
Let a spider run alive.'

Traditional English nursery rhyme

The Hitler Diaries

One

At the age of seventy there is something intensely pleasurable in having a naked girl walk across the small of one's back. At all events, that was the view of Norman Cavendish, who, being seventy and having at that moment a young woman performing that function, felt that he was in a position to know.

'Gabrielle – a little more over the shoulders, please.' A thin voice with a polished accent, a touch petulant.

The girl laughed. She hopped on to one foot, curling her toes into the soft nap of the towel she was standing on and drew the other foot like a touch of breath up the old man's spine until it nestled in the cavity between the shoulder-blades, where the toes could play among the flaccid muscles. The old man sighed.

'Is that all right?'

'Marvellous, my dear.'

The toes danced on the flesh. The old man thought to himself that the sensuous capacity of the skin of the back was much underrated by physiologists. The girl gazed, bored and dreamily, into the heat haze and brushed a strand of hair from her eyes.

The land stretched out northwards, gentle chalk hills rolling towards the Garonne; the air heavy with heat and dust; the sky an irridescent blue. Swallows caracoled after insects; silence except for the dull throb of a tractor motor. In the vineyard Gabrielle watched the machine at work, a strange contraption raised on stilts so that it could straddle the rows of vines like a giant crab.

'Patience, my dear. I'm sure that they will arrive. All in good time.' The old man tapped her leg with his bony finger and she moved her foot. He rolled on to his back and gestured towards a glass. 'Another drink – please.' A wheedling note in the voice suggested that she could refuse to obey and therefore had to be coaxed. 'Do let me have another one and I promise that it shall be my last – for the time being.'

Gabrielle yawned, looked down at the old man and smiled. 'Dr Bouchard says . . .' She reached for the bottle and poured a stream of golden liquid into the glass.

'Dr Bouchard is a fool.'

'As you wish.' She replaced the bottle on the wrought-iron table. 'As for looking forward to your new – guests,' she said languidly, 'not at all.' She looked blankly towards the horizon where a yellow motor-car crept along the distant road. 'In fact I think they're here already.' She indicated the skyline. The old man did not bother to look up. He brushed a fly from the sparse grey hairs of his chest and rolled on to his belly.

'In that case, wake me up when they arrive. If, indeed, it is them.'

The ancient *deux-chevaux* turned off the highway on to the unmetalled road leading to the château, its springs creaking and swaying as the driver negotiated the ruts and shallow bends along the avenue of poplars. At the top of the knoll, the main house was visible through a fretwork of trees, an ochre-washed building with peeling shutters at the windows, a tiled roof and turrets at each of the corners. It was surrounded by a grassed ditch bordered by a hedge. A small château, typical of that part of France.

'This looks like it,' the driver said firmly. He pulled the car to a halt as the man on the tractor, a middle-aged peasant in black beret and faded shirt, jumped from his machine and ran into the roadway waving his arms and jabbering away in French.

The driver stuck a head of shaggy, black hair out of the window and asked, 'What do you want, sunshine? I don't parlez the old français.'

'I'll deal with him, Arthur,' the passenger said. He stood up so that he was above the roof of the car, a tall, fair-haired figure with long-headed, open-faced good looks. 'What do you want?' he asked in French. 'We're here to see Monsieur Cavendish.'

The workman stopped, catching his breath, and continued in his own language. 'You are . . . the two Englishmen . . . that are expected?'

'I don't imagine you're expecting any more.'

The Frenchman took off his beret and wiped his face with it. 'No, no – you must be them. Please, follow me.'

The one called Arthur tapped the door of the car. 'What about this then?' The Frenchman, recognizing the gesture, said in halting English, 'Follow me. Bring the car.'

The driver shrugged his shoulders and turned on the engine. The car lurched forward at a crawl after the shambling figure. 'This'll ruin the bloody clutch!' he muttered.

The drive ended in a small, gravelled circle. A bridge, framed by a pair of limes, led over the dry moat. The two Englishmen got out of the car.

'*Vous avez des fusils?*' the Frenchman asked. He planted himself in front of the two men and looked them up and down.

'What's he after now, Frank?' the driver asked.

'He wants to know whether we have any guns.'

'Guns?' A laugh. 'Ask him what the bloody hell we would be doing with guns? We're invited guests, aren't we?'

'*Nous n'avons pas de fusils*,' his companion said.

The Frenchman nodded. He took a step forward, stared into the eyes of the driver and raised his hands to search the Englishman's denim jacket. A hand swept up and grabbed the Frenchman's wrist and a pair of cold, green eyes bore down the other man's gaze.

'Leave it, Arthur.' The passenger tapped his companion's hand. 'Let him search you. We've got nothing to hide.'

The grip on the Frenchman's wrist relaxed. 'Go on – search me then,' the Englishman said softly and smiled. 'Fuckin' French git.'

The other man ignored the insult. He ran his hands quickly and expertly over the Englishman's clothing, finding nothing. The fair-haired passenger stepped forward and allowed the process to be repeated. The Frenchman pronounced himself satisfied and beckoned them on. They followed him across the bridge. The path led to a large oak door between a pair of classical columns, but their guide turned off the path and led them by the side of the house across a border of turf.

'Nice place,' the fair-haired man said. He walked easily, casting his eyes about to admire the surroundings. He was wearing a tweed sports jacket, open-necked shirt, silk cravat and twill trousers in a gentlemanly contrast to his companion.

'Oh yeah. Bloody marvellous!'

They turned the corner by one of the towers on to an expanse of lawn leading to a swimming-pool. In the middle of the lawn, by a table, an old man lay naked on a towel. Next to him a bronzed female wearing nothing but a pair of briefs and an *ankh* talisman stood nursing a glass of wine. The hand holding the glass cast a dark shadow across her breasts.

Their guide indicated that they were to wait. The two men paused whilst he ambled across the grass, stopped and whispered something into the ear of the reclining figure.

'Show them over!' the old man said cheerfully and raised his hand in greeting. The Frenchman headed back.

'It's okay,' the man called Arthur said. 'That bit I understood.' He walked towards the old man and smiled at the girl.

'Now you will be . . .?'

'Francis Lethbridge and Arthur Harrison,' the fair-haired man said.

'Francis and Arthur . . . I must try to remember the names from the start if we're all to get on together.' The old man got off the towel and began to tie it dhoti fashion around his loins. 'My name is Cavendish – Norman Cavendish – but then, I suppose you know that already.' He shook hands in turn with both men. 'This' – indicating the girl – 'is Gabrielle . . . and that old fool is Henri. You'll get to know them both better.'

The ertswhile guide, Henri, wiped his hands on his trousers, forced his face into a grimace and offered his hand to the visitors. The girl stayed where she was but inclined her head in recognition. She gave them a smile of unconscious sexuality; the sort she gave every man without realizing it. Harrison looked at his friend and raised an eyebrow.

'Is the body-search standard procedure?' Lethbridge sounded unconcerned.

'That? Well, I suppose it is – although it's Henri's doing, not mine, I assure you. He used to be in Algeria, so he sees Arab gunmen behind every stone. Foreign Legion – they won't take you unless you're paranoid. Would you like a drink?' He nodded to the girl, who busied herself with the glasses. 'Henri carries a gun too.' He raised his glass and a pair of shrewd eyes peered over the rim at the newcomers.

'Really?' Lethbridge said softly.

The old man turned to Henri and murmured something.

The other man smiled, wiped his lips and helped himself to a drink from the table.

'I thought that Henri might stay whilst we get to know each other,' the old man said.

The five of them squatted on the grass, Cavendish, with his spindly body and shock of white hair, looking like a California guru, and the girl his acolyte. In the manner of Englishmen meeting, they talked about the weather and the rigours of the visitors' journey.

'People of our political persuasion tend to be of the older generation. When I was invited to accept you as guests, I confess I thought you would be nearer my own age.'

'There are still young people who want to serve their country,' Lethbridge said. Cavendish regarded him curiously, as if he recognized the echoes of English public-school sentiment.

'Shall we be working with Henri?' Lethbridge asked. The Frenchman, hearing his name, smiled and tilted his glass in the Englishman's direction.

'In the vineyard – in the house – wherever. This is a burdensome place to run. We rub along doing what we can.'

Harrison sipped at his glass. 'Is there anyone else apart from Henri and . . . Gabrielle?'

'Casual labour from the village when we can get it – oh, and Ernestine, the cook. She's a widow, so you must call her Madame Bresson.' Cavendish sighed as though repeating a lament, 'There's really no money in this end of the wine business. Not as far as Sauternes are concerned.'

Lethbridge murmured sympathetically.

'The yields are too small and the modern taste has rather turned away from dessert wines. Do you know how much we get per acre? Eight hundred bottles! It's quite uneconomic. Still, one keeps the place up to do one's duty; and one lives off one's investments.' He stood up and tightened his loincloth. 'Shall I show you around the house? I've asked Ernestine to prepare a couple of rooms.'

'We'd love to see the house,' Lethbridge said.

Cavendish led them inside by a porch at the rear. Henri returned to the vineyard and the girl stayed by the pool. As they entered the house they could hear the sound of her radio playing pop music.

Madame Bresson was in the kitchen. She was a fat-faced woman in her sixties, with blackened teeth and grey hair scraped back into a bun, an old-fashioned country woman. She wore a coarse black dress with stockings to match and an apron made from a length of sacking.

The kitchen itself was the roomy, rustic sort: paved floors, a cast-iron stove, scrubbed table and a dresser stacked with crockery.

'This is Monsieur Lethbridge,' the old man said. The cook wiped her hands on her apron, shook hands with the visitor and grumbled something in a thick patois. Cavendish gave her a reassuring pat on the shoulder. 'And this is Monsieur Harrison.' The handshake was repeated. 'Madame is a marvellous cook,' Cavendish said as an aside, pausing to cast a smile in her direction to indicate that his comments in English were complimentary. 'Of course there's no ban on coming into the kitchen, but, if you'll take my advice, you'll treat this place as her sacred temple and keep well clear.' He looked at Harrison who was running his fingers over an array of knives and skewers. The dark-haired man closed his eyes, put down a knife and dropped his hands by his side. 'Whatever you say.'

Cavendish ushered them gently out. 'To tell you the truth, she's a bit of a tartar,' he said, 'but I daren't tell her that to her face.' He led them into a white-washed corridor. 'And now,' he went on, 'I imagine you'd like to see your rooms.'

The old man kept up the small-talk as he showed the two men round. 'What we produce here is Sauternes. Do you know anything about wine? No? Well, it's like no other wine – if you discount some rubbish the Germans produce.'

'How so?' Lethbridge asked.

'*Pourriture noble!*'

'Noble rot?'

'A fungus that attacks the grapes. It reduces the yield but increases the alcohol and sugar content of the finished wine – say eighteen per cent alcohol against ten or twelve.' He raised his hands. 'Of course, with the low yield the price has to be kept up to make the wine pay, but – well, I'm sure you understand.' He opened a door into a small bedroom bright with light from a narrow window. It contained a small bed, a table and a tall clothes-press. 'One of you can have this.' He closed the door and moved on. 'As I was saying, the other problem', he went on, 'is that in waiting for the fungus to develop, you run the risk of a change in the weather and disaster – grey rot!' He opened another door and showed them a bedroom similar to the first.

'We used to have a great deal of good furniture,' Cavendish said apologetically. 'Only two or three years ago I might have offered you a First Empire bed, but one has to sell things.'

'I'm sure,' Lethbridge said.

The old man tugged at his loincloth and gave a deprecatory laugh. 'I imagine you think I'm a terrible snob. No, it's all right! So I am! Of course I'm not really English.'

'No?'

'French. English ancestors, naturally. There are quite a few of us about in the wine business. It gives us a sort of colonial mentality – keeping up the standards against the natives and that sort of thing. Wrong empire though – Angevin – Henry the Second and all that.' He moved the two men on and allowed his hand to drop and graze Harrison's buttocks.

Harrison stopped and pouted his lips. 'You know what, Frank? I think our Norman here is a bit of an old fairy.' He gave a short, hard laugh and the hooded eyes stared coldly above the smile.

Cavendish seemed unperturbed. He opened his palms expressively. 'At my age, you know how it is: any port in a storm.' He opened a third door. 'Just so that you know where it is, this is my room.'

Whatever Cavendish had been forced to sell, he had drawn the line here. It was a tall room, lit from a window that opened on to a balcony. The centre-piece was a Consulate bed, a great gilt and mahogany affair that sat in the middle of one wall framed by a pair of gilded sphinxes. On the opposing wall, dividing two tapestries, was a pier-glass mounted over a Louis Quinze table. There was a large secretaire in the same style, a couple of smaller tables and a boulework cabinet. The effect was grandiose.

'You like it?' the old man asked, turning on his toes on the carpet and facing them.

'Incredible,' Lethbridge said softly.

'It was all like this once – not so many years ago. But taxes, bad investments . . . you know how it is.' The words were lightly spoken but wistful as the old man crossed the room and gazed out of the window. 'Even now I'm sure that you'll find the atmosphere most—'

He moved back from the window and turned to face his visitors. He recoiled from Harrison's green eyes. The Englishman pushed him roughly on to the bed. Cavendish fell badly and groaned with pain. Harrison laughed.

'Do you see this?' The younger man's hand held something against Cavendish's nose but it was too close for the old man to focus. He tried to move back across the bed on his elbows but Harrison seized him by the feet and pulled him horizontally across the covers. The Englishman sat on the edge and leaned across, resting his weight on the old man's stomach.

'What do you want?' The voice was frightened but did not hold the surprise of a man who expected nothing. There was recognition, like Faust meeting Mephistopheles.

'Come on, old man, you know what we want.' The hand moved away from Cavendish's face and he saw that it was holding a long kitchen skewer.

'You are burglars?'

Harrison laughed. 'Hear that, Frank? What would your old headmaster have said if he'd heard you called a burglar?'

'Rather working class,' Lethbridge said in polished Oxford tones.

Harrison leaned over further so that his face almost touched the old man's. The point of the skewer grazed an earlobe. 'No, we're not burglars. Care to guess again?'

Cavendish's eyes darted about their sockets, searching the room as if there could be help. He could see Lethbridge opening the drawers of the secretaire and scattering the papers. Lethbridge asked, 'Do you have a study or is this it?'

'There's no study . . . all my money . . . all my papers . . . everything is in there.'

A smile. 'Most obliged.'

The old man writhed. 'What do you want?'

Harrison's lips opened slowly; his face so close that Cavendish's eyes were fixed on the small irregularities of the teeth, on the individual pores of the other man's skin. 'Listen –

carefully, mind. I've got one question and I want an honest answer.' A little shake of the head, anticipating any reply, 'No, before you say anything, let me tell you what I'm going to do.' The old man lay still. 'Good,' Harrison said. 'Now then. In my hand here I've got a skewer what I took from the old lady downstairs. Understand?' A nod. 'Good, you're not the stupid old git I thought you were. Well, first, I'm going to stick it in your ear – gently to begin with – and then, maybe, twist it round a bit. No prizes for guessing it will puncture your eardrum – not to mention causing you extreme pain and driving you more than a bit crazy.' Harrison paused, watching a tear form in the corner of the old man's closed eyes, and then went on. 'For the time being I propose to leave you with one good ear to listen by, but, if you persist in being deaf to my little question, there's the matter of your eyes. I could simply gouge them out with my thumb or I could give my little skewer a tap and drive it through the eyeball' – he chuckled softly – 'or I could do one of each – for the sake of research.' He breathed out, his warm breath flickering the old man's eyelids. 'Then, when we've entertained ourselves in that direction, we could turn to your nose – underrated object the nose. There's a whole collection of lovely nerves in there that we could cheer up a bit. And, with a knock from one of your handy brass ornaments, I dare say we could drive the skewer through the bone and into the brain – in fact I just know we could!' He paused again. 'All of this is calculated to bring me a bundle of laughs and you a lot of grief.'

'Just tell me what you want to know,' Cavendish groaned.

Harrison sucked in his breath with satisfaction. 'That's better. I thought you'd appreciate an explanation.' He shifted his weight to allow the old man to breathe more easily. 'One question then – where is Helsingstrup?'

The old man writhed at the question as though in pain. 'Who are you? Who sent you?' he gasped.

Harrison grinned and said jauntily, 'We were invited by your old friends right enough, the ones who've kept you in style all these years. Remember the old rhyme? "If you want to live and thrive, let a spider run alive". Well, now you've become an embarrassment to the Spider.'

The old man gave a small exhalation of breath. The pale eyes with their clouded whites stared up at the Englishman.

Harrison returned the stare but the old man's eyes had ceased to blink.

Harrison got off the bed and slipped the skewer into his pocket.

'What now?' Lethbridge enquired sharply from the corner of the room where he was turning over the contents of a chest.

Harrison said airily, 'Would you believe it? The old sod's died on me – and I never even touched him.'

Lethbridge dropped a handful of papers and moved quickly to the bed. He took the old man's wrist and then felt for a pulse in the neck. He bent over, opened Cavendish's mouth and breathed into it several times. Then he struck the body some sharp blows on the chest and listened for the heart.

'Well?' Harrison said.

'He's finished – and so are we unless we can turn something up.'

'Found anything yet?'

'Nothing.'

'Shit!'

'Take it easy. There may be a secret drawer in one of the pieces of furniture, or maybe a wall-safe.'

'Maybe.'

'Then let's look for it!'

They set about searching the room. Lethbridge tore down the tapestries from the walls and the hangings from the bed. Harrison used a candlestick to smash the backs from the cabinets and the bottoms out of drawers. A pair of Sèvres porcelain urns stood on the marble mantelshelf with a clock between them. Harrison took them, broke them apart on the fireplace and rummaged among the shards.

Five minutes later he asked, 'Find anything?'

'Nothing. And you?'

'Just this.' He held up a black revolver. 'Smith and Wesson thirty-eight. He kept it under the bed, suspicious old bleeder.' He flicked open the chamber and spied down the barrel. 'Still, it saves going back to the car for my piece,' he said and pushed the gun into his jacket.

Lethbridge picked up some papers from the floor. 'We'll take what there is. Give me a pillowcase to stuff them in. Then we'd better finish off the business.'

Madame Bresson was at the stove, clarifying some stock in a saucepan when the two Englishmen ambled into the kitchen smiling and chatting to themselves. She gave them the scowl that she reserved for trespassers and placed her hands on her haunches. The dark-haired one, whose name she couldn't remember, came up to her speaking reassuringly in English, though she didn't understand a word. He placed his hand on her right shoulder with a familiarity which disconcerted her, and she looked past him suspiciously at the fair-haired one, who was carrying what appeared to be a pillowcase in one hand and a cushion in the other. She was about to say something when she felt a sharp pain under the breast bone. At first it felt like one of the pains she sometimes got after a good meal; she breathed in sharply. And then a wave of agony hit her.

Harrison removed the bloody skewer as the elderly woman's body fell forward and hit the floor with a dull thump, like so much meat.

Gabrielle got out of the pool and picked up a towel from the grass. Water, falling from her long hair, streamed along the curves of her body. She stretched her limbs and admired her shadow on the grass.

The two Englishmen emerged from the back of the house, walking towards her, laughing and talking. The taller, blond one with the attractive aloofness carried an odd-looking bag and the small, dark one with the unpleasant eyes and the suggestive manners was holding a cushion in front of him – which seemed rather strange.

She shook back her hair and grinned at them. She liked to smile. It came to her naturally. They advanced towards her and smiled back.

Her death was not long and elaborate like the slowed-down action of a film. The bullet from the thirty-eight, fired through the cushion, tore through her and exploded fragments of vertebrae and viscera through the soft bronze skin of her back. Her body was flung in a parabola across the pool and landed in the water.

The two men drove the *deux-chevaux* down the road towards the highway. Henri Dupuy, from his vantage point on the tractor, watched them approach through careful eyes. There was something wrong – he sensed it but couldn't tell what. Maybe it was the speed at which the car was travelling or its unexpected appearance, but the sixth sense that had kept him alive in Algeria warned him that something was amiss.

The car pulled up sharply. Puffs of dust spat out from beneath the wheels. The repulsive little man with the black hair stuck his head out and called towards him. Henri put his foot on the accelerator and the tractor moved slowly forward. All the while he kept watch on the car.

Harrison bit his lip and watched the other man approach. He could tell that the sly-faced bastard was leery of something. Come closer! he muttered to himself. He knew that at this range he could hit the Frenchman – but knowing it wasn't the same as doing it and if he missed . . .

He raised the gun slowly in a double-handed grip, still keeping the barrel below the other man's line of sight. Henri seemed to be hesitating. The Frenchman's hand went into the blue shirt with its sweat stains and mismatched buttons and pulled at something that was held in his belt.

Harrison moved quickly. He straightened his arms and took aim as the other man was clearing his shirt. 'Jesus, that's a fucking magnum he's got!' Harrison yelled. His finger tightened on the trigger as the Frenchman was raising his gun. He fired and fell back with the recoil. Henri took aim.

The car was in gear. Harrison let slip the clutch and hit the accelerator. The car jumped forward and stalled but the distance was enough. The other man's shot smashed through the coachwork harmlessly and passed out the other side. Harrison fired again.

The Frenchman threw up his arms and jerked as though an electric shock had touched him. His gun went spinning into the vines. Something was holding him in the tractor seat. The engine roared as the great machine lumbered forward, crashing through the vines where it was deflected. The engine stormed as the tractor hit some invisible obstruction and then the whole works canted on to one side, rolled over and collapsed, the wheels spinning in the air.

'Let's get out of here,' Lethbridge said.

Harrison turned the engine on, got into gear and the car

sped forward in a shower of loose stones. Harrison was panting like a man who has just run a race.

'Come on, Arthur, we're out of it now,' Lethbridge said and put his hand on that of the other man.

Harrison stared fixedly ahead. 'The bastard! He had a cannon down his pants – and I thought it was only his dick!'

The car disappeared down the road. Behind them, flames flickered around the tractor. There was an explosion. And half a mile away the two men saw the bright yellow flame and the black plume of oily smoke rise lazily to be blown away by the wind.

Two

12 November 1980

If the world of publishing has a centre, then it is New York, and, more particularly, Sixth Avenue, if only because the firm of McGraw-Hill, the world's largest book publishers, has its head office there.

The day was cold and autumnal, the transition from one of New York's unbearable summers to one of its unbearable winters. A yellow cab cruised past the McGraw-Hill building several blocks and deposited its occupant outside a black monolith of reflecting glass and steel which the architects had provided with a small apron of paved ground to prove the civic-mindedness of the owners and to earn the title of 'plaza'. The passenger paid off the driver and walked past the bronze statue of a twisted figure, the benches where the hardier office workers were lunching off hotdogs and cans of 7Up and went into the building.

The lobby had a clean, air-conditioning, aseptic calmness. A security guard in shirt-sleeves leaned on a desk making small-talk with a receptionist who glittered and pouted like a talking doll. A few men in business suits sat around in armchairs reading copies of the *Wall Street Journal*. When the stranger came in, the guard did not bother to look up: the terrorists, when they arrived, would be wearing Che Guevara beards and fatigues.

The visitor was a man, aged about thirty, tall, athletic-looking in the style of a runner and dressed in a tan light-weight suit. His face was sunlamp-bronze with fine, regular features, a firm mouth and a pair of watery-blue eyes that had a cold, ironic look about them. He carried an attaché case under his right arm.

The identities of the tenants were given on a column of stainless-steel plaques by a row of elevators. The visitor scanned it. Listed as occupying the thirtieth and thirty-first floors was the firm of Magruder-Hirsch & Co. The name was stencilled in lower-case letters without serifs, with, underneath, the words *A Division of the Rama Telecommunications Corporation*. There was a logo of intertwined letters spelling 'Rama' for the benefit of those who could read logos. The man read the logo and rang for the elevator.

Barton Magruder, who lent his name to the firm of Magruder-Hirsch & Co, publishers, was sitting at his desk meditating on his lunch, which was scheduled to be with his partner, Nathan Hirsch, at a little French restaurant a couple of blocks away. The thought of lunch distracted him from his immediate problem, which lay on the desk in front of him in the form of a project outline from an English writer he had been keeping on a string for a couple of months whilst he made up his mind.

The writer was Jonathan Grant. He was an ex-journalist with an attractive, incisive style and a nose for a good story, but he had a jinx attached to him. Magruder had a cool head for business and an eye for a straight calculation, but he still allowed a lot of room for gut-feeling when it came to selecting books and writers, where all that mattered was getting under the skin of the great reading public. Grant had got under that skin with a vengeance. He had written three books, all of them bestsellers, but with a twist in the tail: the public bought the books but hated the author.

Grant's field was history, particular the Second World War. He had the industry and the nose to go through the records that were buried in the archives of the victors, and pick out and string together the facts that cut the legs from under popular heroes or demolished favoured myths. For a publishing house tied to a major conglomerate with interests everywhere, including in government contracts, there were limits to the tails that could be twisted. The British and American governments were self-righteous about their role in the war, and a lot of the heroes turned out in the end to have enough clout to embarrass publishers or the corporations that owned them. And so the message was to stay away from writers like Grant.

Magruder liked Grant's latest idea. It dealt with the involvement, and profiteering, of some of the biggest corporations in the war. It was well researched and the conclusions, if they were true, might make a few investors think twice about their money. But Magruder knew that the last thing Rama needed was a wrangle with some of the major internationals and the Department of Defence. It was tough, and so he sighed and pushed an empty coffee cup to join a collection of others on the desk.

Barton Magruder was in the habit of closing his eyes to punctuate his thoughts and conversation. The eyes in question were smokey-brown, almost invisible under a pair of heavy lids that ordinarily sealed them up like tombs with just enough of a crack for a vampire's hand to creep out. His nose was long and fleshy with open pores and hair in the nostrils, and the ensemble was finished with a thin, downturned mouth marked with long lines as though he hadn't heard a good joke in years; which was more or less true, since he viewed life as the routine of a cheap, stand-up comedian.

In publishing, the dour Midwesterner was an anomaly. His father had been a meatpacker who had starved himself to send his son with the aid of scholarships to Harvard, where Magruder had majored in literature before the war with an eye on journalism. In the event, the war had brought him into contact with Nathan Hirsch, an emigré German Jew. They had found an incongruous sympathy and, after the war, they founded their own publishing firm.

The two men made an odd pair. Magruder a sharp-tongued, abrasive businessman and Nathan Hirsch a gentle, introverted scholar; the relationship had earned them the nickname of Laurel and Hardy, but the oddity didn't bother either of them and they got along in an easy, lopsided harness for more than thirty years. Moreover, the business prospered. They hadn't become the biggest, but they had acquired a solid reputation and a good foothold in the market. Then, in 1970, they had been bought out by a conglomerate which already held a film studio, a network of newspapers and interests in television, radio and telecommunications electronics. The two partners now ran the publishing division of Rama Telecommunications Corporation.

Magruder was considering the publishing business with his habitual black misery when he was interrupted by his secretary. It was one of his jokes on life that he surrounded himself with pretty assistants and stayed faithful to his wife. Annette was one of these assistants, good-looking, and dark-haired with a lot of brains. She bossed the elderly misanthrope about and he allowed it with just enough complaints to avoid the suspicion that he had a soft heart.

Annette stood in front of the desk waiting for Magruder to look at her and, whilst she waited, she arranged his papers and piled the empty coffee cups on to a tray.

'Okay, what is it?' Magruder snapped.

The girl stared down the rebuke. 'There's someone outside to see you. He hasn't got an appointment.'

'You need to come in here to tell me that? Why didn't you use the phone?'

She scooped up another cup. 'He was quite insistent and not the usual type, I didn't want him to hear me.'

A flicker of interest crossed Magruder's face. He reached for one of the cups and looked into it to see if his luck was in. 'So what does he want?'

'Well . . .' she hesitated. 'I know it sounds dumb, but he says he wants to offer you the greatest publishing opportunity ever.' She raised her eyebrows and went on. 'How dumb can you get? I tried to stonewall him and fix an appointment with someone else, but it's kind of hard to reply to a statement like that.'

The expression of interest vanished. Magruder had never known a new author who didn't offer the greatest publishing oppcrtunity ever. For that matter he'd never known one who did. The files were full of rejection slips for the daily delivery of unsolicited masterpieces.

'Why are you bothering me? Tell him the usual thing: to leave the manuscript and we'll let him know. Then ask George to take a look at it or farm it out to a reader.'

Annette nodded. She knew what that meant. George was a burial ground for new writers, an ageing editor who was allowed to while away his days till retirement administering the gentle letdown by writing sympathetic letters of rejection. She persisted. 'I know the drill, but I'm not sure that this is just routine. This guy doesn't look like the ordinary characters we get in here. I wouldn't put him down as a writer at all. More the business type – expensive suit and he cleans his shoes. He says that if he doesn't see you today, then he'll walk away and you'll never hear from him again.'

'That's the sort of promise I'd like in writing,' Magruder

said. Then, on reflection, he decided that no one, if he was not totally naïve, would use that gambit unless he really had something. Besides, he had a sneaking respect for Annette's character judgement and this one sounded as though he might be interesting. 'Okay,' Magruder sighed, 'wheel him in.'

Unlike the fictional characters who occasionally landed on his desk, Barton Magruder was unable to identify the styling of the major European tailors at a thousand yards over the open sights of a Kalashnikov, but he could tell the difference between tailor-made and ready-to-wear and put a price on both. The visitor in the tan suit came in the expensive class.

Magruder looked the other man up and down and took in the good looks but wasn't impressed – they applied to half the faggots that Madison Avenue used to push vodka and fast cars. The truth was that Magruder had a prejudice against handsome men as Nature's favourite children. They shook hands.

'I didn't give my name to your secretary, but it's Simon Knights,' the visitor said.

'Take a seat, Mr Knights, and let me see what I can do for you.' Magruder tried to identify the other man's origins, but they were buried under the transatlantic English. Something North European, maybe even British: Magruder didn't have an ear for nuances of accent.

Knights pulled up a chair and sat down. He cast his eyes about the room, weighing up the publisher from the contents. They were off-the-peg executive style: a presidential desk in teak and leather, a drinks' cabinet shaped like an antique globe, a couple of Finnish-designed chairs with matching couch in nondescript oatmeal, and a lithograph which Magruder described as 'the sort hotels buy wholesale'.

'My card.' Knights took out a silver case, extracted a slip and passed it across the desk. Magruder scanned it quickly: gilt-edged with a parchment finish and a stylish typeface. It bore the legend *Simon Knights – General Agent* and an address in Zurich. Magruder considered it and dropped it into his pocket.

'Are you a literary agent, Mr Knight? No offence, but I count on knowing most of them by name if not by sight.'

'No. But neither am I based in the United States. I have an

office in Zurich as you can see, and I travel extensively.'

'As a whatchamacallit – general agent?'

'Exactly. I put people in contact with each other when they have something to buy and sell.'

Magruder nodded but felt no wiser. However, Annette was right when she said that the stranger was out of the usual run. He began to feel curious.

'Okay, I take it that you have something to sell. Why have you come to me?'

'I have a manuscript,' Knights said, 'which needs to be handled by one of the leading publishing houses.'

Magruder nodded, but the reply confirmed his dislike of the other man. It was too smooth, too obviously insincere. 'Fine, so you have a manuscript. There's no point in fencing with each other: what is it?'

Knights answered with a question. 'Tell me – would the diaries of Adolf Hitler be of any interest to you?'

Magruder thought at first that he had misheard. 'I'm sorry, will you put that again?' he said.

Knights smiled. 'I asked if you would be interested in the diaries of Adolf Hitler?'

'Fiction or fact?'

'Fact.'

'I thought that was what you meant.' Magruder moved uncomfortably in his chair. He wasn't used to being thrown, but on this occasion he was stumped for a response. If Knights had been a regular writer, he might have had a feel for what to do, but with a completely unknown quantity he couldn't think whether to laugh or treat the idea seriously. 'Well, I could see it as being of some interest,' he said guardedly.

'Of some interest?' Knights repeated. 'I should think it would be more than that.'

Magruder closed his eyes thoughtfully and then said, 'Frankly, Mr Knights, I don't know you. Every day this firm gets dozens of manuscripts from people we never heard of, and ninety per cent of those manuscripts we sling into the trash can. Hitler's diary, or whatever you call it, sounds like a cut above the average. But when a stranger walks in off the street and offers it to me, you'll understand that I'm not going to roll over on my back and let him stroke my belly. So, like I said, it may be of some interest, nothing more.'

Knights wasn't fazed by the reply. 'I can understand that the proposition may seem unusual.'

'A little. But don't let that stop you. I'm willing to listen.'

Knights paused. 'What do you know about Adolf Hitler?'

'I take it that's a rhetorical question? If you want an answer, I know about as much as the next man and maybe a bit more.'

'What do you know about his writings?'

'*Mein Kampf*?'

Knights nodded. 'Of course. Most people have heard of that particular work. But, tell me, have you ever heard of *Hitler's Secret Book*?'

'I can't say I have. What is it?'

'It was a second book. One that Hitler wrote after he had come to power. It set out in more detail what his goals were and how he proposed to set about them.' Knights spoke without the excitement Magruder would have expected from a crank and he was interested.

'What happened to it?'

'It was suppressed – by Hitler. He decided it was too explicit. You understand: it was one thing to write *Mein Kampf* as an imprisoned revolutionary but quite another to put down the same ideas as a ruling head of state. So the book was never published whilst Hitler was alive. In fact its existence was never even suspected.'

'From what you say, it's been published since?'

'Under the title I mentioned.'

'So? What relevance does it have to any diaries there might be?'

'As an illustration,' Knights said. 'It's too easy to assume that everything is known about Hitler, whereas the truth is that he was a highly secretive man. Today we know all about Eva Braun, but during the war her name was just a rumour and the German public knew nothing of her. Hitler wanted it that way. How much more secretive do you think he would be about keeping his diaries?'

'Assuming they exist,' Magruder said, but he didn't emphasize the point.

There was a tap at the door and Annette came in with a tray of coffee which she left on the table. Magruder picked up the pot and poured.

'Cream? Sugar?' The visitor shook his head. Magruder spooned some sugar into his own cup and stirred it thoughtfully. 'So you – or should I say your principals? – have a diary by Adolf Hitler to sell. What kind of diary?'

'Not one – several. Hitler kept a set during the war which he intended to use as the basis for his memoirs.'

'His memoirs? Of course – everyone writes his memoirs.' The eyes closed. 'Excuse me if I'm slow taking this in, but it isn't every day that I get this kind of offer.' The eyes flickered half open. 'I imagine they would come quite expensive.'

'Ten million dollars.'

'Ten million dollars,' Magruder repeated. He clicked his tongue. 'Well, at least it's a nice round sum.'

If Knights sensed the irony behind the publisher's impassive face he didn't show it. 'It's a difficult idea to take in,' he said.

'No offence intended, but the notion does seem a little far-fetched.' Magruder reached into the humidor on the desk and took a cigar. He threw another one across the desk and pushed a lighter in Knights' direction. 'Smoke? No?' He lit his own cigar deliberately, the deliberation hiding his thoughts. He didn't know whether to laugh at the absurdity or not, but the strange, calm expression on the other man's face persuaded him that whatever Knights had to say was worth listening to. 'Well now,' he went on, 'don't be too hasty to judge from my first reaction. Do you have the diaries with you?' He looked at the attaché case. 'I'm interested enough to take a look.'

'I'm afraid I don't have them with me.'

'Why not?'

'The contents are – shall I say – politically sensitive. At this stage I can only show you a sample. However, I'm sure that you'll find it interesting.'

'Whatever you say.'

Knights looked at Magruder long and carefully and then reached for his case. He opened the clasp and took out a thin folder of papers which he handed across the desk. Magruder picked them up and cast his eyes down the first page.

'This is in German.'

'Naturally.'

'How about a translation?'

'I'm sure that your partner can do that for you. If I'm not mistaken, Mr Hirsch is German by birth.'

Magruder nodded. He wondered How Nat would react when the diaries were mentioned to him. 'I guess he could translate if need be,' Magruder said, but the idea didn't appeal. It was a long time since Nat had considered himself a German. He didn't care to be reminded of the fact.

Knights stayed half a hour. He continued to be polite but uncommunicative beyond the bare bones of the diaries' existence and he stonewalled any probes by Magruder, suggesting that first the publisher should read the sample and then, if he was interested, Knights would give him more details. In the end Magruder shrugged his shoulders and they left it at that with a handshake and a promise from Knights to call.

'But there is one condition attached to the transaction,' Knights said as he was leaving.

'Uh huh, and what's that?' Magruder asked. And the reply surprised him because as far as he could make out it made no rational sense at all.

'There is a closing date for the sale. You must agree to our conditions and take delivery of the diaries by Tuesday 16 December,' Knights said. 'I trust you will remember that date.'

When the other man was gone, Barton Magruder sat thoughtfully behind his desk digesting the conversation. He realized that Knights had taken him at a disadvantage and played him like a fish to screw up his interest in a proposition that no sane man was going to believe in. Well, two could play at that game. He had the germ of an idea. After all, true or false, Hitler's diaries were bound to be interesting.

He wondered how McGraw-Hill had reacted when Clifford Irving had told them he could deliver Howard Hughes's autobiography. Magruder had met Irving once in Ibiza, where the writer used to hang out with a crowd of painters and artists who bullshitted to each other about their talents and lack of recognition. Irving was a handsome, plausible character but Magruder wouldn't have let him take an old lady across the street. A different type from Knights, who was an icebox.

Annette came into the room. 'So?' she said as she collected

the cups on to the tray. 'Was he a cuckoo or was he the real thing?'

'What did you make of him?' Magruder asked.

'He gave me the creeps. But guys that good-looking do. They're always bastards.'

Magruder watched her. He guessed she always went out with guys that good-looking.

'Well? Are you going to tell me what he wanted or do I have to peek at the files?' she asked.

'Tell me first, when did I last fire you?'

'Fire me and I'll tell everyone you're a soft touch.' She paused and looked more serious. Like any good secretary she shared a mental symbiosis with her employer that went beyond the formal relationship.

Magruder put out the stub of his cigar and said, 'I guess it happens to everyone at least once in a lifetime.'

'What does?'

'I just met a man who wanted to sell me Howard Hughes's autobiography.'

'Oh, really?' She cocked her head like a bird. 'I thought that was a fake?'

Magruder sighed, 'Well, whaddaya know?'

Three

Berchtesgaden: 29 June 1944

Today I saw von Rundstedt and Rommel. The former is not the man he was in Poland and the latter has gone to pieces since leaving Africa. They came to me appealing for an end to the war, wailing like a couple of old Jews. It makes me wonder how far the rest of the Army is infected with defeatism. They are a spiritless bunch, the lot of them, with their Von und Zu's*: a crowd of filthy aristocrats not fit to shovel shit! The complete lack of insight on the part of the Army is nothing short of astonishing. Their ignorance of the world-historical currents of Fate is abysmal. They talk about numbers and equipment – how we have so much and the Americans so much and the British so much – utterly disregarding such matters as the spirit of men fired with National-Socialist enthusiasm or the refining hand of Destiny in its selection of leaders.*

Rommel I don't mind so much. For one thing, he isn't an aristocrat, and, for another, his health isn't so good. It would be an easy matter to push him upstairs and have him lecture the troops on morale. On the other hand, it is intolerable that the Commander-in-Chief West should have an opportunity to spread defeatism. Clearly von Rundstedt will have to go. Perhaps von Kluge could put a light to the tails of those gentlemen who have been sitting on their backsides in France for four years.

Here in Berchtesgaden it is scarcely possible to fail to see the hand of the Almighty touching the German people. The day has been brilliantly clear. The meadows are full of Alpine flowers and, when I take the trouble to listen, I can hear the cowbells tinkling and see the girls moving the cattle down for milking. This is really where my soldiers should be. In their lederhosen and handsome jackets. The Bavarians have always been one of my favourite people, though Munich is too cosmopolitan for my taste. Perhaps, when the war is over, I could build a new capital for Bavaria. Maybe Nuremberg. Some day

I must discuss it with Speer. There's no reason why he shouldn't produce some plans now, whilst the war is on. That way we can get down to business as soon as the war is ended. He had a model of Berlin built – splendid! Really, one can see it now, if, like me, one has vision! A truly Germanic capital!

Morelle's eyedrops are very effective, though the effect seems to be wearing off sooner than when he first prescribed them; then it was truly wonderful. At any rate, the strain wore off sufficiently well that I felt able to watch a film.

It was a home movie. Eva has been pestering me to watch it. She had taken it whilst I was at Rastenburg, taking command in the East. She did it to while away the time, she says. I know what she does to while away the time. The place is cluttered with magazines and trashy novels. She really is quite obsessive about films. I suppose it must come from having been a photographer's assistant.

I invited everybody to come and watch, but she made a little moue and said that she intended it only for me and I was feeling so splendid with the weather and the clean air that I agreed. I should have known what to expect!

She had had the film taken in the gardens. God alone knows who was there! It started off with her in her swim suit, grinning and laughing, rather embarrassed and altogether girlish. She cavorted about and did a little dance, one of those Bavarian country dances; but of course she didn't have a partner. It was all quite charming.

There was quite a bit of this sort of stuff, maybe five minutes or so. Of course it palls rather easily and I was dropping off, but she kept nudging me to keep me awake and saying things like, 'Don't you think the costume shows off my shape?' and 'After the war, couldn't I go into films – I have fair hair and I'm every bit as good-looking as Garbo.' All sorts of silly things.

Then there was a cut and the next shot was of her still in the garden in a different swimming costume, and the light had changed a little. The camera was kept at a fixed angle, so I suppose she must have told the cameraman to leave it in one position and go away – at least I hope so. When this part started, she leaned over, nibbled my ear and said, 'Now watch, Liebchen*! This is special. All for you!'*

I wondered what she meant; but then I saw that the mood of the film had changed. She had a moonstruck expression on her face, which I suppose was meant to be passion, and she started drifting about making dramatic poses and looking moodily at the camera. I could see that the strap on her costume was starting to slip from her right shoulder.

At first I thought it was an accident, but she seemed to jerk and it slipped down to her elbow and her right breast was exposed. She moved closer to the camera. I could see the erect nipple – touch it almost.

'What is all this?' I asked.

'Don't you like it, Liebchen*? It's Salome.'*

In the film, she turned and I could see that her back was naked and the costume had slipped down on to her hips and her hands were covering both of her breasts. She faced the camera and ran her hands through her hair. Her face had a languid expression. Her breasts were full and round. It's funny how I had never really been aware of how big and firm they were. And I could see that she must have rouged the nipples.

She began to caress her breasts and pout at the camera, running her tongue between her teeth. You could see the line of hair rising upward from the swell of her belly.

I was so intent on watching that I hadn't noticed that her hand was on my thigh rubbing up and down. I was trying to keep my composure and ignore her.

In the film, the costume had fallen to the ground and she had stepped out of it. She was girating her hips and sort of bending over and backwards from the camera, pushing her pubic mound forwards. It is difficult to describe how peculiar it seemed, there in the silence except for the whirring of the projector.

Eva was writhing at my side, giggling and saying, 'Isn't it marvellous! Look how dramatic it is! You must watch the next part!' And her hand was inside my trousers working at my penis.

She had stopped the dancing part and reached for a towel which she took and used to rub herself down. I thought it was all over, but she must have had another thought because she laughed at the camera and put the towel between her legs and started working herself up on it. She lay on the ground and rolled over, all the time rubbing herself and moaning. You couldn't hear it, but it was moaning.

I could hardly stand it. She was on her knees with her mouth around me and her tongue working away like the devil, and before I knew where we were, I was thrashing around with her, and her bra was on the floor and her girdle around her knees. She was limp and passive, just groaning and saying, 'Do it to me! Do it to me!'

I felt my blood raging within me. My disgust was rising in my gorge, but my urges were too strong. I shouted at her, 'Harlot! Filthy whore!' and struck her as hard as I could across the face and breasts. She just took it – lying there like the dirty strumpet she is, with her mouth slack and open and her tongue glistening wet and lolling on her lips. Eva! Eva! She was Eve all right! Mother of downfall! Drainer of virtue and strength! God, for a moment I could see into her, her suppurating pit of vice, degradation and femaleness!

But I was magnificently astride her! There was no doubting who was the master. I was riding her and bucking her and she was helpless! I could feel my strength rising against her! I would use her and not she me! She would not take me!

I was astride her and my penis was in my hand and I could feel the blood and the seed in it, boiling until it would almost burst! But I was sure that she was not going to have it. No, not her! Not any woman!

There she was, subdued, begging, pleading! Desperate! 'In me*!' she was shouting, 'In* me*!' But I was there, taunting her with my swollen talisman of life and the harlot could do nothing!*

Then it seemed to explode, my seed sprayed on to her belly and I let out a cry of joy! I was exultant! And she lay, degraded and conquered beneath my victory!

Ah, Geli! Geli! Geli!

Four

For a while after Annette left the room, Magruder mulled his ideas over, lost his temper at being treated like a sucker and picked up the day's newspapers for distraction. He scanned a few paragraphs of the lead story on the Polish crisis and then turned the page over because the prospect of a Soviet invasion of Poland scared the hell out of him. Next he caught a short item on the forthcoming trial of Pieter Xanten, the Dutch millionaire antiques' collector – Magruder had been following the story because he felt sorry for the old man, and who could be sure after thirty-five years that he was really guilty of the crimes charged against him? What the hell – he was getting nowhere. He picked up the phone.

'Annette, I've got a lunch date with Nat. If anything happens keep it on ice until I get back.'

The answer was a brisk, 'Okay, but don't forget you have an appointment at two-fifteen.' Magruder put down the receiver, searched on his desk for the stub of a cigar and, catching sight of the papers left by Knights, picked them up and stuffed them into his pocket as an afterthought.

The Escargot sans Maison was furbished French farmhouse style with old furniture, gleaming napiery and sideboards groaning with cheeses and bottles of wine. Nathan Hirsch gave a slow wave of recognition from the table in their usual corner by the Breton dresser and then returned to his eating whilst his partner negotiated the intervening obstacles.

Nathan Hirsch looked like a man who liked eating and very little else. He had a fat, sweat-beaded face with a clout of grey hair and sad brown eyes like a pair of fieldmice curled up in his flesh to get warm. Below the neck his gross body fleshed out a wrinkled suit as though he had once been even fatter and had started to deflate. If he had been a man concerned with appearances he might have gone to a good tailor, but, instead, he went to a little man who spoke Spanish and was cheap. Magruder couldn't recollect anyone who boasted of wearing a Puerto Rican suit.

The gaunt Midwesterner looked around and found a waiter haunting his side, pulling out a chair and waiting expectantly for an order. 'I'll have some *crevettes* and the *carbonnade de boeuf*,' Magruder said without looking at the menu, 'and a bottle of claret, but don't make it that Californian stuff or the one that tastes like it had a teabag dipped in it.'

Nathan Hirsch was dabbling with some bread in an empty soup bowl. He turned his slow, liquid eyes on his partner and said, 'I heard a joke today. A Jewish pessimist dies and appears in front of the Pearly Gates. He asks "Where am I?" and Saint Peter says, "You're in Heaven." So the old Jew shrugs his shoulders and says, "Just my luck. They tell me that hell is like the West Side – and at least there I can afford to pay the rent!" ' He dropped the pellet of bread into an ashtray. 'Funny, hey?'

'It's the way you tell them.'

'I think it's terrible too.' He pushed back the chair and waited whilst the *crevettes* were placed in front of his partner. The latter picked up the fork and prodded them gingerly. Hirsch said, 'What's new?'

'I had a call from Emmett. The usual bullshit.'

Hirsch nodded. Walter Emmett was the senior vice-president of Rama. His field was micro-electronics, but he considered himself a literary expert and had a habit of pushing his fancied writers at the two publishers. Usually they slung them out, but occasionally they would take one if they wanted Emmett's support on a policy or budget decision. At the moment the horizon was clear.

'I told him to go shag,' Magruder said. He added as an afterthought, 'You might drop him a line to smooth him over. Tell him the latest guy is great but the public haven't caught up yet with Bulgarian poetry.'

'Bulgarian?'

'Well, maybe Russian. Some dissident.' He paused, 'Hell, the poems aren't bad and someone will probably want to take them up, but they're not mass-market stuff.' He watched as the fat man meticulously noted that point in his diary. 'What are you eating?' Magruder asked.

'Pork.'
'Your mother would approve?'
'It was a very devout pig.'
The waiter deposited their dishes and did the usual leger de main with the vegetables. Magruder tasted a mouthful of wine, nodded and allowed his glass to be filled.
'I had a weird character in the office just before lunch,' Magruder said. He was unsure how to open the topic: Nat was touchy about anything to do with the past.
'How's that?'
'He looked like a straight business type, but he came out with the craziest proposition I ever heard. I don't know whether to take him seriously or whether he was a nut.'
'What did he want?'
Magruder put down his fork, wiped his face with a napkin and leaned across the table. 'What would you make of a guy who says that for ten million dollars he can sell you the diaries of Adolf Hitler?'
The fat man paused, his knife poised over a slice of meat. 'Are they genuine?' he asked.
'That's what I ask myself. But how could they be? They'd be the hottest thing in publishing since the war – strike that – the hottest thing this century. So why haven't they been published before now? The longer they were held on to the more doubts there would eventually be as to their authenticity. It doesn't make sense.' He paused. 'You don't seem surprised.'
'I'm surprised,' Nathan Hirsch said, but the shutters had come down over his expression. 'Tell me about it.'
Magruder described the meeting with Knights. The fat man listened in silence whilst his partner filled in the details with his usual irony, and nodded on cue when Magruder closed his coffin-lid eyes to underscore a point.
'It's a strange enough story,' Hirsch said when he had done. 'Do you have the papers with you?'
'Right here.' Magruder pulled the folded sheets from his pocket and smoothed them on the table. 'It's all in German.' He pushed them across. 'And that's another thing. Knights made a big deal about secrecy. He said that if I showed the material to anybody else then the whole business was off. I told him, no way: that we'd have to bring in our lawyers on

any copyright angle and also some outside help to validate the manuscript. He seemed to agree to that. He said okay, but if it got back to him that the existence of the diaries was generally known, then all bets were off.'

'So what did you say?'

'Scouts' honour, I wouldn't tell. What else?'

Hirsch pulled the papers towards him and took a pair of dust-smeared spectacles from his pocket. 'That's quite a secrecy restriction.'

'I don't know what to make of it. When Knights raised the point, I was still considering having him thrown out as a crank. Maybe that's what made me listen to him: he just assumed I was going to buy.' Magruder paused and poked the meat on his plate. 'Anyway, read the sample and tell me what you think of it.'

Hirsch adjusted his spectacles and began to read. Five minutes later Magruder interrupted. 'Is there any sex in it?'

'Sex in it? What sort of question is that?'

'Well, it would really stand them on their ear if Hitler was a lesbian!'

A faint smile crossed the fat man's lips. 'Do you really want me to translate it?'

'Why do you think I gave it to you?'

'Very well.' Hirsch picked up the papers and began to read slowly, *'Heute sah ich von Rundstedt und Rommel. Der Erste ist nicht dieselbe Persönlichkeit die in Poland war.'* He cleared his voice. '"Today I saw von Rundstedt and Rommel. The former is not the man he was in Poland . . ."'

The translation took a quarter of an hour as Nathan Hirsch read aloud the language he had not spoken for more than thirty years and then repeated the text in English, frequently going back over a sentence to correct some nuance that he had missed at the first attempt. The fat man's voice was slow, polite and academic compared with the brusque tone of his partner, but Magruder stayed quiet and listened with growing interest.

'It's pure pornography!' Magruder said at last – but he smiled as he said it.

Hirsch put the papers down and folded away his spectacles. 'Presumably it was selected to excite our interest.'

Magruder's mouth snapped shut. 'Yes, well, I guess it does that.' He thought for a moment. 'With that sort of fantasy pornokitsch it's got to be a fake. It's too good to be true. I wonder if there's any more of the sex stuff in it or if this is it? What does all that business about "Geli" at the end mean? You didn't translate that.'

'I don't know what it means. It looks as though it's a name; maybe a place.'

'I guess so,' Magruder said. 'Anyway, for now it doesn't matter.'

'What are you going to do about it?' Hirsch asked.

'I don't know,' Magruder murmured. He caught the waiter's eye and asked for some more coffee. Hirsch asked for some ice-cream. 'What the hell *do* you do when someone hands you a thing like that?'

'You could try finding out whether it's authentic.'

'I think I know the answer to that one. It may be more interesting to discover just how good a fake it is. But then what? Knights says the owner wants ten million dollars for the rights. So it's a negotiating position: it still beats every book on record I ever heard of.'

The waiter returned with the coffee and Magruder asked him for a light. Drawing on his cigar he went back to the conversation.

'Let's say we can persuade people the diaries are genuine: then what do we have?' He thought for a moment and then said, 'You know, if I had to think of a book that everybody in the world would want to read, then this would be it. The war has been over for nearly forty years and yet how many books are published every year that rehash the same old stuff? There must be hundreds. We must have half a dozen in our list alone.'

'About that.'

Magruder nodded. The lines of his mouth drew closer. He took out a pen and made notes on his napkin. 'Since we're talking hypothetically, let's put a figure on US rights. Say four million? UK rights another quarter of a million?'

'Maybe.'

'That's four and a quarter. My guess is that the Germans will fall over themselves to buy if their reception of *Holocaust* is any clue. So we'll say another quarter of a million there, a bit more if we're lucky. Throw in the French, the Japanese and a few others and we'd top the five million mark.' He crumpled the napkin. 'Which still leaves us five million light.'

'Serialization?' Hirsch suggested.

'Sure,' Magruder was unimpressed. '*Time-Life* or one of the others might buy. I can see Ben Vitalis smacking his lips – it would give those guys a chance to revamp their old copy, "Is Hitler Alive and Well and Living in Paraguay: the Public Demands the Right to Know!" But we're talking about a million at most if we take the assumed base figure.' He shook his head. 'We need to be thinking about big money, about films.' He picked up the papers and the crease of a smile split his face, 'Could you imagine this stuff on film?' He gathered the sheets together and put them back in his pocket. 'It's a nice idea though.'

With that remark they dropped the subject and for the rest of lunch talked over general business until Magruder decided it was time for him to go. 'I'll talk to you later,' he said, 'when I've had a chance to think this diary thing through.'

When his partner was gone, Nathan Hirsch wiped a ring of pink ice-cream from his round, plump mouth. He ordered a cognac and paid the bill, and then remained at the corner table staring thoughtfully into his drink. He rummaged in his pockets, turned up a tarnished silver box and took a pinch of Otterburn, a fine snuff with a faint smell of roses. He inhaled then rubbed the excess from his fingers, the brown fragments dusting the front of his shirt.

His expensive doctors told him there was nothing he could do about his weight. They put it politely and said it was something to do with his metabolism. Only the cheap doctors told him they could cure him. They prescribed tablets which gave him the shits but otherwise did nothing. No one, not even Bart, mentioned the true cause of his obesity: the interesting operations by the cold, polite doctors in the concentration camps. The talk of the diaries brought back the memories.

Barton Magruder headed back to the office. A few drinks and his conversation with Nat had left his brain seething with competing ideas and emotions and he was trying to straighten them out. His intellect still clung to his first, instinctive impression that the whole business of the diaries was too far-fetched to be credible: the more realistic scenario was that the diaries were forged and that someone had had the idea of doing a Clifford Irving on the grand scale. On the other hand, the notion of marketing the diaries – forged or genuine – interested him almost as a professional exercise. Thinking of Irving made him wonder how much McGraw-Hill had paid for the Howard Hughes autobiography. He had a feeling that it was three-quarters of a million dollars or thereabouts, and that was back in '71. Take inflation into account and the same book would fetch maybe one and a half today.

One and a half million – ten million. The figures weren't comparable. But, then, maybe the books weren't either? Magruder didn't want to sell Hughes short. There had been a lot of public interest in him because of his lifestyle and the 'is he alive or is he dead?' mystery that hung over his last years. But, at bottom, he was a private individual in the historical as well as the personal sense, who left no impact behind him. If he hadn't lived like a hermit he would have attracted no more interest than the other super-rich tax-exiles who lived out their lives in obscure tax-havens. After you'd described his life and his health fads and speculated whether his aides, the so-called 'Mormon Mafia', weren't in fact the real Mafia, there wasn't much else to say about him. At a guess, two Americans in ten hadn't even heard of Hughes, and seven out of ten didn't give a damn. Outside of the United States, say in Western Europe and Japan, maybe two people out of ten had heard of Hughes. And in the rest of the world – zilch. He was of local, ephemeral interest. In five years nobody would care.

It all made Magruder wonder what McGraw-Hill would be getting if they laid out their million and a half today? Was it anything more than the US rights? Magruder would have loved to see their sales projections. They must have reckoned on some European market, but he couldn't see it as being much. Hughes was too much of an American phenomenon, a gothic twist to the American Dream. Film rights? They would have had them in mind, but Magruder couldn't see that they had much value – '71 wasn't a good year for films and a biopic based on Hughes had 'loser' written all over it. No, when McGraw-Hill bought the rights, they were going to recoup their money peddling the book in the United States: the rest was gilt on the gingerbread.

And against that – the Hitler diaries. Were they, as Magruder suspected, the one book that everybody would want to know about?

He reached the office. Annette blew him a kiss and told him that Jonathan Grant had called again but she had brushed the Englishman off with a story that Magruder was giving his latest plan for a book serious consideration and would let him know. Magruder thanked her, told her to cancel his appointments and then went into his room where he poured himself a stiff drink.

'I hear you want a word with me?'

The long face looked up from the scrap of paper on which Magruder had been scribbling some figures. The publisher was sitting hunched over his desk. 'That's right. Come on in, Jack.'

Jack Robarts inclined his head slightly in recognition of his reception and took a seat without being asked. He was a tow-haired man of about thirty, square-built with a face like a Pole. His manner was polite but abrasive, outwardly self-assured – in Magruder's eyes maybe too much so. He was wearing a pair of expensive slacks and a neatly ironed shirt, hedging his bets to be casual or formal as the occasion demanded.

Magruder took out a fresh cigar and lit it. He sighed deeply. 'I've got a problem, Jack, that I think you may be able to help me with.'

'Name it and I'll see what I can do.'

Magruder hesitated. He had his doubts about Robarts. The younger man had worked for Magruder-Hirsch for two years. He was able and he put in the effort to make things move. But he was too eager, too aggressive in his drive to the top. Magruder was aggressive himself, but he knew that he had a sneaky charm that took the edge off. Jack Robarts thought he was a high-flyer who was being held back. Magruder was old enough to have come across people who had reached their limitations. They either had to admit them and learn to live with them, or try some other way to force a path through. He remembered the old adage that robbery was a lateral-thinker's idea of work. He wondered sometimes what route Robarts would take out of his problems.

For the moment he put his doubts aside. Jack Robarts was head of marketing. He held a master's degree in history and knew his way about publishing better than most. For the job Magruder had in mind he seemed ideal.

'Jack, what would you say if I told you that I'd just been offered the diaries of Adolf Hitler?'

Robarts' face flickered with the same equivocal reaction Magruder had felt – were they real or were they fake?

'I'd say that was one hell of a book.'

Magruder took the other man through the story he had given Nathan Hirsch. Robarts was guardedly enthusiastic: Magruder guessed he was feeling his way to a response, not wanting to go out on a limb. He wondered if Robarts ever let his guard slip. The younger man's ambition left him wound to the point where, sometimes, it looked as though it wouldn't take much to break the spring.

'So that's the story.'

'It takes some believing, but if it's true, we'd have the book of the century on our hands,' Robarts said.

'However, we've got to get to first base. Before we can do anything else we've got to get a feel for the diaries' authenticity. And to get that we need an expert.'

'That should be no trouble. Anyone in the field would give an arm for a chance of working on a document as important as the diaries would be.'

'Maybe,' Magruder said. 'but what we need isn't some professor who'll sit on his doubts and the diaries for a year whilst he makes up his mind. If we lay out anything approaching Knights' asking price, we have to turn the book into cash pretty damn quick.' He paused. 'What I'd like is someone who has the expertise to give a reliable opinion, but whose name could sell books on its own account. What do you say? Take a few days and come up with a name.'

Robarts gave a thin smile. 'I don't need a few days. I can give you a name right now.'

'Like who?' Magruder asked.

'Jonathan Grant.'

Five

13 November 1980

'Jonathan Grant,' Barton Magruder said. He looked as though he was chewing his long nose, weighing up the idea. 'I can't say the notion appeals, but Jack says he's the man, and it makes a kind of sense for what I have in mind.'

The two men were in the bar of the Algonquin where they sometimes took clients for a drink. They had found themselves a quiet spot away from the crowd.

'What's your objection?' Nathan Hirsch asked. The question was rhetorical since he knew Grant's reputation, but he fed Magruder the line so that he could get things off his chest.

'He's got a whatchamacallit – a jinx. He's the only writer I know who can give you a million-seller and still leave you screwed. I'm not saying it's deliberate, but when you find yourself with another guy's prick up your ass, it's no comfort to know that it's only because the bus is crowded.'

Nathan Hirsch sucked in his fat lips. 'I understand,' he said.

Magruder knew Grant by hearsay from other publishers who had handled the Englishman and been burned, and that had been enough to make him hesitate when Grant's latest project landed on his desk looking for funds. After Robarts had brought up the name again, Magruder had made it his business to go into the rumours to discover what the truth was.

'Grant? Sure, I know the sonofabitch!' Magruder's informant said. 'Don't be fooled by the English name. His grandfather was a Polish Jew, name of Kaganovitch or something like that – he came over from the old country, made his pile and bought land. His father was a broker, increased the family grubstake and sent old Jonathan to Eton and Oxford. And after that he turned reporter. That's where the bastard should have stayed!'

As the story went, Grant was not a reporter's reporter. To do that he would have had to qualify his ambition with the back-slapping sociability of El Vinos or one of the other bars that lie in ambush about Fleet Street. Instead he had a cold, hard-headed reputation and when, after three years around London, he disappeared working for one of the news agencies in Indo-China he left behind a reputation for turning in a good story but few friends wondering how Jonathan-boy was getting on.

Somewhere, sometime out there, they said that something had snapped. There was nothing spectacular that you could put your finger on, but one day they hear that Grant is out somewhere in the crud watching the world being made safe for democracy, and the next day they see him back in Saigon applying himself to drink and women in whatever proportions come to hand. No one thinks too much about it. Another case of terminal disillusionment. Another one of the walking wounded in the spiritual rout from the war.

As part of his recovery Grant gave up journalism. His colleagues said that he had lost his edge. Not that he had lost his powers of searching enquiry: on the contrary, they seemed to be enhanced. Rather his judgement was shot through with morbid scepticism, a belief in the story behind the story. At its worst it seemed like paranoia. In 1976 Grant published his first book.

That book, *Nemesis and Pacific Power*, had been about the war against Japan. In it he approved of the Japanese attack on Pearl Harbor and called its author, Yamamoto Isoroku, 'the most original naval tactician produced by the war'. General Douglas MacArthur, he wrote, was 'an actor in the mould of Gary Cooper, masquerading as a conqueror'. Neither judgement was accepted by the public of middle-America, despite the fact that their country's nuclear strategy was predicated on the truth of Pearl Harbor that it made sense to strike first and discuss niceties afterwards. Accordingly the book received vehemently hostile publicity and was duly bought in thousands by people who wanted to disagree with it. The publishers, who had interests in newspapers, found themselves with a handsome profit out of the book. They also found themselves with a handsome loss of advertising revenue as companies with ex-generals on their boards – a surprising number – withdrew their accounts.

Grant's second book was published in England. *The Other*

Holocaust was an account not of the concentration camps in Germany but of the Allied bombing offensive against German cities. It was in the bestseller list for ten weeks and did equally well in Germany. It also brought down a libel action from a British air-marshal which cost Grant fifty-thousand pounds in damages and his publishers a further hundred thousand.

The third book was *Himmler – the Apotheosis of Mediocrity*, for which he returned to the United States. In the serious press it received critical praise for its style and scholarship but in the eyes both of academics and the public it had one flaw. It said the unsayable. It said in the most moderate terms that Himmler had not been alone in planning the massacre of the Jews and that it had gone beyond its intended extent.

As the historical equivalent of pornography, this last book sold two hundred thousand copies in hardcover. It earned the publishers the wrath of the Jewish community, an unattributed bomb through their window and a fire at the printer's plant.

'One thing that Grant has proved is that he has a nose for a story. If there is something in the diaries then Grant will find it out and in short order. Remember we have until 16 December – that's a little over a month – in which to check them out, so time is important.'

'Why is Knights sticking at that date?' Nathan Hirsch asked.

'Search me, I can't find any magic in it, but maybe Grant can tell us. In any case we have to meet the deadline,' Magruder answered. 'The way I read Grant, he has some sort of thing about notoriety, a hang-up about sticking his neck out in public. That's a big plus. If we publish the diaries – and don't get me wrong, I'm only talking hypothetically – they're going to cause a storm among historians. And historians are like lawyers: they won't give you a straight answer for all the "ifs" and "buts". That's where Grant comes out ahead: he'll tell you out loud whether or not the diaries are genuine. In addition, like him or not, his name sells books.'

'But there are drawbacks,' Nathan Hirsch said.

Magruder paused in stirring his martini and let the olive fall against the half-empty glass. 'Sure. From the marketing standpoint, after the Pearl Harbor book, the newspapers could be tricky about taking serialization rights, and, I don't know how cautious the British are about that sort of thing, but the UK rights could be difficult to push after the defamation lawsuit.' He shrugged his shoulders, 'I don't see those problems as insuperable. If the diaries are Hitler's, Grant can hardly be responsible for that. And we can give any takers latitude to change anything that Grant writes by way of preface or notes to cut out anything damaging. Once they can do that, they'll realize that with his fangs drawn, someone like Grant could be a useful additional selling point.'

The fat man listened quietly, put his glass down and ran his fingers across the lip. 'You seem excited about this, Bart. Why, when only yesterday you were laughing at the whole business and saying it was crazy?' The soft eyes searched his partner's face.

'I'd have thought you'd find it interesting too – after what happened to you in the war,' Magruder answered. Hirsch said nothing. He cast his eyes down and raised a finger to order another drink. 'Bad vibes?' Magruder said. His ordinary, flinty voice softened for the fat man; sometimes he felt it was like talking to his conscience. 'Okay, I'll tell you what it is that's getting me under the skin: it's the whole idea of publishing a book like the diaries! When we first talked it over,' he went on, 'I mentioned Cliff Irving. Remember? So, on the way back to the office I was trying to get a feel for what the diaries might be worth if they were genuine, and I made a few calls to find out what McGraw-Hill had in mind for the Hughes autobiography.

'First thing. They laid out three-quarters of a million to Irving, but they recouped that pretty well straight away with two-hundred and fifty thousand from *Time-Life* for world serialization, four-hundred thousand on offer from Dell for paperback and three-hundred and twenty-five from Book of the Month.'

'That's good cover,' Hirsch assented.

'But not all. Their in-house estimate was that they would turn two to three *million* profit on their outlay. And, wait for this, under their royalty arrangements with Irving they guessed at another two million dollars for Irving – or should I say Hughes? But you get my meaning: back in '71 they thought that an autobiography of Howard Hughes would turn in five million dollars' profit for the parties!'

Magruder pushed away his empty glass and picked up a fresh one. 'I'm no economist,' he went on, 'but, at a guess – we can check later – five million in '71 has got to be worth eight or better today. And what for? There's no comparison with the Hitler diaries. If they're genuine – and I'm not saying they are – but if they are then we're moving into something so big that ordinary notions of this business don't apply. It'll be like selling the Hughes' book, Frederick Forsyth's latest and the Holy Bible rolled into one!'

Magruder relaxed and bit into his olive. 'Do you ever dream about doing the impossible?' he asked. 'Or things that may be possible but you know in your heart that you're never going to do them? I remember when Lennie was a boy —' Magruder paused; Lennie was his son who had been killed in a road accident. 'We used to talk about going down the Colorado River – you know, the Grand Canyon and the whole bit. It's been done lots of times. In fact, for all I know they run tours now for old ladies from Minneapolis. But, anyway, fifteen or twenty years ago it was a big deal, but it could be done by a man and a boy. So that's what we planned to do. We got all the maps. We worked out the itinerary. We went half crazy looking through catalogues and magazine articles to decide what to take with us and which brand of equipment was the best. In short, the whole megillah!'

'And did you go?'

'Hell no!' Magruder said wistfully. 'That was the year Elspeth and I went to Bermuda. Lennie went to summer camp.' He sipped his drink. 'But that's the point. It was just a dream but we played it through like it was for real.'

'And it's like that with the diaries?'

'Maybe not exactly,' Magruder said. For once his face showed emotion. 'That was with children, the sort of fantasy you get only once in a lifetime. But I guess it's a little similar. If my feel for the diaries is right, they're the sort of book that guys like us can only dream of getting – which is why I think they're phoney. But,' he opened his hands, 'I can't help playing around with the idea in my head.' He put his hand reassuringly on the other man's shoulder. 'Don't worry, Nat, I'm not about to sign anything!'

'What about Grant?' Hirsch brought the subject round.

'I've had an idea about that. I'll ask Elspeth to invite him round tomorrow night. Grant is hot to get an advance on his latest book, so we have an excuse. We can get a feel then and decide.'

The fat man picked up his drink and raised his eyebrows, '*Mazel Tov!*' he said somewhat doubtfully.

Annette caught Magruder as his shambling, stooping shape was disappearing into his office.

'Mr Knights called just after you went out.'

'Any message?'

'He said he'd call back. He wants to discuss things with you some time tomorrow. I've checked your appointments and you're free between ten and twelve.'

'What do I have in the afternoon?'

'The dentist. It's taken me a month to fix you up.'

'In that case I'm free all day,' Magruder said.

'Suit yourself. But momma is going to take away all your candy,' the girl answered and did a quick vanishing act.

Knights was on the line half an hour later. 'If it's agreeable I'd like to see you at your office some time tomorrow.'

'Okay. Say ten-thirty?'

'That will do.'

Knights sounded as though he was about to put the phone down but Magruder caught him, 'You'll be bringing the full manuscript with you.'

There was a pause at the other end, then, 'I'm sorry but I can't do that. I don't have it with me. That's one of the matters I'd like to talk about.'

Magruder was intrigued but decided to play hard, 'I don't know what you're at, Mr Knights, but to discuss this sort of deal without a manuscript is a hell of a way to do business.'

'This isn't ordinary business,' Knights said, and the line went dead.

Six

14 November 1980

The cut-throat razor traced the outline of the lower half of a face. It was a long, gaunt face that had character but could never be called handsome. The skin was sallow, drawn into hollows at the cheeks and blued with a beard that the razor never entirely removed. The hair was black, flecked with grey, the nose large and straight. The only remarkable features were the eyes, which were grey, pale almost to the point of translucency. The razor removed the last gobbet of lather and flicked it into the bowl.

Jonathan Grant carefully rinsed and wiped the blade and put the razor back in its case. It was an antique piece that he kept from a sense of gallows' humour: it simplified speculation when the means of experiment were poised at the jugular every morning. One day he was going to find his head on the floor.

He wiped his face on the towel and returned to the main room of his apartment. He surveyed the damage again: the upholstery meticulously slashed, the contents of the bar poured into a pool on the carpet, a Chelsea porcelain figure lying smashed on the floor with a corresponding notch on the fireplace where she had broken it. On the mirror there was a message in large letters: *Bastard!* She must have enjoyed that. The mirror was seventeenth century, by Robert Mansell. The message was in diamond.

He put on the shirt he had worn the night before. Apart from those he stood up in, the rest of his clothes were lying in a heap smouldering in the bedroom. He gave a smile on the funny side of tragedy because he had read Kathy so wrongly. When she had flown out of the restaurant he had gambled on nothing more than the usual acid recriminations which she had rehearsed in their fights a dozen times. Instead she had come back, dismissed the sitter and proceeded to destroy the apartment.

It didn't take much to reconstruct the picture. After working over the main room, she had gone into their bedroom, emptied the drawers and closets into a pile in the centre of the bed, poured a bottle of brandy over it and set fire to the lot. Then, maybe she had got cold feet or perhaps she was frightened the fire would take hold before she could remove Joey from the next room. Either way, she had emptied the contents of the soda syphon over the blaze and then collected Joey and left. He wondered at what point she had carved the message on the mirror.

The phone book was still in its usual place and she hadn't cut the wire to the phone. It wasn't his property and she had a curious sense of decency that prevented her damaging it. Perhaps the same sense had stopped her destroying the contents of the freezer: people were starving so you had to clean your plate.

Grant checked the list for likely numbers and rang round Kathy's friends. The responses were variations on a theme.

'Hello, Jeannie? This is Jonathan. Super to hear you.'

'Why are you calling so early?'

'I'm trying to find Kathy. Is she with you?'

'Kathy? Why should she be?'

And then the explanation. Followed by a sympathetic pause.

'But Jonathan, that's terrible!'

It didn't take long to conclude that Kathy had been on to her friends before him and said that she didn't want to be found. Which meant that her friends had rallied round and that Kathy and Joey were both okay. Grant put the receiver down and picked up his coat. He would get a bite to eat, and then perhaps he would do some work on his new book.

The ringing of the phone caught him before he closed the door. It was Barton Magruder, with an invitation to dinner.

Simon Knights appeared on time at Magruder's office. He was wearing twill trousers and a Harris tweed jacket with a yellow waistcoat. The country gentleman effect suited Knights' languorous style, but it confirmed Magruder's dislike of the man.

'Before we go any further,' Magruder opened, 'I'd like to know more about the history of the diaries and I'd also like to know who you're acting for.'

Knights gave an unruffled smile, 'I can see that those matters might interest you.'

'Well?'

'Let me say that I can oblige you on the first but that the identity of my principals must remain unknown.'

'You make them sound like Howard Hughes,' Magruder said, and as he said it he realized that his subconscious fears were slipping in. Was he really heading for a fall like McGraw-Hill with the Irving fake?

'I gather you found the sample I provided . . . stimulating?' Knights said, changing the subject. Magruder wasn't to be sidetracked.

'I don't think you understand, Mr Knights. I believe in your diaries at this point like I believe in fairies. Sure, I found the bit you showed me interesting, but there was nothing in it to make me change my mind. If you're serious about a sale then I want hard evidence that the diaries are genuine and I want my lawyers to be happy that I'm not going to buy a legal wrangle along with everything else. A good start would be to tell me where the diaries come from and who owns the copyright.'

'Very well,' Knights said. 'The copyright is held by the West German Government.'

Magruder didn't know exactly what answer he was expecting, but it wasn't that. 'I see . . .' he said carefully. 'You're acting for them?'

'I didn't say that.'

'Then I must have missed something – I thought you offered to sell the diaries to me.'

Knights fingered the tip of his tie and then commenced plausibly, 'The West German Government owns the copyright under the terms of Hitler's will as successor to the Third Reich and also under various confiscatory laws. But, surely, isn't your real concern not so much who owns the copyright but whether the owner will seek to enforce it against you?'

'That's one way of putting it,' Magruder said.

'Then I can give you two reasons why they will take no action. The first is that to make a claim, the German Government would have to allege the authenticity of the diaries. Now, although you will be satisfied on that point before buying the diaries, you must expect – maybe even desire – the controversy among historians that they will provoke. Do you think that any government would want to involve itself in that sort of controversy?'

'Possibly not.'

'Then consider further. You have read an excerpt from the diaries. I can assure you that it is not the only example of such material.' Magruder raised his eyebrows as Knights said this. 'Can you see the German Government wanting to claim ownership of a piece of pornography?' He smiled as Magruder said nothing. 'The Germans will take the same course as the Russians did over Khruschev's memoirs – namely they will do nothing. Once the book is published the damage is done. The safest course – which the Russians found too – is to deny the whole thing and leave it to the experts to argue over.'

Magruder nodded to show that he took the point. He did and it disturbed him. Magruder knew that with any such work there was bound to be a copyright problem and that didn't worry him: either the lawyers would solve it or the deal would be off. What troubled him was Knights' explanation. If the diaries were a scam he would have expected some pat story that gave good copyright to Knights' clients. Instead Knights had given his principals no more right to print than anybody else. Was Knights' confidence because the diaries were the real thing?

'All right,' Magruder said. 'We'll leave it there for the moment. I'll float your idea with our attornies and see what they come up with.'

Knights just nodded as if indifferent to the problem.

'I still need to know more about how you come to have the diaries and more details of what they consist of.'

'You can have anything short of the identity of my principals,' Knights said.

'Knights wants fifty thousand dollars before he'll hand over the text.'

'That's a lot of money,' Nathan Hirsch said quietly. 'How does he justify it?'

The two men were in Hirsch's office an hour after Knights had gone. The fat man was heaped behind his desk in shirt-sleeves, sweating even in the moderate temperature of the air-conditioned room. There was a bottle of mineral water in front of him and a paper cup. Magruder was standing at the window, pulling at the edge of the gauze and staring out at the traffic in Sixth Avenue.

'The fifty thousand doesn't bother me,' Magruder said dismissively. 'It's what we get for the money. On payment Knights says he'll deliver a copy of the manuscript – only a copy, note – together with some affidavits that are supposed to prove the diaries' history.'

'Why only a copy?'

'Search me. Maybe he's afraid that if we have the original, now that we know the copyright is weak, we'll take it and run: bye bye Mr Knights and his ten million dollars!'

'Or maybe he's afraid we'll know that the diaries are faked once we see the original,' Hirsch suggested.

Magruder sat down on the windowsill and drummed his fingers on the glass. 'Who knows? He says that the diaries cover from 1942 to the end of the war and that they're in Hitler's own handwriting. If he's right, that's a hell of a thing to forge. It would be easier to do the whole thing on a pre-war German typewriter and then think up a story. Even Cliff Irving didn't try to write the whole book in Hughes's handwriting.' He shrugged his shoulders. 'I don't know. Maybe there's some rinky dink I haven't even thought of. Either way, the only thing we get to run handwriting tests on is a photocopy.'

'And for that he gets fifty thousand.'

'I can see his point,' Magruder said. 'Knights claims that what's in the diaries is politically sensitive – don't ask me how – and that once it comes out he doesn't want it tracing back to his clients. He figures that if we pay fifty thousand just for a peek, then we'll be more careful about spreading the good tidings.'

'What did you tell him?'

'I said that I'd think about it. But I'm inclined to pay. What he says makes sense and fifty thousand is nothing in a deal this size.'

'He could take the money and disappear.'

Magruder let the curtain fall. He went over to the desk and helped himself to a mouthful of water. 'I don't think so,' he said, wiping the drops from his chin. 'Not even if we start from the assumption that the whole business is a scam. Irving aimed for a million or more on a deal that wasn't a fraction of this. I don't see Knights as settling for less. You should hear the story he gave me about how his clients came by the diaries. He's gone to a lot of trouble and my guess is that he's after his ten million.'

'So?'

'So, if we hand over the fifty thousand I think we'll get a text and some affidavits just like he says. And if it's a hoax – so what? We still get something we can print.' He held up his hands. 'I know: it wouldn't be genuine – but we could still run the line "Is this book, which emerged under such mysterious circumstances, the diary of Adolf Hitler?" We leave it as a question. Anyone who believes in the Bermuda Triangle will buy it and, if there's any more of that soft porn in there, I don't see how we can miss.'

Knights phoned half an hour later and Magruder told him that the first stage of a deal was on. The publishers would pay fifty thousand dollars for a copy of the diaries and the affidavits. Magruder held out for an option on the book and a credit against the final price. He didn't know whether to be surprised or not when Knights agreed.

'What arrangements for the handover?' Magruder asked.

'It will be in Zurich in three days' time.'

'Zurich? Is this a joke?'

'No joke,' Knights said. 'I have other business which takes me out of the United States, and, for the moment, it isn't convenient to return. You must arrange with your bank for a payment to the Schweizerische Allgemeine Kreditanstalt at their main branch.'

'The whoosit?'

Knights spelled out the name of the bank and gave the account number. 'When you arrive in Zurich, I want you to stay at the Atlantis Sheraton. I'm sure you'll find it an excellent hotel.'

'You'll contact me there?'

'Exactly,' Knights said. 'Now, do you have any questions?'

Magruder could think of a few along the lines of 'Who the hell do you think you are?' but he limited himself to a negative grunt and the line went dead.

Seven

It was evening. In the soft, moist light after the mild sunshine of the day, the roads out of New York City were crowded with people making their way home to suburban Connecticut. Jonathan Grant slipped his beat-up yellow Jensen into the stream and struggled with it out of the city.

The Magruder house stood on the brow of a hill, back from the road, a low frame house of white weatherboard with a red-shingled roof and a garden full of maples and quarrelsome roosting birds. Grant parked his car in the driveway and walked up to the house.

'Mrs Magruder?'

Elspeth Magruder's face broke into a well-bred smile indistinguishable from the real thing. Her careful eyes looked the Englishman up and down.

'Jonathan Grant? I'm sure you must be. My husband told me to expect you.' She stood back from the door. 'Do come in. I hope you've had a pleasant journey.' Grant followed her into the hallway.

He took in the house and the owner. The house was all-electric colonial in expensive style and Elspeth Magruder matched it. She was a tall, angular woman with the sort of well-boned face that looks haggard at thirty and beautiful at seventy. She wore a light cotton dress in a small geometrical print and an art-deco brooch of a milky green colour that might have been made of jade or glass. As she escorted him through the house she made solicitous enquiries about the state of the traffic and asked if he wanted to remove his jacket.

The room which Grant was ushered into reminded him of a movie set lit by Carol Reed. Faces emerged from the chiaroscuro glow of an open fire. A long-case clock beat out a slow, heavy tick. The only thing out of place was a Mochica pottery lute player, which should have been in a museum if it were genuine, and Grant decided that it probably was. Barton

Magruder was bending over the fire lighting a cigar from a wooden taper.

There were four people already in the room. Grant knew Magruder from seeing him at book launchings, where the publisher haunted the fringes of knots of in-conversation like a graverobber. The gloomy American had a mixed reputation: some said he was a hard-nosed type with a face like a stonewall; others said that underneath the granite there lurked a human being. Grant had no views on the subject.

Nathan Hirsch he knew by reputation and description. The fat man was sensitive about hauling his bulk around in public and Grant had never met him, but he had heard that Hirsch was a silent partner with an immense amount of learning and no head for business.

The other two were a married pair. The husband was a thin type with a scrubbed moon-shaped face and a shiny skull covered with wisps of fair hair, who stood nursing a drink as though it were a wet baby. His wife was a pudgy-faced woman with expensive dental work. The two of them were talking about the weather.

Elspeth Magruder made the introductions. 'Jonathan, this is Arthur Grenfell. He is a lawyer who does work for my husband. Arthur, this is Jonathan Grant – the famous writer,' she added with an attempt at sincerity.

The lawyer had a nervous stammer and looked down into his drink as he spoke. 'I'm pleased to meet you, Jonathan. This is my wife, Diana.' Diana Grenfell smiled and said hello, at the same time eyeing Grant like a pack of meat.

'Sherry, Jonathan?' Elspeth said. At her elbow there was a dark-haired youth in a white, duck-tailed waiter's jacket and sneakers who was holding a tray with half a dozen diamond-cut glasses on it and trying not to look embarrassed. Grant took a glass and his tongue curled at the taste of the fino.

Magruder came over and pumped his hand. 'Glad you could make it, Jonathan! Much trouble getting here? I guess not at this hour. Drink? Got one, eh?' He glanced in Grenfell's direction and said, 'I see Elspeth made the introductions so perhaps I could take you away and show you to Nat.' He put an arm across Grant's shoulders and steered him across the room.

Nathan Hirsch levered himself out of an armchair by the

fire and shook hands. 'I've read all your books,' he said in a soft sincere voice, 'and I've found all of them most interesting – though, I admit, some of your conclusions have at times been disturbing.'

Magruder interrupted, proffering another glass of sherry. He eased Grant aside and said, 'I guess you must be wondering why I invited you here.'

'I assume it wasn't just to be the prize in a social pass-the-parcel.'

'I know what you mean. You get handed round like a hot potato with everyone asking the same questions. The penalty of being a stranger. Well, play the game for now and we'll talk things over later.' He looked about him and added, 'I've promised Diana one of my specials – if you'll excuse me for a minute.'

The lawyer's wife cruised over, her husband in tow. 'Somebody talking about me?' she said, letting Grant inspect her teeth. She gave a TV smile and went on, 'I read your book.'

'Oh, super – which one?'

'Oh.' She looked puzzled, 'The one about Goebbels.' She pronounced the name Go-balls.

'You mean Himmler.'

'Yes, that's who I meant,' she went on unconcernedly. 'I thought it was terrible that you said he wasn't responsible for killing all those Jews.'

'I didn't say that. The American press did.'

'Oh, really? I knew I'd read it somewhere. Wasn't it dreadful of them to say that?'

'I don't think you understand Jonathan,' the nervous husband corrected her. 'He means that the reviewers misunderstood his book.' He looked at Grant and the tremor in his voice disappeared. 'It may be more pertinent to enquire whether the book was intentionally written so as to be misunderstood? I believe you made a great deal of money out of it?'

'Me and the publishers,' Grant said, and Grenfell gave a little uncomfortable grimace. 'I suppose we're both tarred with the same brush.' He moved away and sat by the fire next to Nathan Hirsch.

The fat man was staring at the flames. 'And what are you writing at the moment, Jonathan?' he enquired good-humouredly without looking at Grant. 'Bart has something on his desk which I believe belongs to you.'

'I'm just working out an idea. One that publishers haven't found too attractive so far.'

'Am I allowed to know?'

Grant wondered why the fat man hadn't been told by Magruder if this latest idea was the reason for the invitation to dinner. 'It's just an idea about the role of industrialists in war.'

'War profiteers?'

'Partly.'

'An interesting subject. You have anyone in mind?'

'Torkild Rieber. Have you heard of him?'

Nathan Hirsch shook his head. He stooped and knocked a fallen log back on to the hearth.

'He was president of Texaco during the thirties.'

'Oh? And what did he do to earn your righteous anger?' Hirsch asked with gentle irony.

'He violated neutrality by shipping six million dollars-worth of oil to France during the Spanish Civil War. He did the same for Germany later, dodging the blockade by using neutral ports. And he financed a Nazi publicity campaign to stop arms' shipments to Britain.'

'Not a very pleasant character. But perhaps your attitude stems from simple anti-American feeling? Are there no British culprits?'

'Sir Henry Detterding, the head of Shell, which is part British-owned. He became a convinced Nazi and retired to Germany. Hitler and Goering sent wreaths to his funeral. Does that answer your question?'

'Oh, certainly,' Hirsch said thoughtfully. 'As you say – a very interesting book.'

'Damning with faint praise?'

Hirsch laughed. 'Yes, it must seem like that. I can imagine the difficulty you've had with publishers in view of . . . '

'My reputation?' Grant restrained the bitterness in his voice. He decided he liked the gentle fat man.

'You sound like someone with a grudge against publishers, Jonathan,' Elspeth Magruder said. She had come up quietly behind Grant's chair. 'That sounds like a subject fit for discussing whilst we eat. Assuming, of course, that we all arrive.' She looked at her husband and asked, 'Are you sure that Jack Robarts is coming tonight?'

'Certainly,' Magruder said uncomfortably. He wondered where Robarts was.

'Then if he's late,' Elspeth said with a smile, 'he'll have a story to tell us. If he's run into difficulties, I do hope they're disastrous. I find that the most amusing anecdotes are funnier with the horribleness of the incident they relate, don't you, Jonathan?'

Grant fielded the sarcasm in the question. 'Certainly, any Jew must be in stitches when he thinks about the concentration camps.'

She laughed. 'How wonderful! I've always wanted to meet someone who cuts you to size like a Raymond Chandler hero.' She paused, 'But now I've spoiled it, haven't I? You'll be too self-conscious to make another witty remark all evening, won't you?' She turned away from any reply and said, 'Shall we sit down to eat?'

The table was laid with porcelain and silver and the conscript flunkey pulled back a chair for each of the diners. A fat, pleasant-faced woman who answered to Maria served the dishes. The dinner passed with Grant trapped next to the lawyer's wife, exchanging remarks that were as disconnected as the prizes in a raffle, until Elspeth Magruder intervened with, 'You promised to discuss your relations with other publishers.' The malicious dart was sheathed in an expression of polite interest.

'The only ones who talk to me like to live dangerously: they drink Bourbon instead of Scotch.'

From the head of the table Barton Magruder said, 'Perhaps you've brought some of the difficulties on yourself? Haven't you gone out of your way to choose risky subjects and write them up in a controversial way?'

'Only when they sell books, make good history and are true.'

'Even the libel on the Air-Marshal?'

Grant picked up his fork and toyed with a piece of meat. 'That was true too.'

'The judge didn't think so,' Elspeth Magruder said.

'He went to the same school as the plaintiff.' Grant paused, 'Actually, so did I!'

'You sound very bitter about it,' Elspeth Magruder said.

Grant tasted her sympathy and turned his cold eyes on her. 'I *am* bitter,' he said simply.

Coffee came round. As she poured it, Maria whispered into Elspeth Magruder's ear and the latter stood up and spoke. 'I believe that Jack Robarts has arrived at last.' She looked at the maid. 'Bring him in, please, Maria.'

Grant recognized Robarts as he came in. He had met him some time before he had joined Magruder-Hirsch and knew him as a quick dealer who was aiming for the top. He neither liked nor disliked him.

'I guess I owe everyone apologies for being late,' Robarts said. 'My car broke down and I had to hang around until it was fixed. By the way,' he added, addressing Elspeth Magruder, 'your telephone is out of order. I tried to ring through and say I'd be delayed.'

There was a quiet cough from the doorway and Robarts looked round. There was a girl standing there. He turned back to the others. 'Apologies again . . . ' he said with a slight slur on the words. 'You invited me to bring a companion. May I introduce Lisa Black?'

The girl was aged about twenty-three, tall and gangly with a mop of straw-blonde hair in a tangle of curls. She had brown eyes and an open, fresh-looking face that was attractive but too unfashionable to be beautiful. Her dress was green imitation silk, too showy for an informal dinner, and she wore it self-consciously as though she had borrowed it from a friend.

'I hope we haven't been any trouble,' she said. 'The car really did break down. We were stranded with it raining outside for an hour . . . ' her voice ran down and she pushed her fingers nervously through her hair.

There was a moment's general silence and then Nathan Hirsch said in a tender, avuncular voice, 'Come and sit yourself down, young lady. Would you like a cup of coffee?' He stood and offered his seat, which the girl took with evident embarrassment.

'I imagine Lisa would like something a little more substantial than a cup of coffee,' Elspeth Magruder chimed in. 'Maria can serve you with some dinner.'

'That's okay,' Robarts said sharply. 'We don't want to put anybody out. It will only disrupt things if we eat now when everybody else has finished.' His face was flushed and Grant guessed that Robarts had had more than a couple of drinks whilst waiting for the car to be fixed.

'I think you should speak for yourself, Jack,' Elspeth Magruder said. 'Lisa looks positively starved.'

'I should like something,' the girl said gratefully.

Barton Magruder coughed. 'I think that this is the point where the men adjourn for port, or, at any rate, a glass of Scotch. Let's go through to the den.' He rose. 'You get some dinner eaten, young lady,' he said to Lisa and then looked to Robarts. 'I know what it's like, waiting for a mechanic to show. You probably need a drink.'

The den was the publisher's private sanctuary. Grant noted the overstuffed chairs that had seen better days, some broken antique furniture picked up at a bad auction, a hideous Satsuma vase, and, in one corner, a pinball machine. Magruder opened the door of a small refrigerator and took out some bottles. 'What'll everyone have?' he asked. The consensus was Scotch and water. Magruder poured out the drinks and passed round a box of cigars and the five men settled into their chairs.

The pause whilst the cigars were lit and the puffs of aromatic smoke clouded the room didn't mask the tension. Grant noticed that, except for Robarts, the others seemed to be taking their cue from Magruder; the marketing man was already helping himself to a second glass of whisky.

'So what's new in the historical biography business?' Robarts said ironically.

'We've seen the plan for Jonathan's latest idea,' Magruder cut the subject short.

' 'Scuse me,' Robarts smiled and settled himself complacently in his chair.

'We're not here to discuss Jonathan's current project,' Magruder went on. 'Instead I'd like his view on a different matter altogether.' He looked round as if checking with the others. Grant sensed the tension again. A log fell from the hearth with a tinkle of ash.

'And what would that be?' Grant asked.

'A book,' Magruder said. 'A piece of fiction that someone offered to me.'

'Fiction?'

Magruder watched the Englishman's unresponsive face and nodded. 'Tell me, have you ever heard of a diary by Adolf Hitler?'

'Yes, I've heard of Hitler's diary,' Grant said. 'In fact I've read it.'

Eight

'When did you read it?' Barton Magruder asked. He had his back turned to Grant and was pouring himself another drink, avoiding the Englishman's eyes. He corked the bottle and turned round.

'I took notes from it when I was researching my biography of Himmler. That would be a couple of years ago. Why?'

Nathan Hirsch asked, 'What kind of a diary is it? Does it tell you anything – give you a feel for the *man*?'

Grant didn't answer immediately. He felt he didn't have all the threads. Magruder's position he thought he recognized: plain business, whatever it was. But there was something behind the fat man's question that was personal; as if he was involved in an intimate sense.

'No, it doesn't tell you much about the way that Hitler thought,' Grant said at last. 'Perhaps the book shouldn't even be called Hitler's diary, but the name has stuck.'

'What exactly is it then?' Magruder asked. He pushed the cigar box across the table and indicated Grant's glass. 'Another? No? Don't the Scots have a story that if you accept a man's whisky then you're bound to him? Or maybe I'm thinking about the Arabs and salt? Go on with the tale.'

'The diary was kept by a Major Heinz Linge,' Grant said. 'He was Hitler's personal aide and he wrote up the Fuehrer's appointments, who he saw, what he did, what he had for meals – I'm sure you have the picture. Hitler didn't dictate it; so it says nothing about what was going on inside his head. Does that answer your question?'

'Maybe.' Magruder's long, gloomy face churned over the reply. 'What period does the diary cover?' he asked.

'From about October 1944. I don't remember the exact date.'

'1944? You sure you don't mean 1942?'

'No. '44.'

Magruder looked to his partner and then to Robarts. 'What do you say we cut the fencing?' Nathan Hirsch nodded uncertainly. Magruder turned back to Grant. 'Jonathan, my apologies for dragging you out here under false pretences. I do want to discuss something with you, but not what you think.'

'And you've decided to let me into the picture.'

'Something like that. But, before I give any explanation, I want your assurance that, whatever you decide – in or out – what I tell you stays locked up inside and doesn't get told to anyone else.'

'Why should I agree to that?'

'Because I'm offering you the chance of a lifetime,' Magruder said. He paused and his face composed itself into his hard features. 'Publishing is a small world, Jonathan, and you're already on the verge of being pushed off into outer space. I could give you that push.'

'Thanks,' Grant said and waited.

Magruder lit himself another cigar and said, 'I've been offered another diary. It dates from 1942 and is in Hitler's own hand. I want to know if it's a fake.'

The wall clock struck the hour. Nathan Hirsch stirred himself to throw another log on to the fire.

'Well, what do you think?' Magruder asked. He had just finished the outline of his meeting with Knights.

'What does he say about the origin of the diaries?' Grant asked.

Magruder nodded. At least Grant was taking the idea of the diaries seriously. At first he hadn't been sure. Whilst he had told the tale, Grant showed no reaction except an occasional sardonic smile turned on and off like a tap. It disturbed him, just as Knights disturbed him. Grant was a stage Englishman but, he supposed, the stage must have got the type from somewhere. For Magruder, doing a deal was like fishing: there was a bite and then the fish was played more or less subtly and with more or less strength until it was reeled in or the line broke. But here it was as though there were no bite, nothing to play with. And yet buying and selling, which was the name of the game, were the most tangible of relationships.

The drinks went round again, Grenfell refusing. Jack Robarts was dozing in his chair, occasionally opening an eye. Magruder noticed and was only too glad that the younger man was human.

'According to Knights, the diaries were bought by a Frenchman named Boisseau. He was a soldier and did a stint in Cologne in '45. We only have the story from the daughter, since the old man is dead, but it seems that he just picked up the diaries in the street from some guy who was selling war trophies – helmets, daggers, that sort of stuff – to soldiers who wanted something to take home.' He paused and said as an aside, 'I was in Germany myself in '45 – Bavaria. I remember that the Germans would sell you anything they'd got for a few cigarettes or a cake of soap —' He looked at his partner and added, 'Anyway, that was a long time ago. Where was I? Oh, yeah – Boisseau. He was an ordinary type, didn't speak German and didn't read much, so he stuffed the diaries into a drawer and hung the other stuff on the wall. And then a couple of years ago he died.'

'And then?'

'He had a daughter, the one I mentioned, who has sworn an affidavit. She went through the old guy's things, bundled them up and sold the deceased's effects in an auction where a local dealer bought up the diaries, some other books and a few other things of value in a single lot. You know how it is in the antique trade. It's like a refining process. Junk comes in at one end and gets channelled up through the system with the rubbish being discarded until someone recognizes an article of value. In this case it was a book dealer called Gobinet. He took the trouble to read the diaries.'

'But he didn't sell them publicly?' Grant said.

'No. I made the same point to Knights. Apparently Gobinet didn't know what to do with them. He didn't know whether they were genuine and couldn't find out for himself. It seems that he was too scared of what was in them and just wanted to get them off his hands at a good price with a minimum of fuss.'

'So he sold them to Knights' client.'

'So he sold them privately to Knights' client. You got it,' Magruder said. He studied the end of his cigar, licked the end of the loose wrapper and rolled it back into place. 'You know,

I never did get the hang of cutting these damn things.' He looked up again. 'So, what do you think?'

'That the diaries are probably a fake.'

Magruder sighed. He nibbled the end off the wrapper, applied some more saliva and put the cigar back in his mouth. 'I thought you might say that. But is it impossible?'

'Not impossible,' Grant said.

Magruder nodded. He went to the door, opened it, stuck his head out and said in a loud voice, 'Antonio, can you bring some coffee in here?'

A female voice said, 'Are you going to abandon us for the whole evening?'

Magruder turned to Grant again. 'Tell me more.'

'Hitler was a dreamer,' Grant said. 'He was obsessed with the idea of his own destiny. He saw himself as the new messiah, setting the seal on the next thousand years of history.' He paused. 'So you may say that he would have the motivation to keep a diary – the vanity of wanting to preserve his every thought for posterity.'

'Then where's the problem?'

'The problem is that motivation isn't enough. Keeping a diary requires method – and that's exactly what Hitler lacked. He was impulsive rather than methodical. He could never have kept a diary on a daily basis like, for example, Pepys, who was a bureaucrat used to keeping records.'

'But you're saying he could have kept a diary of some sort,' Magruder pressed.

'It's not impossible, just unlikely,' Grant said. 'For example, at the beginning of a year, when a diary is like a new toy, he might have made a few entries, but these would tail off with the novelty. Then, if something caught his imagination, he might make a diary note of it and perhaps keep the diary for a few days until the enthusiasm waned. And so on.'

The door opened and the youth in the waiter's jacket came in with the coffee. He placed the tray carefully and served everybody. Jack Robarts stirred enough to ask for some.

'But you still don't believe in the diaries?' Magruder asked when the boy was gone.

'It isn't a matter of faith but of evidence.'

'You can skip the sententiousness,' Magruder said testily. But the reply made sense. 'Forget I said that, Jonathan,'

Magruder said apologetically. 'Naturally you'd want proof. Hell, I want proof! And that's why I've asked you.' He went over to a decrepit roll-top desk and took out a folder of papers. 'I guess from the books you've written that you must understand German.' He threw the papers across. 'Take a look at these and give me your opinion.' He subsided into a chair and waited.

'I don't give instant reactions,' Grant said when he had read the typewritten sheets.

'We won't hold you to them.'

'Okay. If that's the way you want it.' Grant folded the papers back into their file, whilst the others waited, Magruder impatient, Grenfell composed like a man sure of his limited role, and the fat man leaning forward in his seat with his face in his hands.

'Style,' Grant said, 'possibly Hitler's. But don't excite yourselves: it's easy enough to fake once you've read a few of his speeches.' He looked at Magruder. 'There's no way of telling. Diary writing is a genre of its own; it doesn't necessarily resemble a man's speech or the way he writes letters. So in this case analysis begs the question: you could only test a fake diary against a genuine diary.'

'You've made your point. What about the content?'

Grant picked up the papers and skimmed through them again. 'The diary mentions a meeting with Rommel and von Rundstedt shortly after the Normandy landings. Well, there was one. Von Rundstedt was Commander-in-Chief in the West and Rommel was responsible for organizing beachhead defences. After the landing they paid a visit to Berchtesgaden to urge Hitler to end the war. As you'd expect, Hitler refused and replaced von Rundstedt by von Kluge – which is what the entry is about. I don't know whether the date is correct but it would be easy to check. The point is that it doesn't mean a thing. If I can find out what happened on any given day, so can any competent forger.'

'Maybe. What about the rest?'

'The reference to Morelle's eyedrops is a nice throwaway touch. Hitler complains that the effect of the drops is wearing off.'

'And?'

'They contained cocaine. Hitler was addicted without

knowing it, and, naturally he built up a tolerance to the drug and the effect tended to wear off.'

'Still, this extract is correct on that point,' Magruder said.

'Certainly,' Grant said.

'But it doesn't mean a sure thing,' Magruder anticipated the next remark. 'For the same reason that anything you know could be discovered by someone else. So what does count?'

'Internal consistency – independent evidence. There's no acid test.' Grant picked up his coffee cup and ran his fingers round the rim. 'Maybe you'll never know for sure whether the diaries are genuine.'

Elspeth Magruder came into the room with Diana Grenfell in tow. Her face was a mask of smiles.

'Really, Barton!' she said lightly, 'What sort of host are you to abandon us for so long?' She looked at Robarts with an expression of distaste, and observed, loud enough to be heard, 'The problem with ambitious young men is that they seem to have lost the art of civilized relaxation. Everything has to be carried to extremes.'

Magruder ignored the last remark and checked his watch. 'I guess we have been quite a while.' He looked at the others and added distractedly as though a chain of thought had been broken, 'What say we rejoin the ladies?'

There were murmurs of assent. Jack Robarts stirred from his seat, rubbing his eyes and examining his watch. In the morning he was going to feel like hell, Grant thought, wondering whether he'd fouled up his career.

They made their way back to the other room, where the girl, Lisa Black, was waiting and looked relieved to see them. Magruder invited everyone to a round of nightcaps and proceeded with their dispensation.

The conversation turned to more general matters, breaking up into knots of two with no endeavour to join them together. Grant watched Elspeth Magruder fishing with the girl for a subject on which the girl was ignorant and then treating her to a discussion of porcelain. It was a crude demolition job on the girl's ego.

Diane Grenfell, who had been drinking as an antedote to the same treatment, took Grant by the arm and drew him into a conversation on books. She read two or three romances a week, and Grant, as a writer, must naturally be familiar with them.

'There was this one about a girl who takes a job as a governess. Her employer is a widower, or at least he *says* he is a widower, and he has an ancient family seat in Cornwall – that's in England – but, of course, you must know that!'

'How interesting!' Elspeth Magruder interrupted as she glided past offering drinks. 'That sounds like a plot in the classic romantic tradition. Shades of *Jane Eyre*, don't you think, Jonathan?' She looked round and seized on the girl. 'Well, my dear, have you had an opportunity to look at that figure? Don't you think it was a lucky find?'

The girl fumbled with a small shepherd figurine, holding it in her lap like a Sunday school prize. 'This?' she said. 'Oh yes, it's marvellous.'

Grant went out of the room to get some air. The boy in the waiter's jacket was in the corridor with a tray of glasses, pouring the dregs promiscuously down his throat. Grant asked him where the bathroom was. The door was open. Jack Robarts was sitting on a chair by the washbasin, a damp cloth in one hand, wiping his face between sips of water from a tooth glass.

'How are you feeling?'

'Like shit,' Robarts said, taking gulps of air between words. He looked up resentfully. 'But I don't need any . . . help . . . from you.'

'As you like.'

Robarts got to his feet and pressed his right forefinger against Grant's chest. 'Just 'cause you're in this – don't think it's because you're anything special.'

'I'm not in yet,' Grant said, but the other man seemed not to hear.

'Remember I got you this when you were finished as a writer.'

'What's this? *In vino veritas*?'

Robarts gave a sick smile. 'Don't knock a good cliché.'

'What did your horoscope say for today?'

'Go shag!'

The party began to break up. People were refusing last drinks and looking at their watches.

Elspeth Magruder said, 'I really don't know what we should do about Jack. He's in no fit state to drive and Lisa tells me she can't, which sounds to me quite extraordinary.' She glimpsed Grant coming into the room and eyed him coldly.

Magruder had the relaxed air of a man who has drunk enough to ignore his wife. 'Jack's okay,' he said. 'One too many, maybe. Jonathan, can you fit him in?'

'No trouble, glad to.'

'See?' Magruder said to his wife, 'Where's the problem?'

'No, none at all,' Elspeth said. 'It's really very good of you, Jonathan.'

'I'm just a good Samaritan.'

Five minutes took care of the goodbyes. Barton Magruder accosted Grant as he put on his coat and said, 'I'm sorry we couldn't finish our talk. I'll give you a call first thing tomorrow and maybe we can discuss this a little more.'

Someone helped Robarts into his coat and the girl held his arm. He was trying to look sober and didn't put up a struggle. When they dumped him in the back seat of the car, he went to sleep, the girl sitting next to him, holding his head in her lap, a dim figure in the driver's mirror.

'Where did you meet him?' Grant asked as they drove along.

'A few weeks ago, at a party. I just got my Masters in English Literature and History, and I'm trying to make it in publishing. Jack said he might be able to help me.'

'That so?'

'There's no need to say it like that!' The voice was more spirited than that of the subdued stranger at dinner. 'You make it sound as though I'm some kind of editors' groupie. This is the first time that Jack ever asked me to go anywhere with him.' She hesitated and added illogically, 'He didn't like my dress.'

'Neither do you,' Grant said.

The girl looked at him, watching his eyes reflected in the mirror. 'It belongs to a friend.'

Grant turned on the radio. The announcer offered to play music for all you young lovers out there wherever you are.

'Where do you live?'
'I'm sleeping on a friend's couch. She has an apartment in the East Village.'
'You've only just arrived in New York?'
'Yes. I'm waiting for you to proposition me,' she said more cheerfully.
'Super – why should I do that?'
'Okay, be like that. I only said it to see how you reacted. You're supposed to be excited or shocked or something.'
'I'm shocked.'
'You don't sound it.'
'I'm a method actor.'
'Ever since I arrived in New York I've been propositioned. You know what I mean? Guys say that I can move in with them – for the usual price.'
'But you don't accept.'
She pushed her neat beadwork shoulder bag to one side and said petulantly, 'Why should I? I've got plenty of money. If I wanted to I could move into a hotel tomorrow. My father happens to be a millionaire.'
'Good for Daddy.'
The girl didn't reply. They drove on for a while and outside the rain streamed off the road.
'What history were you studying?' Grant asked.
The girl livened up. 'I'm studying for a postgraduate thesis in European history.'
'I thought you already had your Masters?'
She appeared not to like the question. She fumbled with her bag again then said, 'To tell you the truth, I was at Berkeley – but I goofed off. Now I'm trying to see if I can get a job in publishing. If not, I guess I'll have to see if I can continue studying here in New York.'
'What about Daddy?'
'Don't mistake me,' she said defensively. 'He's a millionaire all right – in hogs if you must know – that's right, in hogs! Just because you never heard of one doesn't mean there are no hog millionaires.'
'I wasn't denying it.'
'You don't have to. Is it because you're English or because you're a writer that everything you say has got barbs in it? You needn't bother to answer that.'

'Thank you,' Grant said. 'In that case I can offer you a bed for the night. The price is optional.'
'Thanks,' she murmured quietly.

A mile down the road Grant slowed the car. He looked in the mirror. 'Jack needs to be cooler,' he said. 'He's sweating like a pig. Take his shirt off.'
'You're joking?' the girl said. 'Do you know what you're doing? He could catch pneumonia.'
'I know what I'm doing. Take it off.'
She hesitated and then slowly eased the sleeping form out of his jacket and unbuttoned his shirt. Underneath it Robarts' chest was matted with ginger hair. For no reason she smiled. 'Are you sure you know what you're doing?'
'Certain,' Grant said. He changed the subject. 'You liked Elspeth Magruder?'
The smile faded. Her face reflected quick changes of emotion, like shower clouds passing over the sun. 'Why mention her?'
'Civilized conversation.'
'Crap! You're as big a sadist as she is. What do you want to do: take me apart and see what makes me tick?'
'I apologize,' Grant said. He looked in the mirror again and she was sitting back peacefully with her eyes closed and a smile on her face like a contented child. 'Take off his pants and shorts,' he said just loud enough so that she could hear.
The eyes opened. 'You're crazy,' she said in a voice that was half indignant but with a laugh underneath. 'You must be some sort of sexual pervert.'
She forced Robarts into an upright position against the back of the seat then unbuckled his belt and unzipped his fly. She tapped Grant on the shoulder. 'That was the easy part. How do I get them off?'
'Kneel on the floor of the car, stretch him out on the seat and then pull.'
'You're the expert.'
A minute later her head appeared again. 'What now, Superman?'
'Now the shorts.'
'You really must be sick or you have a hell of a sense of humour – maybe both.'

'Maybe. But do it.'

There was no reply but Grant could hear her breathing as she struggled with the unconscious body. Then she muttered, 'Goddamn it! Is everybody in publishing a Jew?'

'He turns you on?'

'Oh sure! I always like 'em this way when the moon is full.' Her head emerged and she hung a pair of shorts over the back of the seat. 'Is it full moon tonight? You know I once did a course on astrology?' She waited for a reply and then shrugged her shoulders.

'What now?'

'Now we stop.'

The car pulled off the highway. The road was empty except for stray cars taking people home from New York to their rural idylls. The rain was falling steadily. Grant got out of the driver's seat and opened the rear passenger door. 'I don't like this,' the girl said, 'whatever it is you're up to.'

A car heading in their direction slowed, a face peered through the rainstreaked window and the car picked up speed again. 'That's New York,' the girl said. 'Always help a neighbour who's in trouble.'

'It's the Pharisees and Sadducees who pay the taxes,' Grant said.

The girl got out and stood by the car with a short coat draped over her hair to keep off the rain. Grant leaned over and into the car and took the other man by the armpits.

'Are you going to leave him here? You can't do that!'

'Try me.' He pulled Robarts out of the car, naked except for his shoes. The girl stood behind him, blocking his way. 'Move.'

'No.'

'Why not?'

'Leave him here and I go straight to the police.'

Grant shrugged his shoulders and bundled Robarts back into the car. The girl got into the back seat and pulled Robarts towards her, using her handkerchief to wipe the raindrops from his forehead.

At the next intersection Grant pulled into a roadside diner. 'Do you want some coffee?' he asked. 'Don't worry, he'll be okay.'

She hesitated and then nodded.

The diner was almost empty. Two teamsters were playing a machine and a juke box was hammering out a number by Dionne Warwick. A black in a check shirt and cut-off shorts was pushing a mop around the floor. Grant ordered two coffees and took them to a table.

'Here.' He put the cup down.

'Thanks.' She kept her eyes down, doodling with the spills on the laminated surface of the table. Grant looked at her carefully for the first time, examining the small imperfections that money would have ironed out. He noticed that her nose was just perceptibly to one side; from where her kid brother had pushed a swing at her – if she had a kid brother. She raised her head and stared at Grant.

'What are you looking at?' The light fell on her cheeks and illuminated some pale freckles. She picked up her bag and ferreted out a pack of cigarettes, lighting one. 'What was that all about?' she asked.

'Let's say I shook a dice and came up with a number six. It made me do it.'

'You don't have any dice.'

'I shook them in my head – I must have been lucky. What's your explanation?'

She laughed and worried her lower lip distractedly in the same way that Grant had noticed her run her hand through her hair.

'You know, I once saw a TV programme,' she said, stubbing out her cigarette on the table. 'It was about some people who were invited to take part in an experiment. They were told that they had to pull a switch and it would send a shock into the guy who was being experimented on – it was supposed to test the guy's reactions to pain.'

'What happened?'

'The truth was that the guy wasn't really in pain, just faking. The real subjects of the experiment were the people pulling the switches: just how much pain were they prepared to cause in the name of science?' She paused and a pair of intelligent eyes looked out from behind the lost-little-girl mask. 'Didn't you write a book once about the Allied bombing of Germany?'

'You see a connection?'

'People will commit any atrocity provided you dress it up right. Is that your hang-up?'

Grant put down his cup and took her back to the car.

They took Robarts home to his bachelor apartment and laid him out on the bed. Half an hour later they parked the car in the garage under Grant's apartment building. Lisa stopped him as he led the way to the elevator.

'All that back there – it wasn't a joke, was it?' She looked for an answer in his pale eyes and shook her head. 'You really are a grim bastard, aren't you?' she said in an emotionless voice.

Nine

15 November 1980

Grant was woken by the telephone. It rang for two minutes and then stopped.

'Who was that?' the voice next to him said.

Grant turned over and saw the girl's face emerge from the bedcovers, her dazzled eyes squinting myopically at him. He remembered that she wore contact lenses. In between bouts of passion she had hunted around for something unbroken to put them in and had finally settled for one of Joey's plastic cups with a Donald Duck transfer on the side.

'Coffee?'

She nodded.

Grant slipped out of bed and padded into the kitchen, where he searched among the débris to find the coffee and something to drink out of, coming up in the end with two shallow steel cups out of an egg-poacher. When he returned to the bedroom, she was lying naked on the floor doing yoga exercises.

'You . . . have . . . a . . . scar,' she said between breaths. 'On your back. I saw it when you went out. Where did you get it?'

'Vietnam,' Grant said.

'How?' She stopped her exercises and sat cross-legged, interested.

'Running away – like anyone with sense.' Grant handed her a cup and sat down on the edge of the bed.

'I bet you modest heroes always say that.' The girl looked around the room. 'You lived pretty well here. I mean – until the end of the world hit the place.' She indicated the torn curtains and the broken furniture shoved roughly into a corner. 'What happened? Or maybe I shouldn't be so curious.'

'You shouldn't be so curious.'

'Thanks a lot!' She stood up and picked up her clothes from

a chair. She ran her fingers through her hair. 'Well, I won't say it hasn't been nice. Thanks for the screw, not exactly olympic standard, but okay for an amateur.'

'Sit down!' Grant said. He looked up from his coffee into the hurt brown eyes. She hesitated. He repeated the words, 'Sit down,' and she sat down again and smiled.

'Breakfast?' Grant asked. She nodded. 'Okay. If you put on some clothes, we'll go out and get some.'

'That's fine by me.' She reached for the green silk dress and paused. 'I can't go out for breakfast in this! I'll look like a hooker after a bad night.'

'This is an apartment,' Grant said. 'No room service.'

She sighed, 'Then I guess it'll have to do.' She looked at the dress. 'That's great! It's stained! Have you ever tried to sponge stains out of silk? Jesus, this is all I needed!' She picked up the rest of her clothes. 'I'll see what I can do in the bathroom.'

Grant dressed whilst the girl was gone. When she came back she was wearing a pair of brown slacks and a tartan shirt that belonged to Kathy.

'Where did you get those?'

The girl twirled on her toes. 'You like? I found them at the back of a closet. I thought they'd be more suitable.' She stopped and brushed her hair out of one eye. 'I guess they belong to your wife,' she said slowly.

'Not my wife.'

'Well, whatever.' She looked around. 'What's her name? Kathy? She do all this?'

'That's right.'

'Wow!' She thought for a moment. 'She must really have been mad. Still,' she added, 'I can understand that. No offence, but it must be tough living with a cold bastard like you. If women's lib knew I'd shacked up here last night, they'd be picketing my fanny.' She sat down and gave Grant a cheerful smile. 'Okay, so how about that breakfast?'

At that moment the phone rang again and Grant answered it. Lisa hung by him, leaning against the wall picking the remains of some wheat flakes from the bottom of a packet. The call was from Barton Magruder.

'I promised to call you,' the publisher said.

'I remember.'

'Have you thought over what we discussed last night?'
'Yes.'
'And?'
'I'll do your job for two-hundred and fifty thousand.'
The phone went dead for a moment. Grant guessed that Magruder was talking to his partner. There was a low buzz of voices and then the other man came back.
'I can't offer you a straight quarter of a million. Not when I don't have a guaranteed return.'
'Then make a suggestion.'
'You can have your two-hundred and fifty thousand,' Magruder said, 'but we'll make it contingent. If you authenticate the diaries, then you get paid in full.'
'And if I don't?'
'We pay you twenty thousand and your expenses.' The publisher gave Grant time to think and then asked, 'Do we have a deal?'
'We have a deal.'
They talked over a few details. Magruder was all reasonableness until Grant told him that he would need an assistant.
The response was sharp. 'What for? You know this business is supposed to be confidential. If there's a leak then the deal is blown.'
'You'll have to take that chance,' Grant said. 'The longer I spend on the diaries, the greater the risk of a leak. You don't really think you can sit on this indefinitely? In publishing? Give this three months and McGraw-Hill will put in a bid that will blow you out of the water.'
Magruder got the point.
'Two-hundred and fifty thousand dollars!' Lisa said. 'What for?'
Grant replaced the receiver and was going to answer when another call came through. It was Jack Robarts.
'Has Bart just called you?' Robarts asked. He took the answer for granted. 'Have you agreed to do the book?'
'Who is it?' Lisa asked.
'Jack.'
'Jack! How is he? Does he remember anything about last night?'
'He sounds fine,' Grant said. Robarts was not the kind to

look back on his failures. 'We have a deal,' he said into the mouthpiece.

Robarts sounded relieved on his own account. 'It was me who put your name to Bart. He was nervous about the whole idea.' He paused, 'Anyway, I wasn't calling for thanks. We've got to establish lines of communication.'

'It sounded like Magruder wanted me to talk to him direct.'

'Oh sure! This is one Bart will want to keep a handle on. But just on the strategy – know what I mean? Bart's delegated the detail to me. There's going to be a lot to do if we're going to tie together the US and foreign rights and hit the public all together with the maximum impact. I'll have to be briefed.'

'Then Magruder will keep you posted,' Grant said. He could see that Robarts was searching for an angle and he wasn't going to hand one over.

'Not on the detail,' Robarts insisted. 'Bart won't carry that in his head. I need you to keep in touch, promise?'

'I'll tell you what you need to know.'

Robarts took the promise in the sense he wanted, gave his thanks and rang off. Grant replaced the receiver and turned to the girl.

She was squatting on the carpet, bored with listening. Her hair was in a tangle, a twisted strand curled between her lips, and beneath her shirt her breasts swelled and fell in the way that bras never imitate.

'You sound as though you've stitched together some terrific deal,' she said. She took a piece of hair from her mouth and wound it unconsciously around a finger. 'What are you looking at me like that for?' Her face brightened. 'Isn't that a great cliché? "What are you looking at me like that for?" Bette Davis – or maybe it was Joan Crawford – said it in a movie once. Anyway, what are you looking at me like that for?'

'Did I hear that you were doing post-graduate research in history at Berkeley or was that just a story?'

'He wants my life history and I haven't had breakfast!'

'Well?'

She looked more serious. 'If you want the truth, I wanted to do research but I didn't get started.'

'Why not?'

'I was dating one of the professors – he would have been my supervisor. So, we had a quarrel and he told me that I wouldn't have got the place if I hadn't been sleeping with him. And that was enough for me.'

'You quit.'

'I guess I'm the wide-eyed vulnerable type. I really thought I had it in me to do research, but, as Karl Marx said, he only wanted me for my body: that's the materialist conception of history for you.' She shrugged her shoulders and laughed. 'And that's it!'

She got off the floor. 'I'll pick up my stuff and be gone. I'll let you have the clothes back.' She turned back at the bedroom door. 'It was great, really. Forget anything nasty I said.'

'Are you still interested in research?'

She paused, surprised. 'What into?'

Grant told her.

'Adolf Hitler! Jesus Christ. I mean that is incredible, but incredible!'

Grant offered her a cigarette and they adjourned to the kitchen to make some more coffee.

'And you're going to be paid a quarter of a million dollars for the research?'

'I'd have thought that was nothing to a pig millionairess,' Grant said.

There was a glint of humour in the reply, 'Truth is my father ploughs everything back into the business, so we don't live what you might call millionaire style.'

'I see.'

'You don't believe me? You needn't answer, I can see you don't.' She changed the subject. 'Why is your style so ironic? Or do I mean sarcastic? Somebody said that sarcasm is the lowest form of wit – Socrates or Colonel Sanders.'

'Why are you such a liar?'

'I guess because it suits me. But you see, you're doing it again! When I say something to try to get to know you, you throw a bucket of cold water over me. Are you suspicious of human relationships or something?'

Grant took the point. 'Okay, ask your questions. If we're going to work together we may as well get them over with.'

She paused, 'All right, we'll skip the personal stuff. Why do you only get paid in full only if you say the diaries are genuine? It sounds like an invitation to be crooked.'

'That's what it is,' Grant said. 'Magruder knows that the diaries are probably fakes. He's calculating the percentages on peddling them all the same.'

'Selling a phoney?'

'It's been done.'

She whistled, 'There goes another of my illusions!'

Grant put his coffee down. 'Get your coat,' he said. 'Let's get that breakfast.'

Lisa picked up her coat and slung it over her arm. As Grant reached for the handle on the outside door, she put her hand on his.

'I'm putting a knife to my throat,' she said, 'but there is one personal question I want to ask.'

'Which is?'

'Is Kathy – or whatever her name is – coming back?'

Ten

'Hello, Harvey. Super to see you again.'

Harvey Warfield turned off the power mower and looked up. He had seen Grant's car draw up across the street, but had deliberately ignored it and got on with cutting the lawn. He had decided to be strong and silent.

'Is Kathy here?'

Harvey rubbed his thick, square hands down the sides of his trousers that he wore for jogging and looked Grant up and down. 'What do you want?'

'I just asked you if Kathy is here.'

'Are you looking for trouble?' Harvey seemed midway between searching for a fight and trying to avoid one. Like other big men who lead quiet lives, he cherished the illusion that he was a tough customer to tangle with.

'How's the insurance business?' Grant asked.

'Fine, but that isn't what I asked you.'

'No?' Grant looked past the other man at the neat, white frame-house. 'Are you going to ask me inside?'

At this point the day-to-day, easy-going nature of the big man took over and Harvey wiped his hands again, glanced at the mower and said reluctantly, 'Well, I guess that, since you're here, you may as well come in.'

The house was clean, homely and smelled of cooking. Harvey took off his shoes and called out to the kitchen, 'Lorraine, we've got a visitor. Jonathan's here.' He turned to Grant and, having displayed his toughness, became friendly. 'What say we go in the den and have a beer? Working in the garden always gives me a thirst.'

'That's fine by me,' Grant said.

Lorraine Warfield came out of the kitchen. She had flour on her hands which she transferred to her hair as she tidied it. She stopped dead on seeing Grant and glanced at her husband. Harvey made a little dumbshow, mouthing words to indicate that everything was all right.

'It's nice to see you again, Jonathan,' Lorraine Warfield said. 'It's been a long time.'

'It's good to see you too.'

'We're having a beer in the den, hon,' Harvey said. 'Can you get some out of the icebox?'

'Beer? Oh, sure!' She gave a nervous smile, 'I'll get it right away.'

The den was where Harvey Warfield lived out his big man's fantasies. He was a gun freak. There was a rack mounted on the wall with a line of guns chained by their trigger guards. It was framed by animal heads, each with an engraved plaque giving details of when the owners were shot. There was a table spread with rifle-club magazines and a small bookshelf stacked with gun catalogues and a scattering of paperbacks by Zane Grey. Everywhere there were photographs: Harvey standing over the corpse of a deer; Harvey, Lorraine and the kids by the side of a camper, barbequing steaks; Harvey and a group of buddies in the National Guard. There was a uniform grin on the fleshy face with its short-cropped hair.

'Nice place you have here,' Grant said as they settled into chairs. He pointed to a photograph. 'That one I don't recognize.'

Harvey threw a glance. 'It was taken in 'Nam somewhere,' he said carelessly. Grant knew that he had been a sergeant in the main PX at Saigon and the nearest he had come to the Viet Cong was in training films.

Lorraine came in with a tray holding glasses and two cans of beer. Harvey took one and threw the other across to Grant. He himself ignored the glasses, pulled the ring and took a drink out of the can. The foam spilled over and down his sleeve.

'You can leave the tray, hon.'

'I thought I'd stay.' In contrast with her husband, Lorraine Warfield was dark and petite with sharp eyes and a determined mouth. She sat half on the arm of a chair and swung one foot with suppressed impatience.

'Are the kids okay?' Harvey asked.

'They're fine,' Lorraine said, not taking up the invitation to go. She addressed Grant, 'Joey's a fine child. Gets on fine with the others – I thought you'd like to know.'

'Thanks.'

'I thought you'd like to know,' she repeated. Then she laughed, 'For God's sake, I didn't get myself a drink. Honey, will you get me one?'

'Me?' Harvey said.

'Who else?' Lorraine said acidly. She watched her husband coldly as he left the room. The moment he was gone she turned to Grant. 'Okay, Jonathan, what brings you here?'

'Curiosity? Doing the decent thing? Love?' For once Grant wasn't being ironic. He didn't know why he had decided to see Kathy and the child. Maybe it was the way things finished – Kathy sneaking off with Joey whilst he wasn't there.

'Love? You don't have an ounce of emotion in you,' Lorraine said. The vehemence was half-suppressed as if she was afraid of letting it out in case the statement recoiled on her. Grant wondered what emotions there were in her suburban world.

'Where is she?' he asked.

'Kathy? In bed. She's sleeping a lot. She's depressed and depressives sleep a lot – didn't you know that?'

Grant didn't answer. Harvey came back into the room with a glass of something pink and translucent. He had put on a solemn face, the sort everyone had worn the day Kennedy died. He took a back seat to his wife.

'Why can't you two just cut loose?' Lorraine said. 'I mean, it's not like you ever hit it off like a couple of lovebirds.' She added quickly, 'I'm not trying to break the pair of you up, God forbid, but you've got to look at these things rationally.'

Grant sat back and listened, but she was addressing somebody who wasn't there – an image of how she thought he ought to feel.

'Maybe you're right,' he said. He had to say something. It was enough. Lorraine reached across and in a show of affection placed her hand in a light pat on his knee. 'We're your friends, Jonathan. We'll do anything we can to help.'

'Thanks. I appreciate it.'

There was a knock on the door. It was Kathy. Her face was pale, without make-up, and her dark hair was scraped back and pinned. She was wearing brown corduroy jeans and a denim shirt.

'Kathy, honey, you shouldn't have got up!' Lorraine said.

'It's okay. I'm fine. I heard you talking.' She looked at

Harvey and in a tired voice said, 'Can you get me a cup of coffee?'

She turned to Grant. 'How are you, Jonathan?'

'Fine. And you?'

'Shall I leave you two alone to talk things over?' Lorraine said.

'No. I'd like you to stay,' Kathy said. Her voice was flat and calm. Lorraine lowered herself back into her chair.

'How's Joey?' Grant asked.

'Fine,' Kathy answered. She folded her hands on her lap. 'I owe you an apology for the way I left. I had no right to break the place up.'

'That's okay. Now I've got the only flat in New York with a Dadaist décor,' Grant said and knew straightaway that it was a mistake.

'Can't you even accept a simple apology?' The voice was still calm but the anger was there. Grant wondered what pills she had been taking. Lorraine probably had a cabinet full.

She went on, 'I'm not coming back, Jonathan, if that's why you're here.' She watched his face but got no reaction since Grant didn't know either why he was there except in fulfilment of some obscure rite. Harvey came in with the coffee.

'Why are you here?' she asked. 'Because of Joey?'

'Would that be wrong?'

She laughed. 'But she's not even your child! She has a father in California who sends me two hundred dollars a month.'

'I wasn't supposed to love her then?' Grant asked. The question was a twisted knife and went deep.

'I don't want to go on with this conversation,' Kathy said abruptly and she looked at Harvey. He stared back and then shook himself like a slow-starting car.

'I think I should go if I were you, Jonathan,' he said, and before Grant could reply added, 'and at the same time you could call off your watchdog before I have to take care of him myself.'

Lorraine's flush of sympathy had vanished and in a mocking voice she threw in, 'I know that you have a jealous nature, Jonathan, but hiring a detective – well, that sounds to me like paranoia.'

Grant didn't know what they were talking about but he said

nothing. They had been speaking all along to a different person, playing out a scene as they imagined this one was supposed to be played. He followed their eyes to the window with its view over the expanse of silent street where neighbours were washing cars or clearing leaves off the lawn.

'You don't say you didn't hire the guy in the blue Ford!' Harvey snapped.

'For what it's worth, I didn't.' Grant looked across the street to where the car was parked. A 1977 model with bronzed windows. 'How long has he been watching you?'

'Two days,' Lorraine said. 'There are two of them, taking turns.'

'You're sure?'

'You think I don't know every car in this street?' Harvey said angrily. 'For chrissake, I insured most of them!'

'Then it looks as though you've got a problem there, old boy,' Grant said as he got up. 'Still, I'm sure you'll be able to do something about it.'

He left the room with Lorraine on his heels. 'Where are you going?'

'To say hello to Joey.'

'You've got no right!'

'You know how it is with an arrogant bastard like me.'

She stopped as he opened the door. 'Get out of here!' she said bitterly.

The children looked around as Grant came out of the back of the house. There were three: a boy of seven who was going to grow up to look like Harvey, a girl of eleven with a tomboy face and braces on her teeth, and a fair-haired girl of three wearing a Little Miss Muffet dress and a broad smile. She threw out her arms and came charging across the grass yelling, 'Daddy!'

'Hello, love.' Grant caught her up in his arms and kissed her.

'Have you come to take us home, Daddy?' Joey asked and spared him the lie. 'Can we stay until tomorrow – I've been having such fun.'

'Okay then, love. Until tomorrow.' He put her down and she ran back to join the others.

Grant looked back to the house where there was shouting. He caught sight of Harvey's face at the window. He was talking loudly and waving his arms. Grant walked across the lawn and climbed over the fence into the next garden.

Two lots down he emerged onto the street past a fat man in his sixties who was raking up leaves. They exchanged hellos. The blue car with the bronzed windows was a hundred yards away, facing in the opposite direction. Grant crossed the street and walked around the block to take him to the driver's blind side – assuming he was keeping an eye on the house.

The car was parked by an intersection, the driver was a dark shape, holding something, probably a newspaper. Then, as Grant approached, something happened that he hadn't expected. Harvey came out of the house carrying a gun.

Grant was no expert on guns but it was some sort of carbine, and Harvey red-faced with beads of sweat on his forehead, was holding it across his chest at the ready as the Army had taught him. Grant set into a run as he heard the shot.

It was the driver of the car who had fired, aiming high or he couldn't have missed. All the same, Harvey let out a yell as if he'd been hit, fell on to his belly, closed his eyes and loosed off a clip of bullets into the garden opposite but the car was already gone.

Grant reached it as the driver put his foot down. He threw himself at the car and caught on to the back, scrabbling spread-eagled over the boot. The driver felt the weight of his passenger, turned round and put a shot through the glass of the rear window. Then he pulled the car over and it yawed across the street, scattering the people as they came running out of their houses. Grant lost his grip and tumbled off. When he picked himself up, the car had disappeared.

He made his way back to the house. The door was open and people were collecting outside in the street. They stood back for him to go in.

Lorraine was standing by the door in a fit of indecision, holding the boy.

'What are you doing here!' she shouted.

'Where's your bloody fool of a husband?' Grant said, brushing past her venomous look. He pushed open the door of the den.

Harvey Warfield looked up blank-eyed. He was in a chair by the window, resting the carbine across his knees. Kathy had Joey in her arms and was trying to soothe the child.

'Put the gun away, Harvey,' Grant said. 'The last thing we need is some trigger-happy cop shooting at you.'

'They shot at me, Jonathan,' Harvey said disbelievingly.

'Yes. Well, they would, wouldn't they? With you going out there to make America safe for the cause of freedom.'

'Don't make fun of him,' Kathy said softly. There was a flash of sympathy. 'I saw you chase the car.'

'That was a mistake in my sense of direction.'

'It's Helterskelter,' Harvey mumbled.

Helterskelter. War between the races as foretold by the messiah Charles Manson. And Hitler.

'What has that to do with it?' Grant asked.

'I saw the driver,' Harvey said without turning his eyes from the gun, which he was stroking gently.

'What about the driver?' Grant pressed him.

'He was black.'

Eleven

16 – 17 November 1980

Magruder arrived at Kloten Airport under a slate-grey sky. En route to the hotel he directed the taxi past the address which Knights had given on his business card. It turned out to be a grey, bleak building in bastard Bauhaus style with a doorway flanked by flat-faced, mock-Epstein caryatids. It was the headquarters of the Schweizerische Allgemeine Kreditanstalt, the bank into which Magruder would pay the money.

The Atlantis Sheraton lay outside the city centre on a hill backed by a pine wood full of manicured paths and neatly painted signs telling the rambler not to pick the flowers and how long his walk would take.

The déjà-vu appearance of the hotel didn't bother the publisher. He liked American-style hotels because they guaranteed the hot water. There was an expansive foyer with marble tables and green leather chairs, a shallow fountain pool tiled with the house-logo and a McGregor shop with the name spelled out in tartan. It had all the flavour of nowhere.

There were no messages at the desk and a porter took his bags to the room. Magruder tipped him and then stood for a few moments simply to breathe. He was feeling tired and a little distant – jet-lag symptoms. His usual recipe was a shower, some food and some background noise to reassure him he wasn't in Limbo. He rang room-service for the food and turned on the television set whilst he ran the shower.

There was a film showing. Walter Matthau in *Charley Varrick*. Magruder had an eye for clichés. The older man always got the younger woman. He thought of Elspeth and what he should get her as a present.

After he had showered and dressed, a Turkish waiter arrived with a plate of *Bündnerfleisch* – slices of air-dried meat – and potato salad. Magruder took the plate and settled down to collect his thoughts.

In the film, the patrol car pulled up in the bright New

Mexico sun. The cop in the dark glasses went up to the driver's window of a dusty Chrysler, tipped the lip of his broad-brimmed hat and asked the woman occupant: '*Entschuldigen Sie mir, Ma'am – Ihr Führerschein bitte.*'

Magruder took out the telephone directory. Someone had once told him that Swiss directories were better than most: they gave the full name and profession of subscribers. He looked up 'Knights' but couldn't find an entry. He checked 'knight' in his pocket dictionary and tried the German variants. There was nothing under *Ritter*. Under *Knecht* there was an entry for Saloman Knecht, a furrier with premises in the Bahnhofstrasse. Magruder decided it was time to stop playing detectives and lay back on the bed, closing his eyes and praying for some sleep.

He wondered: what's so special about 16 December that Knights needs to close the deal by then? Here he was, running around and with no idea why. Next he remembered: tomorrow he was going to see Hitler's diaries! It was a thought that should have given him some comfort, but, somehow, it didn't.

In the morning he got a message that a Mr Knights had called and proposed they meet for lunch at twelve-thirty at the Baur en Ville. Until then Magruder was left to kick his heels, buy his wife a diamond clip at a jewellers' in Talacker and stroll by the Limmat, watching the coots bobbing for food.

Simon Knights was on time, looking cold and stylish in an English-cut suit with a carnation buttonhole and a rolled copy of the *Neue Zürcher Zeitung* under his arm. He smiled amiably and held out his hand.

'It's a pleasure to see you again, Mr Magruder.'

Magruder nodded and took the proffered seat. Knights passed the menu and made bland conversation whilst the American worked his way through. When the meal was settled Knights rattled the order to the waiter in German, and Magruder noted that the other man spoke without the nasal tones of the local dialect. Whatever Knights was, he wasn't Swiss.

It wasn't until coffee that they came to the business in hand.

'All right, Mr Knights, thanks for the meal,' Magruder said. 'Now, where are the papers?'

'You mean the diaries? Oh, they're somewhere quite safe – at the bank in fact.'

'Do we go from here to collect?'

'You have the draft for fifty thousand dollars?'

'Naturally, since that was the deal.'

Knights leaned back in his chair and smiled. 'In that case, you will walk away with a copy of the diaries and the originals of the affidavits. Then – maybe in a week or so – I shall contact you in New York and I trust we can then proceed to a conclusion.'

'There's no way I can be ready in a week. The research is going to take longer and I still have to sell the deal internally – I don't command a budget of ten million dollars for a single project like this.' Magruder had in mind a meeting with Walter Emmett in San Francisco. What Rama's senior vice-president would make of the Hitler diaries was anybody's guess.

Knights nodded. He seemed unconcerned, a fact that Magruder couldn't square with the urgency of the 16 December date. Then it occurred to him: was there another bidder?

The two men dodged the blue and white trams in the Paradeplatz and arrived at the bronze doors of the bank. The main hall was a marbled circus ringed by the tellers' positions and on the wall opposite the entrance a large clock shaped like a sunburst marked off the time in the world's major financial centres. Knights gave his name to a severe-looking woman with spectacles on a gold rope, and, as if expected, they were shown through a door into an office marked *Herr Scherer*.

The room was in classical style, pink and fawn with detail picked out in gilt and white. Herr Scherer was behind a desk that looked like a black sarcophagus with ormolu mounts and was littered with commemoration pen sets, plaques and other trophies of successful bond issues and loans managed by the bank. He was a pleasant-faced man with small, weak eyes and a button nose, and was watching currency movements on a desk-top console.

'May I introduce Mr Magruder, Herr Scherer,' Knights said. The banker responded with the usual courtesies but Magruder was taking in the room with its juxtaposition of oil paintings and framed copies of bonds. Knights went on, 'Mr

Magruder is here to collect some documents from your custody. He has with him a banker's draft for fifty thousand dollars. I should be grateful if you would hold it until our business is complete.'

'Of course,' Scherer said as if he understood perfectly what was taking place. The friendly eyes showed no trace of curiosity. He looked at the publisher. 'The draft, please?' Magruder handed it over.

There was a knock and Magruder turned round to notice a second door. Scherer said something in German, the door opened and a bank guard came in. 'Please to follow me,' Scherer said.

The door led by a flight of steps directly to the vaults. At the bottom there was a barred grill of grey steel which the guard opened with a key and locked behind them. The room beyond was laid out like an airport lounge with soft chairs and low tables loaded with magazines. The difference lay in the two massive doors with combination locks set into one wall and the row of cubicles with mirror-doors along another.

The banker opened the door of the strongroom and invited Knights to go in, but, when Magruder tried to follow, Scherer shook his head and indicated the seats. Knights emerged holding a metal box, went into one of the cubicles and, a minute later, came out and beckoned Magruder to join him.

The mirror doors proved to be one-way glass giving a view over the waiting room. Inside the cubicle there was nothing more than a narrow shelf holding a pen, a note pad and a calendar, and, in this case, the open deposit box which Knights had taken from the strongroom.

'Well?' Knights said. 'Are you going to take a look?'

Magruder saw what he had expected to see. But the effect was strangely anti-climatic. The diaries were not immediately visible, being overlaid by some typewritten sheets of stiff paper, the kind lawyers use for engrossments; Magruder had no difficulty recognizing the originals of the affidavits. Underneath there was a large manilla envelope. Knights took it and broke the seal.

The diaries formed a bundle about an inch thick. They looked as though they had been reduced through a dry-copier, two pages of the original to each sheet, and the paper smelled faintly of chemicals. Each daily entry was on a separate page with the date printed in heavy Gothic lettering. The writing was angular and spidery, varying in size from a slovenly scrawl of letters covering two or three lines to a cramped, miniscule script filling the margins. Magruder fingered the sheets and felt in himself a strange emptiness instead of the exhilaration he had looked for.

'What sort of writing is this?' he asked. 'I don't even recognize the letters.

'It's called *Kurrent*. Nowadays it's not often used, but it was once the normal handwriting of any German.'

Magruder grunted and rifled through the rest of the bundle. 'Is there an English translation?'

Knights took another envelope out of the box and handed it across. It contained the translation, closely typed on ordinary bond paper. Magruder muttered his thanks, riffled through more pages and then paused, went back, fingered over the individual sheets and then bit his lip and put the papers down.

'What's the idea?' he said. 'These diaries are nowhere near complete. There can't be more than six months of entries here out of three and a half years.'

'That's right,' Knights said calmly. 'To be exact there are two hundred and five entries.'

'Okay, then where's the rest. If I'm to buy, I want the whole lot. There's no way I lay out ten million and then find that some other guy is coming out with a selection from the diaries at the same time.'

Knights laughed softly. 'You may relax on that count. I assure you: these are the complete diaries. Hitler was not a man of regular habits. He was too busy or too lazy to write up an entry for each day. But for all that, I believe that you will find the diaries most rewarding.'

Magruder looked at the other man doubtfully but then he remembered what Grant had said. The Englishman had known that the only possible diaries by Hitler would be episodic. He swallowed his objections.

A quarter of an hour later Barton Magruder walked out of the bank with the copies and translation in a small attaché case. It seemed to tingle in his hand as he waited to hail a taxi for the airport.

Twelve

'This is your office?' The voice was disappointed. The girl looked around the small room and its contents, a line of old filing cabinets, green and stacked like ammunition boxes along two walls, a desk with brown-gravy varnish and a scarred leather top, peeling wallpaper, fly-specked light-shades and everywhere books and papers thrown together in loose heaps.

'This is it,' Grant said as he turned on the light to supplement the dull snatches of daylight. 'What did you expect?'

'I don't know,' Lisa answered, taking off her coat and looking for a place to hang it. 'I guess – famous writer and all that – it would be . . . '

'The World Trade Center?'

'Well, not exactly.' There was a flash of mischief and naïvety in her smile, 'But you get the general idea – I hope I'm not embarrassing you or anything?'

'That's all right,' Grant said. He took her coat and hung it over the door handle then went to the window and opened it a little. The sound of traffic drifted in. 'No air-conditioning,' he explained.

She looked around. 'Where do we start?'

'You start here with solving the problem of who we're dealing with. Until we get the text, we have nothing else to work on, so Magruder wants some suggestions as to the identity of Knights' clients.'

'And what are you going to do?'

'Browse around the City Library, contemplate my navel and look for inspiration. We have a month at the outside to work on the diaries. Unless we're luckier than we deserve, no regular programme of research can be completed in that time.'

'And contemplating your navel will save time?'

'If it gives me the inspiration to cut corners,' Grant said.

He moved some of the papers from the desk. 'You can use this space. Try not to move the piles of loose stuff – it isn't in any order that you'd recognize. Use any of the books you need and make free with the files' – he gestured at the cabinets – 'but replace anything you take out. If you get thirsty, you'll find some Cokes in a fridge in the loo.'

'Thanks. But aren't you going to tell me where to begin?'

'Begin at the end,' Grant said.

'The end?'

'Hitler's end. He kept the diaries until a couple of days before his death. How they were got out of the bunker may throw some light on who has them now.' Grant took a book from among those on the floor. Lisa read the title *The Last Days of Adolf Hitler*, by the Englishman, Trevor-Roper. 'This should help you to make a list of the characters who were there at the end. I spoke to some of them in connection with my last book – you'll find the notes on file – and some of their diaries and memoirs are around here somewhere if you find a lead that you want to trace.'

Lisa looked around the room. 'This is all stuff you collected for your last book?' Grant nodded. '*The Apotheosis of Mediocrity* – the Himmler book, wasn't it?'

'That's right.'

'I remember. I read all the lousy press reviews.' She looked up into the Englishman's cold, ironical eyes. 'I also read the book. I thought it was good.'

'Thanks,' Grant said.

He returned to the office shortly after ten. It was in darkness except for a light angled over the desk. Lisa was asleep in the chair, slumped forward, her hair lying in a loose tangle over some scattered papers covered with her handwriting. Open files and books lay on the table and the floor and wastebin were littered with crumpled notes, dirty paper cups and the remains of a sandwich.

'Do you want to eat?' he asked. He stood behind her chair and touched her neck gently. She stirred and opened her eyes.

'What time is it?'

'Five past ten. Have you had a meal today apart from —' he indicated the wastebin.

'I had a bite at lunch,' she said slowly, stretching her arms out. She shivered as if noticing for the first time the touch of his hand on her skin. 'I must have been asleep for about half an hour. It's so hot in here.'

'I told you – no air-conditioning,' Grant said. He picked up some of the books and piled them together.

'Wait a minute, I can't see! Where did I put my lenses?' She scanned the desk top with her fingers and finally found them in the upturned lid of a typewriter ribbon box which Grant had used as an ashtray. She squinted and slipped them in. 'I'm going to regret this,' she said in a voice that suggested she wasn't in the habit of regretting much. 'My eyes are going to sting like hell.'

Grant lit a cigarette and watched her shake down her hair and put it into some sort of shape. 'Are you hungry?' he asked.

She thought for a moment. 'I guess I am at that.'

'Good. There's an Italian place a couple of blocks from here. I've booked a table.'

The restaurant was unpretentious, the paint on the chairs was chipped, the chequered tablecloths were neatly darned and there was a pleasant smell of good cheese and oregano. As far as Lisa could tell it was run by a fat middle-aged couple and a girl of about eighteen who alternately waited on the customers and breast-fed the baby at one of the tables.

Grant took the menu out of Lisa's hand. 'We're having antipasta followed by veal. The drink is chianti.'

'Don't I get a choice?'

'Not in here,' Grant said. He gave the order to the girl and then leaned across the table. 'Let me give my news whilst we're waiting. I spoke to Nathan Hirsch this afternoon.'

'Oh? What did he have to say?'

'Magruder called him from Zurich. He collected the manuscript today. He's flying back overnight and we get to see it tomorrow.'

Lisa nodded. 'Good news. The first kick in the tush for Bob Zimmermann.'

'Who's Bob Zimmermann?'

'The guy I told you about – prof at Berkeley who wanted me to screw for victory.' The girl came with the dishes of antipasta. When she had gone, Lisa went on, 'Don't you want to know the result of my first day's effort?' She fumbled in her bag and pulled out a piece of paper. 'How do you want to play it?'

'Just read out the names and we'll discuss them as they come.'

'Okay, then let's start with my favourites.'

'You've got more than one?'

'Three – they all seem to fit and I can't make up my mind between them.'

'Then let's have all three.'

'You're the boss. First among the front-runners then is Heinz Lorenz. I like him because he was at the bunker with Hitler until 29 April – which is the day after the last diary entry. He was caught by the British in '45 and interrogated. He gave a story about being a journalist from Luxembourg, but he soon cracked and out came the truth. Am I going too fast?' No reply. 'Okay. Well, here's Lorenz's tale. Hitler had written a will and a political testament. There were three copies to be taken out by Lorenz and two others, the idea being to get them to Hitler's successors.' She paused for effect. 'The way I see it, if Hitler wanted to get his diaries out of Berlin, he would have sent them by the same route as his will. So the most likely candidates are Lorenz or one of the other two.'

'What about them?'

'If I had to pick, I'd go for SS Standartenfuehrer Wilhelm Zander – genuine SS type who wouldn't crack under interrogation; he had the documents for Doenitz, who was going to be Hitler's successor. So what's more natural than that he should have the diaries?'

'He was caught?'

'Near Passau in December '45. Like I said, he didn't talk, but someone else showed where his documents were hidden.'

'But no diaries.'

'He might have hidden the diaries separately.'

'Why?'

Lisa shrugged her shoulders. 'Who knows?'

'Okay, who's next?'

'Major Willi Johannmeier. His job was to get the will and political testament to Field-Marshal Schoerner – what was left of the Army was commanded by Schoerner.'

'And?'

'He was caught and the documents were recovered from a garden of a house near Iserlohn.' She looked up from her notes. 'You don't like any of them, do you?'

'They were caught. Two of them confessed under interrogation and the papers were found in all three cases. If they'd had the diaries, why didn't they show up?'

'I'm out of guesses. How about some more names? Major Freytag von Loringhoven – I think that's how you say it – Captain Gerhardt Boldt and Lieutenant Colonel Weiss? They all got out on 29 April ahead of Zander's crowd. They could have carried the diaries with them.'

Grant shook his head.

'Why not?'

'They all made it to the West. If any of them had the diaries, they've managed to keep the secret for nearly forty years. After that length of time even old old Nazis talk – to Allied interrogators, to the press, to old friends.

'Unless there's something in the diaries that makes talking impossible,' Lisa said.

They drove back to Grant's apartment in silence. Lisa sat huddled in her coat, demolishing a candy bar that she had found in her pocket like a greedy child. Grant watched her from the corner of his eye – a mixture of shrewdness and childlike ingenuousness that he couldn't grasp.

He fixed himself a drink. The girl stood in the doorway watching him hunt for a clean glass among all the cheap crockery they had bought that morning.

'What's wrong with you?' she asked. 'I don't understand you at all. One moment we're having a quiet conversation about what might be in the diaries and the next you pay the bill and bundle me out of the restaurant. There's nothing consistent about you.'

'Real people aren't consistent. Isn't that what Jack Robarts is on about?'

'You jealous?' She was about to laugh but he turned from pouring his drink and she saw the unreflecting pallor of his eyes. 'No – I guess not. That would be too simple.'

'I'm not concerned with your secondhand psychoanalysis,' Grant said. He downed his drink and looked from the empty glass to her face. 'Can I get you one?' She nodded. Grant reached for a teacup, poured some Scotch into it and handed the drink over. 'This is Laphroaig. Single malt. You can taste the peat in it.' She took the glass hesitantly and sipped the contents. Grant went into the next room and sat down. 'Okay. Who's your next candidate?'

The night wore on and the list grew shorter. Grant listened and only occasionally commented.

SS Brigadefuehrer Johann Rattenhuber. Head of Hitler's detective guard, with access to Hitler's study and therefore to the diaries after the Fuehrer's suicide. Captured by the Russians.

Hermann Karnau, Erich Mansfeld and Hilco Poppen. Members of detective guard. Too low-ranking to have had access to Hitler's study in the ordinary course but may have taken the diaries in the chaos at the end. All three were captured by the British or the Americans. No reference to the diaries in their interrogations.

Hanna Reitsch. Female air ace. At the end, when Goering was deposed from the succession, Hitler had her fly in the new Luftwaffe chief, Ritter von Greim. The promotion was fatal to von Greim, who was wounded during the flight and committed suicide within a month, but Hanna Reitsch made it out again with various papers and letters.

She is a distinct possibility. She carried out messages for Doenitz, so she might have taken the diaries with her,' Lisa said.

'She is a distinct possibility. She carried out messages for head. 'If she had taken the diaries, she would have told.'

'I guess that's right,' Lisa admitted reluctantly.

'I'm afraid so. Who's next?'

Some of the names on the list were people whom Grant had met. Like Heinz Linge, compiler of the appointments book falsely known as *Hitler's Diary*; he had been captured by the Russians and held prisoner for ten years. Grant had talked to him for an hour one spring day in the airport lounge at Frankfurt and if he knew anything more, he wasn't going to say: he had died in February.

Another man that Grant knew was Hitler's personal pilot, an ancient Bavarian named Hans Baur, who had stomped up and down the bedroom of the Hamburg hotel where they had met. He had ended his days with ten years in a Russian prison, a wooden leg and a grudge against Albert Speer, Hitler's architect and crony, which he sounded off about at every opportunity.

Others Grant knew by name. Erich Kempka, the chauffeur who had burned the body. Werner Naumann who spied on everyone on behalf of Goering. Admiral Voss who spied on Werner Naumann on behalf of the Navy. There were Hauptsturmfuehrer Schwaegemann and Dr Stumpfegger; the secretaries Frau Christian and Frau Junge, whom Lisa had already written to in the hope of stirring some recollection; Frau Manzialy, Hitler's vegetarian cook; General Krebs; Rittmeister Boldt; General Burgdorf; Colonel von Below; Weidling, the Commander of Berlin; the pilot Beetz; the bodyguard, Harry Mengershausen, who had helped in the destruction of Hitler's body.

Some of them were little more than passersby caught up in the wreckage of the Third Reich: Walter Wagner, the local official, who had no other function than to marry Hitler to his mistress; Professor Haase, the surgeon brought in to destroy Hitler's dog Blondi and her pups; Baroness Varo who was there for no particular reason at all; and, like a bad joke, a tailor whom nobody could remember except that they thought he was called Mueller.

Lisa yawned and folded away the papers. It was three in the morning.

'Well? You've had your lot. Take your pick. Or maybe you want to dig up the corpses to see if they ran off with the diaries?' She stretched her legs and shivered. 'You know, I could just drink a glass of warm milk. Can I get you one?'

'Pass.'

'Suit yourself,' Lisa said. She went into the kitchen where Grant heard her rattling among the pots. He looked at his own notes taken during her explanation and said, 'There's one person who was at the bunker, whose name you haven't mentioned.'

'Uh huh? And who is that?'

Grant ringed the name and watched it stare back from the page.

'Martin Bormann,' he said.

Thirteen

19 November 1980

The five of them met at Magruder's usual restaurant. Grant brought Lisa and the two publishers had Jack Robarts in tow. Magruder looked shaken by his travels, his eyes were closed and tired when he wasn't speaking and the skin of his face hung in waxy folds. He proposed drinks and then said, 'So Lisa is acting as your assistant?'

'Lisa is eminently qualified to help,' Jack Robarts threw in. He looked at Grant as if he were doing him a favour, but the truth was that, if any blame were to be placed, he felt exposed for having first introduced her.

'Yes, thank you for reminding me,' Magruder said. 'I'd forgotten that Jonathan got to know Lisa through you.' If he had doubts he didn't show them but his comment made Robarts look uncomfortable.

'Do you always discuss people like cattle when they are present?' Lisa asked cheerfully.

'I stand corrected.' Magruder looked over his glass at her and smiled the nearest he could manage to a fatherly smile. 'I for one am glad to have you with us.'

He looked at his drink. 'I'd better not have too many of these – I'm feeling like a corpse already and Nat has arranged some sort of Jewish clambake this evening.'

'You really don't have to come,' Nathan Hirsch protested.

'You should tell Elspeth that!' Magruder said and put a hand on his partner's shoulder.

The waiter brought the remaining drinks and took the orders. When he was gone, Magruder leaned over the table and came out with his question.

'Okay, Jonathan, you've had time to think it over. Can you tell me who in God's name we're dealing with?'

'Did you get a copy of the diaries?' Grant asked.

'I have it in the safe,' Jack Robarts said. There was something smug in his voice and Grant guessed he was signalling that keeping custody of the diaries was a sign that he was allowed to play with the big boys.

'We have the text,' Magruder confirmed, 'but I want to know more about the angle that Knights is hiding from us – something about the diaries that he doesn't want us to know. The best clue might be to know who he's working for.'

Grant weighed up the options that he and Lisa had discussed.

'How about the Russians?' he said.

'The Russians?' Magruder repeated. 'Are you sure?' He looked around at Nathan Hirsch whose quiet face registered no change and then at Jack Robarts who was nodding as though he had guessed all along. The Russians for chrissake! He thought to himself. He caught a flash of Knights sitting down at an editorial conference with the man from Dzerzhinsky Square – he wondered how writers always knew that KGB headquarters were in Dzerzhinsky Square? Maybe it was in the telephone book.

'I said I can only give you the most likely explanation, I can't guarantee it's true,' Grant replied.

'Okay, so it's the Russians. I guess it had to be somebody – but why them?'

Grant told him. He took Magruder and his partner over those last few days in the bunker between the final diary entry and the arrival of the Russian Army. The story came out about the couriers who got out of Berlin only to be caught and their documents recovered; that and the tale of the others who made it to the West.

'If the diaries were brought out to the West, why haven't they been published before now?' Grant said.

'They were left in a drawer – maybe the story of the old Frenchman is true.'

'Nobody who was there at the bunker could have failed to recognize the diaries for what they were. And they weren't the sort of trophy that gets peddled to a French soldier.'

'Any other evidence that it's the Russians?' Magruder asked.

'The long delay before publishing, the use of an intermediary: they both have a Russian style about them. They waited twenty-seven years before releasing Goebbels' diaries; I imagine Hitler's would give them even more pause for thought.

In the Goebbels' case they used an intermediary too.'

Magruder listened. He trusted the Englishman's judgement. 'Okay,' he sighed at last. 'For what it's worth, we're dealing with the Russians. Where do we go from here?'

'You have the affidavits. I propose to talk to the old man's daughter and the two dealers who are supposed to have handled the book. It may not tell us much about the diaries but it could give us some clues about Knights.'

'That sounds fine by me.'

Jack Robarts caught the older man's eye. 'I've been in touch with a firm of handwriting experts,' he said. 'They say they can run tests even on a photocopy – not as good as the original, but they promise a better than even chance of being right.'

'Let's hope so,' Magruder said in a slow, tired voice. 'It might save us all this trouble.'

Fourteen

20-21 November 1980

In the departure lounge at Kennedy a face unwrapped itself from the crowd and the owner pushed a way through towards Grant.

'Jonathan Grant as I live and breathe! Whaddaya know! How's the world treating you?'

Grant focused on the face and searched the slot in his memory. By his side, Lisa looked up at the small, neat man in the rumpled safari-suit and snappy hat with the silk band.

'Max Weiss.'

'So who's the memory man?' A laugh and Grant caught a whiff of peppermint breath hiding halitosis; the smell gave the other man away like a signature. The newcomer put a hand on Grant's forearm and said, 'I never thought you'd recognize me. "I'll never forget old Whatshisname." How many times have I said that? But you I knew straight away, though don't ask me when we last me.'

'Singapore. I was going west – you were going east.'

'That's right!' Max Weiss shook his head. He looked past Grant's shoulder at Lisa. 'I don't know how you managed that one. All the hotels, all the cities – they're getting to seem the same. Even the stories are the same story. The whole world is becoming homogenized and processed – Kentucky Fried Life. Who's the girl?'

Grant did the introductions, names and places. What he couldn't explain to Lisa was the nature of friendships that sprang up over a single encounter in a bar in no particular city where two journalists just happened to be chasing the same story. They were the credit cards of the business, useful to have in the pocket and always overdrawn.

'So what takes you over to Europe?' Weiss asked. The tired eyes in liver-coloured folds of flesh seemed to Lisa unusually cold and attentive whilst the words tumbled over his tongue like junk food. 'Chasing a story still?'

'I'm out of the game – ever since Vietnam.'

'Uh huh. I heard about the books but never had time to read them. They tell me they're good. Is that what takes you on this trip?'

'Something like that. Research. And you?'

The other man shrugged his shoulders. 'I'm a stringer for one of the Tel Aviv papers. They want me to cover a story in Germany.'

'This is the Paris flight.'

'So I'm chasing a rumour, a chance to make a few dollars en route.' He looked behind him at the passengers filing out to the aircraft. 'Maybe a drink at the other end, huh? For old times' sake.'

'Maybe,' Grant said and picked up his airline bag.

The drink was sooner than Paris. They found Max Weiss in the next seat in the row, his shoes off, displaying a pair of violet socks. His eyes caught theirs and a smile came out. It was a thin one, guarding two rows of discoloured teeth.

'Looks like you can't get rid of me. Let me buy you a consolation Scotch.' Weiss eased around in his seat and tapped a finger against the headline of his newspaper. 'You following this story?'

'The Xanten case?'

'That's the one.' Weiss kept pressing the smile and opened the page to show the banner. 'These guys don't know whether to sympathize with the old man because of his age or with the victims.'

'Even murderers look appealing when they have white hair and are confined to wheelchairs,' Grant said. Or talk in soft accents and wear medals for their crimes, he thought. He remembered the gentlemanly figure of the air-marshal giving evidence in the Strand lawcourts, when Grant and his publishers were buried under damages for libel.

'How old is he?' Lisa asked.

'Nearly eighty,' Weiss said. 'Does that make a difference? He was forty-four and in pretty good health when he killed those three hundred people.'

'Perhaps I don't know what makes a difference,' Lisa said.

Takeoff killed the conversation. The shots of Scotch came round; Lisa picked up the newspaper and read the story whilst Grant gave in to the other man's need to reminisce and agreed that he'd never forgot old Whatshisname.

Pieter Xanten, so the story went, was a Dutchman, millionaire and antique collector. He was also SS Major Peter Zanthen, wanted for the murder of two hundred and eighty-six innocent women and children during the German retreat of January 1945. He had never returned to Holland. Instead, after the war he had settled in Düsseldorf, got some capital from somewhere and built himself an engineering business that was one of the largest private businesses in Germany. On the way he had assembled a fabulous collection of porcelain. Admired and respected as a founder and acme of the *Wirtschaftswunderung*, he was recognized in the street by a survivor of the massacre and was now, at last, to face his trial.

'I'm covering the hearings,' Max Weiss said. Lisa had noticed him watching her whilst pretending to talk to Grant. 'I report the usual bleeding-heart complaints about the unfairness of a trial after all this time, let bygones be bygones.' He paused. 'But the dead can't bury the dead. The corpses just lie around and stink.'

'But why the interest in Israel?' Lisa asked. 'None of the victims were Jews.'

'I guess they weren't,' Max Weiss said. 'But you know how crazy the Jews are. To them even a bunch of Polish peasants are human beings.'

From the air Paris was laid out in a translucent haze of altitude and light. Grant remembered that Lisa had said she had never been to Europe. Maybe she was looking at the same view and seeing the yellow brick road that sometimes led to the Emerald City.

At the Hertz desk he swapped promises with Max Weiss that neither intended to keep. As they walked away to find a taxi they saw his limp shape folded over the desk arguing with the clerk about a car.

On the way to the hotel Lisa put the question that had been bottled inside her ever since she heard the idea from Jack Robarts. 'Why is Bart bothering with our work if he can get some expert to verify the handwriting?'

'Because he's too careful to be caught by that one. McGraw-Hill had two firms pass on the handwriting of the Howard Hughes forgery. They said it was genuine.'

They reached their hotel, unpacked, showered and slept off

the jet-lag. Grant woke first and whilst Lisa curled and uncurled in her sleep, her face in a halo of golden hair, he took some papers from his bag and for the first time read the Hitler diaries.

She woke in time for breakfast. Grant watched her eat it with relish whilst he turned over the pages of the morning's news. The news wasn't affected by jet-lag; Poland was still in a mess between the Party and Solidarity, and Pieter Xanten's lawyers were trying to get the trial date postponed because of the old man's health.

After breakfast Grant put a call through to Gobinet, the book dealer. It was answered by a young assistant with a nasal voice and acne that was visible over the telephone. Monsieur Gobinet was out but he could give them an appointment for two o'clock. Which left the morning free.

Grant took Lisa to see some of the lesser tourist spots, the lovely gothic church of St Severin, the Halle aux Vins and the auction rooms of the Hôtel Drouot. They lunched at the Restaurant Magny in the Rue de Mazet, where Flaubert, Sainte-Beuve and Turgenev were once part of the clientèle. Lisa drank in the atmosphere with almost painful avidity.

The Librairie Gobinet nestled among the other bookshops off the Boulevard St Germain. It had a green-painted front and shuttered windows with a display of tired oil paintings, some illustrated books on hunting and a couple of old cartographies with hand-coloured plates. The opening door brushed a small brass bell and caused the assistant to turn away from his book. He was the owner of a pair of pebble glasses and the nasal voice Grant had heard on the telephone. He didn't have acne.

'Monsieur Gobinet?'

They were shown into a room at the back of the shop where the proprietor had his office and the collectors' items were evidently kept. Large bookcases with diamond-leaded panes lined the walls and the books stood in ranks of gold-tooled calfskin and bone-white vellum.

A figure hunched behind the desk, fiddling with a large reading glass looked up from some papers and a pair of brown, swimming eyes examined the visitors.

'You have the advantage of me' – the voice was cracked as if arrested in puberty – 'Monsieur . . . ?'

'Grant. I was given your name by Mr. Knights.' Grant stopped, wondering whether the vacant look in the other man's eyes meant that he was ignorant of the name. 'He told me that you had handled certain diaries. I have your affidavit.' Grant passed it across the table.

'I understand,' Gobinet said, scanning the first page and letting it fall on to his other papers. 'I don't know your Mr Knights; I was approached by a lawyer, Maître Lullien. But, certainly, that is my affidavit.' The Frenchman twisted in his swivel chair and stared momentarily at a small group of lovers in Parian-ware that stood on his desk. The movement was reflexive, as if whichever way he turned he could never feel comfortable. He paused and sighed and then picked up the affidavit again. 'You have some questions about this?' He leaned across the desk and passed the paper back, and as he did so, Grant could see that the dealer's spine was deformed.

'I have one or two.'

'Anything within reason.'

'Does that include giving me the name of the purchaser of the diaries?'

Another twist in the chair. 'I did say "within reason", Mr Grant. If my client was not prepared to reveal his name to you, I am certainly not prepared to do so. But, I am forgetting myself. Please take a seat, and may I offer you any refreshment? No? Then, please, your other questions.'

Grant put them. 'Let's start with your story. Would you tell it me again, in your own words.'

'To check whether I am being consistent? By all means. Where shall I begin?'

'With Charbonnier.'

Gobinet nodded. 'As you wish. Charbonnier was a dealer in – what shall I say? Antiques seems too gracious a word – furniture and bric-à-brac. He had a small shop in Amiens which he used to stock out of small, local auctions – principally with the effects of people who had recently died.'

'Why do you talk of him in the past tense?' Grant asked. He had Charbonnier's affidavit with his papers and was proposing to pay him a visit next.

'Because he is dead,' Gobinet said. 'He was an elderly man and he died, let me see, two or three months ago. Heart failure, old age, however one calls it.' He gave a smile that was intended to be disarming. 'But before that unhappy event, he brought to me the diaries from the estate of Monsieur Boisseau.'

'Why should be bring them to you?' Grant asked.

'It was a long-standing arrangement. You will understand that he was not a dealer in books; but, naturally, in his business he would acquire quantities of books along with items that were more in his line of business. So, once every month or so, he would make up a package and send it to me and I would pay him at my valuation.'

'He trusted you to do that?'

'He accepted my valuation, naturally. The alternative was for him to become his own expert in books, which, frankly, was not worthwhile for the quality of the books he was buying. Of course, if he thought that a book was more than usually valuable he would draw it to my attention and we would negotiate a separate price; but in his business that was very rare.'

'What about the diaries?'

Gobinet looked down at his fingers splayed on the desk top. 'He had no idea what they were. He could not read German and did not know whom they were by – which is not surprising since the one name that usually does not appear in a diary is that of the author. As far as Charbonnier was concerned they had nothing more than curiosity value and he did not bother even to bring them to my attention.'

'But you recognized them for what they were.'

Gobinet protested mildly. 'Oh, no, not immediately! To be frank, I normally took no interest in Charbonnier's packages and left them for my assistant. It was he who drew my attention to the bindings – have you seen them, by the way?'

'No.'

Gobinet raised his eyebrows. Grant speculated that he was wondering how far he could let the fiction run. 'You surprise me, monsieur. Well, let me say that the bindings are quite attractive: black leather with a silver motif and an eagle and swastika embossed in the centre. My assistant wanted a price for them as Nazi memorabilia.'

Grant let the story flow. Gobinet's voice, passing over his clipped, fussy expressions, hesitated between uncertainty as to how much the Englishman knew and how much he was ignorant of. Grant allowed everything to pass.

'Do you speak German?'

'As a matter of fact I do,' Gobinet said. There was a note of pride in his voice that was unusual for a Frenchman.

'So you read the diaries.

A nod. 'Though let me say that I am no expert and have no head for details.'

He deftly avoided the next question, 'If you want me to tell you what was in them, I'm afraid I really can't be expected to remember.'

Lisa gave an audible sigh of disappointment.

'Maybe not,' Grant said. 'But you knew that the diaries were of enormous interest. Why did you sell them privately. You could have auctioned them. Or sold them to a publisher.'

Gobinet's face assumed a serious expression. 'I am a seller of rare books, not a publisher. When I saw the diaries I regarded them only as a rare find of interest to the collector. If I had been an antiques' dealer who had just purchased a rare piece of furniture, would you expect me to commission copies?' He paused and watched carefully for any hint of a reaction. 'Moreover I had my clientèle to consider. I suspect that it will not come as a surprise to you to learn that many of my clients are, shall I say, of the Hebrew persuasion? They would not have been pleased if I had associated myself openly with the diaries.' The Frenchman sat back in his seat and said sneeringly, 'Although a Jew yourself, Mr Grant, you have found to your cost how vindictive members of your race can be.'

'That sort of guy makes me feel unclean,' Lisa said as they left the bookshop.

'He probably makes himself feel unclean,' Grant said. 'That's why he's like that.' He slipped an arm around her waist. 'That's my platitude for the day. Now let me whisk you to Fairyland – or at least to get you a drink.'

They found a café and ordered drinks. Lisa played with her lips thoughtfully against the glass and then put it down.

'Do you believe any of that?' she asked.

'Gobinet's tale? If he had any idea of what was in the diaries he would have sold the story for money.'

'So where does it get us?'

'Nowhere.'

'Why should he lie?'

'Because the diaries are fakes and someone had paid him to give them a history,' Grant said, 'or because the truth of the diaries is something that can't be told.'

Lisa laughed. 'You're lapsing into mystery again!'

Grant turned his pale eyes on her and gave her a thin smile. 'Maybe it's my paranoia.'

'Maybe.' The smile died. Her face was thoughtful for a moment and then her childish sense of fun sneaked through. 'You know I never thought of you as Jewish.' She paused to see how far she could go. 'Now that I think about it,' she added, 'I can't say that I've ever noticed that your . . . '

Grant smiled as he caught her meaning.

'It isn't,' he said.

Fifteen

22 November 1980

It was a drab mining village half an hour's drive from Amiens. The main street held a brick mock-Byzantine church, a straggle of small shops and cafés advertising Stella Artois, and a *mairie* with the inscription *Liberté, Egalité, Fraternité* over the entrance and a tricolor twisted around the flagpole. Drab streets of small houses went off at right angles, terminating at the canal or the railway line, and beyond the slate-coloured mounds of spoil bare fields spread out under a leaden sky.

Grant turned the hired Renault into one of the side-streets and drew up alongside the broken pavement.

'This is it?' Lisa asked. She checked the street sign. 'Okay, which house?'

Grant indicated a sprinkling of parked cars. 'Guess.'

Lisa looked and saw the pink Mercedes.

'Madame Caillot?'

The woman at the door was blonde, but a pair of brown eyes looked out from under dark eyebrows.

'My name is Grant . . . ' he didn't have time to finish.

'You must be the Englishman,' she said indifferently. She examined them both carefully but without any show of concern. 'You'd better come in. I was told to expect you.'

'Who told you?' Grant asked.

Unlike the book dealer, she didn't put up any pretence. 'Monsieur Knights. He telephoned and said that one of these days you would show up. It's about my father, isn't it?'

'Yes.'

'He said it would be. I told the whole story to the lawyer when I made the statement' – she shrugged her shoulders – 'but if you want to hear it all again, that's okay by me.'

They followed her through the door and into a small room at the front of the house.

'My husband's working,' she threw away as she closed the door, 'but he couldn't help you. He knows nothing about the business – he hated my father. Can I get you anything – a cigarette, a drink?' She gestured at a bar that stood incongruously in a narrow alcove, teak-veneered and sparkling with glass. 'New,' she said, seeing the expression on Lisa's face. 'Bought it with the old man's money.' She helped herself to a drink. 'He was a real old miser – no furniture, no holidays, no enjoyment, no nothing – but had a stack of money shoved into an old mattress.'

Grant took a cigarette. 'He paid for the car, too?'

Her eyes brightened. 'Sure, he paid for that too – you like it? Pink was my choice. They said we couldn't have a pink one but I got it resprayed.' She gave them a defensively defiant look. 'Why the hell shouldn't I have it the colour I want? After all, I earned it.'

'Earned it? I thought your father left you the money.'

There was a pause during which Madame Caillot swallowed a few large mouthfuls from her glass and poured herself another stiff drink. 'Of course I earned it,' she said at last, 'slaving after the old man until he died, I deserved everything.'

'And got it,' Grant said.

The woman stared back at him. 'Yes, I got it.'

Grant changed the subject. 'Did you ever read the books?'

She laughed. 'Me?'

'Do you know what they were?'

'I wasn't interested. My father brought them back from the war, that's all I remember. They were black with a fancy pattern and an eagle on them. He used to keep them in a drawer with his medals – never even looked at them. I would have thrown them out, but, instead I sold the furniture and the whole lot in an auction. I don't even know now what's in them, except that it was important enough for someone to want me to give a statement to a lawyer saying what little I did know.'

Grant unfolded the affidavit. 'Is this your statement?'

'Probably.' Her eyes drifted aimlessly down the page.

'Cologne – mean anything to you?'

'Scent?'

'Did you mention it to the lawyer?'

'Why should I mention scent?' She gave Grant a smile as

though she was too clever for him, then seemed to have doubts. Her fingers curled gently around the top of the bar as thought its touch gave her reassurance. 'Cologne – maybe I did say something about scent. My father told me a lot of things. I don't remember them all now.'

'You told the lawyer that your father bought the books in Cologne from a German soldier,' Grant said.

'I remember now. That's what he told me. The name had me confused.'

'But now you remember.'

She looked Grant boldly in the face. 'Yes, now I remember.' She sat down and nursed her drink on her lap. 'Anything that's in that statement: if you put it to me, then I remember. Understand?'

Grant understood.

There was a noise from outside, a key turning in the lock.

'My husband,' Madame Caillot said.

'Who knows nothing,' Grant said. 'Then we don't need to stay, do we?'

'No more questions?' She smiled as if she had won something.

'No. I have what I wanted.'

She watched his face and her expression became more guarded. 'You'd better be going,' she said abruptly. She looked unconsciously at the bar as if she doubted it would still be there.

The door opened and a big, square man with heavy, somnolent eyes came in. He was wearing a zip-fronted jacket, and his fists were pushed into his pockets.

'You'd better be going,' the woman repeated as Caillot glanced around the room and muttered something rapidly in French. As they left, the door slammed behind Grant and Lisa and they heard the sound of raised voices as they walked down the street.

'Okay, what now?' Lisa said as they sat in the car and stared at the outline of the railway viaduct that dominated the centre of the village. 'Do we wait for another chance to see Mme Caillot when the Incredible Hulk has gone out or do we return to Paris?'

'We go back to Paris. Knights has paid for a story and true

or false it's the one that our friend is going to stick to.' With that Grant started the engine.

The village was behind them in less than a kilometre, or so the roadsign with its red bar striking out the name said. And, except for two blocks of cheap apartments, the roadsign was right: there was nothing around but sodden-looking fields, the occasional walled farm and, in the distance, the pitheads and coaltips of the next village.

They pulled off the road for a cup of coffee at the nearest halt after town. It was a hamlet that didn't warrant a name, half a dozen houses, a Total filling station and a café standing in its own parking lot. A truck and trailer with a Swedish flag blazoned on the side and a couple of Ford tractors stood on the bare earth whilst their owners had a few drinks inside.

They took their coffees to a couple of high stools by the window where they could watch the rest of the bar and keep an eye on the car. The Swedish truck-driver was minding his own business over a beer and two locals were hammering at a pinball machine.

Grant was finishing his drink when he heard the noise of a car. 'We've got a visitor,' he said.

'I've heard that cliché before,' Lisa said and finished her drink before grabbing her bag. 'In the films it always spells trouble. Isn't that Caillot's car?'

The vivid pink Mercedes had pulled up suddenly in the parking lot and was swaying on its springs whilst the dust settled. Four doors opened and the big Frenchman and three more like him got out.

'What do you think he wants?' Lisa said.

'I don't think he's come here to make a full and frank confession.'

'Knights sent him?'

'I doubt it. This is just his bonehead idea of loyalty. Knights doesn't want us hurt, but Caillot doesn't know it.' In evidence of the truth of that last remark, The Frenchman took out a clasp knife and buried the blade to the hilt in one of the tyres of the Renault.

The door of the café opened and Caillot came in with his three cronies. Size apart, the blue dust-scars on their faces gave them away as miners. They had that vacant determination of men who don't understand the quarrel but know well enough which side they are on.

Caillot didn't go in for sophisticated approaches; he came straight towards Grant and picked up a glass that was sitting next to the Englishman's cup. Fingering the glass he spoke.

'You came to my house.'

'That's right. I saw your wife. A marvellous woman.'

'She says you called her a liar.'

'Really? She must be very sensitive to atmosphere,' Grant said and knew that was the end of the conversation. Caillot jabbed with his right hand to smash the glass it was holding into the Englishman's face, but he was too slow. Grant slipped from the stool and, as the other man came at him, he grabbed Caillot's arm, pulled him forward at gut height into the seat, and, as his body folded and his feet came up, Grant grabbed them and catapulted the Frenchman's bulk in a somersault. There was a crash and a cascade of glass as Caillot careered through the window.

His three companions were too surprised to react. Their minds were still in neutral when Grant seized Lisa's arm and opened the door. Outside he pushed her into a run towards the nearer of the two tractors. They reached it just as Caillot's friends came out of the bar, picking up their leader.

As Grant expected, the keys to the machine were in the ignition: who stole tractors in broad daylight? He pushed the stop-control in, wrenched the two gear levers into neutral and turned the key. The engine leapt into life.

Their four pursuers raced for the Mercedes. Grant swung the Ford round and followed them. There were iron ballast weights on the bracket in front of the tractor and he knew just what they were good for.

The Frenchmen had reached the car and were flinging open the doors as the tractor came at them out of a cloud of stone-dust. They scattered when it became clear that it was aimed straight at the centre of the bonnet, smashing the radiator into scrap with the impact from the projecting weights. Grant pulled the machine into reverse and headed for the fields.

Caillot, however, was more determined than Grant had given him credit for. A hundred yards behind them, they heard the sound of the second tractor starting up. Grant glanced back and saw it lumbering out of the car park, Caillot behind the wheel, with one man with him in the cab and two riding shotgun on the outside.

'There's a lot of insanity in these small communities,' Grant muttered. 'That clown seems bent on getting himself killed.'

'I think he's got similar intentions towards us,' Lisa replied and steadied herself as they jolted over the rough grass and climbed an incline.

With a main gear, high/low gear and dual power, the Ford 7700 offers sixteen gears to take advantage of every load and every nuance of ground. It didn't take Grant long to realize that Caillot, whatever his intellectual limitations, knew more about using them than he did. The gap, which had opened to four hundred yards, began to narrow rapidly.

The two tractors did a circuit of the field then pirouetted past each other only a few yards apart but in opposite directions. Through the mud-streaked cab screen, Grant glimpsed his adversary's grim, blood-stained face.

Each circuit, each pass, each turn – Caillot from experience had the edge. In the silent countryside the two machines roared and swung at each other whilst the gap inexorably closed. And then, suddenly, Grant's tractor stopped. The wheels were still turning, churning the waterlogged ground and kicking up great clods of earth where the plough had passed and the two machines had ripped up the ground. Caillot's machine, with the two men hanging on the side brandishing tyre levers, came swinging round fifty yards behind.

Punishing the engine wasn't helping Grant out of the wheel slip. He glanced at the floor controls and spotted the differential lock, hit it until it engaged and then crashed through all the gears he could find for one that gave him traction. And then – painfully slowly – the big Ford lumbered out of the rut.

Caillot didn't miss his chance. He swung his machine over, too late to nudge Grant's tractor into further trouble, but one of his friends leapt on to the cab step and smashed a tyre lever into the screen in front of Grant, shattering it.

The hand dropped the lever and tried to grab the metal frame by the broken screen. Lisa saw a pair of eyes mixed with fear and ferocity and, without thinking, she grabbed hold of the hand and dragged the wrist over the broken glass. A fountain of blood sprayed the cab and with a cry the man lost his hold and bounced off the rear wheel to the ground.

The two machines were running parallel. Grant wrenched the wheel to the right. Caillot tracked him. The tractors careered up the slope of the field sending clods of damp earth flying behind them. Five yards apart they beat a path through the mud and rank grass.

The slope sharpened and then levelled off. Caillot was closing, nudging the rear wheels, trying to upset the delicate balance of the machine on the slope. Grant knew that it was only a matter of time before he was beaten unless . . .

As the ground levelled off, Grant stamped on one of the two footbrakes and locked the left-hand wheels. Immediately he wrenched the wheel round and felt the whole vehicle rock as he pulled it into a hairpin turn – he prayed that it wouldn't turn over.

On the last piece of the slope, Caillot followed suit. Grant saw the other tractor's wheels lock and the big Frenchman, his face frozen in a mask of hatred, yank with all his strength to bring the machine round. The big Ford swung obediently but, unlike Grant who had taken advantage of the crest, Caillot had the slope against him. His vehicle teetered, straining to keep its hold on the ground, and then, slowly, like a dying whale, the right-hand side lifted and the wheels spun in the air. The man remaining on the step threw himself on to the earth whilst Caillot wrestled to bring his machine under control. Then, suddenly, after the long, swaying movement, it collapsed on to its side. The engine gave a roar as the wheels churned the air, and there was a crash and splintering of glass as the cab struck the earth.

Grant watched briefly as Caillot struggled out of the wreckage and then drove slowly back to the road.

Sixteen

24 March 1945

Hildesheim! One of the last beautiful places. Flattened. I can hardly write for grief. Goebbels is right: we should denounce the Geneva Convention. These terror-bombers are brute beasts, barbarians! They should be strung up whenever they are caught! This is all Churchill's idea. The man is an animal. When I have him, I shall have his entrails paraded around Hildesheim for the crowds to spit at.

The reports say that the Pope is furious with the Americans over Yalta. Jew-Roosevelt has sent someone to the Vatican to bribe the old man to keep quiet. Little does he know what Yalta has done to me!

Where now the Miracle of the House of Brandenburg?

The last time I mentioned Helsingstrup it was with hope. The next time will be to report a hanging!

Seventeen

Whilst Grant was beginning his researches in Europe, life in New York was not entirely uneventful as Magruder-Hirsch geared itself for the biggest production and marketing effort in its history. On Friday, the same day that Grant was meeting Gobinet in Paris, Magruder received a telephone call at home. It was from Herb Mirisch, one of Rama's PR men. Five years before, Magruder had helped him out of a fix and he repaid the favour by feeding the publisher any information that spilled through the keyholes at Rama's headquarters.

Magruder picked up the phone and caught the name.

'Herb? Nice to hear from you.' He checked his watch, 'Is this a social call that it couldn't wait for the office? Where are you calling from, it must be the middle of the night there in California.'

'I'm in Washington.'

'DC? What are you doing there?'

'The Defense Department dragged us out here yesterday – and I mean everyone. Emmett came in person.'

'The Lockheed contract?' Magruder asked. He knew that the aircraft deal was the only one large enough to cause Rama any major problems.

'You got it.'

'So?' Magruder was curious. 'How does that affect me? All I know about the Lockheed programme is what I read in the papers. So Rama is six months behind – I should worry?'

'Listen!' Mirisch said. He sounded agitated. 'If you don't know, I can't tell you because I don't know myself. I can only repeat what I hear. You'll have to piece the story together from that.'

'Then let me have it,' Magruder said.

There was a pause at the other end. 'Okay, now hear this. We arrive in Washington this morning and go straight to the Pentagon. Naturally Emmett and his pals go inside for a meeting and yours truly stays outside the room waiting for someone to decide that they want a press release. And there I stand, watching the other side arrive – except that there is no one from Lockheed!'

'You sure? They weren't talking about the Lockheed deal?'

'They were talking about it all right,' Mirisch came back. 'But this wasn't the Lockheed guys bitching about their delivery deadlines. This was the Defense Department putting on the heat for their own reasons.'

'How do you know?'

'Because when I stand outside and watch the Defense brass going in, who should be going in with them but someone I know from the State Department. Now why the State Department? Rama is doing something which impairs our relations with other countries?'

Magruder listened but the drift escaped him. 'Is that it?' he said at last.

'No, not all. The Rama guys come out of the meeting looking sticky as though they've been under a lot of pressure and they look at me like I'm dirt and say the last thing they want is a press release. Instead they start having a crack at Emmett and say that he's got Rama into this mess and it's up to him to get them out. . . . And then I hear your name mentioned.' Mirisch stopped and waited. 'Did you catch that, Bart?'

'I heard you,' Magruder said. He heard but he didn't understand.

'Let me spell it out for you,' Mirisch said. 'Rama is being pressured by the Defense Department over the Lockheed contract. And the reason is that you, Bart, are doing some sort of deal that the Government doesn't like one little bit.'

Having checked the story provided by Knights and his affidavits, Grant decided that he and Lisa would have to divide their forces if they were to meet the deadline date. He felt that he had to return to the States, partly because there were developments that he thought Magruder should know about, also because there he would have access to captured Nazi documents held in the American archives. For Lisa he had another task that required her staying in Europe.

As Grant expected, the manuscript contained a mass of

comment on troop positions and other day-to-day details of military operations, reflecting Hitler's preoccupation with the minutiae of the conduct of the war. In itself it was no great problem to check the details in the diary entries against a history of the various campaigns, but Grant knew that such an approach ignored the fact that Hitler's knowledge wasn't that of a historian reporting after the event. Instead of the facts, the genuine diaries, if they existed, would contain the omissions, mistakes and downright lies as they came to Hitler through the reports of German high command, OKW. Lisa's job was to get at those reports through the records held in Germany at the *Militärgeschichteforschung* in Freiburg.

On Monday morning Barton Magruder found the Englishman working on the manuscript in the empty room reserved for him next to Magruder's own office. It was the thirteenth day since Knights had walked through the door with his incredible offer, but Magruder wasn't superstitious.

'You look as though you've been here all night,' Magruder said. Grant's pale eyes had exhaustion underneath their restlessness and he needed a shave.

'I have,' Grant said simply. He took a drink from a half-squashed can of Coke and waved a hand for the publisher to sit down. 'You don't look so good yourself,' he said.

'At my age I travel badly. I still haven't recovered from the Zurich trip and I'm booked on the red-eye special tonight for San Francisco to see if I can raise some money from Rama to finance this crazy business.' He paused. 'How was your trip?'

Grant told him.

'So you think Knights is covering up a fake?' Magruder asked when he was done.

'Perhaps,' Grant answered. 'Or he could be simply protecting his clients. There could be something in the diaries that would be dangerous to them.' He watched Magruder to see if the publisher found the idea too far-fetched. Magruder shook his head with the air of a worried man.

'I want to tell you about a call I got on Friday,' he said.

He told Grant the story given to him by Mirisch. 'What I don't see,' he said when he had finished, 'is what's in the diaries that can be giving the State Department or anybody else problems.' He picked up the papers and riffled through them. 'For chrissake, I've read them and I just don't see it! I mean, as a book they are going to be a sensation to make the headline writers shoot themselves trying to find big enough words, but the bottom line is that they're *history*. Who gets that uptight about history?'

'Not about this history,' Grant said. But there was something in his voice.

'There's another history?' Magruder asked.

'When do you see Knights again?'

'Are you changing the subject? I'm meeting him later today for a progress report.'

'Then ask him why the diaries have been edited.'

There was a pause, then Grant invited Magruder to the table. 'Read this entry.' The sheet in front of him was headed *24 March 1945*.

'So? I've read it before. It's all gibberish.'

'The last paragraph mentions an earlier entry. It isn't in the copy Knights gave you.'

Magruder looked at the paper again. 'This stuff about Helsingstrup? What's that? A person? A place?'

'It's the name of a lake in Finland – I checked in the atlas. It's also the title of a Swedish noble family according to the *Almanach de Gotha*. The connection is that Finland was part of Sweden two hundred years ago.'

'Okay, so where does that get us?'

Grant smiled. 'Nowhere,' he said.

Magruder ordered some coffee. When it came, he spooned in the sugar and watched the coffee creep up the spoon and dissolve the granules.

'I've got some news of my own,' he said. 'Jack's handwriting guys came across with a report over the weekend.'

'The writing?'

Magruder shook his head. 'The manuscript. What we have isn't an ordinary commercial photocopy. It's a print taken from a film.' He reached into his pocket and pulled out the report. 'I won't go through the technical stuff, but the guts of it is that our text was taken from an enlargement.' He read out the next part, ' "from film type ORWOSNP 15." '

'East German microfilm,' Grant said.

'You know already?'

'I've heard of East German records being kept on that type of film, that's all.'

'It fits in with your theory that the Russians are somewhere in back of this thing.'

'It's consistent,' Grant said, 'but not conclusive. The East Germans export both cameras and film.'

'You sound as though you have another theory about the diaries?' Magruder said.

'An idea,' Grant said. He felt suddenly tired as the options began to spin inside his head. 'Just an idea.'

The librarian was a pretty girl who was trying to make herself look plain under some obscure notion of how a librarian was supposed to look. She had a hesitant nervous smile that people sometimes have when they are trying to be polite but don't understand a word you are saying.

'Can you give me that again?'

'*Vem är Det.*' Grant spelled it out. 'It's a sort of Swedish *Who's Who*.'

'And you want the 1939 edition?' The same look of incomprehension masquerading as intelligence.

'Or as near as you can get.'

She finished writing the words and the point of her pencil broke. She looked up from her paper. 'Have you tried the Swedish Embassy? I mean, we can get the book for you – but really – well, I mean, it might be simpler . . . '

'I'd really appreciate it if you could help me with this,' Grant said. He let the Englishness of his voice flow over her.

'Oh, well. If we can be of service . . . ' she said.

From the City Library, Grant returned to his apartment. He stopped at the janitor's office to collect his mail. The janitor was an Irishman who claimed to have fought in the Easter Rising. If he did, then the IRA were recruiting six year olds. Grant and he used to exchange republican and loyalist banter.

'So your visitor left?' the old man said as he handed over the letters.

'What visitor?' Grant asked.

'Dark suit – aged about thirty. He said your outside phone was out of order and I had to let him in the main door. He didn't come down again, so I guessed that he'd found you at home.'

'You probably missed him when he came down,' Grant said and stuffed the mail into his pocket.

The door of his apartment was closed and showed no signs of being forced, but that meant nothing. Grant slipped his key into the lock and hoped that the wards would turn without too much noise. As the door opened he saw a man in a dark suit, his back towards him, reading his notes.

The intruder turned round. He was young, fresh-faced, with neat hair and a shirt with a buttoned-down collar and a sober tie. If he wasn't carrying a gun, he might have been a business-school graduate. Grant anticipated the hand reaching inside the other man's jacket and grabbed instinctively for the nearest object, a small pedestal table with a telephone on it. The other man was still looking surprised and hesitant, as if he were only a bureaucrat doing his job and this wasn't supposed to happen to him. As Grant threw the table, he caught it on the arm and sent it spinning into a corner. His gun followed it.

They stared at each other as if neither knew what to do next. Is this what violence is? Grant wondered, so accidental, unpremeditated? The intruder was already coming for him in a textbook karate stance. Grant sidestepped, grabbed the table from where it was lying on the floor and swung it at the other man's head. It connected with a force and solidity Grant hadn't expected, and the other man, his face still holding the expression of hurt surprise, cannoned against the wall and collapsed.

Grant had no time to think about what he had done. Another man was standing in the open kitchen doorway, a muscle-bound type with the dangerous, slow-seeming movements of a fighter that contrasted incongruously with his discreet banker's suit.

Instead of charging in as Grant expected, the second man paused, looking for an opening, changing his weight from foot to foot as Grant swung the pedestal table in front of him. He sensed the initiative slipping away. He knew that if he traded blows with his new opponent he was going to lose. The other man knew it too. He stayed squarely in the doorway, restricting the opening for Grant to swing the table, knowing that he couldn't hang on to its weight indefinitely. Grant had to make his move.

He glanced at the gun lying on the floor where the first man had dropped it. His opponent followed his glance and Grant saw his chance.

Momentarily he let his grip on the table relax and moved towards the gun. The big man threw his weight on to that side and came at Grant to keep him from reaching it. A hammer-blow from a fist glanced off Grant's ear as he retreated from his feint. He threw himself flat against the wall as the other man crashed past him and careened against the entrance door to the apartment.

Grant raised the wooden table to bring it down on the big man's head but saw that there was no point. His opponent was in no fit state to do anything. He bent down and lifted the gun out of the other man's jacket and then went into the kitchen to fix himself a drink and decide what to do next.

As he stepped through the door, he felt a blow to the head.

Eighteen

25 November 1980

Following his conversation with Grant, Barton Magruder went for his meeting with Knights. The rendezvous in Central Park was Knights' choice and Magruder had no idea why.

The other man was late or Magruder had the spot wrong. Either way he found himself walking in circles around a park bench to keep the circulation in his legs going, whilst, around him, even in this cold, a group of Puerto Rican kids were playing ball and others were lounging around on the grass, eating and looking like they had nothing to do. It was an eternal mystery to Magruder: who was doing the work?

He caught sight of Knights rolling down one of the avenues in an open carriage like a tourist. The other man was wearing a tan-coloured suit with a cream shirt, and had a yellow rose in his buttonhole. Magruder's own concession to colour was a red stripe in his blue tie.

'Have I kept you waiting?' Knights asked. 'I suppose I must have.'

'You suppose right.'

'Well, I'm here now.' Knights was unconcerned. 'Shall we walk whilst we talk or will you hop in?'

'Do you have an aversion to offices – you know, the places where people ordinarily do business?' Magruder answered, but he climbed on board. The driver touched the horse with his whip and the carriage went off at a trot.

'The weather is more pleasant than it has been. Besides,' Knights added more seriously, 'if I call at your offices with any more frequency, people may start to ask why. And then . . . '

They sat in silence for a minute or two, watching the sights. Then Magruder took out a handkerchief and ran it round the neckband of his shirt. 'Do you mind it we get out and sit a while?' he said. 'Movement makes me think of aircraft.'

They stopped and Knights paid off the driver. A small child holding a frisbee was standing a few feet away, staring at them with wide, ignorant eyes until an older child came up, yanked the toy away and dragged the child screaming down the path.

The publisher planted himself on a bench and sighed. He wasn't as fit as he thought. He looked up at Knights who was still standing, and, suspecting the other man of trying to steal a psychological advantage, snapped, 'Sit down. I can't stand looking up when I'm talking.' He waited and then went on. 'Okay, have you read the draft contract that I gave you last time?'

Knights opened his attaché case and took the draft out. He handed it across to Magruder. 'You'll find I've made a number of small amendments which I'm sure your counsel will find acceptable. I've also drafted some terms as to payment.'

Magruder took the draft. 'By the way,' he said, 'when do we get the rest of the manuscript?'

There was a scarcely discernible flicker in the other man's eyes. 'What do you mean?'

'The bits that you edited out.'

Knights maintained the unruffled exterior, but Magruder knew that he had scored a hit.

'I see,' Knights said calmly. He paused. 'Shall we walk a little?'

'Why not?' Magruder said cheerfully.

'I gather you don't know what's in the missing part,' Knights said as they walked.

'I have an approximate idea.'

Knights stopped. He fixed his pale blue eyes on the older man and said quietly, 'I don't know how you know that there are parts of the diaries missing.' He raised a hand to stop any reply. 'But I know for certain that you have no idea what it is that's missing.' He turned on his heels and carried on walking. Magruder hurried after him.

'What's all this about?'

'We cut out a small part of the transcript.'

'I know damn well you did that! What I want to know is why?'

'For your own good.'

'Nuts!'

Knights halted. 'Certain parts of the diaries are politically sensitive – *still* politically sensitive.'

'After more than thirty years? Come on, you've got to be

joking!' Magruder laughed, but underneath he was uneasy. He sensed that Grant had been uneasy too.

'You don't know what you're talking about,' Knights said coldly. 'There were a lot of things done during the war that never came to light because the people responsible are still alive and powerful, or because governments that are still in office would be discredited.'

'Like what?'

'The Katyn massacre.'

'The murder of some Polish officers by the Russians – is that what's in the diaries? Where's the big deal in something that everyone knows?'

'That was just an example. At the time the British and the American governments went along with the Russian story that the Gestapo were responsible – at the time it was a convenient explanation. In that particular case the truth came out.'

'But you're saying that in this case there's something in the diaries that people suspect yet can't prove?'

'Not people,' Knights said. 'Governments. The man in the street suspects nothing, but certain governments do. They can prove nothing – and in all likelihood wouldn't wish to.'

'How do I know you're telling me the truth?'

'You don't.'

'Terrific.'

'Be realistic, Mr Magruder. There is enough in the diaries for your purposes. You'll make your profit if you publish what you have already. The rest is bonus.'

'You intend to let us have the rest then?'

'Certainly. We have kept back the sensitive parts as a matter of security. Once we have a deal, you may have them and publish or not as you see fit.'

Magruder was mollified. 'Okay. I don't like it, but I guess I've got to live with it. What do you say we sit down a minute and I take a look at the changes you've made to the draft contract?'

'If you want to do that, shall we go to the Metropolitan Museum of Art. I believe it's quite close by. You can read the contract and I can admire the paintings.' He smiled at the publisher's look of surprise. 'You forget that I'm a visitor to New York.'

Fifteen minutes later they were in the Met. Knights stalked Nelson Rockerfeller's collection of primitive art whilst Magruder read over the contract. The gallery was busy with a crowd of tourists, students and schoolkids chaperoned by their teachers, all of them walking by oblivious of the two men.

The reading took five minutes after which Magruder took off his spectacles, slipped them into his pocket and sighed.

'You can't be serious about this section on payment.'

A bearded type who looked as though he was working his way through college by taking gaggles of middle-aged women from Little Rock on museum tours said to his charges: 'The term "primitive" is inaccurate in that it manifests itself in a style of art deriving from quite opposite perspectives.' He brushed past Magruder with a look of annoyance and went on, 'Take this example' – he waved his hand at a painting of Noah's ark – 'without my telling you the name of the artist, can you tell me this: is this painting of a familiar children's subject the work and simple technique of a childish mind, or is it in fact a work by a far more accomplished hand, consciously adopting the style and perspective of a child as a device to convey a more profound visual or philosophical message? Can you tell me that?' Nobody could.

'Do you hear me?' Magruder repeated. He shook the typed draft. 'There's no way I can accept that payment provision.'

'Why not?'

Magruder kept his voice low. 'Because your draft calls for the payment of ten million on signing.'

'Less the deposit.'

'Sure – less the deposit.'

Knights raised his eyebrows. 'Isn't that what we agreed?' He maintained his cool, galling manner.

'We agreed ten million – I don't deny it – but there was nothing said about payment on signing the contract. You don't understand this business. You'll have to take your money on some sort of royalty or instalment basis: there's no way I can raise this sort of finance in advance of sales.'

The bearded guide continued his piece, 'The dichotomy between natural primitivism and the primitivism assumed by the academically trained artist – you have examples in the two pictures in front of you – means that a canvas can have two meanings, solely dependent on what we know of its author: that is, it can be simple, naïve and sincere or the product of an approach that is imitative, over-sophisticated and affected.' He looked back at the assembled ladies and added, 'Come on folks, this way. One more room and then it's back to the souvenir shop.'

Magruder waited until they had passed before turning to Knights again. He spoke slowly and emphatically, 'We don't carry this kind of working capital.' He waved the contract. 'You've got to remember that Rama is a conglomerate and we're only a part. There's no way I can sell Rama a high-risk deal like this.'

'Then you'll have to sell some of the rights.'

'Okay, that's fine with me!' Knights had stated what Magruder would have to do in any event: paperback rights, book-club sales, foreign sales, newspaper serialization – Magruder-Hirsch wasn't geared to handle them all. 'That's what I planned to do once we were signed up. If I can release the manuscript to the trade, then just maybe I can raise the money.'

Knights shook his head. 'That was just a suggestion. Whatever you do, there's to be no mention of the diaries to any outsiders before we sign the contract.'

'But that's impossible!' Magruder's voice echoed round the gallery. He stopped and looked around at the eyes of the visiting crowd which were fixed on him. He lowered his voice. 'I can't pre-sell rights blind. What do I have to give? You're driving this deal into a dead end. I've told you: I just don't carry that sort of clout inside Rama and I can't turn outside for finance. Just maybe I could come part way towards meeting you if I could pre-sell some rights. But do you realize what you're asking? Nobody, and I mean *nobody* can command ten million up-front, not even for the biggest thing to hit publishing since Shakespeare.'

If Magruder expected a reaction, he got none. Knights said impassively, 'The problem is really yours. I'll report what you've said to my principals; but you shouldn't expect a different response.' He checked his watch and added, 'I must be going. I'll keep in touch to see how you're getting on.' He held out a limp hand for Magruder to shake and then walked away down the gallery.

Watching Knights go, it occurred to Magruder for the first time that whoever was behind Knights wasn't interested in this sale, that the whole negotiation was for some other purpose. He tossed the idea around in his head for a while, but in the end he couldn't make any sense of it.

Nineteen

26 November 1980

Grant was awakened by the sound of poultry clucking. His head ached, his mouth tasted of ether and he could feel the pulses in his temples. He flexed his limbs slowly, feeling his body systems turn on one by one. He decided to try to open his eyes. The light filtered in slowly and an image resolved itself. He was looking at a white cockerel.

The bird gave a sharp head movement and fixed him with a staring pink eye.

'C'mon man! Ain't it time you snapped out of it?' it said.

'Jesus Christ!' Grant muttered. He risked a shake of his head to see that it was still on. He felt his hands. There was pressure at the fingertips as if the blood flow were constrained. He tested them gingerly and found that he was bound by the wrists.

Pieces of sensation dropped into their slots. He was in a room – dank, smelling of moulding paper and stale food. The white cockerel was in a wicker cage suspended a foot away from his head.

The bird looked up from preening its feathers. 'Lordy, Lordy, do I perceive some life?' The accent was mocking. 'Hallelujah!'

'You're a pretty intelligent bird,' Grant said, but couldn't hear his voice. The bird said nothing. 'I'd like some water,' Grant said. His voice had found bottom gear and came out as a croak.

'The man wants water! The man shall have some water!'

'Thanks.'

A chair scraped. Grant looked round and saw a vague figure silhouetted against the window. A face with a faint penumbra of hair. The figure rose and opened the door, and Grant sensed that he was alone.

'He's gone to get the water?' he asked the cockerel. 'What's wrong? Lost your voice, old man?'

His eyes began to focus more clearly. He could distinguish the tone of the walls, a putty colour streaked with white efflorescence and faded images of flowers in red. There was an empty chair facing him. To the side of it a bare wooden table. An unshaded light bulb hung from the ceiling. The floor was of bare boards, rough and paint-splashed. Grant had never seen the room before.

The door opened again and the man came in carrying a cup. He was a black, six feet tall or so and built to match. The face was long, with an Afro haircut, the mouth not unusually thick and topped by a pencil-line moustache. The nose was thin and beaked, reminding Grant of an Arab. There was a notch out of one nostril.

'A cup of water for the master,' the black said, addressing the empty room. He passed the handleless cup over and shook some drops from his fingers.

' 'Scuse fingers. Afraid us poor black folks don't run to glasses, no sir!' He beamed an expanse of yellowing teeth in Grant's direction and deposited himself on the empty chair, where he struck a pose of thoughtfulness and pulled his face in contortions as if wrestling with some problem.

Grant watched the circus impassively. If he waited long enough, maybe the pounding in his head would go away.

'I can't get the cup to my mouth.'

The negro looked at the cup which was held uncertainly in Grant's bound hand.

'The man can't drink the water! Sure is a problem!' The other man rolled his eyes. 'Sweet Jesus inspire me! What is I going to do?' He clasped his hands together and wrung them.

'Try cutting the Amos and Andy talk and letting my hands free.'

The negro turned around sharply and gave Grant a murderous look. Then his face broke into a smile and he dragged his chair to the Englishman in front of him, his face so close that Grant could feel his hot breath.

'So whitey don't like the Uncle Tom talk? Can't say I care for it myself.' The voice had changed to a neutral accent. The owner leaned back in the chair. 'So you want to be set free? Well, I'd like to do that, but I saw what you did to those two dumb honkys yesterday.'

Grant registered that he had lost a day. 'You hit me on the head?'

'Give the man a prize! Sure I hit you. I waited in the kitchen until the other two saw to you or – as it turned out – you came through the door all unsuspecting.' He mimicked Grant's English accent, 'Discretion is the better part of valour, don't you know?'

'And now what are you proposing to do?'

The negro sucked on his teeth. 'Well now, that really depends on you.'

'You can start by releasing me from this chair – I take it that since I'm still alive you have no fatal intentions?'

The other man laughed. 'You got a lot of cool, mister, but you're right. For the moment we have no intentions of killing you.' He dipped his hand into the pocket of his blue jacket and produced a knife. 'Not for the moment.' He got out of his chair and moved behind Grant. 'Now, Mr Grant, I'm going to cut your hands free. I'll tell you now that this place is in Harlem, not Sesame Street. I think you know what that means.' He slit through one of the cords and Grant felt his legs free. 'If by some miracle you got away from me, I'd only have to holler and one of the brothers would stop you before you got a block.' The knife passed through the cord tying Grant's hands. 'Of course, I'm telling you this just to put the thought of escape out of your head. The truth of the matter is – well, I guess I'd kill you.'

Grant said nothing. He rubbed his wrists where the rope had bitten in and moved his feet to feel the blood returning.

'Does my freedom run to stretching my legs?'

'Take a tour of the room if you want to.'

'Thanks.'

Grant got to his feet holding the chair. His legs felt weak.

'Looks like I may have overdone the warning. With legs like those you ain't going nowhere fast.'

'So it would seem.' Grant gripped the chair tightly waiting for his sense of balance. In the meantime he checked out the rest of the room. It wasn't much. At the back there was a small stove, a table and a painted cabinet holding some junk crockery. Next to that an alcove hung by the rags of a faded curtain and behind it a bed that had been slept in. Otherwise nothing except the white cockerel watching from its cage.

He took a step out from the chair and held out a hand to catch at the wall, which, obligingly, came out to meet him. He paused whilst the blood pounded in his head and the skin of his face tingled.

'What did you give me?'

'Nothing dangerous,' the negro said equably. 'The effects will wear off.'

Grant nodded and proceeded to feel his way around the walls of the room. He stopped at the window and looked out at some children playing in the street by a broken hydrant that was spraying water. Across the way was a tenement building and a small store. The name of the store had been Minsky's Drugstore, but someone had painted it out.

'Don't think you'll be finding your way back here,' the negro said. 'When you go, so do we.'

Grant turned away and staggered back to his chair.

'Okay,' he sighed. 'So you've turned over my apartment and brought me here. Do you want to talk?'

'I call that a businesslike suggestion.'

'Fire away – you seem to know the topic – I don't, Mister . . .'

'Brown – call me Mr Brown. Tell you what I'll do, Mr Grant, I'll read your fortune. Ever had the cards read?'

'No.'

'You've been missing something all your life.'

Brown reached for his jacket and took something from the pocket. Grant looked up at the white cockerel. Around its neck it had a necklace strung with a piece of bone.

'This is what I call the "modern tarot",' Brown said. He dealt half a dozen photographs face down on to the table. 'You heard of the tarot?' He spread the deal. 'Now take your pick.'

Grant turned a photograph over. It was of Kathy and Joey.

Someone had taken it from inside a car. At the bottom of the print was the edge of a newspaper showing the date. Kathy was in the driveway of Harvey Warfield's house about to get into her car to go shopping. Joey was standing on the lawn holding a shoe in one hand.

'This was taken today?'

'That's what the newspaper says.'

'What do you want?'

Brown picked up the photographs and shuffled them together. He watched the Englishman. 'You know there's no way you can stop us getting at them.'

'I asked what you wanted.'

'You're in the middle of a deal for a manuscript,' Brown said slowly. 'You don't have to agree or deny it, just listen. If the deal is completed you will take delivery of the papers for your employers.'

'Go on.'

'Instead of doing that, you will follow instructions from us where to take them.'

'I'm to hand them over to you?'

'Not to me personally, but you get the general idea.'

'That's it?'

'That's it.' Brown pushed back his chair and rose. 'You're free to go, Mr Grant.'

Grant got up. His legs were still unsteady, his coat was on the floor in the alcove. Brown was waiting by the door.

'I know what you're thinking,' Brown said, 'but heroism isn't going to do you any good.'

He opened the door and at that moment a gun barrel came through the doorway and hit him across the face. The big negro collapsed back into the room and was followed by a broad-shouldered red-faced man wearing a blue suit and a snappy little hat with a snakeskin band. Three more of the same type piled in behind him.

The newcomer looked at Brown who was lying on the floor nursing the gash on his cheek and snapped, 'Get on your feet, mister, this is the police!' He caught sight of Grant. 'And who the hell are you?'

Grant looked at Brown. 'I'm a customer – having my fortune read.'

'Then it should have told you to beware of strange niggers. Give your name to Johnson here and then get the hell out.'

Brown looked up from the floor and gave an innocent grin. 'Shi-it, man! What you want? I ain't done nothin'.'

'Save it! You're busted along with your friends downstairs.'

Brown played the dumb street-nigger, 'C'mon, man, what I done?'

One of the other men pulled open a drawer and produced a package. He turned to the red-faced man, 'Lieutenant, looky here! There's got to be a pound of marijuana here.'

'You got to be kidding!' Brown shouted. 'C'mon, Lieutenant, you ain't gonna bust me on a dumb conjurer's trick like that.'

'Ain't I though?' the lieutenant said and he pulled Brown to his feet. 'Move it!' He spotted Grant and added, 'And get *him* out of here!'

Grant pulled on his jacket and followed the man named Johnson down the stairs. Out on the stoop two more men were keeping the curious back. There was a wagon parked in the street and a couple of uniformed cops were bundling two negros into the back.

As Grant paused on the stoop, Johnson gave him a push in the back.

'Don't hang around this shit heap! There's a subway two blocks away.'

Brown emerged blinking in the sunlight. He looked around and then at the wagon and suddenly his expression changed to one of panic.

'I ain't getting in there!' he said, and as he said it he turned and threw a punch at the lieutenant. The other man caught the blow on the forearm and felled Brown with his gun butt. The negro crumpled on to the steps and was hauled up.

Grant glanced at Johnson who was by his side. 'What's a nice Georgia boy like you doing in New York?' he asked.

'You heard the lieutenant,' Johnson hissed. 'Get the hell out of here.'

The apartment had a déjà-vu appearance. Brown's associates had taken it apart with a thoroughness that even Kathy couldn't match. However the telephone was still working. Grant fixed himself a drink and made a call.

'Bob? This is Jonathan . . . good to hear you too. I want to ask a favour of you. A drugs bust in Harlem today' – he gave the address – 'can you run a check on it. I counted three negros and seven officers – two in uniform and five in plain clothes. One of them called Johnson. They were under a lieutenant with a face like a cement mixer – tough nut, pushing retirement . . . thanks.'

He rang off and dialled again. Kathy answered the phone.

'Jonathan?'

'Are you alone in the house?'

'Yes. Why?'

'Where's Harvey?'

'Where should he be? He's working and Lorraine has taken the children to visit her mother. What do you want?'

Grant hesitated.

'Look, I can't explain. I want you to take Joey and move out of Harvey's place.'

'What is this, Jonathan? Where am I supposed to go?'

She was frightened and Grant wasn't sure he could help her.

'You've got other friends – try them. If necessary, book into a motel. Don't worry, I'll send you some money.'

The voice changed to animosity and then to tears. 'What are you up to, Jonathan? Can't you leave me and Joey alone? Damn it, aren't we entitled to be left alone! If this is some sort of trick to force me to come back, then it isn't going to work.'

'It's not a trick, believe me!' Grant insisted. 'If you stay where you are, then you're in danger. Can you get that into your head?'

'Oh, sure! I can see I'm in danger – from you!' Kathy's voice was rising with emotion. 'Don't you ever let go of anything? Leave us alone, Jonathan! Leave us both alone!'

The phone went dead. Grant replaced the receiver. He felt that, in some way, the diaries were a knife that had just cut out part of his life.

Twenty

Barton Magruder had always found his relations with Walter Emmett difficult. The senior vice-president of Rama had come into the corporation via a Boston upbringing and MIT which made him a mixture of dilettante, businessman and technocrat; and shaking the pieces so that the right bit came up at the right time could get to be a problem. In general he was inclined to be benevolent towards Magruder-Hirsch, regarding the publishing business as the up-market end of Rama's interests in the media and good for the conglomerate's image as a Liberal American Institution rather than a faceless multinational engaged in secret corporate freemasonry. But this view and his own aesthetic leanings, which pushed him towards dumping artistic oddities on the publishing house, conflicted with his commercial ideas which required that Magruder-Hirsch turn in a profit representing an adequate return on investment.

Magruder flew into San Francisco on the evening flight and arrived with more drinks and dinners inside him than he wanted. He snatched some sleep and then, taking the lawyer, Grenfell, along, presented himself at the Rama building.

Emmett was in a sprightly mood. He was a dark-haired, intense man with a Clark Gable moustache that was turning white. He wore a dove-grey suit and hand-made shoes. As if to draw up the battle lines he had brought along his own lawyer.

'Bart, it's good to see you! Have you met Sam Rubin before? He's one of our in-house attorneys.' Emmett paused whilst the handshakes went round then enquired, 'How was the trip?'

'So, so, nothing special.'

Magruder's slow eyes took in the room. It was large and walnut panelled with a carved fireplace holding unburnt logs; there was a long conference table also in walnut with Queen Anne legs and claw and ball feet, and on the wall a Dutch seascape with barges. The publisher guessed that Emmett had chosen the room to convince him that Rama was taking the project seriously and that whatever was said was final.

'I was impressed by your presentation,' Emmett said. They hadn't taken seats so Magruder recognized the remark as a prelude, not to be taken seriously. They made themselves comfortable around the table.

'I mean that sincerely,' Emmett emphasized. 'It was clear, concise and well argued. I liked it. We all liked it.'

'Thanks,' Magruder said.

'Of course – it's got it's problems. But then, what doesn't have problems? Then again, I imagine you can iron those out.'

'Probably.'

'You should see the problems we have on the Lockheed contract. The technical side is six months behind and we have the Defense Department breathing down our necks.' Emmett sighed and looked to Rubin for a cue.

'I heard you were having difficulties,' Magruder said. He waited for the other man to come in.

'One of the things that causes us difficulty in your case is the copyright position,' the lawyer said. He was a youngish man, bland faced and conservatively dressed, and his voice revealed him to be a New Yorker.

Grenfell moved uncomfortably in his seat and shuffled his papers. 'Our English lawyers advise us that we have a pretty good position over there,' he murmured in his hesitant alto. He glanced at his notes, 'Under Section 13 of their Enemy Property Act 1953, we think we can make out a case to extinguish any German copyright.'

Magruder watched Emmett nodding as if he understood. But Rubin wasn't to be sidetracked.

'That's pretty interesting, but we're not chiefly concerned with the British.'

'Sam has a point,' Emmett said. 'After all, our primary market is the United States.'

'Well I can see that,' Grenfell hedged, '. . . but these things have to be considered globally.'

The remark trailed off into silence and the four men sat back in their chairs waiting for the next round.

'Still, you thought it was a good book,' Magruder said.

Rubin replied with a question to Grenfell. 'Just how do you put your US position?'

'Well, we think there may have been a vesting —'

'Under the Trading With The Enemy Act? Come on, that isn't going to fly for a minute.'

'What's he talking about?' Magruder asked Emmett.

'I think Sam should give you the details,' Emmett said smoothly.

'Sure, I don't mind doing that,' Rubin jumped in.

Magruder looked at Rubin then at Grenfell and knew he had backed the wrong horse. He lit a cigar whilst he thought.

'When it comes down to it, Walter, this is really a commercial not a legal problem,' he said. It was an appeal to Emmett's business masculinity.

'I don't know – it's difficult to see it in that light once the lawyers have become involved.' Emmett threw the ball back: it was the publisher who had first dragged in Grenfell.

'The problem is quite simple,' Rubin said. 'If there had been a Section 39 vesting – and I emphasize "if" – then maybe the German copyright would have been extinguished. But even then we'd need a Section 10 Presidential License – which we don't have. And if there isn't a vesting then I don't see we have any right at all.'

'I assume all that means something,' Magruder said. 'Do you follow it?'

'Not the detail, perhaps,' Emmett said, 'But I'm sure you understand the drift. We don't have any right to print the book.'

The meeting adjourned for coffee and they talked about wives and children. Afterwards Magruder took up the discussions.

'Do you see US government or the Germans wanting to associate themselves with this book?' he asked Emmett. 'You've read it. Parts of it are pure pornography.'

Emmett avoided the question. 'It isn't just the governments, Bart. What's to stop a pirate edition being run off. If we have no rights, then anyone can print.'

'I don't believe that,' Magruder said. 'Any house with the size to handle this has a reputation to lose.'

'I'm not sure we can take that risk, Bart.'

Magruder looked to Grenfell, and then to Rubin again.

'Don't we have any rights in the translation?'

'We don't have any rights at all. The Germans, or whoever the copyright holders are, have the translation rights.'

Magruder was thinking fast. 'That's not what I mean. What I want to say is, don't we have copyright in the actual words used in *our* translation?'

'Sure – but there's nothing to prevent anyone running off a new translation from the German text.'

'Except that we have the text. So long as we hold on to that no-one can do a new translation: they can only plagiarize ours – and that we can stop.'

Rubin turned to Emmett and said slowly, 'Bart has a point. It's crazy but I think it works.'

'It would mean holding up publication of the German edition for say twelve months, but that should be manageable,' Magruder said.

Emmett looked doubtful. He picked up Magruder's report from the table and scanned it. 'Your projections assume a substantial return from German sales.'

'Not so. The cash figure is large, but only marginal against the viability of the deal: the US remains the big market. In any case we're only talking about deferring the income for a year. That wouldn't even make a scratch on Rama's books.' Magruder looked into Emmett's face and made an appeal to vanity. 'Walter, don't you want to launch the biggest deal in publishing history?'

The remark hit. Magruder could see that Emmett wanted to do it but there was something else holding him back. Emmett looked away and stroked his moustache. When he turned to face the publisher he had come to a decision.

'You're still asking me to take a risk, Bart, but I'll tell you what I'll do. If you can pre-sell two and a half million dollars worth of rights, Rama will come in for the other seven and a half.' He raised his eyebrows. 'That's only fair isn't it? If you can sell that much, it will demonstrate that the market has confidence in the book.'

The offer was smoothly done but Magruder knew it was the kiss of death. He could see that Emmett was under an instruction to kill the deal and only his self-esteem was preventing him from saying so outright. Magruder wondered who was breathing on Rama's neck – and why?

'You know there's no way I can do that,' Magruder said quietly. 'The owners of the manuscript won't allow its existence to be advertised, so how can I invite anybody to buy the rights? What are they supposed to be buying? I should go along to Ben Vitalis and tell him that *World-Time* have a great opportunity to buy into a book, but unfortunately, I can't tell him what it is? He wouldn't give the idea house-room.'

Emmett shook his head, 'It's the best I can do, Bart.' He reached into a silver cigarette box that lay on the table and asked Sam Rubin for a light. Then he turned to Magruder again. 'Do you ever bring Elspeth out here to the West Coast?'

'She doesn't like to travel.'

'I sympathize, but she doesn't know what she's missing. I have a boat and wondered if you and Elspeth would care to spend a week cruising?'

'I'll bear it in mind,' Magruder said. He glanced at Grenfell and the lawyer began collecting his papers to leave.

'By the way,' Emmett said, 'whatever did you decide about Orshov?'

'Orshov?' Magruder remembered: the Russian dissident poet that Emmett had been pushing in his direction for the past six months. 'We made up our minds to publish,' he said.

Emmett smiled. 'I'm glad you decided to do that.'

Twenty-one

27 November 1980

Outside the United Nations building a crowd of demonstrators marched quietly in a small circuit or lounged on their placards, talking to their friends. There were about two dozen of them, mostly serious-looking young men and women. They took no notice of Grant as he walked into the building.

The day was fine and cold. Sunlight glinted from the wall of glass. Two policemen kept an indulgent eye on the procession. A few tourists took snaps of the building or speculative shots of the people coming and going, in case they might be famous. A tall, broad African in a striped, flowing robe, smiled at the crowd, stopped obligingly to be photographed and then got into a sleek black car. The placards did another circuit with their message: *Soviet Hands Off Poland!*

A tall, handsome figure in the public concourse checked his watch, spotted Grant and came towards him.

'Jonathan! It's good to see you again.'

'And you too, Sven.'

Sven Gunnarson was a tall, fair-haired Swede with a taste in burgundy-coloured shirts with white collar and cuffs and dark, well-cut suits. He looked like one of these people in newspaper photographs who stand, unremarked, next to the famous and powerful.

'I'm late?' Grant asked, checking his own watch.

'Not at all. I had an idea it might be lunchtime. Would you care to join me?' Gunnarson spoke in the lilting bloodless way of Scandinavians.

'That sounds like a good idea,' Grant said.

They talked of incidental matters on the way to one of the restaurants inside the building.

'Did you have any difficulty with the demonstrators?' Gunnarson enquired.

'No. They seemed a good-tempered lot.'

'Obviously you don't look like a diplomat,' Gunnarson

said. Grant was wearing an open-necked shirt with a linen jacket and dark slacks.

'Normally they leave me alone, but sometimes I get mistaken for a German and receive some abuse about being a fascist pig or similar – an occupational hazard. Yesterday there was a crowd of Poles demonstrating in support of the workers' union, Solidarity.'

'It's the same crowd today.'

'I thought so,' Gunnarson said. 'Volatile people, the Poles. It wouldn't take too much to set them off and bring the Russians down on their heads.'

'That's what you expect to happen?'

'Who can say? I only know that it's something no Western government wants. It would destabilize Europe – ruin détente with the Soviets.' He smiled. 'But, then, I don't suppose you came here to talk about that.'

The restaurant looked from high over the Manhattan skyline. The Swede caught the eye of a waiter, introduced himself and asked for the table he had reserved. It was in a quiet corner hung with sand-coloured drapes.

The restaurant was filling up with a miscellany of diplomats, mostly male: smooth Europeans who looked as though they had come straight from their tailors; glossy-faced Africans, ebony-black and sleek-looking; a variety of brown-skinned Asians. Most of the non-Europeans wore some sort of ethnic dress – the sort they will make up for you in Saville Row, Grant thought. But maybe that was cheap cynicism – there hadn't been a world war since the United Nations was created.

Gunnarson ordered the food and the conversation continued in the same flat, guarded tone. The Swede talked with emotionless suavity of his work at the UN, retailing a few anecdotes which he laughed at drily, and occasionally interjecting a political observation as if testing Grant out. Their talk drifted towards the past.

That past acquaintance was fairly brief. Grant had run into the Swede in Saigon, during his tour with the news agency in Vietnam. Gunnarson was working for the World Health Organization but Grant had seen him hanging around the chief American spookhouse, which may have meant everything or nothing, since, by 1975, the CIA were keeping open house, buying rounds for anyone prepared to drink with them and burning the files that even Langley didn't want to know about.

Whatever the truth, Gunnarson was a mine of information. He knew everyone and had the entré to anywhere he cared to go. He said it was because of his neutral status and maybe it was. He was affable, obliging and, when it suited him, prepared to talk. And what he said had a knack of being accurate. He was a man who, if he didn't know something, could find out fast. And that was why Jonathan Grant had arranged to meet him.

Gunnarson put down his knife among the remains of some Roquefort cheese and dabbed his lips with a napkin. He sipped at a glass of port.

'Why did you approach me with your question? You could have made the enquiries yourself or hired an investigator.'

'Possibly,' said Grant, 'but I need a lead quickly.'

Gunnarson considered the answer. 'Helsingstrup?'

'He was a Swede,' Grant said. The library had come up with a 1938 edition of *Vem är Det*. It had an entry for Sigurd Olafson – Baron Helsingstrup.

'So you came to see me.'

'Presumably you can help or you wouldn't have invited me here.'

The other man nursed his glass in his hand. 'May I ask what your interest is?'

The question wasn't unnatural, but Grant tested it to see what the Swede might mean in his oblique way. 'Is there something special about the name?'

A smile. 'You're answering a question with a question. I believe I was first.'

Grant had prepared an answer. A number of Swedes had been involved as linkmen with the Allies in the various plots against Hitler's life. Helsingstrup? It was plausible.

'Where did you come across the name?' Gunnarson asked.

'When I was researching my book on Himmler I came across the name in some of the files of his intelligence chief, Walter Schellenberg. It set me thinking on a line for a new book about the conspiracies against Hitler.'

Gunnarson nodded to show he understood, and Grant waited for an answer. As the other man thought over his response Grant got an impression that the Swede was under some form of instruction and didn't know how far he could go.

'I don't like to press you, Sven. If I thought that it created problems, I wouldn't have asked you.'

'Not at all. There is no problem, just some embarrassment. You are on the wrong track if you think that Helsingstrup was involved in any anti-Hitler plots. You see: Helsingstrup was a dedicated Nazi.'

'Is that a joke?' Grant asked.

'It is difficult for a Swede to admit,' Gunnarson went on, 'but despite Sweden's neutrality during the war, there were Nazis in the country just as there were followers of every other political persuasion. Norway wouldn't have been alone in having its Quisling. Sweden, Britain, the United States – there is never any shortage of collaborators.'

'What do you know about Helsingstrup?'

'He was a member of the minor nobility, something of a playboy, but he fancied himself an intellectual – a romantic nationalist. He wasn't deeply involved in political circles, but when war broke out he was able to make himself useful to the Germans. As a neutral capital, Stockholm was a major centre for diplomacy and . . . intrigue for want of a better word. Someone with Helsingstrup's connections was able to introduce the Germans into respectable gatherings to fix meetings and so on. I don't believe he was ever a spy: certainly there was never any question of prosecuting him after the war.' He watched Grant for a reaction and continued, 'His wife was also well-connected. She was one of the Chartronnais.'

'The Chartronnais?'

'A group of old Anglo-French families involved in the wine trade. I believe they got their name from the Quai des Chartrons in Bordeaux. All very English. They tell me that there's even a cricket club there.'

'Go on.'

'There's very little I can tell you. Immediately after the war, Helsingstrup disappeared.'

'Dead?'

'He may well be by now, but if you mean was he murdered, then I doubt it. The facts suggest that he had planned in advance to disappear if Germany lost the war. He sold up all his assets for cash and simply vanished. Bolivia, Switzerland, you may take your pick.'

'But why disappear at all?' Grant asked. 'He wasn't a criminal.'

'Perhaps he knew too much,' was all that Gunnarson could offer.

And that was it. Whatever Helsingstrup had really been up to, Gunnarson wouldn't, or maybe couldn't, say. Somewhere, perhaps, there was a clue lying in some discarded file, say a couple of lines in a routine intelligence report, a departmental memorandum in Walter Schellenberg's sinister Sixth Bureau of the *Reichsicherheitshauptamt* – the Nazi security service. If there was, then Grant had missed it when he went over those same files looking for clues to the truth about Himmler.

He was left with the credible but tantalizingly vague picture of the vanished Swedish playboy, living in the make-believe world of a wartime neutral capital – a world of dilettantes and cranks who thought that the war could be ended by the right word in the right place among the circle of passé nobility, socialites and black marketeers. Grant was reminded of Garbo's film of *Grand Hotel*. He could see Helsingstrup in that gilded, tawdry luxury of svelte women and tuxedoed men among the smoke and velvet and the elegant carosserie of pre-war motor-cars.

'And what are you doing these days?' he asked Gunnarson.

The other man waved his hand and said casually, 'Oh, it's just some liaison work to keep the Swedish Government abreast of developments at the UN. And you, are you still chasing women?'

It was a question that wasn't looking for an answer. Gunnarson snapped his fingers for the waiter and paid the bill. As far as he was concerned, the interview was closed.

They strolled out in front of the building, blinking in the sunlight. The demonstrators were represented only by a token picket.

'They go for lunch about now,' Gunnarson said. He held out his hand to be shaken. 'Look, it's been very nice seeing you again and we should do this more often.' He smiled as he discharged himself of this piece of insincerity and then paused. 'I have one more piece of information for you,' he added as if by afterthought. 'You can have it for what it's worth. Part of Helsingstrup's property was a vineyard owned by his wife – the Château Charlus. It makes quite a passable Sauternes. Just before he disappeared, Helsingstrup sold it to an Englishman by the name of Cavendish. As far as I'm aware, Cavendish still owns it. It's possible he can help you.'

Grant had a feeling that Gunnarson knew more but was unable to tell. He wanted to know why Cavendish should be expected to know anything about a man from whom he had bought some property more than thirty years ago, but there was no chance to ask the question. Gunnarson was smiling past him at a small man in biscuit-coloured uniform hung with braid and medals. The Swede excused himself and took hold of the stranger's hand. 'Eduardo,' he said. 'How good it is to see you after all this time!'

The two men disappeared into the building, leaving Grant to watch their backs.

From the United Nations building, he returned to the Magruder-Hirsch offices. Jack Robarts caught him before he could see Magruder.

'What's new on the research front? Got something to break to Bart? If so, I'd better warn you, he's been like a bear with a sore head since he came back from San Francisco.' He scooped Grant up by the arm and marched him away towards his own office. 'Let's get some coffee and talk things over. Confidentially, Emmett gave Bart a tough time. Rama won't come across with ten million unless Bart can demonstrate that he has a winner. And, frankly, who can say that in this business?'

They found a coffee machine and drew two rations. Robarts took his cup and pushed open the door to his office.

'This is where it's at – the powerhouse of Magruder-Hirsch.'

Grant looked around. It was a regular office: a desk, some cabinets and a set of shelves holding a miscellany of books. There was a view of Sixth Avenue through the window.

'Between ourselves,' Robarts went on, 'I think that Emmett is looking for a way out.'

'Why would he want one?'

'The Defense Department has a lot of leverage over Rama

on account of the Lockheed contract – they have six hundred million tied up in some new aeroplane. If the State Department know about the diaries and are getting nervous, then a word in the right ear and . . . know what I mean?' The sentence trailed off with an enquiry in Robarts' voice. He was wondering what Grant knew about the missing portion of the text. Grant wasn't prepared to tell him.

They looked at each other for a moment over their drinks and then Robarts changed tack.

'Look, Jonathan,' he said. 'Bart has asked me to pull in some of the world's major houses so that he can try to sell them some of the rights in the diaries. I know these guys – you can't sell them a book completely blind. I need some bait. Is there nothing you can give me?'

'Nothing.'

'Not even a reason for Knights' deadline of 16 December?'

Grant shook his head. 'That least of all,' he said.

Magruder saw Grant straightaway. The publisher seemed gloomy and preoccupied whilst Grant explained what he had been able to learn about Helsingstrup. When Grant proposed returning to Europe to trace the Englishman, Cavendish, Magruder nodded as if he weren't interested, but told him to go ahead.

Next Grant called Lisa. He asked her how the work was going.

'So far everything checks out,' she said. 'But there's no way that I can cover everything in the time; so I'm having to select. By the way, for what it's worth I researched the entry that mentions Helsingstrup – remember, there was a reference to some place called Hildesheim.'

'I remember.'

'Well, it checked out okay. It's a town, a small, no-account place. The Allies flattened it in a bombing raid on 23 March.' She paused, 'Another bunch of heroes like your friend the Air-Marshal.'

The bitter recollection of the lawsuit came back to Grant.

Lisa went on, 'If you allow twenty-four hours for OKW to put its report together for Hitler, it makes sense that the reference turns up in the entry for the twenty-fourth. I don't see any connection with Helsingstrup though.'

'There isn't,' Grant said. 'The connection is somewhere else in the same entry – maybe the reference to the Yalta Conference.' He paused and thought for a moment. Then: 'Look, I think we should take a chance on the military details if so far everything you've examined checks out. If the diaries are forged, then the forger could easily have gone down the same route as we're taking, and we could be wasting our time trying to catch him out on a slip of detail.'

'Okay, so what next?'

Grant told her of his researches in New York.

'Someone was running Helsingstrup as an agent in Stockholm. If so, there's a chance that his name is on file somewhere.'

'Where?'

'Try the German Federal Archives in Koblenz. There may be something in the *RSHA* papers on Sweden. Alternatively he may have been working for military intelligence, so check into any *Abwehr* files on the same topic. As an outside chance, there may be something in the reports for the German Foreign Office.'

'That's a tall order,' Lisa said.

'I'm not asking you to read the stuff – just look for the name.' Grant was aware of the tension in his voice but before he could apologize the line was cut off. There was no purpose in calling back just to say he was sorry.

Jack Robarts was waiting for him when the call finished.

'Some policeman friend of yours called whilst you were in with Bart. Some enquiry you made about a drugs bust in Harlem – are we all researching the same book?'

Grant was in no mood to banter. 'What does he want?'

'He said he wanted to see you. Straightaway.'

Twenty-two

A policewoman with her hair in a bun, flat shoes and a pretty face led Grant into Lieutenant McCluskey's room. It was a box stolen off a larger office, with pale-green partition walls, the usual furniture and a large nude calendar with the compliments of a garage.

Bob McCluskey was behind his desk. In one of those mismatch relationships that work, he had married a writer whom Grant knew, and they had met at a party. He was a stooping, hoarse-voiced, melancholy character.

'Come on in, Jonathan, pull up a chair and just give me a second to put this stuff away,' he said and shovelled some papers into a drawer. 'It's good to see you.'

'It's good to see you too.'

McCluskey nodded as if he habitually didn't believe anything he was told. He picked up the telephone and told the switchboard to hold any calls for the next half-hour. Having done that he put his hands together and pulled the fingers into a cat's cradle. 'Let me see,' he said, 'it must be six months since I last saw you. At Marcia's wasn't it?'

Grant said he supposed it was. He looked away out of the small, square window into a courtyard crammed with fire-escapes and ventilators that gave off curls of steam.

'We should meet more often,' McCluskey was saying as Grant turned round. 'Have a drink – maybe come and have some dinner with Barbara and the kids.'

'That would be . . . '

'Nice? Maybe it would.'

Grant took a chair. 'My enquiry caused you problems,' he said. It was a statement, not a question. McCluskey didn't bother to deny it.

'When you asked me to do a favour – well, naturally I did it. After all, we've been friends for a while and it isn't as though you call me every day so that you can get facts to beef up newspaper copy.'

'You sound as thought you have a complaint.'

'Maybe, maybe not. It depends on whether you were frank with me. It seems to me I'm entitled to that.'

'Then ask me something.'

McCluskey gave a street-wise look, 'Okay, so what's your interest in a Harlem drugs bust?'

'A book – I'm looking for a new theme away from the war.'

'Uh huh. Why don't I believe that?'

'You have a suspicious mind.'

'I thought you were the one with the suspicious mind.'

'In my case it's paranoia.'

McCluskey turned his eyes away and glanced at what looked to Grant like a report. 'How are Kathy and Joey?' he asked casually.

'You heard about that,' Grant said, grasping the drift.

'From the local police – they kiss and tell.' McCluskey put the report aside. 'They tell me that was a negro too.'

'So Harvey said. I didn't see.'

'Any connection with your drugs story? I don't like to press you, Jonathan, but when you start enquiring about Harlem and then I learn that some black has been taking potshots at you – well, the ting-a-ling of coincidence starts ringing in my ears.'

'Mine too, old boy, but I don't know what the connection is. Maybe I've kicked an ant's nest and don't know it?'

'Sure, sure,' McCluskey said. He sounded tired. 'C'mon with me. I want to show you something.'

The something was a mortuary. Down among the banks of refrigerators, stacked like left-luggage lockers, an elderly man with a walrus moustache and a white coat was about to make an incision into a freshly laid-out corpse. He looked around as McCluskey and Grant came in and waved a scalpel in recognition.

'You're too early for this one, Bob. Give me a couple of hours and I'll have him stuffed and ready for the oven.'

'Which one is it?'

'The Fernandez case – the stiff from the East River – did he jump or was he pushed?' He turned his weak eyes back to the table. 'Well, here goes to find out.'

McCluskey said, 'Sorry, Joe, that's one of Frank's.' He glanced at Grant and whispered. 'There's a guy who likes his work.' He moved over to the refrigerators and pulled open one of the numbered doors. The corpse slid out on rails.

'Know him?'

It was a negro Grant had never seen before. He shook his head.

'You sure?'

'Certain.'

McCluskey shrugged his shoulders and slotted the body back into the box. He opened the next door along. Another negro.

'This one?'

'Is this a lottery or is there some reason why I should know him?'

'I take it you don't?'

'No.'

'Okay, whatever you say.' He closed the door.

'You haven't answered my question,' Grant said.

McCluskey let his hand rest on the handle of the third box. He turned to Grant and said, 'Look, Jonathan, I don't like playing walk-on parts in my own cases. You ask me about a drugs bust in Harlem – three blacks arrested. I check and find that no-one knows anything about it. Funny? You bet! And then, this morning three corpses turn up, which doesn't mean anything except that there are two police uniforms found with the stiffs and I remember you tell me there are two uniformed cops at the pinch. All of which is giving me food for thought when suddenly two guys from the FBI descend on my back and start asking questions about these three customers – and about you.'

'Interstate trafficking. The FBI could think I know something,' Grant said.

'Manure! I know the narcotics crowd. They're a relaxed bunch who like to talk over a beer. These two characters were from Washington: strong silent types with freshly ironed shirts and all the buttons on their suits. Know what I mean?'

'I'm sorry I can't help you, Bob.'

McCluskey nodded. The muscles in his hand tensed and he pulled open the refrigerator door.

'Take a look at this one.'

It was Brown.

The skull had been beaten in, the eye sockets were empty

and there was a crust of blood round the rim of the nose, but Brown was still recognizable. Just.

Grant looked for the identity tag and found it tied around the left ankle. The corpse was listed as John Doe – identity unknown. Then he saw the white enamelled bowl placed neatly by the side of the body. It contained a penis and a pair of testicles.

'Those were stuffed in his mouth,' McCluskey said. He looked up from the corpse. 'Seen enough?' He didn't wait for an answer but closed the refrigerator door. 'Let's go back to the office.'

'Him you know,' McCluskey said as they settled over cups of coffee.

'I didn't say that.'

'I'm not stupid. You didn't need to. What I want to know now is whether you can tell me anything I don't know already.'

Grant shook his head. 'I still can't help.'

McCluskey sighed. 'Did you know that these guys were CIA?'

'The killers?'

McCluskey laughed. 'Christ no! The stiffs, would you believe it?'

Grant was stunned but the explanation began to fall into slots. He remembered what Jack Robarts had told him earlier that day about State Department pressure on Rama.

'I thought the CIA weren't supposed to operate inside the country?'

'Why do you think that nobody's claimed the corpses?'

'Then how do you know where they come from?'

'The two guys from the FBI let it slip. One of them said, "Would you believe that three of our guys could fuck it up and get themselves killed?" '

'That suggests they were FBI.'

'And then he laughed. You don't laugh at your own team.'

They finished their coffee and threw the cartons into the bin. McCluskey eyed Grant speculatively. 'You aren't going to ask who did it?'

'You know?'

'Who but not why.' McCluskey took a photograph out of his desk, and passed it across. Grant recognized the ugly features of the supposed lieutenant of police who had led the raid.

'Would you believe that yesterday afternoon he was killed in a shoot-out over a traffic violation? The address of a cold-store was found in his wallet, and when we checked it out, we found the three dead guys trussed up and hanging by their heels next to the sides of beef. No wonder he was edgy when the cops stopped him.'

'Do you know who he is?'

McCluskey nodded. 'A guy named Walter Krauss. Respectable married man with his own business in the wholesale meat trade. Nothing about him to call attention except for some way-out political views.'

'Such as?'

'Before the war he was a big shot in the German American Bund.'

'A Nazi?'

McCluskey reached over and took back the photograph. 'You better believe it,' he said and laughed sardonically. 'Those guys in the CIA got themselves sandbagged and killed by a bunch of geriatric stormtroopers!'

'Thanks for the information,' Grant said. He took his coat from the back of a chair and got up to go.

'I don't know why I gave you so much,' McCluskey said. 'I thought favours were supposed to be a trade-off.'

'Friendship?'

'Maybe.' McCluskey held open the door. As Grant was stepping out he put a hand on the Englishman's shoulder and stopped him. They stared at each other for a moment and then McCluskey mumbled, 'I don't know what business you're into, Jonathan, but it's clear as hell that the government wants to stop it.'

'I'm grateful for the warning,' Grant said. McCluskey let his hand slide back to his pocket. 'Perhaps we can have a drink together some time.'

'I don't think so.' McCluskey looked at his watch. 'But it's been good seeing you again.'

'And you too.'

'Sure . . . ' A pause whilst he searched for words, 'I've never understood this thing of yours, Jonathan . . . this searching for an angle behind what the rest of us can see.'

'I just want to know the truth – there's nothing else to it.'

'And how much are you prepared to sacrifice? Your future? Your friendships?'

'I don't see it like that,' Grant said as he turned away.

Twenty-three

28 November 1980

'That's it, gentlemen. Any questions?'

Barton Magruder looked around the room assessing the reaction of his listeners to his veiled presentation of the Hitler diaries. The range was from bafflement to hostility, neither of which surprised him. What was more astonishing was that in virtually no time from Rama laying down the line that Magruder had to pre-sell some of the rights, Jack Robarts had managed to get representatives from a dozen publishing houses and newspaper syndicates together to hear Magruder expound a message that was scarcely more than Jack had been able to tell them over the phone. The worrying side of the problem was that news of the diaries was leaking by the osmosis of rumour all over the street. Magruder suspected that the men in front of him knew or suspected more than he had told them.

His message was that Magruder-Hirsch had got a book – a memoir if they chose to call it that – of a major figure from the Second World War, and when it came out it was going to raise the roof in publishing, historical research, and any other roof you cared to name. But – and here was the rub – Magruder wasn't free to tell them exactly what the book was.

It was a bare story and even when padded out with passion and hyperbole – except that Magruder knew that his talk about 'the find of the century' wasn't hyperbole – it failed to cut any ice. The more cynical suspected that Magruder's game was a simple hype for a book that might or might not be good but wasn't worth the ten million he was rumoured to have paid. The two Englishmen, burned by the libel disaster suffered on the only one of his books that London had handled, were visibly turned off when Grant's name came up. That left a residue of those who were curious and who thought that Magruder was choosing a hard road if all he had in mind was a hype. They were angling for facts.

The Frenchman raised his hand. He was a dapper character with iron-grey hair and a soft voice loaded with sybillants.

'Monsieur Lequesnel.'

'Speaking hypothetically, you understand, can you tell me: assuming that we were to put money into this book, what guarantees would we have of a financial nature? Guarantees that we should at least recover our investment?'

Magruder handled the answer carefully, nurturing the spark of interest. Some of the others were sitting up and listening.

'It would be unusual. Ordinarily we would expect you to take the risk in your own markets.'

'Ah, yes! But this is not ordinary. From what you have told us, we have not the information on which to base any assessment of the book's value. So I ask you again: would there be any financial guarantees?'

'Let me say that we would give consideration to the position of any participant,' Magruder said.

From the back of the room, Ben Vitalis spoke up. The big man from *World-Time* magazine had come in person, which Magruder hadn't expected: he put it down to Jack Robarts' work in selling his guts out.

'Is that really so, Bart?' Vitalis asked. He was a balding, ascetic type with half-moon spectacles and the near-English accents of Boston. 'Isn't it the case that Rama could finance this whole operation out of petty cash? Some of us here are pretty sympathetic, but isn't the truth that Rama – Walter Emmett, I guess – is looking for someone to shoulder part of the risk? Because, if that's so, any question of financial guarantees is out.' He looked at his neighbours and poured himself a glass of water.

'I can only repeat that we're prepared to talk to anyone who wants to come in,' Magruder said, but he knew that the point was lost. Vitalis's guess was right and it was a fatal flaw in the deal. Without guarantees, any buyer would be taking the risk blind. And no one was going to do that.

'Any more questions,' Magruder asked, and, for form's sake, a couple were raised to make him go over the points he had already made. And with that he wound the business up.

'Okay, if there are no more questions, Jack has laid on some drinks and snacks. Just follow him into the next room.'

The room emptied, leaving the two partners.

'Where do we go from here?' Nathan Hirsch asked.

'Nowhere. That was the last shot we had. Dream's over. Next time Knights calls, I'll tell him the deal's off,' Magruder said. 'And you can call that Russian poet – Emmett's protégé. Tell him he knows what he can do with his book.'

'We have a contract with him.'

'Break it! If Walt wants this to be a commercial operation, he can't expect us to take his deadbeats.'

The fat man smiled. 'Revenge?'

'So it's petty-minded? Who cares?' Magruder folded away his papers. 'Let's have a drink.'

It was then that the door opened and Ben Vitalis came in. He was holding a glass and masking a smile.

'I've got to admire the effort you put into your pitch, Bart. Ever thought of trying for politics?'

'Publishing isn't politics?' Magruder said. His half-closed eyes examined the other man suspiciously. He turned to his partner. 'Nat, can you get me a drink? Scotch and water.' The fat man took the hint. Being excluded didn't disturb his gentle manner.

Magruder turned back to Vitalis. 'You have something on your mind, Ben?'

Vitalis laughed. 'Not if you think I'm going to buy into your deal blind.'

Magruder nodded. He sensed there was something there. 'You have some other proposition?'

Vitalis took a sip of his drink and put the glass down.

'I know about the Hitler diaries,' he said.

When Grant arrived, he found Jack Robarts plying his guests with drink. The PR man caught sight of him and sloped over. He had a bottle in his hand.

'Drink?'

'Scotch. And what's yours?'

'Tonic water.'

'Giving up alcohol, old man?'

Robarts' expression was blank. 'During the day,' he said.

Grant looked around the room, recognizing a few faces. The two Englishmen nodded in his direction and carried on with their conversation.

'Ever felt you weren't popular?' Robarts said.

'I'll survive.'

'Maybe, but I'd start making up your expenses if I were you.'

'Why?'

'Because,' Robarts said, 'you're about to get paid off. Bart just tried to sell the deal to this crowd' – he nodded towards the group of publishers – 'and they wouldn't buy. Rama won't come in for the full ten million – so it looks as though this is the end of the road.'

'You sound quite cheerful about it,' Grant said.

Robarts' expression froze. 'Look, I know you don't like me, but I've put a lot of work into this project. That these guys are here at all is nothing short of a miracle. So don't make it sound as though I'm not involved.'

Grant didn't argue the point.

Robarts' mouth lifted in a half-smile, 'What the hell – who cares?' He shrugged his shoulders. 'By the way, I never believed your story that the Russians have the diaries. I don't think you did either.'

'Is that so. What leads you to that conclusion?'

'The Linge diaries,' Robarts said. He took the whisky bottle and poured himself a shot. The gesture was defiantly self-conscious. 'I thought to myself, "What's in the Linge diaries that's important?" '

'And the answer?'

'Nothing – the Linge diaries aren't significant at all. It's the fact that they were always known as "Hitler's diary" and how they were found that counts.'

'Go on.'

'Okay, then let's take the history. 2 May 1945 – the Russians capture the Fuehrerbunker. The Russian secret police, the *NKVD*, descend on the place and stop anyone else from going in. No Americans, no English – they have the place entirely to themselves. So what are they doing? Naturally they're going through the bunker with a fine toothcomb and carrying everything back to Moscow for analysis.'

'That sounds reasonable.'

'Except that it didn't happen! Months later the Russians allowed the British and Americans in and instead of finding the bunker as clean as a whistle there were papers all over the place. More to the point, a British officer went into Hitler's room and there, lying in open view on a chair, was the Linge diary. So of course, if you believe it, he was allowed by the Russians to put it in his pocket and walk off with it. Not just any old diary, but a diary of Hitler's movements, a diary dealing just with Hitler, so much so that everyone called it "Hitler's diary".'

Grant lit a cigarette and inhaled slowly. 'So what does it mean?'

'That the Linge diary was *meant* to be found.'

'Why?'

'Because there is another set of diaries – the real Hitler diaries,' Robarts said. He finished the Scotch and poured himself another. 'My guess is that, like Goebbels, Hitler had a copy of the diaries made before the end, and that's what the Russians found. And they didn't like what was in it. Their problem was that they didn't know how far Hitler had kept his diaries a secret: there was always a possibility that someone who knew the Fuehrer's habits would know that he kept a diary. And if that came out, people would begin to look for it.'

'That's quite a problem.'

'Sure, and this is how they solved it. They let another "Hitler diary" be found – the one kept by Heinz Linge. It was a neat way of side-tracking investigation. Whenever anyone asked whatever happened to Hitler's diary there was a ready-made answer. It was the diary kept by his valet and there was nothing in it to embarrass anybody!'

Grant stubbed out his cigarette. He could see Nathan Hirsch at one of the doors beckoning to him. He finished off his drink and asked, 'All right, if the Russians don't have the diaries, who does?'

Robarts shook his head. 'That I don't know,' he said. 'But if you want my guess, I'd say that somewhere in back of this thing, we're dealing with a bunch of old Nazis.'

When Grant joined Nathan Hirsch he was with his partner and a stranger. Magruder introduced Ben Vitalis. The publisher looked pale but calm.

'Ben runs *World-Time* magazine,' he said. 'We were hoping to sell them serialization rights.' He hesitated. 'But now he has something to tell.'

Vitalis was relaxed. He shook hands with Grant and said, 'I've just told Bart: I know about Adolf Hitler's diary.'

'Now that Jonathan's here,' Magruder said, 'perhaps you'll tell me how you found out.'

'Don't worry, Bart,' Vitalis said. 'I'm not about to tell the whole world.'

'Maybe not, but I'd still like to know who told you.'

'Jack Robarts – he came to me yesterday with the whole story.'

'Jack?' Magruder murmured. 'Why the hell should he do that?'

'Greed, ambition – the usual things. That young man wants to get to the top fast and doesn't much care how he does it. He offered me a deal. He told me about the diaries and said that your financing had cratered.'

'For chrissake!' Magruder exclaimed.

'Wait a minute,' Vitalis went on calmly. 'If I weren't being straight, I wouldn't be here now.'

Magruder quietened down. 'Okay, Ben, go on. I've got nothing against you.'

'Fine.' Vitalis paused and poured himself a glass of water then offered the jug around the table. 'Jack also told me that you had a copyright problem. Not to labour it, he told me you didn't have copyright and couldn't stop anyone else from jumping in ahead of you and publishing – the end of the story being that for some small consideration and a job he could deliver the text.'

Magruder stood up and walked to the window. He parted the drapes and stared out into the street. Finally he asked, 'And what do you propose to do?'

'Running pirate editions isn't my style,' Vitalis said. He shrugged his shoulders. 'I didn't come here with any preconceptions – I'm prepared to talk. Provided you answer some questions.'

'The copyright problem doesn't scare you?'

'I talked to our lawyers. They confirmed that you have a problem, but they tell me that it's manageable so long as you hold on to the German rights. I noticed that there were no Germans invited to your little party, so I guess that your advice is the same.'

'That's right.'

'Good. Then tell me what Rama's hang-up is? Why won't they finance the whole package? Don't tell me that the returns won't cover the investment because this book is going to outsell anything that's ever been printed except maybe the Bible.'

'It's the telecommunications deal with Lockheed and the Defense Department.'

Vitalis nodded. 'I hear that Rama is behind with delivery.'

'You hear right. That gives the government a lot of leverage if we do something they don't like.'

'And why don't they like the diaries?'

Magruder told Vitalis about the missing portions. 'We don't know what's in them, but it's something scary – both to the US Government and maybe to the Russians as well.'

Vitalis took out some cigars and offered one to Magruder. He chewed over the idea as he cut and lit the cigar. 'All right,' he said at last. 'I can see that the Defense Department would employ the Lockheed contract as a threat – but would they use it? I don't think so. The Administration would be too scared of it coming out that they had used government contracts to suppress freedom of speech.'

'Maybe, but Emmett isn't about to take the risk.'

'If you're right, Rama won't produce any finance at all. How much has Walter promised you?'

'Seven and a half million.'

'Then the question is: will he renege if you come up with the other two and a half?'

They were silent for a moment and then Magruder gave a lugubrious smile, 'I don't think so,' he said.

'Why not?'

'Because now that there's been one leak, Walter has got to see that there will be more. This thing is too big to have the lid kept on indefinitely. And once the story breaks, the State Department isn't going to make any fine distinctions about who is responsible: they're going to blame Rama.' He shook his head in amusement. 'Whichever way Walter plays it – publish or just let the story come out – his contracts are going to be at risk. And in that case, he may as well publish and be damned.'

'Then it looks as if we may have a deal,' Vitalis said.

Twenty-four

29 November-5 December 1980

The day following the meeting with Vitalis, Grant flew down to Washington, taking with him his papers and a stack of unopened mail. As he had told Lisa, whilst she searched the German records for a trace of the elusive Helsinstrup, he was going to cover the same ground in the National Archives. It wasn't entirely unfamiliar ground.

Three years before, when he was researching the Himmler book he had looked over the surviving papers of the Reichsfuehrer SS. Those in the National Archives were on microfilm, recorded under the reference T175.

On this occasion there was an underlying irony. He had written what he had hoped was the definitive biography of Himmler, but if his suspicions were correct, there was something there, something so far unknown, that would reveal Himmler in a new light and destroy Grant's own book.

In the back of his mind he had the image of the mysterious Swede: sportsman, playboy, Nazi agent. Like the mark of the beast, the hallmark of Himmler's henchman and spy-chief, Walter Schellenberg, seemed stamped on his brow. In the crazy world of Hitler's entourage, Himmler had waged a private war with the Reich Foreign Minister, Joachim von Ribbentrop. At stake was the conduct of Germany's foreign affairs, a chance to end the war – and to succeed the Fuehrer.

On Himmler's behalf, Walter Schellenberg had a stable of agents operating out of the neutral capital of Stockholm, where contact could be made with the diplomats of other neutrals and with the Allies. Helsingstrup, with his ready access to high social and diplomatic circles, was tailor-made for the job.

That was the theory. No one except Schellenberg could have given the answer. But Schellenberg was dead, lying in a Turin cemetery: 3rd *Ampliemento Campo Est.* His grave was number 1763.

On Sunday morning after his arrival the day before, Grant got round to opening the mail he had brought with him. Amongst all the trash and the unanswered demands from the Internal Revenue Service, he found a letter addressed to Lisa, care of Magruder-Hirsch. Since it was reasonable to suppose that it was related to their joint researches, Grant opened it.

Dear Dr Black,

Thank you for your most kind letter. It came to me as a great surprise that after all these years there should be someone to take an interest in those of us who played a small part behind the scenes during the last war. May I say now that I believe it to be a most excellent project that you should write a history of the experiences and feelings of humble secretaries like myself.

I do not know whether I can be of any great assistance to you. If your interest is in the life of Herr Hitler [here the letter betrayed signs of hesitation over what the writer should call the Nazi dictator], then I am sure that there are many who can tell you more than myself. Indeed I am most surprised that my name should have come to your attention. It is true that I did work near to Herr Hitler on occasions when temporary clerical assistance was required; but this was only for very brief periods. My official post was with the Naval Ministry. Of course, if you are interested in other German leaders, I may say that I have worked closely with Admiral Doenitz, and on occasion I worked for Herr Doktor Goebbels.

If my story is still of interest to you, I shall be pleased to help. My memories of those days are still very clear. For example, in answer to your query whether Herr Hitler ever kept a diary, I am able to say quite definitely yes. If it is detail like this that you wish, then I am sure you will find me most useful.

Fraülein Gisela Herder.

Grant read the letter again. It carried a Düsseldorf address, the paper was scented, lavender in colour with a sprig of flowers printed in one corner – it was the sort on which a Victorian lady might write a note, but the Victorian ladies were all dead. The writing too, in brown ink, was in a neat, old-fashioned italic hand. It didn't answer one question: who the hell was she?

It was lunchtime in Washington, early evening in Koblenz when Grant was able to reach Lisa on the telephone. She was pleased to hear from him and seemed eager to tell him some tale of her own, but Grant stopped her with his news of the letter and the mention of the diaries that it contained. But which diaries – the Hitler diaries or that of Heinz Linge?

'Who is this "Gisela Herder"?' Grant asked.

'Remember when you suggested I get in touch with Hitler's old secretaries? Well, I pulled her name out of your files.'

'She was one of Hitler's secretaries?'

'Depends what you mean. She wasn't on the permanent staff, but on a couple of occasions she had a temporary posting. You never interviewed her – at least I never found anything in your papers.'

And there it was. Grant looked at the name again, but it meant nothing. It was just one of hundreds who might have been able to help him in his biography of Himmler. He had worked through the list: chauffeurs, filing clerks, faceless bodyguards, any of whom, despite the insignificance of their jobs, might know something. He remembered the driver, Kempka, a man of no account except that he had burned the corpse of the dead Fuehrer. Some of the people Grant had interviewed, some he had not. In the end it was a guess who was important.

Grant had spent a long summer in Germany interviewing forgotten people. For the most part they were solid and respectable people who assured Grant earnestly that they had never been Nazis personally – though, of course, they had been forced to join the Party in order to get advancement. They talked freely, regretting the past, yet it seemed to Grant that they regretted the present even more. They were colourless men and women with gentle manners and inexpressive speech that could not convey their obscure feelings about what had happened to their lives.

There were exceptions. Grant met an SS sergeant who was running a backstreet garage in Essen. Yes, of course he was a Nazi and why not? Europe would be communist if it were not for what Germany had done. The Jews? Just look at all the trouble in the Middle East! Did Grant think that America would be backing Israel if it weren't for the Yiddish politicians in the United States? The man had said all this from the underside of a large Mercedes he was fixing for a Jewish customer.

In the end it had been necessary to select from the names those who looked as though they had something to contribute. And so Grant had excluded the name of an obscure copy-typist. The irony came to him as he envisioned her. A middle-aged woman, still unmarried as she made clear from the emphatic 'Fraülein' of her signature, a woman still nourishing her core of snobbish respectability: styling herself a secretary when she had worked in a pool, and awarding Lisa a doctorate to which Lisa had laid no claim in her letter. He looked at her reply again and thought he understood the significance of the paper and the neat, precise handwriting.

And yet for thirty-odd years she might have been sitting unknowingly on the biggest historical secret of the century.

'Do I get my news in?' Lisa asked at last.

'Fire away,' Grant said.

'Guess who I ran into in the Federal Archives?'

'I give up.'

'Max Weiss!'

'Max?' Grant made no secret that he was puzzled. What was the reporter doing in Koblenz? 'I thought he was covering the Xanten case in Frankfurt?'

'The trial isn't on yet; the old man is still trying to get postponements.'

'You talked to Max?'

'I couldn't help it when I ran into him, face to face, between a line of stacks. Naturally I asked him what he was doing there and he said he was just researching some of the background to the case.'

'Did you believe him?'

'I have a suspicious mind – must have got it from you I guess – so I turned my charm on one of the archivists and found out what sort of stuff Max was asking for and get this: Max was after the same as me – Schellenberg's files on his Swedish operations!' She paused to let the message sink in and then went on, 'Jonathan, I read everything I could lay my hands on concerning Xanten. He was never anywhere near Sweden.'

The rest was unspoken. They knew who was in Sweden.

Grant wondered whether he had a race on his hands to find Helsingstrup.

On Monday morning, when Washington was back in business, Grant's plans were slightly changed because of the letter from Germany, and instead of visiting the National Archives as planned, he got in touch with a contact in the office of the Chief of Military History and asked for access to the routine interrogations carried out by the US Army as part of the denazification programme carried out in Germany after the war. The result he wanted came through on the following day: the record of the interrogation of Admiralty typist, Fraülein Gisela Herder. On the same Tuesday night he put through a call to London.

The operator's voice said, 'Sir, your call is through.'

A muddy voice murmured, 'Jonathan? What time of night is this to be calling me?'

'Freddie?'

'The very same. Super to hear from you and all that, but it's three in the morning and I've had a bloody rough night.' A pause, then, 'Where in God's name are you, anyway? The line's as clear as a bell, so you can't be in London.'

'I'm in Washington.'

'New Zealand?'

'That's Wellington.'

A yawn on the other end of the line, 'Oh, *that* Washington. Sorry, but my geography isn't too good at this hour of the day – or night – whichever it is.'

There was an off-stage complaint and a groan of 'Can't you tell I'm on the phone?' Then, 'Sorry about that, old man. The troops are muttering. Look, is this a pencil and paper job? Because, if it is, I'll just have a pee and get the necessary.'

'I want you to take down a name,' Grant said when Freddie Thornton came back. He spelled it out: Gisela Herder.

'Got it. Who is she?'

'A clerk in the German Admiralty during the war.'

'Pretty ancient history,' Thornton said cautiously, sensing a story.

'Maybe.'

'Any more details?'

Grant gave her date and place of birth, which he had got

from the American record, and heard a pencil scratching the surface of the paper as Thornton took note. He recognized the other man's instincts in reaching for a pencil and paper before he had even known what the call was about. Freddie Thornton was a Fleet Street hack. It wasn't a description that Freddie would have objected to – he regarded it as the appellation of an honourable profession. And, like all journalists, he gave and owed favours, debts which he repaid, more or less, when he sensed a story.

'What do you have to do with this Herder woman?' Thornton asked. Addressing someone else he said, 'Sling me a smoke, Sal, there's a love.' Then, 'Sorry, old man, just getting a life-saver . . . this old bird, Fraülein Herder?'

'I'll have to save the explanations for another time,' Grant said.

Thornton accepted the refusal with equanimity. 'So I'm whoring on credit? Okay, so what do you want?'

'Ever heard of a *Persilschein*?'

'*Persilschein*? After the washing powder? Wasn't it some chit that the Allies used to give to Germans who'd been laundered and cleared of being Nazis?'

'That's it.'

'I get it, this Herder woman had one.'

'She got it from the Americans,' Grant said, 'but when they picked her up, she was on her way to Hamburg.'

'British occupation zone.'

'You're ahead of me, Freddie. It's possible that she was processed again by the British, and, if so, her interrogation should be on record. I'd like you to fish out the transcript for me.'

'Piece of cake. Is that it?'

'That's it,' Grant said.

'What do I do when I get it?' Thornton asked.

'Call me at this number,' Grant said, and he gave it. 'It's the Hotel Steinberger in Frankfurt.'

Twenty-five

On Monday 1 December, whilst Grant was still in Washington, two Englishmen arrived in Paris and booked into a small hotel near the Gare d'Austerlitz. It was a small, run-down place where the rooms at the rear overlooked the railway lines and the rattle of the trains kept the guests awake.

The owner operated from a glass and mahogany booth carved out of the lobby. He was a small, squint-eyed man with wisps of black hair plastered across his scalp and a pair of down-at-heel slippers which he dragged around when he walked. Without stirring from his seat he put down the remains of a sandwich on his newspaper and asked what the newcomers wanted.

'Two rooms – next to each other and at the front of the hotel,' the taller man said.

The Frenchman looked the other up and down. Fair-haired, clean-looking, in a good-quality suit. He cast a glance at the second man. Not so good, a darker type with an edgy, trouble-making look and a zip-fronted leather jacket.

'Two rooms together and at the front,' the proprietor repeated. 'You have a booking?' He pulled an old register from the back of a shelf and made a show of turning the pages with a greasy thumb. 'No booking . . . I don't see how I can help you.'

'My friends in the police tell me you let rooms by the hour,' the fair-haired man said. He took a wallet from his jacket and peeled out some notes slowly.

'The police,' the landlord said slowly. He eyed the money. 'How long do you want the rooms for?'

'A day. Perhaps two.'

'For two days it will be five hundred francs.'

The Englishman pushed the notes across the counter top.

'And the names?'

'Karl Marx and Friedrich Engels.'

The Frenchman gave a lopsided grin. 'I understand. I have

two German guests.' He put the register away without bothering to write in the names. He reached across to an old roll-top desk and took out two keys with zinc tags. 'Rooms five and six.' He threw them from where he was sitting and the dark-haired man caught them.

'Thanks,' he said in English.

Room five was a box ten feet square, chiefly occupied by a large bed. For the rest there was a chest of drawers with a small gas-ring on top of it and a stained washbasin with a freckled mirror above it.

The fair-haired man threw the suitcase on to the bed and went over to the window, drawing back the thin curtains. 'Check there aren't any nasties lying around, Arthur,' he said and stared out into the street.

It was quiet. The window gave a clear view to the other side. A patisserie that was running down its stock of cakes towards close of business; an osteopath with a shop-front window painted white and labelled with the name of the practitioner. And, between the two, a door marked Hotel Barzin, which was half-open, revealing a flight of stairs leading to rooms above the adjacent premises.

'Bugger me, Frank, if we don't have an iron!'

Francis Lethbridge let the curtains fall and looked around. Harrison had found an iron and an ironing board.

'Just the job. I'm sick to the teeth of flea-bitten hotels and never getting a decent shirt. Is there any soap in the sink? I may as well wash some socks whilst I'm at it.'

Lethbridge didn't answer. He pulled a bare wooden chair to the window and positioned it so that he could look out. Harrison opened the suitcase and began to rummage among the clothes. At that moment there was a tap on the door.

It was a girl.

'What does she want?' Lethbridge asked. The girl was standing in the doorway, dark-haired and sparrow-like with brown eyes and soft lips over a boyish, skinny body. She wore a plain blue dress and carried a cheap silver evening bag with a tarnished clasp.

'She looks like a whore,' Harrison said. 'Our friend downstairs must have thought you needed entertainment and sent her up. There's probably another one next door waiting for me.'

'*Tu désires une amie*?' she addressed Lethbridge slowly, uncertain if he understood French.

Lethbridge nodded and she looked in Harrison's direction. '*Il va rester*,' Lethbridge said and it was her turn to nod in understanding. Whether the other man stayed or not was a matter of indifference. She put down her bag and looked around the room. Harrison opened the ironing board and placed it by the window.

'It's okay by me, Frank,' he said. 'I'll keep look-out whilst you . . . Like I said, I'll keep watch.'

The girl listened to the conversation with a look of incomprehension on her face.

'*Comment t'appelles tu*?' Lethbridge asked.

'Marie-France,' the girl said, '*et toi*?'

'Karl.'

She laughed softly as though it pleased her and then opened her bag and powdered her face.

'Did I ever tell you,' Harrison said, 'that I used to be a sales rep?'

'No.' Lethbridge watched the girl unbutton the front of her dress.

'It was for a firm that made fire extinguishers. That's the truth – bloody fire extinguishers!' Harrison laid one of his shirts over the ironing board and tested the temperature of the iron with his finger.

The girl slipped the dress from her shoulders and sat with it gathered around her waist. She wore no bra. Her thin body looked cold and frail. Her breasts were small and pointed with thin curls of hair around the nipples.

'It was a bloody awful game,' Harrison went on. 'The trouble with fire extinguishers is that nobody ever replaces the bloody things. I used to visit places that hadn't bought one for fifty years. I'd point out that the one they had wouldn't work if they tried to use it – sometimes there wouldn't even be anything in the bastard – but they weren't interested.'

The girl looked at Lethbridge and then drew her dress over her hips revealing a pair of tights. Over the left thigh there was a small hole, neatly stitched and sealed with a drop of nail varnish. She took them off.

Harrison started to iron his shirt. 'I always said: no more for me! No more sodding hotels, living out of suitcases and washing my underpants in the sink. Change my line of work. The high life – know what I mean?' He gave a short, bitter laugh.

The girl slipped under the sheets of the bed. Lethbridge watched her coolly and then took off his clothes and laid them carefully over the chair.

'We used to have this story – about sales reps,' Harrison said as he folded his shirt and took another one from the case. 'Do you know how a landlady tells if you're a rep? She sees whether you clean your shoes on the curtains and piss in the sink.' He looked more carefully at his shirt, 'You know this one isn't too bad. It must be the drip-dry I bought in London.' He picked it up and examined it against the window light, then stripped down and changed shirts. 'By the way,' he continued. 'I don't like to interrupt you two whilst you're having fun, but our friend has just come home.'

Across the street an elderly man with white-blond hair was on the steps of the Hotel Barzin exchanging words with the concierge.

Five minutes later Lethbridge got out of bed and dressed whilst the girl sponged herself down at the sink and put on her clothes.

'Is he still there?' Lethbridge asked.

'Looks like it.'

'You sure of his identity?'

'I'd know that old bugger anywhere.'

The girl was waiting at the door, clutching her evening bag.

'She wants paying,' Harrison said.

His companion pulled some notes from his pocket and stuffed them into the girl's hand.

'It beats reading a book in a waiting room,' Harrison said and, abruptly, as the girl was about to leave, he grabbed her and pressed his lips forcefully against hers. For a moment a look of mutual loathing passed between them.

The concierge was toasting her feet on a broken-toothed gas fire in the little booth tucked behind the street entrance to the Hotel Barzin. She displayed no interest when the fair-haired Englishman picked up the register and flicked over the pages.

Lethbridge put a finger on one of the entries. 'Langstrom – room seventeen. He's been here two months.' He threw a smile at the concierge who nodded and returned a gummy smile.

'I told you that old bastard Cavendish knew something,' Harrison said.

The second floor was a straight corridor of broken oilcloth running the length of the two shop frontages. The noise of a mixing machine percolated upstairs from the patisserie.

'Imagine trying to sleep with that sodding thing blazing away,' Harrison said. He checked the cracked bakelite numbers on the doors. Fifteen, sixteen, seventeen – a brown door with panes of frosted glass and the shadow of a curtain behind it. An old mortice lock on the door.

Lethbridge tapped softly on the glass.

'*Qui est-ce*?' a voice said.

No reply except for the gentle tap.

'*Qu'est-ce que vous voulez*?'

The sound of elderly breathing and footsteps across the bare floorboards of the room. A silhouette appeared in the glass.

'*Qu'est-ce que vous voulez*?' the voice repeated.

The two Englishmen heard the sound of a chain being slipped into place and a key being turned in the lock. A crack of pale light appeared at the edge of the door and the profile of a face glanced sideways round the rim.

'Baron Helsingstrup?' Lethbridge said quietly and watched the look of terror in the old man's eyes. The face recoiled as Harrison's fist smashed through the pane of glass and his gun fired six times at the retreating figure.

Twenty-six

7 December 1980

Lisa was waiting by the Selbstfahrer Union desk in the arrivals hall when Grant arrived on the evening flight. He was tired and let her drive him through Frankfurt's quiet Sunday streets to their hotel in the Bethmannstrasse. On the way they compared notes. Lisa had turned up nothing new in the archives at Freiburg and Koblenz either to prove or disprove the authenticity of the diaries. She had managed to arrange an interview with Fraülein Herder in two days' time.

'Which doesn't leave us much time – a week – until the deadline. And so far I've drawn nothing but blanks.'

Grant told her about New York, including the dead negro.

'What are we supposed to make of it?' Lisa said. 'The State Department doesn't want the diaries published, so they're putting pressure on Rama and setting the CIA on you. And on the other side you have a bunch of musclemen headed by some ageing Nazi who save your hide. Just who are the good guys and who are the bad guys?'

'Perhaps they're all bad guys,' Grant said.

That night they drank two bottles of wine and went dancing in the Lipizzaner bar. Afterwards, on the way back to their room, Grant checked at the desk for messages. The girl gave him a cute smile and told him that Mr Thornton had called and left a number at which he could be contacted.

The number was that of a night club. Grant could hear the music in the background whilst an attempt was made to find Freddie. When he arrived at the phone, he was drunk.

'Jonathan, old sport! Hope I didn't disturb the sweet fruits of sin and all that. Looking for a bit of the same myself later on.'

'What made you call?' Grant asked.

'Thought that was my question? Got the impression that your enquiry was urgent, so couldn't let life, liberty and the pursuit of happiness stand in the way of an answer, could I? I was sitting here – brought the old better half out on the town – and thought, Must call Jonathan! So here I am! Anything to get away from the cabaret. One of those northern comedians – all tits and bums and no sense of humour. So, like I say, here we are, ready, willing and able!'

'What did you find out?' Grant pressed him.

'No joy, I'm afraid. Oh, there's a record of interrogation of this Herder woman all right! But couldn't lay my hands on it.'

'Why not?'

'I ran into one of those young, snotty bastards at the ministry of what-not. Full of apologies, like to oblige and all that, but the record was with the papers of the – what did he call it? – Combined Services Detailed Interrogation Centre!'

'Which means what?'

'Classified, old sport! Not to put too fine a point on it: your Fraülein Herder's interrogation is still bloody secret!'

'What do we do next?' Lisa asked when Grant told her. 'Putting it another way: why did you pull me out of Koblenz back to Frankfurt?'

Grant poured them each another drink: the conclusion of Freddie's call had sobered him up. 'We've got an appointment tomorrow at the State Procurator's office.'

'Why are we seeing a lawyer?'

'Because I want to find out about some Nazis,' Grant said.

'Okay. Explain.'

'The State Procurator's office handle the investigation of fugitive war-criminals. Ever since I was rescued from the clutches of the CIA by a bunch of American Nazi-sympathizers, I've been asking myself: why did they do it?'

'Because there are some Nazis who want to see the diaries published?'

'So far so good. And who has the greatest interest in seeing the diaries published?'

'The people behind Knights who are doing the selling.' Lisa paused. 'That's a pretty neat syllogism, but there's one flaw in it. I thought we'd decided that anyone who made it free from the bunker carrying the diaries would have published before now?'

'Not if he needed to avoid personal publicity.'

'Like a war-criminal?'

'It fits.'

Lisa laughed, 'Come on, Jonathan, the only person who escaped from the bunker and fits into that category is Martin Bormann!'

At the Procurator's office they asked for Herr Spruengli and were told that he was out.

'I have an appointment,' Grant said.

The secretary sympathized, 'I'm sorry, but a case has come up urgently. Herr Doktor Spruengli is in court.'

Finding the court was no problem, but what they didn't expect was the sight of Max Weiss sitting on one of the public benches eating mints from a paper bag. The surprise was mutual.

'Hey, Jonathan, what gives? Trying to make a few dollars out of journalism again? What's your interest in the Xanten case?' The reporter pushed a notepad into his jacket pocket and offered the bag of mints. 'Not your taste, huh?'

'They're holding the trial here?'

'Not yet,' Weiss looked at them curiously. 'I guess you haven't heard: Xanten's lawyers are in there arguing for the case to be withdrawn because their client is unfit to stand trial – the old man tried to kill himself last night.'

'You're covering the story?'

Weiss glanced past Grant at Lisa. 'Didn't I tell you that's why I came to Europe. You sound as though you didn't believe me.'

'I believed you,' Grant said. He glanced at the courtroom door. 'What's the result going to be?'

Weiss's face lightened. 'They'll turn the old man down. He doesn't know it but his lawyers are too smart for his own good. They've tried so many tricks to postpone the hearing that no judge believes a word they say. If Xanten were to die tomorrow, the court would dig up the body and put the bones on trial.'

The conversation stopped there as the doors to the court opened and the lawyers and their assistants poured out. Max Weiss approached one of the defence counsel and started to interview him. Grant stopped a pale, robed figure who was striding away with an assistant in tow.

'Herr Spruengli, my name is Grant.'

The lawyer stopped. He was a grey-haired man of fifty with

fierce dark eyes over a face that for the rest of it seemed friendly enough. He looked at Grant and said, 'We had an appointment. My apologies for missing it; if you had asked my secretary I'm sure that she could have fixed one for another day.'

'I only have one day in Frankfurt.'

Spruengli searched around for a bench and, having found one, sat down and sent his assistant to find some coffee.

'Did you succeed in avoiding the adjournment?' Grant asked.

Spruengli allowed himself a smile, 'It was a satisfactory result. The trial will still go ahead. Is that what you're interested in, the Xanten case? The letter of recommendation from Professor Holz didn't say.'

'Not exactly. I didn't know before today that you were prosecuting Xanten, though I should have guessed that the Procurator's Office for the State of Hesse would be handling the case. I think maybe I should like to know some of the background to the case.'

'Well, perhaps I owe you that since I cancelled our appointment,' Spruengli said affably.

In the outline the story was simple enough. Two brothers, Pieter and Cornelius Xanten had been running a small family business in Amsterdam when the Germans invaded. They had both played a part in right-wing politics before the war, and they seized the opportunity to side with the Nazis and joined the SS. Cornelius Xanten was lost sight of, but Pieter Xanten had reached the rank of major and served on the Russian front. On 21 January 1945, Xanten and some Waffen-SS troops under his command had been digging a defensive position in a small Polish village as part of the German rearguard against the Russians, when one of his men was killed by one of the villagers. Xanten lost control, rounded up nearly three hundred peasants from the surrounding area and had them shot and buried in a mass-grave as a reprisal.

'After the war he couldn't return to Holland where he was known as a collaborator,' Spruengli went on, 'but in Germany he felt that he was safe because, as a Dutchman, it was unlikely that he would be suspected of war-crimes. From somewhere or other he managed to get together a considerable sum of money which he used to found an engineering business. His problems started when our tax authorities started an investigation into his financial affairs and then, by chance, he was identified by one of the survivors of the massacre.'

'And what's his side of the story?' Grant asked.

'He denies more or less everything,' Spruengli said as if that was a piece of audacity that he couldn't believe. 'He says he was never in the Waffen-SS and claims that he spent the whole of the war working at one of the ministries in Berlin. Major Peter Zanthen, he says, was a name used by his brother Cornelius. In other words, we have the wrong man.' Spruengli finished his story and checked his watch. 'Can I invite you to lunch?' he suggested.

The lawyer took them to a *Bratwurststube*. His manner continued to be cheerful and hospitable. Only when they had settled in their booth over some beers did he ask why Grant had wanted to see him.

'I wanted to ask some questions about Martin Bormann,' Grant said.

The other man's face lost its good-natured expression. 'Why do you want to know?' he asked.

'I'm doing some research.'

'For one of your books? I have read them.'

'You sound suspicious.'

Spruengli let himself relax. He opened his hands, 'There's nothing that we want to hide, Mr Grant. I'm sorry if I gave the contrary impression. But, you must understand, the Bormann case – whatever the evidence, there will always be people who refuse to believe that the man is dead.' He picked up his beer and took a sip. 'Do you fall into that category?'

'I'm open to persuasion.'

'Then what can I tell you? If you want to believe that Bormann is alive, there are masses of sightings from eye-witnesses to support you. But, on the other hand, there is no Bormann to come forward and confirm them. If you want hard evidence, on the other hand, there is the body.'

'You have the body?' Lisa asked. Spruengli nodded.

'Although people have claimed to have seen Bormann alive, there have always been witnesses to his death. Arthur Axmann, who was the Hitler Youth leader, said that he had seen Bormann's body in the Invalidenstrasse near the old

Lehrter station. Axmann knew Bormann well, but back in 1945 people were naturally suspicious that a Nazi like Axmann might have been shielding Bormann and there was no corroboration of his story. That is, until 1972.' Spruengli paused and took another sip of beer. 'Two workmen were doing construction work on an exhibition park opposite the Lehrter station and came across two skeletons. Because of their location we were naturally interested and tests were run to determine the ages of the dead men and checks were run to compare the teeth of one of the skulls against Bormann's dental records and some bridgework that was done for him.' Spruengli shrugged his shoulders. 'What can I say? The body was that of Bormann. The other corpse was probably that of Dr Stumpfegger who was in Bormann's party and went missing at the same time.'

'Can I see the records?' Grant asked.

'It's a little unusual but I can probably arrange it.'

Lisa looked at Grant to see if he was interested in taking up the offer, but Grant changed his line of questioning.

'Bormann was believed to be carrying some documents with him when he escaped from the bunker —'

'He had a copy of Hitler's will and political testament,' Spruengli said and anticipated the next question. 'They were not found with the body. But is that surprising? They were made of paper, after all.'

'But no traces of the wrappings or anything?'

'No, nothing.'

From the meeting with Spruengli, they returned to the hotel. Lisa called Fraülein Herder and confirmed the meeting for the following day. Grant called Magruder and gave him a routine report. Afterwards they had a drink and Lisa quizzed Grant.

'Do you really believe that Bormann is alive? I mean, is truth really that corny?'

'No. I accept what Spruengli said.'

'Then what's the point if Bormann's dead?'

'The point is that I believe he was carrying the diaries when he died. Do you remember the documents?'

'Sure, Hitler's will.'

'That's just supposition. No one knows for certain just what he was carrying. It may have been the will or the diaries or both. But he was carrying some documents – and they were never found.'

Twenty-seven

9 December 1980

The address in Düsseldorf was an old apartment building with bars to the ground floor window and a heavy door that opened on call to the occupiers. There was a row of enamelled bell-pushes, each labelled *stossen*, and a frame of tarnished brass slots holding cards with the names of the inhabitants. Grant recognized the brown ink and neat italic script of Fraülein Gisela Herder.

Gisela Herder – the American records said – was born in Stuttgart in 1920. Her father was a municipal official and her mother came from a family of small manufacturers. She had a normal childhood and an undistinguished school career ending in her attending a commercial course and learning to type. In 1938 she became engaged to Hans-Jurgen Bauer, a lieutenant in the Wehrmacht, but they did not marry: he was called to the war and, as a tank commander, was killed in action in July 1943. At the outbreak of war she joined the German Admiralty as a typist-clerk and served there, with the exception of brief absences, until the end of hostilities. Her absences from the Admiralty included two short periods on Hitler's staff: the first in February and March 1943 at the Fuehrer's headquarters at Vinnitsa in the Ukraine and the second in January 1945 in Berlin. In the first case the appointment arose because the move to the Vinnitsa headquarters was organized by Admiral Puttkammer who had applied to his own department for assistance, and on the second occasion Gisela Herder was selected to serve the Fuehrer because of her earlier experience. She was not and had never been a member of the Nazi Party.

'They didn't ask her a single important question,' Grant said. 'What did she do at Hitler's headquarters? Who came to see him? What did she hear? What did she type?'

'Didn't they cross-examine her?' Lisa asked.

'I imagine that some lieutenant straight out of high school asked her: "Now, Fraülein Herder, will you take this pencil, go into the next room and write me a statement? By the way, were you ever a member of the Nazi Party? No? Well that's fine! Collect your *Persilschein* on the way out." '

'You make it sound like a joke.'

'That's how it happened.'

'Then I guess we'll have to do what the Americans back in '45 didn't do.'

Or the British. But what had the British asked? Freddie Thornton had given his opinion: 'Of course, it doesn't matter a toss that we can't see the CSDIC records. If they'd got so much as her name out of her they'd keep it secret. Seems to be a reflex action. As if the British were ever capable of keeping a bloody secret! My guess is that there's fuck-all in there or someone would have told.'

'Fraülein Herder?'

'Yes?'

The figure in the doorway was of a woman aged about sixty, plump and apple-faced with grey hair braided and wound into coils on each side of her head. She wore a simple brown dress decorated with a cheap, glass-studded brooch.

'My name is Jonathan Grant. This is my assistant, Miss Black, who wrote to you.'

'Miss Black' – the elderly face lit up – 'of course! You wrote me such a charming letter. I was looking forward so much to meeting you. Please, do come in!'

The voice was crisp and polite as though Fraülein Herder had learned English by reading Jane Austen's novels. The room had the same old-fashioned feel, a place of over-stuffed chairs and heavy furniture smelling of wax, and on the wall a sepia-tinted photograph of a man with a Kaiser Wilhelm moustache.

'Would you like some tea?' she asked as they settled on a sofa. 'I don't normally drink tea, but I knew you were coming and I bought some – but, then, don't you only drink tea at particular times of the day?'

'Tea will be fine,' Grant said.

'And for me too,' Lisa said and glanced at him. 'How terribly English.'

When she had left the room Grant examined the bric à brac scattered about. He picked up a photograph in a grey, steel frame. A young man with fair hair, dressed in the black uniform of a tank commander. It was signed 'Hans' and bore a date, January 1943. Six months later the young man would be dead.

Fraülein Herder came back with a tray and some tea. She saw Grant holding the photograph but registered no emotion. 'Will you pour, Mr Grant?' she said cheerfully. Whilst Grant poured, she chatted amiably.

'I was so surprised to get your letter – and such a novel idea for a book! I said to my mother straightaway that I must try to help.'

'Is your mother here now?' Lisa asked.

'Asleep, the poor dear. She normally sleeps at this time of day. But what was I saying? Of course, your book! Are you trying to speak to all of the Fuehrer's secretaries? Have you seen Christa Schroeder and the others – I forget their names – I'm sure they could tell you more than I could.'

'We wrote to them,' Grant said blandly.

'They must have been full of stories.' She paused and looked at her cup. 'Is it customary to have cake or sandwiches with one's tea?' she asked.

'It isn't necessary,' Grant said. 'Please, do go on.'

She told them her story. In February 1943 she had been approached by Admiral Puttkammer to join his staff in the move of the Fuehrer's headquarters from Rastenburg in East Prussia to Vinnitsa in the Ukraine. She had no idea of the reasons for the move.

Vinnitsa, she recalled, was an unpleasant place. The headquarters were in a set of log cabins in a small wood and in summer suffered from plagues of mosquitoes against which people had to take a foul-tasting medicine, Atabrine; but, at the time she was there, the problem was simply the discomfort of snow and cold.

Whom did she remember there? Grant asked.

She had really taken little interest in the comings and goings of the generals, she said. She had a recollection of General Zeitzler, one of the commanders on the eastern front, and General Jodl, who was chief of OKW operations staff; and in particular she remembered the hirsute and repulsive Dr Morelle, Hitler's personal physician. Martin Bormann she was sure had not been there.

What had they discussed? She didn't know. There had been a difference of opinion between two of the generals and Hitler had visited them at Zaporozhye to resolve the problem, but Fraülein Herder had no idea what the quarrel was about. There was a lot of talk about the coming offensive against the Russians – Operation Citadel, in which her fiancé was to be killed – but it was too technical for her to follow. She remembered far more clearly the late-night 'tea parties' that Hitler used to have, when he would regale the staff with cream cakes and conversation that went on until everyone was exhausted.

'Does all of this help you?' she asked.

'It's all super stuff.'

As they reached the end of her stay in Vinnitsa, they paused and she volunteered to make some more tea. Grant walked around the room and stared out of the window at a black saloon parked in the street. A mongrel dog padded past and halted to urinate on one of the wheels. A clock chimed. Fraülein Herder returned with the tea and a plate piled high with cream cakes. Grant came back to the table and picked up his notes.

In January 1945, she went on, she had been asked to rejoin the headquarters staff; she had no idea why, but in the chaos towards the end it hadn't seemed strange and there had been plenty to do during the two weeks that she was there. Hitler she hardly saw during this time. When he did put in appearance, she was startled at the change: he was a sick man, old before his time and shivering uncontrollably down his left side.

The story went on, a string of unconnected glimpses of people and events from her small perspective. Grant took notes but was careful not to push the narrative in any direction – avoiding pressure towards the question he most wanted to ask: had she really seen the diaries?

What had she told the British interrogators? The humdrum gossip of secretaries? The speculation about who was going to marry whom among the narrow circle of the Fuehrer's staff? About political and military events she knew almost nothing. Martin Bormann and the other leading Nazis were shadowy figures who hardly made any impact on her life.

Reason told Grant that Freddie Thornton was probably

right: there was nothing on the British files. But in his heart Grant couldn't believe it. There was something there, something that compelled the American State Department to pressure Rama, something that kept Fraülein Herder's record locked in some obscure filing cabinet in a British ministry. Either that or he was going crazy.

'I must say, you're the first people who have ever shown any interest in my story,' she concluded.

'You were interrogated by the British and Americans,' Grant said. 'What did you tell them?'

There was a flicker of hesitation. 'So I was. I'd forgotten. It was such a long time ago. I suppose I told them the same things I'm telling you.' Her eyes turned away and lighted without interest on the photograph.

'Your fiancé?' Lisa asked.

'My fiancé? Oh, the photograph! Yes. He was killed.' There was no emotion in the voice.

Suddenly she said briskly. 'Have you got any more questions? There's no hurry, you understand, but my mother will wake up soon and she is nervous of strangers.'

'You really have been most helpful,' Grant said. His notes brushed Lisa's hand as he picked them up and she looked at him and said: 'There was one thing.' Her voice suggested an afterthought.

'Yes?'

'In your letter, didn't you mention a diary kept by Hitler?'

'Did I really?' She picked up a small turquoise bonnet. 'Is this your hat?'

'I think it's meant to keep the teapot warm.'

'So it is.'

'The diary?'

'Ah yes. I did see it once – not to read, you understand – it would be on the occasion that I was in Berlin.'

'You saw Hitler writing in his diary?' Lisa asked. She caught her breath softly.

'The Fuehrer? No, no, my dear child! It was Major Linge, dear Heinz Linge. *He* kept the Fuehrer's diary.'

The door closed softly behind Grant and Lisa and the red plush curtain that screened the draughts rattled back to its accustomed place. Fraülein Herder moved to the window and, her fingers playing with the curtains, watched her two guests get into their car and drive off. Behind her the bedroom door opened and a voice said in English:

'Give the lady a coconut! I heard the lot. Great job.'

She glanced at the dark figure in the doorway and then, going to the sideboard she began to remove the pins from her hair.

'I mean that, honestly! A great performance. What do you think, Frank?' he said back into the bedroom. 'It can't be often that our friend has an audience, so give praise where it's due. Like I said: great job.'

The woman took the pins from between her teeth, dropped them into her bag and shook out her hair. She reached for her comb. 'I don't really care to know your opinion,' she said softly. 'What I did was done from political necessity.'

'You're not the only one with beliefs,' Harrison said. 'Frank and me – believe it or not – we're both working for the cause.'

She turned round again to face Harrison and snapped the clasp of her bag. The Englishman looked away.

'The rest is up to you. I don't care how you do it. Get rid of them, but it must appear an accident.' She looked past him into the bedroom at the two frightened women.

One was her own age, with grey hair braided and coiled around a small, heart-shaped face like that of a little girl. The other was an old lady, wispy-haired and balding, wrapped in a pink, quilted bedjacket.

Harrison turned his head and smiled at them and then looked back.

'Don't worry,' he said. 'Old ladies don't trouble me. Kicking the old and helpless gives me a bang. It's people like me and Frank that give sadism a bad name. Can I help you on with your coat?'

'Thank you, no,' the woman said and picked up her bag. She walked to the door and drew back the curtain. 'I shall expect your report in due course.'

Harrison's mouth opened in a slit of ironic humour. 'Certainly, miss. One report.' He went back into the bedroom and heard the door slam behind him.

Lethbridge got off the bed where he had been lounging and

slipped a gun into his waistband. He eyed the two women and checked their bindings.

'Make some tea, Frank. I was dying of thirst whilst that lot were talking,' Harrison said. He pulled up a chair with its back opposite to those on which the two ageing women were tied and sat astride it, facing them, his chin resting on the back of the seat and his hooded green eyes regarding them intently. Lethbridge could be heard whistling in the kitchen.

'Well now, what are we going to do with you? A couple of nice old ladies to get mixed up in this sort of business, aren't you?'

The two women were gagged and could say nothing. Fraülein Herder kept her eyes tightly closed as if she could not bear to open them, but her mother stared out with cold, grey eyes.

'How much sugar?' Lethbridge called out.

'Two.' Harrison looked at the two women and absent-mindedly fingered a spot on his cheek. 'Did I ever tell you that I used to sell fire extinguishers? No, I don't suppose I did.' He stood up and stretched his legs. 'Anyway, as part of the job-training, as the saying goes, we had to learn all about fire risks – so as to demonstrate them to the customers.' He looked about the room and his eyes fell on the paraffin heater standing against the wall. 'Take this for example.' He raised his foot and tilted it with his toe until it fell over, 'Too easy to knock over, see what I mean?' He watched the contents of the heater spill across the floor.

Lethbridge came in with the tea and glanced idly about him. 'Can't say I like the smell.'

'Me neither.' Harrison took the cup and sipped at it. 'Christ, Frank, this is burning!' He blew on the tea and then, abruptly, laughed. 'Burning! Did you hear me, Frank? Burning! Joke, eh?' He put the cup down and picked up a lace mat from under a small ornament on the dressing table. 'Pretty.' He bent down and soaked it in the spilled paraffin.

'Old ladies – living alone – can't be too careful about fire,' Harrison said as he applied the soaked rag to the bindings and gags of the two women. 'I saw lots of cases – terrible.' He threw down the rag. 'Hang on a tick whilst I wash my hands.'

Coming out of the bathroom he met Lethbridge.

'Well?'

'They'll go up fine, no trace of them being tied up. In fact, not much trace of anything.'

'Then let's go,' Lethbridge's voice was urgent.

'Whatever you say,' Harrison said cheerfully. He took a box of matches from his pocket and went back to the bedroom.

'Well, this is goodbye, ladies!'

The cold eyes of the old lady met his scornfully. He turned away and dropped a lighted match. A wall of flame went up behind him.

'Sadism,' he said softly. 'If you haven't tried it, don't knock it.'

'What did you say?' Lethbridge asked.

'Nothing. Just thinking. Let's get the hell out of here.'

Twenty-eight

9-11 December 1980

After their interview with Fraülein Herder, Grant and Lisa found a hotel for the night and Grant put through a call to New York to give his report to Magruder. The publisher was philosophical about the failure and confined himself to reminding Grant that, with a week to go, he was fast running out of time. He asked what Grant proposed to do next.

'And what do we do next?' Lisa asked.

'We try the Englishman, Cavendish,' Grant said. He had no expectations that a man who had bought some property thirty-five years before could give him any leads either as to Helsingstrup or the diaries, but the options were narrowing and time was closing in.

He tried the number of the Château Charlus. It rang for a long time and then a sleepy voice answered.

'May I speak to Mr Cavendish?' Grant asked.

There was a pause at the other end and the sound of people talking among themselves. When the speaker came back, the voice was crisper and clearer.

'This is Cavendish speaking,' he said.

The next day Grant and Lisa left Düsseldorf and by evening were in Bordeaux, lodged in a hotel off the Esplanade de Quinconces. There Grant was fixing them each a drink when Lisa gave an exclamation and dropped the newspaper she was reading. Grant picked it up; it was one that he had bought in the hotel that morning.

'What is it?' he asked. He scanned the headline, the usual headline dealing with the Polish crisis and the by now almost equally inevitable paragraph on the Xanten case. Lisa took the paper and pointed out the story she had noticed. It was the report of the death of two elderly ladies in an apartment fire.

'It says it was an accident,' Grant said. He passed over her glass.

'Do you believe that?'
'It frightens you?'
'The business with Caillot when we spoke to the old Frenchman's daughter, what happened to you in New York and now this – sure it frightens me.'
'Do you want to get out?'
Lisa shook her head. 'You don't understand, do you? There isn't any getting out where you're concerned. Tell me – are Kathy and Joey out of all this? They're not, are they? And they don't even know the first thing about what's going on.'
Grant watched her. She avoided tears, but her eyes were bright with moisture. He finished his drink and poured another.
'Don't I even get some show of emotion?' she asked. 'Or are you like a robot that's been programmed to go chasing after what it thinks is "the truth" – and to hell with the humans who get in the way!'
She went over to the window and stared out at the traffic. Grant came behind her and put his arms around her waist. She let herself relax and her face rest against his.
'Maybe tomorrow we'll know the truth,' he said.
'Maybe,' she said and brushed her hair out of her eyes. 'Until then I want you to make love to me. I don't mind if the feeling is counterfeit – but do it as if you cared.'

The following morning they hired a car and drove the fifty kilometres to Langon, a small town in the Sauternes country where they had lunch. From there they took the D8 road south towards the village that gives the wine its name. Lisa was in a more cheerful mood and joked about her fears of the previous day. The gaiety went about as deep as the skin.
North of Villandraut Grant turned off the road.
'This is it?' Lisa asked. Ahead of them on the chalk of the hillside the turrets of a large house were silhouetted against the hard blue of the sky.
'The Château Charlus – and maybe a lead to Helsingstrup.' Grant looked about him at the ill-kept, ragged lines of vines. They looked as though someone had been tending them and then for some reason stopped; there were knots of mould where the grapes had rotted and not been cleared. He wondered why.

They passed the dry moat and the pair of pollarded limes and arrived at last at the gravelled parking place. There were no other vehicles there. At the windows of the house the peeling shutters were open, but behind them, drapes of sacking masked the interior.

'This place is empty,' Lisa said. She kicked her feet in the dust. 'What now – take a look and see if there's anyone about?' She set off along the path between the box hedge and the house. Grant heard her say, 'Hey, there's a swimming-pool here!' She was staring into it when Grant joined her.

'It sure looks as if no one's around,' she said, studying her reflection on the dull shimmer of green algae. Grant cast his eyes around the uncut grass and at the other side of the pool caught sight of a lizard crouching stiff and transfixed under the shadow of a garden chair.

Just then they heard a noise and turned round.

A small door had opened and a man was lounging in the shade. For the place he looked incongruous in his city suit and natty hat with a black-silk band.

'Who are you?' Grant asked.

'My question, monsieur. Who are you?' The man took a pack of cigarettes from his pocket, lit one and stamped the match out on the gravel.

'My name's Grant. How did you get here – I didn't notice any cars?'

'There are garages,' the Frenchman said. He looked Grant up and down. 'We were expecting you, of course; but we didn't know exactly when you would arrive.' The voice was a drawl as if he didn't personally care. 'Will you come in please and join us?' With that he slipped one hand in his pocket like a stick-up guy from an old film. Maybe that's where he got the image from, Grant thought and allowed himself to be led into the house; Lisa followed.

The kitchen looked unused. There was a basket of rotten peaches in one corner and everywhere the sweet smell of decay. In the corridors there were dust-sheets hanging loosely from the furniture. The Frenchman led them to a door on the ground floor and tapped it gently.

'I'll be waiting outside,' he said as he opened it.

The window faced directly into the sun and the air was filled with the blue light of dust particles hanging in the air. Grant noticed a bookcase and an escritoire, both covered in sheets; and then his eyes focused on the desk and the vague outline of a man sitting with his back to the sunlight.

'Good afternoon, Mr Grant, Miss Black, please take a seat.' The figure rose and indicated two chairs in front of the desk. The voice gave every indication of friendliness. Lisa thought she might have believed in it, except for the gun that lay on the desk-top next to the speaker's right hand.

'I wouldn't let the gun trouble you, Miss Black,' the stranger said, catching her concern. He picked the weapon up and flicked open the empty chambers. 'I was merely cleaning it when you arrived.' As his eyes adjusted to the light, Grant observed the other man's small, sharp eyes which belied the pleasant, easy-going expression. 'May I introduce myself – the name is Legros. You were expecting to see Monsieur Cavendish perhaps. I'm afraid that he has been dead for some weeks now.'

'I spoke to him two days ago,' Grant said.

Legros smiled apologetically, 'A little deception on my part.'

'What happened to Cavendish?'

'He was murdered. I represent the French authorities in the investigation.'

Grant nodded. Legros hadn't used the word 'police'; and Grant guessed that if he asked for the other man's credentials, he wasn't going to get any.

'Why do you want to see Monsieur Cavendish?' Legros asked. The Frenchman was relaxed. He poured himself a glass of Perrier water from a bottle on the desk. 'Let me tell you now that I'm familiar with your background. In fact I happened to read one of your books. About Himmler – very interesting.' He took a sip from the glass and waited patiently for an answer. Grant suspected that if he wanted to walk out of the room nobody was going to stop him; which inclined him to stay.

'I'm researching for a book,' Grant said and ignored the sharp glance from Lisa. 'A follow-up to the one on Himmler.'

'Indeed? What sort of follow-up?'

'On German diplomacy during the war. Particularly in Scandinavia.' It seemed as good an explanation as any. Better – Legros was listening intently and his round, amiable face suddenly assumed an expression of seriousness. 'Himmler had agents in Stockholm, negotiating with the Allies. The intrigues make a good story.' Grant let the explanation fall there, suggesting there was more.

'Yes, as you say, it should make a good story,' Legros said at length. 'But why should it lead to an interest in Monsieur Cavendish?'

'I heard that he bought this château from a Swedish nobleman, Baron Helsingstrup.'

'And this Helsingstrup . . . ?'

'Acted as a diplomatic go-between for the Germans in Stockholm. He went to ground after the war; but, first, he sold the château to an Englishman, Cavendish.'

Grant waited for the question that had troubled him ever since Gunnarson had first mentioned the dead man's name – why should Cavendish be expected to know anything about Helsingstrup and his whereabouts? The question didn't come.

Instead Legros said, 'You are misinformed about Monsieur Cavendish's nationality. He was French, not English – one of the Chartronnais.'

The word struck a chord in Grant's memory. 'Helsingstrup's wife was Chartronnais.'

'Cavendish was her brother. A somewhat disreputable character. The father willed the estate to the daughter rather than see the son destroy it. But, then, you must know all of this.'

'Yes,' Grant lied.

'And, equally, you know what Monsieur le Baron was involved in?'

'Yes.'

'Indeed?' Legros' eyes searched Grant's face for the truth. Then, 'You will please excuse me if I make a telephone call?'

'We can go?'

Legros hesitated. 'You may go at any time, but I would advise you to stay. That is not a veiled threat. It is merely possible that, if you stay, you will learn something of interest.' The Frenchman didn't wait for a reply. He went out, closing the door behind him.

'What was that about?' Lisa asked.

'He's gone to call his bosses in Paris.' Grant took some

cigarettes from a box on the desk and lit one for himself. He wondered what the Frenchman knew about Helsingstrup that he didn't? And whether he was ever going to find out.

Legros' call took half an hour. When he came back into the room the same friendliness was there, but the voice was urgent.

'You will come with me to Paris?' he asked.

'Today?'

'Straightaway. I assure you that it will be to your advantage.'

Grant looked past the Frenchman at the open door. Legros' companion in the dark suit stood menacingly in the doorway.

'We'll be delighted,' Grant said.

There were three cars, grey, anonymous Citroëns. The front and rear cars were filled with slab-faced types in overcoats who reminded Grant of the characters he had seen in films of French riot police in action. It gave a grim kind of comfort.

At Langon the convoy picked up another vehicle. Nothing was said, but Grant saw it travelling behind them.

'We're being followed,' he remarked to Legros. 'A black saloon with diplomatic plates and a driver who doesn't care that we know.'

The Frenchman didn't bother to check in his mirror. 'It's a Russian embassy car,' he said casually. 'The Soviets can't display any official interest, so they register their concern this way. I shouldn't let it disturb you – would you like some music on the radio?' He leaned forward and turned it on. 'I'm sure you understand,' he added.

'I understand,' Grant said as if he meant it. He only wondered what it was he understood.

They arrived at Paris in the dawn light, the streets shimmering where they had been washed. The river was wanly grey. Grant recognized the embankment they were driving along.

'This is the Quai d'Orsay,' he said.

'Naturally,' Legros said without further comment. It was unnecessary because they were already outside the building of the French foreign ministry.

'Wake up,' Grant whispered into Lisa's ear.

'We're there?' She uncurled on the seat. 'Where is "there", by the way?'

'The Quai d'Orsay.'

'Uh huh.' She raised her head and peeked out of the window. 'Nice building.'

There was no ceremony. Legros, suddenly crisp and officious, snapped orders to his henchmen, doors were opened and Lisa and Grant were ushered briskly inside and bundled into a lift. It stopped at the third floor. Legros led them out into an empty corridor lit only by a faint night-light and then to a door. He opened it and showed them into a room where three men were waiting.

The pecking order was immediately evident. They were sitting round a long walnut table, two men in sober business-suits with files open in front of them and, in the chief position, a man of about fifty with steel-grey hair and a long nose. He gave his name as Dumergue, and got straight down to business.

'What exactly brings you to France, Mr Grant?' The English was good, the accent barely noticeable.

'A book. I told your colleague about it,' Grant answered. He wondered who exactly Dumergue was. In the French foreign ministry evidently, but how high-ranking? In a service more hidebound than most, the Scottish tweeds and the cravat suggested that he didn't have to care much about what other people thought of him.

'Legros mentioned a successor to your Himmler book. I find that strange. I had heard that you were working on a book about war-profiteers. How is that one coming along? Have you found a publisher for it yet?'

'Not yet.'

'My sympathies. Have you finished the writing?'

'Not quite.' Grant returned the other man's civility and waited for the barb in the questions.

'But it must be nearly completed. You took a large sample to Simon and Shuster, and to McGraw-Hill, I believe. And they both rejected it.'

'You seem to know quite a lot.'

'Please don't think we wish to intrude on your privacy,' Dumergue sounded mildly apologetic, 'but your call to the late Monsieur Cavendish – it made us curious.'

'So you had me checked out.'

Dumergue gave an easy, unembarrassed laugh. 'Well, you have it there. It seems impossible to reveal that one has been prying and then put a good face on it. But, believe me, there is nothing sinister in our enquiries: we were simply puzzled by your interest in a dead man.'

Some coffee and croissants were brought in and Dumergue invited Grant to join in. The Frenchman helped himself while he talked.

'It must have been difficult to work on a new project at the same time as the book on war-profiteers. How on earth did you find the time?'

'I tried hard.'

'Of course. What does surprise me, however, is that you offered this new book to publishers only quite recently. The work must have taken some time in preparation and yet you didn't seek an advance. In fact, though you clearly needed the money, you had two books in preparation and no advance.'

'I only had notes,' Grant said. 'Nothing I could sell.'

'Then you still have some writing to do – and some further research too?'

'Yes.'

Dumergue nodded. 'How long will it be before you publish? Some months? A year?'

'A little time. I can't say exactly how long.'

'But not in the near future?' Dumergue pressed.

He was near to his point. Grant decided on a show of righteous indignation. 'Is this an interrogation?' he demanded. But Dumergue was too shrewd to be thrown.

'Can you tell me why Magruder-Hirsch should be buying prime advertising space in three weeks' time?' he asked.

Lisa looked up sharply. Dumergue caught the movement and focused on her. 'Perhaps you could help, Miss Black?'

'She wouldn't know,' Grant said.

'You didn't know that Magruder-Hirsch were set on publishing in three weeks' time?'

'I don't know what they intend to do,' Grant answered – which was true: he had never asked Bart about the marketing side of the operation. Three weeks! Someone had to be putting on heavy pressure.

The conversation ground to a halt. Each man knew that the

other had something to trade. Grant had the diaries, which he suspected Dumergue had no knowledge of. And the Frenchman had what? Dumergue looked at his colleagues and Grant registered the scarcely perceptible nods; he knew what they meant – it was time to trade or to start pulling fingernails. Grant had no guarantee which.

Legros emerged from the back of the room. 'Come with me please. We have something you would like to see.'

'There's no obligation to go,' Dumergue said in a tired voice. 'But I think we've been fencing long enough, don't you?'

Grant didn't answer. He picked up his coat, and slung it over his shoulder. Lisa followed him out of the door.

Legros didn't take them far, only a few doors along the same corridor. By now the main lights were on and there were people about. Legros took out a key and slipped it into the lock.

'Are you going to lock us in there?' Lisa asked.

Legros gave his usual affable smile. 'Not unless you wish it.'

'Well, if it's all the same with you . . . '

'Naturally,' Legros said and stepped back for them to go in.

It was a bare room with three plain, wooden chairs, a table and a window looking out on some trees. By the window a man turned away from the view and examined the newcomers through dull, blue eyes.

'Allow me to make the introductions,' Legros said. 'Mr Grant, this is Monsieur le Baron Helsingstrup.'

Twenty-nine

The man in the room was tall, ageing, and had a tired look as if at some point he had given up caring. The face was long, with a thin mouth scratched in a hard line under a chiselled nose; the hair was white rather than grey and drawn thinly across a high domed skull. In his youth he had probably been handsome in an ascetic, Nordic way, and the vestiges of his good looks haunted his face and lingered in the pale eyes and the long, delicate fingers.

'Who are these people?' he asked Legros. The eyes passed over Grant and Lisa as if they weren't there.

'Monsieur le Baron,' Legros said, 'may I introduce Monsieur Grant and Mademoiselle Black.'

'My pleasure,' Helsingstrup said with crisp indifference. He gave no sign of recognizing Grant's name.

'Monsieur Grant is an Englishman – a historian. He wishes to speak to you, and we . . . we should be grateful if you would answer his questions.'

'Are you going to stay?' Grant asked Legros.

'I haven't been asked to,' Legros replied. He opened the door. 'If you want me, just pick up the telephone.' He indicated the black telephone lying on the floor with a coil of flex around it. Then he went out.

For a moment the three of them looked at each other. Helsingstrup stood behind the desk, his right hand unconsciously rubbing across his ribs as though he were in pain. His plain, collarless shirt was unbuttoned at the neck and Grant caught a glimpse of the bandage that was wound around his chest.

'You've been injured,' he said neutrally.

Helsingstrup looked up from his musing. 'I was in an accident,' he answered blankly, then looked around him. 'Forgive me, will you take a seat?' He came out from behind the table and pulled out a chair for Lisa to sit on.

'Thank you.'

'And you, Mr Grant?'
'Thanks.'
Helsingstrup remained standing. He returned to the window and stared out of it, his back to his visitors, his right hand fingering the seams of his trousers and then creeping back to massage the pain in his chest.
'Why do you want to speak to me, Mr Grant?' he asked suddenly. He spoke English in a clear, high-pitched voice without accent except for its lack of emotion.
'I'm a historian. I like to speak to the witnesses of the events I write about.'
'Grant . . . I recognize the name now – I regret that I haven't read any of your books. Didn't you write something about Heinrich Himmler? There were articles in the newspapers' – a glimmer of irony in his voice – 'the Jewish press didn't like you.'
'And you don't like the Jews?'
Helsingstrup turned round and smiled sadly. 'The Jews?' he murmured. 'They mean nothing to me. I am a Swede: why should I hate the Jews?'
'I guess the Nazis just loved the Jews,' Lisa murmured. She bit her tongue as she spoke. She knew that they couldn't afford to antagonize.
Helsingstrup's eyes grazed her face but he didn't appear disturbed; rather he seemed to pity her. 'So? I was a National Socialist. But do you think that that was all there was to it – anti-Semitism?'
'It seemed to be,' Lisa said softly.
'In retrospect,' Helsingstrup answered, 'only in retrospect.' He took the remaining chair and leaned across the table. 'What do you want to know, Mr Grant? Whether I am one of your Nazi bogeymen, strutting around in my varnished jackboots, stamping on the faces of the helpless? If so, you have been watching too many films. Do you think that an ideology which offered only that image could ever appeal to people other than psychopaths?'
'I'm not here to express my views,' Grant said. There was something disquieting and passionate in the other man's face. 'I just want to hear yours.'
Helsingstrup shook his head. 'I don't think so.'
'Why not?'

'Because you are trapped by the present, whereas I . . . I did not become a Nazi *now*, Mr Grant, with all the benefit of hindsight, but in 1936. To understand, you would have to make a leap in imagination, ignore your mythical Nazis in favour of real people. I doubt that you can do it.' He looked at the telephone. 'Shall I call Legros?'

'It depends on whether you want to try me.'

'Why should I?'

Grant remembered Nathan Hirsch and his question about the diaries: what do they tell you about the man? Even someone who had suffered still desired to understand his torturer.

'Because, if you can't persuade me, then no one will ever understand. Everything you believed, everything you did, will remain incomprehensible.'

There was silence. Helsingstrup's hand dropped to his pocket and there was a rattle of pills. He pulled out a bottle, uncapped it and took out a tablet. Grant pushed across the carafe of water that stood on the table; he watched the other man taste the pill and wash down its bitterness. Helsingstrup closed his eyes.

'I was a communist once – did you know that?'

'No.'

'I joined the party in 1932.' He opened his eyes. 'Can you understand that?'

Grant saw the image of the lost, idealistic generation at Cambridge in those years, the Philbys, Macleans and Blunts who fell into the Soviet net.

'I think so,' he said.

'Those like me, we considered ourselves visionaries when the rest of the world was sunk in bourgeois torpor. It seemed obvious. The old world had been smashed by the Great War and the capitalist democracies were like graverobbers arguing over the possessions of a plague victim. And then there was the Depression.'

'But you weren't affected by the Depression.'

Helsingstrup laughed ironically. 'Because I was rich? Do you think that made me insensible of the general suffering? I was young and wanted what the young always want: justice, fairness, truth!'

'Instead you became a racing-driver and an international

playboy,' Grant said and as soon as he spoke he recognized that he was trying to reconcile the irreconcilable, to force human actions into a coherent whole.

Helsingstrup snapped his fingers. 'Everyone retreats from horror into fantasy. Why do you think that the cinema was so popular in those years? My fantasy was merely more elaborate because I had money.' He hesitated. 'Perhaps it was lack of moral courage. We felt powerless: and what we couldn't face we tried to avoid. Have you never done the same?' He looked at the Englishman, who remembered the abyss of drink and women that followed his return from Vietnam. Grant pushed the thoughts out of his mind.

'So you joined the communists.'

'Yes. They made it easy for me. They said that the Soviet Union needed people with good connections, who could counter capitalist propaganda. I could carry on as before and still further the Proletarian Revolution. It was an opportunity to assuage my conscience.' He paused as though the thought were new to him.

'What did you do for them?'

'I wrote articles in the press, made introductions, greased the social wheels. It was all to persuade people that they would not get shot when the revolution came.' He bit his lip, 'Of course, it was all lies. The communists were shooting peasants who simply wanted to keep their own farms, and then they began shooting anyone who might conceivably disagree with Stalin.'

'You became disillusioned?'

'After 1936 the signs were there that Stalin was a megalomaniac. People I had known in the Soviet Union – good communists – began to disappear. The Western economies might be struggling in blind self-interest, but it was no better in Russia. I went to Moscow in '35 and saw for myself. In the towns one could scarcely buy food and in the countryside it was an open secret that people were starving.' Helsingstrup's face showed the pain of recollection. He went on, 'Only in Germany was there a mood of optimism and a sense of real revolution. The Nazis seemed to have escaped from materialism and from the blind forces of economic law by the power of human ideals and human will. In Germany there was a sense of something spiritual.'

'If you call the Holocaust "spiritual",' Lisa said disbelievingly.

Helsingstrup was impatient. 'You forget that in 1936 there had been no Second World War, no massacre of the Jews! There was only failure, everywhere except in Germany. The Nazis were offering visible prosperity and a sense of purpose. Oh, there was oppression, certainly, but every system has oppression built into it, if only oppression of the poor. And in the case of the Germans, they were in the throes of a social revolution.' He paused. 'And as for the Jews, all that Hitler was proposing at that time was their deportation from Europe. What did they want? They were asking for a homeland of their own and Hitler seemed to be offering it. I had no strong feelings about the Jews, but the spiritual message of the Nazis was the West and its culture. The recognition of that fact was fundamental to the system, to its unity and purpose. The Jews were outside it and incapable of assimilation.'

'They were scapegoats,' Lisa said.

'No! They simply did not fit. The Nazis demonstrated what could be achieved by a sense of common purpose. Capitalism was too obsessed with self-interest to find one, and the communists were dragged down by the pursuit of material goals. Hitler offered the spiritual lead to socialism and European unity – I firmly believed that. What motivated people was idealism: when Hitler conquered Europe, all the defeated countries provided volunteers for the German Army – even the French! How could that be so? Where were the native German units in the British and American Armies? There weren't any. Explain that to me!'

In the silence that followed Grant asked, 'What did you do for the Nazis?'

Helsingstrup appeared not to hear. 'Those of us who were Nazis represented the best and most noble of our generation. No one has the right to judge us out of hindsight!' He got up from his chair and went over to a picture on one of the walls, a cheap engraving of the Siege of Paris. He examined the inscription and then stared at his reflection in the glass.

'I wrote articles and talked to friends,' he went on. 'Many of them agreed with me. Liberals, communists – they came over to National Socialism. It was all so obvious to anyone who could see.'

'Did you do anything else?'

Helsingstrup looked round. 'Oh yes,' he said and turned back to the picture. 'When war broke out we used our influence to keep up supplies of Swedish iron ore to Germany and to maintain Swedish neutrality against those who wanted our country to join the Allies.'

'That wasn't all,' Grant said. It was a statement, not a question. He wanted to keep the other man talking. 'There was diplomacy. How did that start?'

Helsingstrup began slowly. 'It was in – I think it was 1942 at a reception. I was introduced by an acquaintance, Count Folke Bernadotte, to a German friend. I knew that Bernadotte was in touch with both the Germans and the Allies and I assumed that the man I met was a diplomat.'

'Who was he?'

'Walter Schellenberg,' Helsingstrup said, and Grant knew that he had found the key to unlock the other man's mystery. But could he turn it?

'Schellenberg was acting for Himmler,' Grant said.

Helsingstrup nodded. 'There was no method to German diplomacy. Himmler, Ribbentrop, Hess, Canaris – they all maintained a network of contacts and they were fiercely jealous of each other. Personally I didn't care for Schellenberg. He was an opinionated man and a born intriguer.'

'What did he want?'

'At that first meeting? Oh, to know if I had any friends who were still communists. I told him I did. Then he asked me if I knew the Soviet ambassador to Stockholm, Madame Kollantai. It happened that I had been introduced to her at some diplomatic reception or other. She was an exciting, interesting woman, an old revolutionary – I'm surprised that Stalin allowed her to survive.'

'The Germans gave you a test?' Grant said. He needed to say something, to nudge the other man towards his confession without indicating that he, Grant, did not know what it related to. 'There had to be a test.'

'Yes, there was a test. Naturally the Germans were unwilling to trust me with anything important until they were assured of my loyalty. So I was asked to deliver various packets to destinations in the Stockholm area – all sorts of nonsense with dead letter-boxes, contacts, codewords.'

'They wanted to see whether you would deliver the packets unopened which, naturally, you did.'

'Yes.'

'And then?'

'I was asked to arrange meetings, usually for Schellenberg. Sometimes they were with Swedes, sometimes with Russians. In the ordinary way I would act as interpreter.'

'These were diplomatic meetings?'

'Usually.'

'Who represented the Soviets?'

'Normally they were low-level people, embassy and trade-mission attachés,' Helsingstrup said, and Grant caught the word *normally*.

What did it mean? So far Helsingstrup had done nothing more than confirm Grant's guess that the Swede was a diplomatic go-between, acting in the hazy fantasy-world of a wartime neutral capital, communicating half-baked schemes for peace, of which there had been dozens, the most spectacular being that of Hess. Was there something different in this case? And, if so, what?

'But the meetings weren't always "normal", were they?' Grant said with what he hoped was a convincing show of knowledge.

'No, not always. Schellenberg lost interest in the small fry that the Soviets scattered around Stockholm. He asked me to use my contacts and arrange a meeting with Andrei Vishinsky.'

Vishinsky was the Deputy Commissar for Foreign Affairs, second only to Molotov. Grant knew that he was close, but he could only guess how close.

'What did you do?' he asked.

'I passed the message on to my Russian contact,' Helsingstrup said.

'You thought the whole suggestion nonsense?'

'Yes. So long as the diplomatic conversations were kept to underlings, they could always be denied. Schellenberg's request, on the other hand, meant serious talks. I thought the proposal was fanciful.'

'But the Russians didn't,' Grant said. It was a statement. He didn't allow Helsingstrup the chance to think. 'Refresh my memory about the dates. This was . . . ?'

'July '44,' Helsingstrup said. Then he went on, 'My contact came back and said that Vishinsky would be prepared to meet with Schellenberg – he proposed a rendezvous at Uppsala. I was introduced to an *NKVD* major, who made all the arrangements.'

'Where exactly?'

'I don't know.' Helsingstrup shrugged his shoulders. 'I was blindfolded. All I can tell you is that it was in a country-house about twenty kilometres from the city.'

'What was your part in the negotiations?'

'I was to interpret for Schellenberg. However, Vishinsky insisted that as few people be present as possible; so his own man interpreted for both sides.'

'Do you know what was discussed?' Grant pressed.

'Not at the time. Schellenberg came out of the meeting looking pleased with himself, and Vishinsky disappeared into one of the stables: there was a radio antenna nearby, fixed to a tree and I assumed he was reporting to Molotov. But that was all. Schellenberg wouldn't talk but he was in fine spirits and took me to dinner.'

'What then?'

Helsingstrup looked up from some scraps of paper on which he had been doodling with a blunt pencil.

'I can still remember what we ate. And what we drank – Château Mouton Rothschild 1928. Schellenberg joked about the expense. "The money is forged," he said. If it was, nobody questioned it.'

Grant looked at the drawing of a spider's web growing on the page. The Swede began to shade in the gaps in the mesh.

Helsingstrup continued, 'A week later my contact gave me a message for Schellenberg. I passed it on. The reaction from Berlin was immediate. I had a reply the same day and was told to hold myself available to meet an important Soviet official and conduct him to Germany. The official was Vishinsky.'

'Vishinsky went to Germany?' Grant had difficulty suppressing his astonishment.

'We flew to Wustrow – Himmler's headquarters was there at Ziethen castle.' Helsingstrup smiled, 'Himmler was almost delirious with pleasure. You understand, Ribbentrop and the rest, who ought to have been informed, knew nothing of the business: Himmler was congratulating himself on pulling one over them.' He laughed wanly at the recollection. 'It was an extraordinary sight. Of course, I'd never met Himmler before. He was a baby-faced man with dirty fingernails and vulgar manners, like a booking-office clerk. It seemed impossible that he should be the next most powerful man in the Reich after Hitler.'

'Wasn't Vishinsky recognized at Ziethen?' Grant asked, breaking the train of reminiscence deliberately. He wanted to dominate the other man so that his answers became reflexive, without holding back.

Helsingstrup shook himself. 'Not at all. There were lots of foreigners about and we passed him off as a Ukrainian collaborator – like Vlasov – or some such thing.'

'He was on his own?'

'No, he brought the *NKVD* major with him to act as interpreter and another man, a civilian. The three of them were closeted with Himmler for two days and I was left kicking my heels in the corridor.'

Grant nodded and took out a cigarette. He passed one to Lisa who was listening impassively as if she couldn't believe what she was hearing.

'Do you mind if I open a window?' Helsingstrup asked. He slid the panes against each other and paused, looking out on the trees, as if suddenly moved by the view of the city. His mouth formed some words silently but then closed and after a moment he merely observed, 'Do you think it will rain today?' He glanced at Grant and his face looked old and very tired. He went on whilst Grant thought over his line of questioning, 'I left Europe immediately after the war – for South Africa. I spoke good English and I thought that nobody would look for me there – which was true; nobody did.'

'But you came back.'

'I'm afraid my tastes were too civilized for me to exist for ever outside Europe. So I came back, first to Spain and then, five years ago, to France. I had hoped that . . . ' he broke off. 'May I have a cigarette?' Grant pushed the pack across and Helsingstrup took one. He held it between the middle and ring finger in a way that Grant had only seen women do. 'Where were we?'

'You told me about the meeting between Himmler and Vishinsky. Why did they meet in Germany? If the Russians were worried about security, surely it would have been more sensible to meet in Stockholm? Himmler could have gone there.'

Grant recognized that he had made a mistake as soon as he spoke. Helsingstrup eyed him curiously as if he didn't understand the question.

'There would have been no point,' he said. 'It was Hitler that he wanted to see.'

He took a long pull at the cigarette and then stubbed it out, all the while watching Grant intently. 'We went to Rastenburg, the three Russians, myself and Schellenberg. Himmler had made separate arrangements – I think he went ahead to prepare Hitler.'

For what? Grant reflected. To talk about peace negotiations? What was there about these negotiations above all others that made them so special, so sensitive, that people would kill to suppress knowledge of them?

'So Vishinsky saw Hitler,' Grant said.

There must have been a question in his voice because Helsingstrup suddenly smiled and became pensive.

Grant thought, He's realized I don't know!

Thirty

'What do you think of the problems in Poland?' Helsingstrup said, abruptly changing the subject, pursuing some interior train of thought. 'Will the Russians invade or not?'

'I can't say,' Grant answered. He tried to follow the oblique logic, wondering why the troubles of Poland should concern the other man. He dimly followed the reasoning. 'Your meeting with Hitler – that was in August '44?'

'The eighth,' Helsingstrup assented.

'The Warsaw Rising had started.'

Helsingstrup nodded.

The Warsaw Rising – two hundred thousand Polish casualties in a desperate bid to eject the Germans from the city, in anticipation of the imminent arrival of the Soviet Army. A futile and heroic gesture like so much in Poland's poignant history, and one that was put down by the Germans in a savage and furious bloodbath. The implicit question behind the old man's enquiry was: were the Poles, under the banner of Solidarity, preparing themselves for just such another disaster?

Helsingstrup collected himself. 'The meeting with Hitler was to discuss peace proposals,' he said. The words had a cathartic effect on him. His face seemed suddenly composed.

Grant said nothing. He waited for the other man's sense of release to flow through him. He knew well enough the opiate effect of confession, the highs, the lows, the need for another fix that only the listener with his gift of absolution can give. Once, in Saigon, in the débâcle of 1975, when the Americans, having failed to win the war by force of arms, were trying to do the same trick with mirrors, Grant had gone out drinking with a lantern-jawed New Yorker, who claimed to be in public relations, which meant he was CIA. They had wound up in the same whorehouse, screwing by turns the same empty-faced Eurasian girl. Between bouts, they had made their confessions over a table of empty bottles, telling their true-life horror stories in bad French so that even the girl should understand what they had done to her people. The message was still the same: *Tell me that it's not my fault!*

Helsingstrup was making the same request and Grant knew that he alone had the power of absolution. Until, by a smile, a word, a touch, he showed that he forgave, the old man would talk. 'You understand,' he was saying. 'You have the ability to see with the eyes of time.'

'How did you get there?' he asked – an easy question first.

'To Rastenburg?'

Grant nodded.

Helsingstrup sounded disappointed, as though more should have been asked. 'We had a car – a six-wheeled Mercedes. Schellenberg drove.'

'You must have been conspicuous – three Russian passengers.'

'We wore SS uniforms.'

'Unit?'

'The Viking Division – I remember that we had armbands with the name on.'

The SS Viking Division! That would be Schellenberg's idea. There was an irony in the selection: the choice of a non-German unit but one with an Aryan name. The three Russians had jokingly been made honorary members of the master race; the humour had the typically mocking, game-playing quality of the secret police. And in character too that Schellenberg should never tell anyone. Perhaps a hint here and there, an allusion trailed obliquely in conversation, but the essential story kept to himself, his last secret, to be taken with him to the cemetery in Turin.

Helsingstrup now seemed eager to talk. 'Do you want to know about Rastenburg?'

'Tell me,' Grant said. His eyes caught Lisa's. She was sitting mutely, avoiding any move to break the rapport between the two. Grant turned away and looked at the floor. He could see Helsingstrup's feet; the French had removed the laces from his shoes and pink circles of flesh were visible through the eyeholes.

'Do you know that part of Poland, Mr Grant?'

'No.'

'The Masurian Lakes. Where the plain drains down into the Baltic. Forest, mosquitoes, frogs, but most of all the forest. Trees – everywhere. They were the *Urwald* – dark, mysterious, as if the German race-memory were living in them.' Helsingstrup closed his eyes as though the feelings were beyond his powers of expression. Then, sensing the anachronism of his sentiments, he added apologetically, 'Can you understand that? It is important. You must realize that we – I mean all of us – were living in a world of images, not ideas. Do you see? When I went to Rastenburg and saw the lakes and the trees, I was convinced that Hitler was right – convinced by *them*, not by Hitler.' He raised his eyebrows expecting an answer and then looked down at his feet. He grinned sadly. 'You've noticed that my shoelaces have been removed. My belt and tie too.'

'They want to make sure you don't kill yourself.'

'Yes. Don't you find that astonishing? I came here to prevent others from killing me, and they conclude that I may want to kill myself. The workings of the bureaucratic mind!'

'But you don't want to kill yourself.' Grant intended the remark as a statement but it came out as a question. Helsingstrup reacted sharply.

'Why should I want to kill myself? Because I am responsible? Guilty?' The voice was sorrowful rather than angry. Grant recognized the other man on the brink of disillusion, talking not to Grant but to the image of someone he had waited more than thirty years to confess to. Give him an image! Grant thought to himself.

'Perhaps to take the responsibility of others,' he said, feeding the other man the most gross of images – of Jesus meek and mild who died for our sins. It wasn't entirely inappropriate: Helsingstrup had spent his life asking the same question, whether of Marx, Hitler or Jesus – or Grant. 'What must I do to be saved?'

'Perhaps, perhaps,' Helsingstrup said quietly. He stared into his hands. 'What were we talking about?'

'Rastenburg,' he said and gave the other man a moment to pull himself together. 'Did you see the Fuehrer's headquarters?'

'Yes, yes,' Helsingstrup murmured as if the factual details bored him. He looked for comparisons around the walls of the room. 'It was a great concrete building. There were no windows or chimneys, just some iron doors that let a little fresh air in. It was a stifling, claustrophobic place; but Hitler was always afraid that the Allies would bomb it or launch a paratroop attack so the building had to be proof against both. The whole area was like a concentration camp. SS everywhere.'

'The *Fuehrerbegleitungkommando*.'

'That was their name – men who were ashamed of not being on active service and others who were afraid of being sent to the Russian front.'

'That sounds like a quote. Who said it? Schellenberg?'

'Yes,' Helsingstrup admitted. 'I think he despised them on both counts.

Grant thought: Yes, of course, Schellenberg again, mocking everyone who wasn't part of his great game – mocking even Grant, who had spent three years unravelling the barren soul of Heinrich Himmler, only to be ignorant of this attempt at a diplomatic coup: peace with Russia. In whatever circle of Hell he was in, Walter Schellenberg must be laughing himself crazy.

'And so you met Hitler,' Grant said, pulling himself back to the subject. 'How exactly?'

'We were shown into a room – a briefing-room I suppose. Hitler was there already with Himmler; they were poring over a map of Poland.'

The pose was studied for the benefit of the three Russians, to impress them that Hitler was still the powerhouse of German strategy, even though he had been injured by the bomb placed at his headquarters on 20 July. Vishinsky knew of the Stauffenberg plot and it was important that Stalin should understand that the Fuehrer was well and that Germany was not about to collapse because of his death.

Hitler looked up, turning his pale, grey-blue eyes on the Russians. He held his hands in front of him, the right one over the left wrist to minimize the tremor that was increasingly affecting that side of his body. His face held the expression of commanding serenity shown in his portraits and which he used as a foil to his browbeating tantrums.

Himmler was flushed with excitement and Vishinsky was shrewd enough to guess why. Where were all the others? Ribbentrop, who as foreign minister should have headed the negotiations? Keitel, the OKW chief, who would have to conduct the necessary military staffwork? Albert Speer, the armaments head, who knew what raw materials the Reich needed to continue the war? Himmler had managed to exclude them all. This was going to be his triumph that would set the seal on his claim to the succession.

Hitler continued to ignore the Russians. He went over to a large wall-map and stared at it for a minute or so, his back turned to his visitors. The three men, wily to the same theatrical traits in Stalin, waited patiently for Hitler to decide that he had achieved the necessary effect. The room was silent except for the rumble of the air-conditioning and the click of a moth's wings against a lampshade.

Suddenly Hitler spoke, 'What are you going to do with Rumania?' he asked sharply, and, as if it were his to command, added, 'I need thirty thousand tons of oil.'

Vishinsky waited placidly whilst the *NKVD* major translated to the third man who made a note of the figure in a small, brown pad.

'We require the oil for Soviet industry,' the Russian said.

Hitler snapped his fingers, 'You have Baku and the Caspian oilwells. Without Rumania the Reich's only significant source is Nagykanisza. We must have the oil.'

Vishinsky didn't reply.

Himmler reached for a piece of paper and pushed it across the table to the Russian. He was evidently nervous. 'This is a schedule of our iron ore requirements,' he said. 'It covers a twelve-month period.'

'You have the iron ore at Krivoi Rog,' Hitler said. He reached into his memory for the figures he carried there. His unsettling ability to carry statistics in his head and roll them out at strategic moments was a trick which the Fuehrer's intimates knew and respected. 'Production there is one million tons per month.'

Vishinsky glanced at the third Russian who nodded to confirm what Hitler had said and noted the request. Hitler appeared to ignore any reaction on their part and went on, 'The Reich has been receiving supplies of Finnish nickel from Petsamo: these must continue. We have also imported Turkish chrome: for this an alternative source must be found.' He continued with his list of German requirements for food and raw materials, quoting exact quantities and referring to Himmler's delivery schedules. The three Russians listened quietly and took notes.

'Why were they talking about iron and oil?' Lisa asked.

Grant answered the question without referring to Helsingstrup. 'They were talking about tanks and aircraft.'

'Why? I don't understand. They were making peace.'

Grant shook his head. 'No. They were talking about peace with the Soviet Union – that wasn't the same as peace.'

'The British and the Americans would have carried on with the war,' Helsingstrup explained, 'and for that Germany still needed tanks and planes and the fuel to operate them. Peace with Germany meant nothing to Stalin unless the Reich stayed as a buffer between himself and the West.'

'But . . . ' Lisa didn't finish. She saw now what Grant had recognized, the massive betrayal of his allies contemplated by Stalin. Beyond that, Grant knew that there had been other peace feelers to the West and had no doubt that there were some there who would have betrayed the Russians if they had had the chance.

In the quiet recitation of events, Grant discerned the almost incredible banality of the meeting. Seven men in a stuffy room, discussing and settling the fate of Europe on pieces of paper shoved into their pockets.

In the bunker the three Russians sweated under the lightbulbs, only a whim away from a bullet in the neck in the cellars of the Lubyanka. As Vishinsky conceded that economic problems need be no insuperable obstacle to peace, he felt an urgent need to go to the toilet and, making his excuses, he quit the room leaving the *NKVD* major and the unnamed third man to face Hitler and his staff. The major made hesitant small-talk with the Fuehrer about Wagner's music and Hitler explained his plans for rebuilding Bayreuth, whilst Schellenberg smiled cynically at the young Swedish nobleman, Baron Helsingstrup, and played with his fingers against his lips, smoking a non-existent cigarette. The conversation petered out and the two remaining Russians asked to confer outside the room.

They watched the door close and then Hitler turned to the others. His face was a mask of triumph. 'We've done it!' he exclaimed. 'Those three have been told by Stalin to make peace. The last thing he wants is a successful general for a rival – he saw what Stauffenberg and all that *Schweinerei* did to me.' There was a pause and Hitler's face grew grey with the recollection of how close to death the conspirators' bomb had brought him. He collected himself and went on in the same exultant voice, 'Believe me, if Marshal Zhukov ever took Berlin, it would be 1938 all over again and Stalin would put him up against a wall within a week.'

There were general nods of agreement. Hitler's political sense was rarely wrong and everyone present knew of the pressures that were already driving the Allies apart.

The Russians came back into the room and Vishinsky asked for a map. Himmler, in his role of indispensable dogsbody to the Fuehrer, had one to hand and unfolded it on the map table. Whilst Schellenberg lounged at the back of the room with feigned disinterest, the young Swede at his side, the two Nazi chiefs and the Russians stared for a moment at the sight of the continent of Europe laid out before them, and then Hitler casually asked for a pen.

Vishinsky took one out of his pocket and handed it across. 'A German pen,' he said and gave a wry smile, 'we took it from a prisoner.'

Hitler, who was not without a sense of humour, replied, 'The Soviet economy has difficulty in producing pens?' The *NKVD* major translated both remarks.

Helsingstrup later surmised that the territorial proposals had been thrashed out beforehand at the meetings in Sweden and with Himmler at Ziethen castle, because this part of the proceedings was settled with surprising quickness and a few bold strokes of the pen on the unfolded map.

The division was a recognition of military reality, assigning to Stalin's portion the major part of Eastern Europe, leaving to Hitler's share part of Czechoslovakia and Hungary. As the pen was poised to divide Poland along the line of the Vistula, obliterating that country yet again from the map, Vishinsky observed, 'Poland is not a state: it is a form of mental illness, a hallucination. Surgery is the best cure.'

Helsingstrup stopped and asked for another cigarette. His face was pale and his hand shook. Grant watched him and wondered. There was something else – there had to be. The negotiations he had described showed the cynicism of the Russians but no more than that. They had been fruitless. There had been no peace. The conversations between Vishinsky and Hitler had merely gone a little further along the road marked by all the other abortive attempts at peace from Hess onwards. What was it about this particular meeting at Rastenburg that made it so important *now* that people should die to suppress knowledge of it?

'What happened?' Grant asked. 'It all came to nothing.'

'Vishinsky had seemed so positive,' Helsingstrup said. 'At the time it was a mystery to the Germans that Stalin failed to confirm the agreement.'

'But later it became clear?'

'After the Yalta Conference,' Helsingstrup said. Grant understood but the other man went on. 'Stalin didn't trust the West. He was frightened that they might do a deal with the Nazis and turn them against the Soviet Union. After all, the Russians were in control of Eastern Europe and it was exactly to prevent the Germans from being in that position that Britain and France had gone to war. So why should the West allow Stalin to do what they had stopped Hitler from doing?'

'But they did,' Grant said.

'Yes. And that was what killed the negotiations. As the date of the Yalta Conference came nearer, Stalin realized that Roosevelt was prepared to concede him as much as the Germans could and without the same risk. Suddenly the Germans had lost their bargaining strength and Stalin refused to confirm Vishinsky's deal with Hitler.'

Grant remembered the garbled diary entry for 24 March 1945, when the realization that he had been cheated finally broke with full force upon Hitler and he gave vent to his resentment in incoherent ramblings. There was to be no repeat of the Miracle of the House of Brandenburg: Frederick the Great had been saved by the Russians; Hitler would not be.

Still there had to be more.

'What was supposed to happen whilst Stalin made up his mind?' Grant asked. He had a vision of the Russian armies poised to strike in Poland whilst in Warsaw the brave fathers of today's Poles rose against the Germans and died for it.

Helsingstrup shuddered with cold – except that the room

wasn't cold. 'The Russian advance in Poland was to stop,' he said. His fingers unconsciously foraged among the cigarette stubs in the ashtray. 'The Germans asked for some evidence of Soviet good faith and that was what was agreed.'

The Russian advance in Poland was to stop. The words sounded innocuous but Grant knew that they meant that the Germans were given liberty to slaughter or maim two hundred thousand Poles in Warsaw whilst the Russian Army waited within easy reach and did nothing.

'Who agreed to that – Vishinsky?' he asked.

'No.'

'Who else then? The *NKVD* major? Hardly. The third man then? Who was he?'

Helsingstrup looked as though the pressure on him was about to become intolerable.

'Can't you see that you're torturing him?' Lisa said quietly.

Grant turned to her. 'What do you expect? Mercy?' The thought suddenly came to him: She feels sorry for him!

Lisa's eyes showed pain and she asked with the same understated emotion, 'Is this what you'd do to me if I stood between you and whatever name you give to your obsession – truth?'

Grant had only to think of the danger in which he had placed Kathy and Joey to know the answer. Lisa knew it too; she didn't look for a reply but just turned away and stared into the palms of her hands.

Helsingstrup remained pale and unmoved, locked in his own thoughts. Grant knew that he couldn't let him go – not now!

'The third man. What is his name?'

Helsingstrup looked up. He was tired and beaten.

'Alexei Kosygin,' he said.

After his confession the old man remained where he was, his face still buried in his hands. Lisa moved next to him and sat with her arm around his shoulder and a hand resting on one of his wrists.

She sees only him and not the thousands of Poles who were killed, Grant thought. But perhaps it was as well: there had to be someone who responded to the immediacy of suffering. No one could live with the collective suffering of mankind. Grant left her to it and went over to the window where he could look out and see Paris carrying on like any other day. But what he saw was Warsaw, not Paris.

As the Germans retreated through Poland in that late summer and autumn of 1944, the pro-Western Polish Home Army attempted to fill the vacuum. On 28 July the Russians reached the Vistula river, on which the city of Warsaw stands, and during the first ten days of August established three bridgeheads south of the city on the German side of the river. On 1 August, the Poles in the city rose against the Germans in the expectation of imminent attacks by the Russians against the German positions. It was an expectation that was to be cruelly disappointed. Whilst the Wehrmacht slaughtered and blasted their way through the city, no Russian attacks of any significance developed though on other sectors of the Eastern front, notably Rumania, the Red Army was sweeping aside German defences. More sinister in its import, the provision of Western support for the rising, in the form of airdrops of supplies, was prevented for a month by the refusal of the Russians to allow American aircraft to use Soviet airfields. Only in January 1945, by which time Stalin was secure in his knowledge of the gains to be made in Eastern Europe, did the Russians advance those last few miles to capture Warsaw. By then it was too late for the Poles.

Alexei Kosygin! Until his retirement one of the two most important men in the Soviet Union, the partner of the Soviet leader, Leonid Brezhnev, ever since the downfall of Khruschev. It was no wonder that, with the mess in Poland, the Russians were scared that the ghost of their past crime against the Poles should be firmly laid at the door of the present leadership. The effect of such a revelation in Poland would be incalculable.

Grant had to ask himself if he really believed it. Was Kosygin in truth there? Grant recalled Helsingstrup's description of the negotiations, of Hitler's economic demands scrupulously noted down by the third member of the Soviet team. He recalled too that Kosygin had a history of involvement in industrial and economic planning and, after the war, was to become the Soviet Union's planning chief. The fit was compelling.

A chair creaked behind him. Grant turned and saw Lisa

sitting on her own, her face cast down and her hands in front of her. Helsingstrup had moved away; it was his chair that Grant had heard. The confession was over. The old man realized that there was no forgiveness there or anywhere else. He would try to pick up the pieces and get back into hiding.

Helsingstrup picked up a pencil from the table and began to draw again. 'Do you have any more questions?' he asked. For an intended exit-line it was clumsy, but he was in no state for finesse. Grant took the opportunity.

'The peace negotiations failed. Where did that leave you?'

'A dead man. The Russians would have killed me if they had got hold of me. Because I *knew*!'

'But Schellenberg must have made arrangements to get you away.'

Helsingstrup shook his head. 'I was expendable. Schellenberg didn't care whether the Russians killed me or not.' He glanced at Grant's face and Grant recognized the look of someone who wanted to know whether he had been believed.

He's back in his prison, locking the doors behind him; Grant said aloud, 'How did you get by?'

Helsingstrup smiled ironically, 'I discovered how useful it was to be a rich man. I transferred all my property to my brother-in-law.'

'Norman Cavendish. And your wife?'

'She was dead – car crash.'

'How did you get to South Africa? You couldn't use your own passport.'

'I had contacts – diplomats. They arranged a Vatican passport. The Holy See was giving them to displaced persons.'

'And your money?'

'I told you.'

'You said "transferred" your property to your brother-in-law. Why didn't you say "sell"? Didn't he pay you?'

There was a bitter laugh. 'Him? He was a parasite who couldn't pay for the clothes he stood up in – he stole . . . ' the words trailed away.

'He stole your money?'

Helsingstrup evaded the question. 'I had funds held in a Liechtenstein *Anstalt* – I thought they would be unidentifiable.'

And so they would be, Grant thought – except to the KGB who could get behind the secrecy protecting a Liechtenstein front company without working up a sweat. Helsingstrup's naïvety was incredible.

'How did you get the income?'

'I drew it monthly.'

'Where was the account?'

This time Helsingstrup didn't risk looking at Grant.

'Liechtenstein,' he said. 'A bank in Vaduz.'

'Name?'

'I forget.'

'Are you sure the bank wasn't in Zurich? Perhaps the main branch of the *Schweizerische Allgemeine Kreditanstalt*?' Grant had suddenly remembered the name of Knights' bank.

'No!' Helsingstrup said. Grant heard the lie.

The old man reached for the water and gulped down a glass full. He wiped his mouth on the cuff of his shirt leaving a dark stain. 'I've had enough questions,' he said.

'Just one more.'

Helsingstrup hesitated. As Grant guessed, the Swede had to know what the worst was if only to deny it.

Do I ask him about the diaries? Grant wondered. There was no reason for the other man to have heard about them, all the reason to suppose he hadn't. It was enough that he was a witness to what Grant now knew was in the missing portion. But then, in a sense, Grant owed a favour to the French, who were no doubt assiduously listening. It was obvious that they had not known about the diaries and that they had allowed him to interview Helsingstrup in order to discover what he knew.

'Have you ever heard of a set of diaries kept by Hitler?' Grant asked.

Helsingstrup's eyes opened wide. It was surprise and relief. He smiled as if there was something that Grant had missed. He shook his head.

'No,' he said. 'I've never heard of any Hitler diaries.'

Thirty-one

Legros was at the door too soon, opening it to let them out. Grant looked at him and wondered whether in the Frenchman's eyes knowledge of the diaries' existence was a sufficient trade-off for Helsingstrup's secret.

Dumergue and his two colleagues were where Grant had left them.

'Why is Helsingstrup here?' Grant asked.

The Frenchman glanced at his companions for cues and then said, 'I see no reason why you shouldn't be told. After Cavendish's murder there was an attempt on the Baron's life. Realizing that there was no other safety for a man with his knowledge, he came to us for help.'

'Who tried to kill him?'

'Two Englishmen.'

'I thought the KGB grew their own assassins?'

Dumergue changed the subject. 'You mentioned some diaries, where are they?'

'On offer to Magruder-Hirsch,' Grant said.

'And they intend to publish them?' Dumergue sounded as though he sincerely didn't believe it. He muttered to his colleagues, '*Ils sont incroyables les Americains. Est-ce-qu'ils désirent la guerre*?' One of them gave a what-can-you-expect shrug. Dumergue turned back to Grant. 'You must realize that that is quite impossible.'

'The State Department seem to agree,' Grant said, thinking of the pressures on Rama, which were suddenly quite comprehensible.

'With the present difficulties in Poland, you can't simply announce that one of the top men in the Soviet leadership once authorized the destruction of Warsaw.'

Grant listened and knew that Dumergue was only speaking the truth. Nobody, not least the US Government, wanted to destabilize Poland: it was one more step towards

Armageddon. In anybody else's scale of values the truth came below disaster. The French interest was obvious enough: Helsingstrup had forced his problems on them by turning up on their doorstep and now all they wanted was to suppress the facts in order to prevent embarrassment to their amicable relations with the Soviet Union.

'What are you going to do with Helsingstrup?' he asked.

'Release him. He's not under arrest.'

'The Russians will kill him.'

'We shall give him police protection.'

'You're not that naïve. The Russians will still get to him.'

Dumergue didn't bother with a denial. 'The Quai d'Orsay is not a hotel,' he said and left it at that.

Grant looked at Lisa and then at the Frenchmen sitting impassively about the room and knew that like Helsingstrup he too had been written off as expendable. Himself, Barton Magruder, Nathan Hirsch, Lisa and anyone else who knew. No government would lift a finger to help them.

Legros came into the room carrying a sheet of paper that Grant recognized as the one the old man had drawn on. Dumergue unfolded it and let Grant look. It was the drawing that Helsingstrup had done of a web. The Swede had etched and shaded the interstices and underneath had written something, a line from an old nursery rhyme:

'If you want to live and thrive
Let a spider run alive.'

It was still only mid-morning when they left the Quai d'Orsay and the city was still flexing its muscles for the day, looking as if it wondered what to do with the sun. There had been a shower and the pavements were steaming. The *bouquinistes* were debating whether to stay open and the passersby carried poplin raincoats folded over their arms.

On the drive to the hotel Legros was quiet. Grant guessed that the Frenchman had troubles of his own, but at the entrance to the lobby Legros shook his hand with a finality that promised to be fatal and drove off without looking back.

'They think we're in a hole and we're never going to get out,' Lisa said. Her tone was resigned. She slipped her arm through Grant's and hung close to him as they pushed through the doors.

'Never say die, old girl.'

Lisa laughed. 'Do the British really talk like that?'

'Not often. But it's good to remember one's roots when up against the rougher sort of native.'

Lisa smiled and kissed him on the cheek.

The hotel was old-fashioned. The proprietor was a small, crab-faced man who looked as though he thought Dreyfus was guilty. He was suspicious that his two guests carried no luggage – it was floating adrift in the car pool at the Quai d'Orsay except for an airline bag – but settled his doubts for rent in advance. Grant and Lisa went to their room and lay on the bed in silence.

When Lisa woke up, the room was in half-darkness. The heavy curtains had been drawn and Grant was sitting at a marble-topped washstand reading by the faint light of a lamp with a scorched parchment shade. She smoothed down her dress and ran her fingers through her hair, then drew back the curtains on a view of white tiles and chimney pots at the rear of the building.

'Where did you get the book?' she asked.

Grant closed the pages and put it down. 'I went out whilst you were asleep.'

'What's it about?' She took it and read the name on the spine: Ladislas Farrago. She flicked over the pages and stopped at the slab of illustrations. 'It's about Nazi war-criminals,' she said. 'I thought you accepted that Bormann was dead?'

'I do.'

'Then what?'

Grant closed the book and laid it aside. 'Do you remember the rhyme that Helsingstrup wrote?'

'Sure. Something about a spider. If you leave it alone then you have good luck – it's an old superstition.'

'Particularly in this case,' Grant said. He opened the book again and pointed at the page. 'What is the German for "spider"?'

'*Die Spinne*,' Lisa said. She looked at the words and saw the same word spring from the page. 'I don't understand?'

'It's here in the book and in a hundred others, *Die Spinne*. It's the name of a Nazi lifeline organization created after the war to help fugitives. It's similar to the Odessa, if you like, but unlike the Odessa it doesn't confine itself to former members of the SS.'

'It helped Helsingstrup?'

'I think he was forced to go to it when his brother-in-law cleaned out his money. They paid him a monthly allowance channelled through the same bank that Knights uses.' Grant paused whilst his ideas followed the new pattern. 'And then *Die Spinne* tried to kill him,' he said.

'Not the Russians?'

'They wouldn't have used a pair of Englishmen.'

'But why?'

Grant didn't know, but logic was pushing him in the same direction as his instinct. 'Let's say that *Die Spinne* have the diaries. For some reason that we don't know about yet, they have to sell. Who would they sell them to? A firm of American publishers? Ask yourself: who would pay most?'

'The Russians,' Lisa said. She thought it through. 'But they would want more than the diaries. They'd want the whole package: the text and anyone who could swear to the diaries being genuine.'

'In which case *Die Spinne* would have to deliver the heads of Helsingstrup and Fraülein Herder as part of the bargain,' Grant said. He smiled, 'We've been had! Don't you see? Magruder-Hirsch is in the deal just to force the price up!'

At that moment the telephone rang and Grant picked up the receiver.

'Someone knows we're here?' Lisa asked.

'I placed a call to Bart whilst you were asleep,' Grant said.

Barton Magruder was in session with his partner when Grant's call came through. He cleared the operator off the line and launched in.

'Jonathan! Where the hell have you been these last two days? Do you have anything for me, because, believe me, the ship is coming apart here. I've had to fix a date for publication. Emmett says that the Defense Department sent some guys down to Rama with bolts through their necks, threatening to crater the Lockheed contract unless Rama shows that it has American interests at heart – for which read "unless we pull out of the deal with Knights". Walter says he can only take that sort of pressure so long as he knows we – you and me – have something for him. So he's fixed a deadline. Do you hear me?'

'I hear.'

'Damn right you do! But that's not the only thing. The town is flying with rumours. I've stopped the leak through Jack Robarts by promoting him – just until we can close the deal and I fire the sonofabitch – but bits of the story are still getting around. People are smiling at me and offering to buy me drinks, know what I mean? Maybe Knights has heard something. He called me earlier and he's burning to close.'

Grant let Magruder fire his shot and then said simply, 'I have something for you.'

'You do?'

'But not on this line.' Grant gave Magruder a number. 'It's a bar. I know the owner. Give me twenty minutes to get there and then call, but don't use the line from your office. Got it?'

'I got it but I don't believe it,' Magruder said, but the phone had gone dead.

Nathan Hirsch enquired, 'Has anything gone wrong?'

Magruder threw up his hands, 'He only thinks that the line is bugged!'

'What are we supposed to do?'

'Call him back on another line. Is there a payphone in this building?'

'In the lobby.'

'Okay, let's go.'

Magruder grabbed his coat but was stopped by the fat man still sitting on his desk.

'C'mon, what are you waiting for?'

'What are you going to use for money?'

'Christ!' Magruder started turning out his pockets. 'See what you got, Nat. I have about fifty cents. How much do you think we'll need?'

'I don't know – twenty or thirty dollars?'

'Do we have a petty cash drawer? No, wait a second! Doesn't the company have telephone credit cards?'

'I don't have one. Do you?'

'No.' Magruder pressed the intercom for his secretary. 'Annette, do we have any telephone credit cards?'

'Yes.'

Magruder breathed a sigh of relief. 'Let me have one.'

'Sorry, boss, but senior executives only.'

'For chrissake, I am a senior executive!' Magruder stormed.

'I know,' Annette said evenly, 'but I'm not. You'll have to ask Jack Robarts or Leo Carson to lend you theirs.'

'Fine. Put me through to Jack.'

'Sorry, boss, he's out at lunch; so's Leo.'

'Oh God!' Magruder said and sat down. He thought for a moment. 'Annette, get me somebody from the place upstairs, the firm of attornies – Shadrach, Meshach and Abednego.'

'Sarrow, Mond and Abend?'

'That's it! Ask if I can use their telephone.' He turned to the fat man. 'Would you believe any of this? What is a man supposed to do when his telephone is tapped? You'd think that the FBI or somebody would put out some guidance, wouldn't you?'

'I believe it's the FBI who do most of the telephone tapping,' Nathan Hirsch said.

Annette came back. 'Boss, I've got somebody from Sarrow, Mond and Abend. The partners are all at lunch, so all I could get was an assistant. His name is Bob Lister and he's only twenty-two so go easy on him.' Another voice with a polite New England accent broke through.

'Mr Magruder, sir? This is Bob Lister. Can I help you?'

'I hope so,' Magruder growled and then caught himself. 'Can I use your telephone?'

'Isn't yours working? Do you want me to call the telephone company?'

'No, I just want to use the telephone,' Magruder said with steely civility.

There was hesitation. 'Well . . . I'd surely like to help. I guess you'd better come on up.'

Ten minutes later Barton Magruder was speaking to Grant.

'What do you have for me, Jonathan?' Magruder asked. 'Let me tell you that I hope it's good. Knights says he'll call me daily from now on to check if we're going to close and I'd like to tell him we have a deal.'

'We have a deal,' Grant said.

There was a pause at the other end, then, 'Jesus Christ!' in the undertones of a man who didn't believe it. Then, 'I can't tell you how happy this makes me, Jonathan, but what makes you so sure the diaries are genuine?'

Grant told him the story of how he had found Helsingstrup and then gave the Swede's account. He mentioned the destruction of Warsaw and Kosygin's involvement, but he left out the political implications – whether Magruder drew the same conclusions was up to him. He also left out his private theories about the identity of Knights' clients and the possible competition. That line of thought led into dark places and Grant knew in his own mind that he was going to have to follow.

The publisher listened in silence and then said, 'Look, Jonathan, it'll take me two days to clear this business with Emmett and Vitalis and to arrange the money transfer from the bank. Knights says he wants to make the handover in Zurich, which is fine by me and I'll tell him that. Since you're over there you may as well take delivery. When I've spoken to Knights, I'll call you back to fix a time and place to meet him. Once you have the diaries, call or telex me using the codeword' – he paused and suddenly thought of his wife – 'Elspeth. That'll mean that everything's kosher. I'll then call the New York bank and tell them to transfer the money to Switzerland. Have you got that?'

'Yes.'

'Good.' Magruder paused and when he spoke again his voice was friendly, even affectionate, 'I owe you a lot of thanks. It isn't often that a man gets a chance to pull off the big one.'

'Happy to oblige,' Grant said. He felt suddenly sorry for the melancholy American.

'Fine . . . fine . . . Well, I guess that's it . . . '

'That's it.'

'Let's hope that this is the one occasion in your life when the publisher doesn't get left in the shit.'

Thirty-two

13 December 1980

The courtyard was shadowed by the building, but, looking up, Helsingstrup could see the bright blue of the sky and a few scuds of broken white cloud. He glanced down on to the cobbles; there was a grey car waiting for him with the engine running and a driver in the seat; otherwise nobody except for a typist staring out of a window with lack-lustre eyes, dreaming of her boyfriend.

'That's right, the car's for you,' the man behind him said superfluously. He urged Helsingstrup gently down the steps like a polite doorman showing the way out to an unwelcome guest.

'Where am I being taken?'

'To a safe house,' the man said. 'The driver knows the address. You can stay there until everything blows over. Don't worry.' He put an arm round the elderly man and escorted him to the car, pausing to open the passenger door. Helsingstrup thanked him, maintaining the pretence that a favour was being done.

'Do you want your stuff in the back or in the front with you?' The man held out a small canvas bag holding some toiletries and a change of underwear. Helsingstrup made room at his feet; his legs ached from a throbbing varicose vein.

A voice said, 'You didn't sign.' A stranger was coming down the steps. The escort and the newcomer exchanged a few whispered remarks.

'He says you didn't sign the release form for your possessions,' the escort explained. Helsingstrup opened his tired eyes to see a sheet of paper clipped to a board being passed to him through the car window. 'Just check the list and sign,' the man said.

'One of my shirts is missing,' Helsingstrup murmured. As if they cared.

'Well, sign anyway,' the escort said. 'If it turns up, we'll send it on to you.' Helsingstrup signed.

The driver spoke. 'Bloody paperwork, eh! Makes you sick!' He slipped the car into gear and they glided out of the courtyard and on to the embankment by the Seine.

'You're not French,' the driver said indifferently.

'Swedish – you don't know about me?'

'None of my business. I'm just the babyminder. I take you to a safe house and then hold your hand.' The driver glanced away from the road to catch a closer glimpse of his passenger. Helsingstrup noticed the other man's muscled look, as if he could take care of himself; he had small, wrinkled eyes and a cleft worn into his front teeth by the stem of a pipe.

Helsingstrup remembered Dumergue's parting shot before he had left the Quai d'Orsay.

'There's nothing to worry about,' Dumergue had said smoothly. He took a mint from a small box of lozenges and transferred it to his mouth. 'Sincerely, Baron, you are very important – one might almost say "unique" – as a witness. We are very concerned to take care of you.'

They were in the large conference room where Grant had been interviewed. It seemed empty because Dumergue and the old man were alone, as if the others associated with the business had found an urgent need to be elsewhere.

'We have a number of safe houses in the Paris area for the use of people whose well-being is important to us,' Dumergue went on. 'You can stay in one for as long as may be necessary.'

'How long shall I be there?' Helsingstrup said. He looked out of the car window at the traffic. When will they come? he asked himself. They won't be able to leave me alone. Sooner or later they'll find me.

'Did you say something?' the driver asked.

'This safe house – how long shall I be there?'

'Don't be impatient' – the driver misunderstood him – 'you'll only be there two days.'

'Two days?' Helsingstrup suppressed the latent panic. 'They said I was to be protected for as long as necessary.'

The driver was unimpressed. 'How long is "as long as necessary"? Someone has to make a guess. And in your case it's two days.'

'And then? What happens afterwards?'

'How should I know? They'll probably provide you with new papers – a new name. After that you're on your own. You'll make out all right.'

Helsingstrup stared at the other man's blank face and then turned away. He knew the thoughts that had gone through Dumergue's mind: 'We offered him protection for as long as necessary – those were the very words I used,' Dumergue would say with the taste of menthol still on his breath. 'We cannot be held in any way responsible for his death.'

The house was small and suburban, set in a quiet avenue of lime trees. The driver who by now had given his name as Leclerc – which was probably false but served its purpose – put the car in the garage and carried Helsingstrup's bag inside.

'Shouldn't there be two of you?' Helsingstrup asked.

'Still worried, monsieur?'

'If I'm to be constantly guarded, shouldn't there be at least two of you?'

Leclerc grinned. 'I wouldn't keep thinking about it if I were you. Someone will turn up.' He switched on the television set then went into the kitchen to make some coffee. From there he shouted, 'You can take your pick of the bedrooms. And if you get fed up of the TV we can play cards.'

'Will you be here all the time?'

'Probably.' Leclerc came out of the kitchen. He had taken off his jacket and was wearing a gun in a shoulder holster. 'They may want me for something else, in which case they'd send a replacement. But, frankly, that's unlikely. I mean it's unlikely that they'd want me for something else, not unlikely that they'd send a replacement.'

'I understand.'

'Do you?' Leclerc said and Helsingstrup detected a wistful note in the other man's voice and wondered why. The Frenchman subsided into an armchair and faced the television screen. 'Coffee's in the pot. There are some beers in the refrigerator. Just help yourself.'

The old man nodded. He wondered at Leclerc's remark. Why was it that he would not be required for anything else?

The afternoon passed. Leclerc seemed to have an insatiable appetite for television. Helsingstrup drifted about the house, occasionally staring out of the window, disturbed by the sound of passing cars, only to see mothers with their children talking to other mothers. He tried a book; there was a selection to choose from – Zola, Simenon, Ian Fleming. Whose taste? Perhaps the aggregate taste of all those who had sought refuge in the house.

The house itself lacked identity; it was like a curious hotel. The refrigerator where the beer was kept had a lock to it and a sheet of paper on the door, listing the contents, to be ticked off as they were consumed. The coffee came in catering sachets.

Leclerc's eyes drifted away from the screen and he noticed Helsingstrup by the window. 'Come away from there,' he said. 'Do you want to make yourself an easy target?' To Helsingstrup he sounded unconcerned, as though he were just repeating a formula.

'Do you play chess,' Leclerc asked. He turned off the television. 'I learned the game – from a Russian. They're crazy about it and this defector was no exception. He was a great player. Do you want a game?'

'No thanks.'

'Suit yourself.' Leclerc turned the set on again. A children's programme faltered on the screen.

'Do you ever see people again – after they've left here?' Helsingstrup asked.

'No, never.'

'Do they all make it – establish a new life?'

For a moment Leclerc showed some sympathy. 'I wouldn't know. They wouldn't want us around. Not afterwards, would they?'

'I suppose not.'

'You believe it. After all, they come out of here with new identities; and often with quite a bit of money. I sometimes wish that instead of retiring me they would give me the same treatment.'

Helsingstrup looked away from the titles on the bookshelf and examined the other man. How old was he? Forty-five? At what age would he retire? It was difficult to say in his job.

'I've got twelve months to go until my time is up,' Leclerc

said. He added hastily, 'I don't have to go – they give me a choice. I fancy opening a little business of my own.' He gave a smile of self-satisfaction in contemplation of himself as a businessman, and, watching him, Helsingstrup knew what it was about the other man that troubled him. He looked expendable.

Night fell. Leclerc did the rounds of the house, drawing the curtains. No relief had arrived and he was increasingly edgy.

'Why don't you go upstairs and read a little there? It isn't as if you're watching television,' he said.

'It's safer upstairs?' Helsingstrup asked, but all the same went to his room. He sat on the edge of the bed, thinking.

Downstairs he heard Leclerc pick up the telephone and dial a call. Out of the low murmurings Helsingstrup could pick up only a few words.

'Sure the old man's safe . . . two men promised . . . aren't I supposed to sleep? . . . I want help . . . ' There was a long gap as if someone were giving an explanation. If so, it failed to impress, for Leclerc muttered '*Merde!*' and slammed the receiver down. Helsingstrup heard him light up a pipe and turn the television on again. The news for the umpteenth time that day – Poland, the Xanten case – war and rumours of war.

There was no one coming to relieve Leclerc – Helsingstrup knew that fact as if it had been spelled out to him by Dumergue. Only the poor devil downstairs didn't know. Going to the French authorities had all along been a mistake. He was an embarrassment to them and to their precious détente with the Russians.

He was struck by the chilling realization that his safety lay not in the ambivalent embrace of the Quai d'Orsay but in publicity. If he had told what he knew to the press, the Russians would have prevented *Die Spinne* from touching him for fear of confirming his story.

Thinking along this line, it came to him that an approach to the press was still possible – if only he could get out of the house!

Helsingstrup put on his coat and went carefully downstairs, his footsteps masked by the sound of the television. He glimpsed Leclerc through the doorway. The Frenchman was nervous. He was peering through the window across the empty street, his left hand unconsciously squeezing a beer-can.

The door of the kitchen to the rear of the house was double-locked and chained, but to unlock it seemed to pose no problem. It was only when he did it that Helsingstrup tripped the alarm bells.

Leclerc was after him as soon as he made his run, tearing through the kitchen, pulling his gun from its holster. Helsingstrup heard him calling his name up the stairs, thinking at first that someone had broken in rather than the opposite, but it took Leclerc only a second to realize the truth.

It was dark at the back of the house, with no more light than the urban haze. Helsingstrup headed for the shadow of a fence; behind him he heard more bells jangling and guessed he had tripped a pressure alarm in the grass or broken an electronic beam. Then suddenly the small garden was flooded with light.

'Come back inside,' Leclerc said. He waved his gun in Helsingstrup's direction but there was no menace in the gesture. His tired voice said wearily, 'We're both too old for this game.' With that he let the gun fall by his side, his other hand resting on the switch that controlled the spotlights. He stood there for a moment in the open doorway, watching the old man cowering under the cover of the fence, nursing the pain in his chest.

'Well? Are you going to come in?' Leclerc said.

Helsingstrup looked up. Is he under orders to kill me if necessary? he wondered. But he didn't find out whether his fears were justified. There was a thud rather than a shot, and Leclerc was lifted by an invisible force and spread-eagled against the wall, his chest emblazoned with blood.

Then Helsingstrup started running.

He was in a quiet street without any recollection of how he got there. The sensations of his ageing body labouring under the strain of running blacked out all conscious processes and, in the end, he stopped not because he was safe but because he could run no further.

He looked about him. A road, a few parked cars, some railings, and, behind them, the beaten earth and sparse grass of a children's playground with the outline of a slide framed against the glow of sodium lights in the night sky. Knowing that he had to rest and think, Helsingstrup squeezed through a gap made by the children in the iron palings and stumbled to the shadow of a bush were he fell to his knees in a litter of dead leaves and Coca-Cola tins.

Slowly his breathing eased and the world slid more firmly into focus, the white noise of motor-cars, snatches of music and, somewhere, the distant rattle of a train. He looked around at the expanse of playground lying grey and dead under the diffuse light of the city, the skeletons of metal apparatus throwing long shadows on the rank grass. Slowly he moved to ease the pressure on his buttocks from the damp earth and massaged the painful veins in his legs.

What to do? He was on his own, cut off from the resources of his apartment and his well-lined bank accounts; and if the French didn't get him, the two Englishmen sent by *Die Spinne* – he guessed they had shot Leclerc – certainly would. The same thoughts recurred. He had to get publicity!

He had no idea where he was, but there had to be a café nearby where he could make a telephone call to a newspaper. He struggled to his feet. There was a temptation to stay in the anonymous security of the darkness and loneliness, but he knew it was an illusion. The reality came as he moved: he heard the snap of a shot breaking a branch somewhere in the trees and his heart began to pound again.

Two men were climbing over the metal railings. They must have seen him as he stepped out of cover. He started to run again, keeping to the broken shadow of the bushes, hoping that the fence would delay his pursuers for long enough to get out of the railed-in trap he had set for himself. A second dull shot was snapped off in his direction.

He reached the far side of the playground – more palings. Climb them or find the gate? Footsteps behind him left no time for decision; his reflexes compelled him to take the shortest route over and he could only pray that they didn't see him or that the distance was too far for a shot to have much hope of success. On both counts he was wrong.

One foot was in the gap between two rails at the top of the fence when the bullet slammed into his shoulder and threw him to the ground on the far side. He felt the crack of knee and elbow as they hit the stone of the pavement and lay there in shock.

Seconds or hours passed – he didn't know which except that he was still alive. His right arm hurt him as if it were broken and there was a burning sensation from the same shoulder, but nothing to see except a tear in his coat and a few beads of blood. Helsingstrup got to his feet and looked around him. The quiet suburban street was gone. On this side the playground bordered a fairly busy road with passersby staring as they walked and hurrying off back to their own lives. On the other side of the road there was a café.

Helsingstrup felt a faintness coming over him as he staggered through the door and collapsed on to a seat. The bar was quiet, the proprietor standing behind the zinc obsessively minding his own business and two Algerians in blue overalls sitting sullenly over a bottle. A whore wandered in off the street, took a speculative look around and pushed off to the next stop on her beat.

'You want a drink, m'sieu?' the barman enquired as if selling them wasn't his business.

'Cognac . . . ' Helsingstrup put his hand tentatively to the injured shoulder and felt the moistness of his blood. He fingered the tear in his coat and guessed that the bullet had only grazed the skin. He reached in his pocket and found a few coins and a couple of notes stuffed there. The drink came. 'Do you have a telephone?'

'In the corner.'

He looked around and spotted the instrument half-masked by a wood and glass partition; using his left hand he pushed to his feet, paused whilst the room took a swim, and then made his way to the booth.

Two directories, torn and minus covers, lay in a corner. They were damp and smelled of urine. Painfully Helsingstrup stooped to pick them up, placed them on the narrow wooden shelf by the phone and leafed through one trying to find the number of *Le Monde*.

'What's up? Trying to call a friend?' A hand swept down and replaced the receiver on its cradle. Helsingstrup looked up into the dark eyes of the Englishman.

'Come along with us, eh? We might have a few things to talk about. Don't want to be causing a fuss, do we? What do you say?'

The old man turned around. The other's fair-haired companion was standing by the door, the barman watching them all with indifferent eyes.

'Don't look to him for help,' Harrison said. He nodded towards the barman and then indicated the two Arabs. 'This place is full of fucking wogs knifing each other most days of the week. Who cares as long as nobody dies before he's paid for his drink. So what do you say?' He smiled at the barman, 'How's business, eh? England for the World Cup, eh?' Then he turned to Helsingstrup, 'See what I mean? Ignorant sod – doesn't even support England.'

Helsingstrup let his hands fall by his sides. He was a dead man if he went outside, but he was equally dead if he stayed. His instinct was to cling to the last moments of survival. He allowed himself to be led out into the street.

They stood on the pavement. 'What do you want with me?' he asked, recognizing the banality and pointlessness of the question.

Harrison smiled thinly. 'Don't worry. It's just a few of our friends who want to talk to you. Get the car, Frank.'

'Are you going to kill me?'

The other man sounded hurt. 'What, us?' He glanced up and down the road as if waiting for a taxi. 'Trouble with you is you're too self-important. Who'd want to kill an old has-been like you? The world's passed you by. It's ordinary working blokes like me who've got to carry on the fight against the Reds and the niggers.' He nudged Helsingstrup in the ribs and gave a sharp laugh. 'Honestly, there's just a couple of blokes who want to know what it is you've been telling people.' He moved Helsingstrup along the pavement. 'Let's pretend we're just taking a stroll – just nice and easy and not too fast.'

Slowly they walked a few yards, the Englishman holding the old man's coat-sleeve, pausing to stare at the reflections of the traffic in shop windows, looking for Lethbridge to bring up the car. Helsingstrup realized why they hadn't killed him at the café: they had left their car somewhere near the 'safe house' and wanted to be certain of their escape.

'Do you want to know why I am being killed?' he asked.

Harrison's eyes turned momentarily away from the glass. 'No. And don't tell me.' He looked past the old man along the street. 'Where the bloody hell is Frank?' Passers-by brushed against them as they loitered in a doorway. A woman carrying two bags of late-night shopping paused to transfer them from one hand to another and shift the burden. Three labourers, talking in loud voices as they walked, stopped to argue the toss about something. Harrison watched the stream of cars impatiently.

The blue Citroën came crawling along the pavement, Lethbridge's pale, elegant features visible through the windscreen. 'This is it,' Harrison said as his partner leaned over to open the passenger door. It was all he had chance to say before all hell broke loose.

Harrison's snake-like eyes caught the familiar movement. One of the labourers was reaching into his jacket with a look of determination. The Englishman anticipated the move even before it was completed and his own gun was out and firing.

'For chrissake let's get out of here!' he yelled to Lethbridge as he dropped one of the men and the other two reached for their own weapons.

In the car Lethbridge saw the move as it was coming, hammered his foot on to the accelerator and pulled the car hard over with his partner hanging on to the swinging door. But he was too late. He had reckoned without the woman, who, even as he reacted, had dropped her bags and was sliding a shotgun out of one. He caught the flash of lights from oncoming traffic and the blare of horns and then the discharge of two barrels at a range of five yards through the windscreen of the car slammed him back into his seat.

As Harrison swung himself into the driving seat, the weight of Lethbridge's collapsing body kept the accelerator down. Quickly he grabbed the steering wheel and dragged the car back on course as it sped away. He reached over the bloody mess, opened the driver's door and pushed the corpse as hard as he could. One foot caught against the sill and for a few seconds the dead man bounced on the tarmac, dragged by the speeding vehicle, before he was freed and left on the road: Harrison spared it a glance and then was gone.

Helsingstrup was on the pavement where he had fallen when Harrison had released his grip. A hand helped him to his feet and he was hastily bundled into another car. A small man in a tired-looking safari suit passed a cigarette to him.

'For your nerves,' Max Weiss said. 'You are a very lucky man.'

Thirty-three

14 December 1980

To Grant, Zurich was a city that had succeeded in making prosperity unattractive. To reinforce that impression the hills around the city had trapped a cloud and mist and rain were sitting on the lake; and in the streets people went about their business, square and well-fed, in decent, sober clothes, looking as if they were selling each other life insurance.

Knights' instructions, relayed through Barton Magruder, were to stay at the Eden Au Lac, a half-hearted classical building on the Utoquai, which boasted one of the better restaurants in the city. On their arrival, Grant and Lisa unpacked their cases and went downstairs for dinner.

Two churches dominate the Zurich skyline. On the west side of the Limmat the green spire of the Fraumuenster looks down on the banks and shops of the Paradeplatz and the Bahnhofstrasse where Zurich tries its best to look like everywhere else. On the east side stands the Grossmuenster with its twin towers and around its feet a maze of small streets where the casual visitor may find an osteopath or a night club as the mood takes him.

The Club Ibiza advertised *Girls! Girls! aus London und Paris! 24 Stünden! Für die echte good time!* A dark-haired man in a red tuxedo jacket, who looked as though he'd had all the good times he could take, stood on the step, paring his nails and opening the door for customers.

'Knights asked to meet us in this place?' Lisa asked as she and Grant went in. 'This place' was a single room with about a dozen tables obscured in darkness except for the pencil torches carried by the waiters and the light from a film-projector that was flashing stills on to the curtain covering the stage.

'Wait till you see the show,' Grant answered.

'That's what I'm afraid of.' Lisa looked at the makeshift screen. The pictures were cartoons out of *Playboy* magazine.

Someone had fumbled with the frames and the English captions were in reverse, but nobody seemed to mind.

They took a table back against the wall where they could see everything, and when the waiter came they ordered drinks, two Loewenbrau beers.

'I don't like beer,' Lisa complained.

'Would you like champagne at fifty pounds a bottle? It's what the hookers drink.'

Lisa sighed, 'Okay, I'll stick to beer.'

There was a fanfare and a roll of drums which switched with the audible click of a cassette to the slow strum of a sitar and an enthusiastic voice boomed in English, 'From the jungles of Jakarta where love is still in the raw, the Club Ibiza brings you the beautiful Rani! Here to continue the good time, ladies and gentlemen, a hand for the beautiful Rani!' A trumpet ignored the sitar and the curtain was drawn back.

'Hey, she really is quite good-looking,' Lisa said admiringly as an olive-skinned girl in a flowing silk robe cut to the waist struck a demure pose.

'What did you expect?'

'I don't know – I kind of guessed she would be silicone from the waist up.' Lisa watched the girl slip the velcro fasteners and let her robe drop. Underneath she was wearing nothing but a pair of gold nipple-covers and a G-string and her oiled body glistened in the strobe lights. 'They don't waste much time getting down to the meat, do they? What's an Indonesian girl doing here anyway?'

Grant indicated the bar. Lisa followed the gesture and noticed three more girls lounging on high stools next to a couple of well-heeled customers. The shape of the eyes and the cheekbones was unmistakable. They hovered like frail puppets on the men's arms.

'White man's fantasy,' Grant said. 'They come down from Holland. The Swiss see so few dark-skinned girls that they can make a killing in a place like this. Then, when they get too fat or pregnant, the Swiss kick them out.'

'That's a pretty cynical attitude.'

'The Swiss are into hypocrisy like the Los Angelenos are into coke.' Grant turned back to the stage where the girl had removed her G-string and was grinding her neatly coiffeured pubic mound in the audience's face. The lights went out and the same irrepressible voice chimed, 'Rani, ladies and gentlemen! Your hand please for Rani!' but nobody took up the invitation to clap.

Lisa checked her watch. 'Are we just supposed to wait here? Not that this isn't entertaining in a lesbian sort of way, but I can think of better things to do.' She paid no attention to the fanfare, the drumroll and the voice offering the next good time. From the corner of her eye she saw a door open beside the stage and the slim figure of the Indonesian girl slip out and into the bar where she slid easily on to a stool and put her hand on the shoulder of one of the florid-faced drinkers. Her glance drifted to a television set above the bar. Lisa looked at the picture and then at the stage. 'What is this?' she said to Grant. 'They can look at the stage but those characters at the bar are watching the same show on the TV set.'

'People are too real. The customers want images.' Grant finished off his beer and a waiter strolled over idly waving his torch to take a fresh order. He cast a scornful eye at Lisa and Grant was suddenly reminded of the old, stale joke pinned up among the bottles in a thousand English pubs: *We don't serve women in this bar – you have to bring your own.* Here they did.

The waiter came back with the beer. The voice full of fun was announcing the next attraction and Grant caught the words, 'And now, all the way from Sao Paolo! You thought *he* had died in Berlin, but here *she* is! Ladies and gentlemen we give you – Adolphine!' At that moment the house lights went on.

Grant kept his eyes on the stage. A spot was fixed on the curtain and the image of a swastika was projected on to it. Then suddenly it was flung back revealing the girl. There was a ripple of laughter from the audience and it was easy to see why. The girl was black.

She was tall, her height exaggerated by a pair of shining riding boots and her figure visible under the black SS jacket that hung open to the waist showing the ebony curve of her belly and the half-hidden swell of her breasts. Her face had an expression of arrogant humour and in her hand she carried a whip with the thong trailing down inside her breeches.

Her act was a stylish strip done with routine flair against the background of a small dais draped with a Nazi flag. She held a chair on which she gyrated so that the audience could have their standard peeps. Grant watched, knowing that the trappings were not just coincidence. They were a hint, a clue, or maybe just somebody's idea of a joke.

'Are you enjoying the show, Mr Grant?'

Grant turned away from the stage in the direction of the voice. The newcomer had already pulled up a chair and was ordering a drink from the waiter.

'My apologies if it isn't to your taste,' Knights went on. 'It isn't particularly to mine either – or am I just voicing the fashionable line that striptease is boring? At all events, I still enjoy coming here' – he threw a panoramic glance at the customers – 'it has all the interest of a visit to the zoo. Or perhaps you don't share my anthropological bent?'

'It's as good a place to meet as any,' Grant said and threw the conversational ball back to Knights.

'I confess I wasn't expecting Miss Black to accompany you.'

'I hope you've no objections,' Lisa said, bridling slightly. Knights' pasteurized English made her uncomfortable, and something in her quiet home-town background distrusted men who wore heavy gold bracelets and sported pocket handkerchiefs in flowered silk. 'I did a lot of the spadework on this project and Jonathan thought I might like to be in when the deal closes.'

'That sounds reasonable,' Knights said smoothly. 'And let's hope that we'll be able to finish with this matter quite shortly. What are your arrangements with Magruder-Hirsch, Mr Grant?'

Grant put down his drink. 'Magruder needs final approval from Rama and then has to set up the funds. He promised to call me when he had both and after that it's up to you.' He checked his watch. 'It's eight pm in New York. They'll be closing business in San Francisco. If Rama have agreed to put up the money, Magruder will call me tonight – he's no great respecter of other people's sleep.'

Knights wasn't very disturbed at the prospect either. He smiled and said, 'If he does call and gives his agreement, we shall make preliminary arrangements tomorrow to complete the contract. I shall telephone you in the morning to check.'

The arrangements made, Knights relaxed and took a sip of his drink. 'Well, that's settled. You are obviously satisfied with the result of your searches.' He raised an eyebrow in enquiry and his hand drifted to finger a gold Star of David which was held on a chain around his throat.

'It would have been easier with some honest co-operation.'

Knights was amused. 'But not as interesting.'

Grant waited but the other man offered no further explanation. Grant checked his watch again and eased back in his chair. 'If we've no other business I'd like to go back to the hotel and find out if Magruder has called.' He picked up Lisa's coat. 'You'll please excuse us.'

'It's been my pleasure.'

'Yes.'

Grant ushered Lisa to the door. She looked over her shoulder at Knights who was lounging in his seat, staring at the black stripper.

'Did you see that necklace he was wearing?' she remarked to Grant.

'He's playing games with us.' Grant was impatient.

'You're hurting my arm!' Grant released her as they stepped out into the street. 'That's better,' she said. 'What sort of games?'

'The secrecy game – I-know-something-that-you-don't-know.'

'Uh, huh? Well, he's picked the guy to play it with. I thought you invented the rules.'

Successful businessmen may have ethics, but they rarely have ethical doubts. When Barton Magruder learned from Grant of the complicity of Kosygin in the destruction of Warsaw, it fixed in his mind as advertising copy and remained that. Nathan Hirsch in his own quiet way pointed out the political dynamite implicit in the revelation, but Magruder put it down to his partner's congenital nervousness and chose not to think about it.

The reaction in Rama was different. It bordered on panic. Walter Emmett kept his nerve and fought off the rout, using the first technique for managing a business disaster in a large corporation: he tried to persuade as many people as possible that they were implicated in the fatal decision.

On 14 December, Magruder was called out to San Francisco to a crisis meeting of the board. Fritz Harfeld, president of the general electronics division, was there; so was Harry Warren of telecommunications. They were looking to the Lockheed contract and their general defence business and both were hopping mad.

'Jesus Christ, Walt!' Harfeld turned on Emmett. 'Didn't we tell you not to make waves – and now you've given us a goddam *tsunami*!'

That was for openers. In support they had brought along Otis Osgood, Rama's senior counsel, who disowned the legal advice that Emmett had taken and accused him of going to the legal department behind his – Osgood's – back. He had armed himself with a couple of legal memoranda that his department had prepared for Emmett and had underscored all the qualifications his staff had written in so that if necessary – like now – they could stand their advice on its head.

Emmett looked around for support among the others but got none except for Joe Katurian of the media division, who puffed his pipe and said he 'sincerely sympathized'. Magruder watched all this and thought Emmett was lost. Then he discovered why Emmett was senior vice-president.

In the middle of the row there was a rap at the door and when Harfeld opened it, there was a figure in the doorway, an old man in a wheelchair accompanied by a nurse. It was the old man, General McKinnon, whose family had founded Rama. From the expressions on everyone's faces Magruder knew that Emmett was the only one who had expected the arrival. As far as the rest knew, the Old Man was plugged into his kidney machine in his house somewhere up in the San Joaquin Valley.

'I believe there's something you want to tell me,' the Old Man said.

Emmett told him. The whole story, labouring the point about Warsaw. He waited for and saw the gleam in the General's eye.

'I always knew those commie bastards would sell their mothers if they got the chance,' the General said. 'It's about time we kicked their butts.'

At this point the waverers fell in behind Emmett and when the vote was taken only Harfeld and Warren held out against the deal.

At eleven forty-five Zurich time, Barton Magruder called Grant. He repeated the call the following morning.

Eleven forty-five was also the time at which the replacements always arrived to take over the midnight shift from the German civil-police guard at the sanatorium north of Wiesbaden where the Dutchman, Pieter Xanten, was held awaiting trial.

The building was the house of a former steel magnate, constructed with all the solidity, pomp and vulgarity of the Wilhelmine Empire. The walls were still hung with portraits of the German colonizers of East Africa, looking every bit as grand and as uncertain as their British imperial contemporaries.

The two replacements signed in at the night desk with a brisk good-evening and soon their feet echoed down the clean, tiled corridors towards the small room where the old man was lodged. Outside the room the two policemen being relieved looked at their watches and counted the seconds. The changeover was as smooth and as regular as normal.

The two off-duty guards exchanged a joke with the nurse at the night desk and went out by the main entrance. They saw the police Mercedes parked under the shadow of a tree twenty yards from the door.

Inside the house, one of the relief guards opened the door to the patient's room. Xanten was visible as a shape huddled on the bed under the weak glimmer of the night-light. The guard extended a hand to shake him, but, before he could touch the reclining form, the old man sat bolt upright and his thin voice, like an exhalation of breath, snapped, 'About time! Give me a gun!'

In the lobby the night-nurse looked up from the pages of a woman's magazine at the two guards and her patient walking towards her down the corridor from the private rooms.

'Where are you going with Herr Xanten?' she asked, folding the magazine on her desk top.

'He's being moved to Frankfurt for the trial.' The taller of the two guards took out some orders and snapped them open in front of her.

'Why wasn't I informed?'

'Search me.'

With her eyes the nurse did exactly that and her hand glided towards the telephone. 'It seems highly irregular to move a patient in the middle of the night without even informing the hospital authorities.' The hand had picked up the receiver and was poised to lift it to her mouth.

'It is quite all right,' Xanten said in his soft, old-man's voice and his hand slid into the pocket of his dressing-gown.

The nurse hesitated, fatally. Xanten's gun was out even before she could scream and the sound of the shot was no more than a sigh from its silenced barrel. The guard leaned over and arranged her body in the chair with the eyes closed and the magazine across her chest covering the neat hole. Then, with Xanten walking between his guards, the three men strolled out of the building.

Thirty-four

15 December 1980

Barton Magruder's call came through as Grant was taking his morning shower. The American kept it short: Rama had approved the deal and the finance was arranged.

When Grant went into the bedroom Lisa was dressing and listening to the radio.

'We're in business,' he told her. 'Rama is providing the money.'

Her voice sounded her relief. 'We're not the only one's coming to the end of a hard road. Max Weiss must be raring to go after his wait in Frankfurt.'

'What do you mean?'

'Nothing in particular. It was on the news: the Xanten trial opens tomorrow. Max can get down to a stretch of real reporting. Hey, what are you doing?' Her voice held a note of alarm. As the words came out Grant's face had changed as if suddenly everything had been made clear, and he grabbed at the telephone.

'What have I said?' she asked.

'What is the date tomorrow?'

'The sixteenth – Knights' deadline. It has something to do with the Xanten case?'

'We wondered what was going to happen on the sixteenth that made it so important to the deal – well, now we know one thing that was scheduled to happen!' Grant broke off there. Spruengli was on the other end of the line.

'I want to talk to you about the Xanten case,' Grant said.

'How did you know?' Spruengli sounded astonished. 'The news hasn't broken yet, so how did you find out?'

'About what?'

'Xanten! He escaped last night from the sanatorium where he was being held!'

Grant let the lawyer calm down and tell him the story. A nurse and two policemen had been killed in the breakout and the German police were already searching.

'I wish them luck,' Grant said. He paused then added, 'If you catch Xanten, I suggest you try him for the murder of the policemen – I'd forget about the original case.' He put down the receiver.

'Why should they forget the original case?' Lisa asked.

'Because Pieter Xanten never slaughtered those Polish villagers. He was telling the truth when he said that he was in Berlin at the time.' There was no opportunity for further questions because the telephone rang and this time it was Simon Knights.

'Did you speak to Magruder?' Knights asked.

'He just called.'

'And?'

'We close whenever you say.'

Grant heard an exhalation of breath and then, 'Excellent! There are some prior arrangements to make. I shall have a car collect you at your hotel. Shall we say ten o'clock?'

'What kind of arrangements?'

'You sound suddenly suspicious.' The voice was amused. More games – Grant thought. He was reminded of Walter Schellenberg playing his games of diplomacy whilst the world burned. People like Knights were unreal: they lived out images of themselves as if they were followed everywhere by a movie camera.

'All right. I'm not suspicious. I'll be outside the hotel at ten,' Grant said and put down the phone. He let the jumble of his thoughts take a spin around his head and then focused on Lisa. 'It's time to get packed. We're leaving.'

'This is it – we close today?'

'You're taking the next flight to New York.'

Lisa's eyes opened; then she sat firmly on the bed. 'The hell I am! Hey, who was it said that?'

'Albert Schweitzer.' Grant reached for her suitcase and placed it open on the bed.

'Well, nuts to the whole idea! The deal was that I stayed to the end. You can't break our arrangement.'

'Sue me,' Grant said. He pulled open a drawer and began to turn out its contents. Lisa watched him without moving as he piled some clothes into her case. He paused, his eyes caught hers. He stumbled over the words without thinking. 'I believe there's a convention that a man is supposed to stop the woman he loves from getting into danger. Knights is about to turn dangerous.'

Lisa's reply showed that the words hadn't fully sunk in. 'You sound as conventional as my father,' she said.

'Which one, the millionaire or the other?'

'I take it back. You sound like my mother.' She watched Grant snap the suitcase shut, 'Except that you don't know how to pack. Here, give it to me!' She reached over and dragged the suitcase towards her.

'I'm glad you see reason,' Grant said.

Lisa didn't respond. Her hand poised itself over the suitcase lock and then halted. She looked at Grant and asked softly and uncertainly, 'Did you just say that you loved me?'

The car that Knights sent was a black Volvo. The driver was standing with the passenger door open, a small, stooping man who looked as though he carried his own personal raincloud; he wore a small black hat with a feather and a shiny blue raincoat with dark stains over the shoulders as though it never had chance to dry out.

'Herr Grant?'

Grant nodded and slung his suitcase into the back of the car. The driver waited for him to get in and then slipped the car into the stream of traffic along the Utoquai.

'Where are we going to?' Grant asked. Almost immediately they had slid off the main highway and up a street lined with cement-grey villas hiding behind cast-iron railings. The driver didn't answer.

The road ran roughly parallel with the lake which was visible in the breaks between the buildings. On the far side of the water, Grant could see grey-green hills and the transmitter on top of the Uetliberg from which he could tell their general direction. The driver remained silent all along, concentrating on the road except to turn on the radio and pick up an Italian broadcast.

The route following the line of the lake didn't last. The driver turned left and they started to climb a hill between rows of the same large, dull houses with their tarnish-green shutters. Then the houses became less frequent and bigger, fronted by high walls overhung by the dripping branches of trees. The Volvo turned into the drive of one of these houses.

The porter carried Lisa's case out of the hotel. She looked up at the break in the watery sky and then down the steps to the taxi that was waiting for her. Mentally she was damning the English and all their works, but she composed her face and got into the car.

'Take me to the airport,' she told the driver. He nodded and set the meter.

The drive through Zurich didn't interest her. Like Grant she had decided that she didn't care for the place; so instead of watching the sights she settled into her seat and conducted a mental argument with the man she loved in which she scored all of the best points. She only took notice when the driver said something.

Lisa opened her eyes. They were already on the fast stretch of the highway to Kloten. She recognized a car showroom and the façade of a furniture hypermarket. The driver was tapping the petrol-gauge and muttering in hesitant English, 'Gasoline . . . need gasoline . . . *verstehen Sie*?' He indicated a filling station that was visible half a mile away.

'You need to fill up? Sure, that's fine by me,' she said. 'I'm in no rush.' She settled into her seat again and amused herself with the thought that even cabs ran out of gas sometimes. Even though it had never happened when she had been in a cab before.

Grant stood at the long window and stared across an expanse of uncut lawn at a dark cluster of yew trees. The room he was in was large, cold and empty except for a pair of bentwood cane chairs with frayed seats and a carpet that was too small and only emphasized the emptiness. The walls were washed a pale green with paler patches where pictures had once hung, there was a large carved stone fireplace that someone had stuffed with red foil to give an idiot's impression of flames and, lost in the space, was a small electric fire with a single bar that glowed to no effect. The driver, hunched like a crow in his raincoat, stood by the door, cracking his knuckles.

A tap and the driver opened the door. Simon Knights came into the room, full of the same brittle bonhommie of the previous evening. He extended a hand to be shaken.

'Jonathan, I do apologize! This place' – he waved a hand –

'well, not as comfortable as one might wish, eh? Perhaps you'll permit me to offer you some hospitality. Where is Miss Black, by the way?'

'She had to go back to New York.'

'Really? No doubt there were publishing arrangements that she could help with.' Knights seemed unconcerned. 'I'm sorry that she won't be present for the handover of the diaries. Well, shall we find a more pleasant spot to have a drink?'

'As you like,' Grant said and followed Knights out.

'What can I get you?' Knights said as Grant sat down. This time the fire was real enough, as were the oak panels, the bookshelves and the Aubusson carpet. 'I anticipated whisky, but if there's something else that you'd prefer . . . '

'Scotch will be fine.'

Knights busied himself amongst the glasses and handed one to Grant. 'I gather you've spoken to our friend, Baron Helsingstrup.' He smiled, 'Yes, I know all about that. I suppose that I should have told you everything at the beginning, but, in view of the delicacy of the matter, we weren't sure what the reaction of Magruder-Hirsch would be and we didn't want to reveal the information only to find that we had no deal: in which case there would undoubtedly have been leaks and publicity, all at no profit to my clients.'

'And who are your clients?' Grant asked.

'You don't know?' The voice was disbelieving and mildly reproachful. 'Well, be that as it may, I have to maintain confidentiality. Would you like a cigarette?' Knights reached a box from the mantelpiece. 'They're Sullivans – or would you prefer American cigarettes having lived there so long?' Grant took one and allowed Knights to light it.

'I should be interested in your speculations,' Knights went on.

Grant watched the other man's cool ironic gaze. Games, always games.

'About the identity of your clients?' Grant asked.

'If you like.'

'Okay. Will you prompt me if I go wrong?'

'Perhaps.'

'I suppose I can't ask for better than that.' Grant drained his glass and began.

'The fundamental question has all along been how did the

diaries get out of the bunker? The date of the last entry was 28 April and the Russians captured the bunker on 2 May, from which it follows that either the diaries were carried away between those two days or the Russians have them.'

'That seems logical,' Knights admitted.

'Do you mind if we open a window?' Grant asked. 'The heat is making my throat dry.'

'Would you like another drink?' Knights said as he opened one of the panes. Grant shook his head. 'Very well. You were saying?'

'We know now that the Russians don't have them, which leaves as the only alternative that someone who was there at the end removed them.'

'The only alternative? What about the couriers that Hitler despatched?'

'They were caught and in every case the papers they were carrying were recovered. Those included Hitler's political testament which provided for the succession after his death: back in 1945 that was more important than the diaries and there's no way that the couriers would have hidden the diaries and yet given up the political testament.' Grant paused. His throat felt dry and he was hot. He looked at the window but it was open and the draught billowed the curtains. 'Can I have some water?' he asked.

Knights pressed the bell-push by the fireplace and asked for a carafe of water from the erstwhile driver. 'Do go on,' he said whilst they waited.

Grant coughed and heard the distant, cracked sound of his own voice. He murmured something about the heat and next Knights was pouring water from the carafe into a glass. 'Please – drink some water,' Knights said, his hand hovering in front of Grant's face.

Grant's voice rambled on. 'Some of the Nazis who escaped from the bunker were caught by the Russians. Most of them made it to the West and were captured by the British and Americans: they were interrogated and they talked.'

Knights' arm was by now around the Englishman and he helped hold the glass and force sips of water down Grant's parched throat. He took a handkerchief and wiped Grant's lips. 'But no one who was interrogated mentioned the diaries?' he asked. Grant shook his head.

'It had to be someone who took the diaries but was never caught.'

Knights prompted him. 'Bormann? You're talking about Martin Bormann? Do you think he's alive?'

'No . . . no . . . dead . . . Lehrter station.'

'He was killed near the Lehrter station? Go on.'

Grant tried to stand up but Knights held him down. Grant grabbed the other man's hand. There was a ring on the little finger with an image graven on a blue stone. Knights pulled his hand away but not before Grant had seen the carving on the ring. It was a spider – the emblem of *Die Spinne*. The recognition momentarily cleared his head of the oppressive heat.

'There were no papers found with the body,' he murmured. 'Someone else came across it and took them.' He looked up and caught Knights' quickened interest. 'It was someone who thought that he was safe from being questioned because he wasn't a German.'

'His name?' Knights demanded softly.

Grant smiled. 'Xanten . . . Pieter Xanten,' he said and passed out.

Thirty-five

16 December 1980

Consciousness came back ebbing and flowing like waves on a beach. States of mind dropped back into his personality like pegs into holes, one at a time leaving unfilled gaps. The first peg was amusement: he wanted to laugh, tell jokes, sway around like a drunkard, smiling in people's faces. It faded. He felt peculiarly lucid, detached, looking down on himself with perfect proportion. That passed too. His clear mind had seen the dark side of his life, the unconsidered, unadmitted motives, the fears hidden behind the show of action, and these came out from their hiding places and stalked around him screaming, 'Look at me for once!' He screamed in turn and woke up.

He found himself on a narrow bed, naked, his skin burning with beads of sweat. His neck ached, his mouth was dry. His right arm was swollen with needle punctures from whatever chemical-sleep had been pumped into him.

'How are you feeling?' a gentle voice said.

Grant risked a turn of his head and saw Lisa sitting on a bed at the other side of the room, pale and dark-eyed but intact.

'You don't seem surprised to see me,' she said. 'I guess you suspected it might happen all along. It was a nice try to get me out, only somebody sandbagged me at a gas station en route for the airport. That's life I guess!' She tried to smile. Grant began to move his limbs one by one. 'There are some clothes at the end of the bed,' Lisa said, 'and there's a washbasin. You'll feel a lot better once you've freshened up. I think there's even a razor.'

Grant made it to a sitting position. He ran a hand over his chin and felt the stubble: somebody had taken a day out of his life. 'Where are we?' he asked, not expecting that she would know.

'Still Switzerland I guess.' She gestured towards the window. 'You can see the Alps.'

Grant looked around and saw through the bars the blue-white of the snow, the dark bands of the trees and the massif of the mountains. It was daytime. If they were still in Switzerland, it had taken Knights the better part of a day to get him here. Bavaria? It was possible that they had slipped over the border into Germany to some haven kept for Xanten by his ancient Nazi friends. Grant turned at the sound of Lisa's voice.

'They were asking me questions . . . '

'Who?'

'Knights and a creepy Englishman with a Cockney accent. They wanted to find out what I knew about Max Weiss. I didn't understand at first who they were talking about since they kept calling him "that Jewboy reporter" like it was an insult, but then I realized it had to be Max.'

'What did you tell them?'

'What could I say?' She shrugged her shoulders. 'They were excited – I'd say downright worried – I got the impression that something had happened in Paris involving Helsingstrup and Max was mixed up in it. Then I remembered that I'd found Max in Koblenz looking through the old Schellenberg files as if he'd guessed about Xanten and the diaries all along.'

'Did you tell them about what happened in Koblenz?'

'No. Since Knights didn't appear to like him, I assumed that Max must be one of the good guys.'

Grant nodded and got to his feet. He looked around the room. The walls were of plain pine boarding and bare of any decoration. There were two simple metal-framed bedsteads and a clothes-press made out of beeswaxed pine painted with sprigs of alpine flowers. In the corner there was a washbasin and a pair of towels.

Grant splashed himself down with cold water until his circulation felt as though it was working. Then he dried himself and tried out the electric shaver. Feeling more like a human being, he put on the clothes, some slacks, a shirt and a pair of black, thick-soled slippers such as the Chinese wear.

'Who is Max working for?' Lisa asked.

Grant shook his head. 'I don't know. If I have to guess I'd say it's some Jewish revenge group, the same sort that grabbed Eichmann. His interest is probably in Xanten rather than the diaries: he wants to break up *Die Spinne*'s organization in Germany, and Xanten and his companies are the key to how the whole operation is financed.'

'I still don't understand.'

Grant sat on the bed and, the ideas still forming in his brain, struggled to explain. 'Do you remember what Spruengli told us about Xanten's defence?'

'Xanten said it was a case of mistaken identity: at the time of the massacre, Xanten was in Berlin.'

'That's right. Now just suppose Xanten was telling the truth; he was working in some government office right up to the end. And when it came, then just like everyone else he tried to escape from the Russians.'

'So?'

'So in Xanten's case his escape route happened to cross with the one that Martin Bormann had taken, and when he reached the Lehrter station he stumbled on Bormann's corpse. Although Bormann wasn't well known, he had appeared in enough photographs with Hitler for Xanten to recognize him and so he stopped and checked the body over.'

'And found the diaries,' Lisa said.

'That's right. But there was probably more than that. For months Bormann had been preparing a bolt-hole for the Nazis in South America and squirrelling away funds to keep them there. The amounts must have been massive and the only man who would know the full extent was Bormann himself. So, when Xanten took the package of papers that Bormann was carrying he probably had with them the contact list, the account numbers, the facsimile signatures – in short, everything Bormann would have needed to unlock the money.'

'I think I can guess the rest,' Lisa said. 'Xanten came back to Germany where he was safe as far as he knew, and he invested *Die Spinne*'s money in his engineering business. It would be a cover for making payments to his fellow Nazis. . . . But why should he sell the diaries if he already had money?'

'Because suddenly he didn't have money. Spruengli told us as much: the German tax authorities started turning Xanten's companies over, which must have put a stop to the deals he was doing for *Die Spinne*. On top of that he found himself under arrest and all his business affairs under scrutiny. That must have been enough for him to want to turn all his liquid assets into cash. And the diaries which it had been too dangerous to sell before just *had* to be sold.'

'To us or to the Russians. That's just terrific.' Lisa gave a pale smile and said hopefully, 'Well, so far we're still alive and maybe nobody intends us any permanent harm.' She looked at Grant for some sign of agreement, but he was staring out of the window.

Grant guessed from the height that there were two floors below the one they were on and nothing above; the sun was throwing shadows of the bargeboards at the eaves across the glass. There was a narrow space directly below the window and two cars parked on it. Beyond the space fresh snow stretched away to a clump of trees that thickened into a wood.

He looked to the side as far as he could. To the right the mountain sloped sharply upwards and disappeared from view. To the left it went downhill between folds of ground and he could see for about a mile. There was more snow and trees and, in the distance, a large steep-roofed chalet of a size that suggested it might be a hotel. Beyond that there was nothing.

'If your horoscope says that the future isn't too bright, maybe you'd better think of a way out of here,' Lisa suggested.

'Any ideas?'

'The usual stuff, slug the guard and fight your way out with your sword. I'll leave the details to you.'

'I forgot to pack my sword,' Grant said and turned to the sound of a click as somebody slid back the judas-hole in the door.

The door opened revealing two men. There was an incongruity in their appearance, each of them aged about sixty and each of them with the determined look that Grant had seen too many times in professional soldiers. He didn't have to be a small-arms freak to recognize the M16 carbines they were carrying.

'You will please come with us,' the bigger of the two said. He jerked the barrel of his gun towards the door and, since the alternative to agreeing promised to be fatal, Grant and Lisa followed him. It wasn't far, two flights of stairs to the ground to the door of one of the rooms.

The room was in the same warm pine and alpine theme as the rest of the house with a few trimmings imported to give the impression of a gentleman's study. Some chamois heads looked down plaintively from the walls at a collection of old prints, a pair of green-leather button-backed chairs invited you to sit on them and in a large free-stone fireplace a stack of logs burned on the wrought-iron dogs and blew a faint, resinous smoke into the air. It was a comfortable, friendly room that a European gentleman with amateur sporting tastes might have chosen. Except that in pride of place, on a turned mahogany pedestal, there was a bronze bust of Adolf Hitler.

Simon Knights was lounging in one of the chairs, reading a book. The ski-pants, the brightly patterned sweater and the snow-goggles pushed carelessly off the forehead suggested that he had just come in from skiing but Grant thought it as likely that Knights was faking it for effect. Playing games, living to his images – that was Knights' style. Grant suspected that the house, wherever it was, belonged to Knights: the effect created by the room was too contrived for the owner to be real.

'Can you arrange a snack for our guests?' Knights asked one of his henchmen. He turned to Grant and Lisa. 'I imagine you must be hungry. We dine at eight but I fancy you would like something before then. Can I get you a drink? Something not quite as powerful as last time.' He smiled with mild apology.

'Where are we?' Grant asked.

'Oh, at a little place near Lucerne. I'm sorry for the treatment that I was forced to administer, but we had to bring you here without the risk of your knowing more than was necessary.'

'And why have you brought us here?' Grant asked.

'To complete the business of course! Did you think that I might have a more sinister motive?' Knights' blue eyes glittered with insincerity.

'We're free to leave then?'

The other man brushed the question aside, 'I shouldn't think you would want to leave without the diaries. Would you?'

There was a knock at the door and the big man came in with some food and a couple of beers with the cold mist still clinging to the bottles. He placed them on the table and removed the tops with a soft hiss of gas.

'Help yourselves,' Knights said. Grant did and whilst he did so he examined the view from the window for a clearer idea of the terrain. It looked no better, the same expanse of unbroken snow and the dark contrast of the trees. The only new note was a figure about a hundred yards away, a man with a shouldered automatic rifle, pausing in his patrol to light a cigarette, and, by his side, the brown silhouette of a waiting dobermann. Grant had encountered dobermann guard-dogs before. He didn't relish the prospect of meeting one again.

There was a sound of laughter from outside. The door opened and two men came in talking cheerfully. They stopped as they saw Grant and Lisa, and the shorter of the two, a stockily built man with a broad, Slavonic face, round-cheeked and good-humoured like everybody's favourite uncle, nodded in their direction and then glanced at Knights, inviting an introduction.

'Jonathan Grant, may I introduce Comrade Golubyev,' Knights said and added, 'our friend represents a competitive bidder.'

Golubyev examined Grant with a pair of cold eyes that belied the good-natured impression and commented in English, 'I compliment yourself and Miss Black on your researches into the diaries.' He turned away and took a drink that was handed to him by his companion. The latter spoke to Knights.

'Don't I get introduced then?' he said and Lisa felt a pair of green eyes strip her naked.

'Of course,' Knights answered. 'Jonathan, Lisa, this is Mister Arthur Harrison.'

'A pleasure,' Harrison said. 'A real bloody pleasure.'

Golubyev addressed himself to Lisa, complimenting her on her dress. Grant directed his attention to Knights.

'I didn't know that this was supposed to be an auction.'

'I don't recall telling Magruder-Hirsch that they were the only bidder,' Knights said and extended his arm as if he meant to put it around Grant's shoulder but then thought better of it. 'I really shouldn't worry, though,' he went on. 'Our friend will have to come up with a considerably better offer than yours before we could accept.'

'For some reason that doesn't give me any comfort,' Grant said. He glanced at the window again and saw the sky dimming and the disc of the waxing moon glimmering over the snow. He checked the clock over the fire. 'I think I'd like a rest before dinner,' he said.

'But of course. I'll have you taken back to your room.' He turned to Golubyev. 'Perhaps, Alexei, you would like to continue your conversation with Miss Black over dinner. She and Jonathan have had a tiring journey.'

The Russian's eyes twinkled and he remarked, 'I look forward to dinner. It isn't often that one can conduct business in such a friendly atmosphere.'

Back in their room Lisa threw herself on the bed and sighed, 'What now? That creep Harrison was looking at me like a slaughtered lamb.'

'Anticipation on his part,' Grant said. 'If the Russians buy the diaries, then we get fed to the lions. In this case Harrison. Remember, as far as the Russians are concerned, this is a package deal: they get the diaries and the elimination of embarrassing witnesses.'

Lisa shuddered. 'What are you going to do now?'

'Sleep,' Grant said and lay down on the bed.

The judas-hole sliding back woke him. A voice snapped, 'Wake up if you intend to eat!' Grant gradually opened his eyes and focused on the light suspended from the ceiling, following the wire from it to the switch on the wall by the door. The door opened and Harrison was lounging in the corridor with an automatic rifle on his hip and a predatory look on his face. One of the geriatric guards was there for support.

They went downstairs again, passed the room they had first been in and halted at a door at the end of a corridor. Harrison opened the door.

Three men were sitting at a long, walnut table that was laden for dinner with cut-glass and porcelain. Knights and the Russian were seated opposite each other, chatting like old friends. It was no strain on the intellect to guess that the man at the head of the table was Pieter Xanten.

He looked old and tired, the sound of his failing lungs could be heard as a soft susurration, and his head with its falling jowels rested forward on his chest; but the eyes were sharp and alive, following the conversation of his guests. He had the sensual, commanding face of a man used to power.

A servant stepped forward from the back of the room to pull out two chairs and then went over to the old man and adjusted the scarf that he was wearing even in the warmth of the room. The conversation stopped and the eyes turned in the direction of Grant and Lisa.

Xanten made a token of rising from his seat and then subsided back into his place. He raised his glass towards them and said in a soft, breathless voice, 'I wish you welcome, Mr Grant.' Grant muttered a reply and the waiter was already serving soup and pouring wine. Lisa glanced over her shoulder and saw that Harrison had taken a position against the back wall where he was helping himself to a bowl of peanuts and waiting expectantly like a dog for scraps.

Lisa sipped nervously at her soup, catching a glimpse of the old man when she dared.

'I see that something interests you,' Xanten said. 'Is it that I'm not eating? I'm afraid that at my age the appetite for most things is diminished.' He smiled but for a second his eyes revealed the bleak abyss of his extinct cravings for power, women, success, the drives that had made him abandon his native country for Hitler's creed.

'Miss Black is merely ill at ease,' Knights suggested. He made a counterfeit attempt at urbanity. 'Talking about the weather seems somehow inappropriate to our little gathering.'

'There are other questions which you would like to ask but daren't, is that it?'

'I guess so,' Lisa said.

'Then feel free.'

Here goes! she thought. 'I always understood that war- . . . you people . . . would be based in South America.'

'Some are and some are not,' Xanten said. 'It is a matter of convenience and safety. You may forget your fantasies. There is no secret "Fourth Reich" growing to life in the Amazonian forest' – as he spoke his eyes softened – 'for better or worse, the struggle was lost. Those of us who survived are now old men, asking for no more than to be left in peace.' He paused and looked at Knights. 'We rely on the few who will listen to preserve our ideals.'

'Napoleon on St Helena?' Grant asked.

'Napoleon?' Xanten tasted the idea. 'Perhaps you are not

so far from the truth. He too was condemned and reviled, but history has come to recognize that he was a great man.'

'And you expect that history will say the same thing about Hitler?' There was no irony in Grant's question.

'History is a court whose judgements are always appealed,' Xanten said. 'You should be more aware of that than most.'

The waiter took away the dishes and served the next course. Knights poured the wine. A silence descended over the table, broken only by the sound of cutlery clicking against the porcelain of the plates and the rhythmic hiss of the old man's breath. Then Knights spoke.

'Really you should be complimented, Jonathan, on uncovering Fraülein Herder.' He looked across at Golubyev and went on, 'Even our friends in Moscow had no idea of her existence until your correspondence drew her to the fatal attentions of Mr Harrison.'

Lisa remembered that her letters had brought Fraülein Herder into the light and the remembrance made her feel sick. Knights observed her and seemed pleased.

'Fraülein Herder, it seems, had the misfortune to come across the diaries whilst working for the Fuehrer. Of course the poor woman never read them, but that scarcely mattered. What signified was that her testimony would have served to authenticate their existence. And that did not suit Comrade Golubyev and he insisted that her removal should be part of our deal.'

Golubyev took a sip of his wine and said calmly, 'The lady you interviewed was a substitute provided by Herr Knights. The real Fraülein Herder was eliminated out of political necessity.' He looked at Lisa. 'I'm sorry if that distresses you, but, in a sense, she was a casualty of the war. Her death would have been unnecessary but for the decision to sell the diaries.'

'Oh, sure,' Lisa said. 'You're sorry for having murdered her, but the responsibility was someone else's. I seem to have heard that before.' She turned to Knights. 'Thanks for telling me, I enjoyed the story. Does making people suffer beat sex?'

The silence was like a chill. Lisa bit her lip. 'I guess murder isn't a good subject for conversation over dinner.' She watched Knights, whose hands were frozen around his glass of wine. His face had a pale, deadly look.

Grant intervened. 'I thought we were going to talk business.'

'Yes, of course, so we were,' Knights said.

'Then can we see the diaries?' Grant said. Golubyev seconded the idea. The Russian sounded calm and friendly, as if he regarded Grant as no competition at all. It wasn't a reassuring thought.

Knights led the party to the basement of the house, a cellar that had probably started life as a root store and been transformed when somebody poured in massive concrete walls and barred the entrance with a steel door that looked as if it would withstand a nuclear hit, and maybe it would. It was fitted out for living in, half a dozen beds lining the walls, each with a bedroll on it, and a stock of provisions, still boxed, stood in one corner. It was tenanted. Another middle-aged man of the same military type as the guards was sitting by a high-powered radio with, close at hand, an array of weapons sufficient to embarrass anyone who came into the cellar without his agreement. When Knights opened the door, the guard was ready with an automatic pistol that would have cleared the room in two seconds.

'This is our nuclear shelter,' Knights said. 'And the diaries are kept in a strongbox here.' He opened a metal door that was recessed into one of the walls. The guard cleared a space on his table and Grant noticed the brown liverspots on his hands. They were hands that should have been holding grandchildren.

Knights took a metal case out of the safe and opened it on the table.

'There you have them, gentlemen,' he said and stood back.

The four volumes were each wrapped in plastic film with a sachet of desiccant crystals to keep out moisture. The diaries themselves were as the French bookseller had described them, though Grant doubted that he had ever seen them. The black covers had small brown spots on them and the silver pattern had tarnished, but the embossed eagle was still sharp and the general condition looked good.

Knights picked up the volume for 1944 and unwrapped the film. He flicked through the pages and found the entry that they all wanted to see.

It was all there, crammed on to the paper in miniscule writing which must have cost Hitler trouble since his eyesight was poor and documents for his personal use were usually prepared on a large-face 'Fuehrer-typewriter'. But on this occasion, sensing triumph, or at least revenge on the hapless Poles, Hitler had taken pains to set out the story in detail – everything as Helsingstrup had described it and more that the Swede had forgotten. The effect on Golubyev was stunning. He allowed Knights to close the book and said simply:

'I am satisfied. I will buy.'

Thirty-six

Snow had started to fall. The trees were dark smudges on the whiteness and the hotel, visible earlier, was now just a suggestion of lights somewhere down the mountain. Grant turned away from the window and heard the click of the key as Harrison double-locked the door. Lisa paused in pacing the room, feeling Grant's eyes on her, and asked, 'What will you do after all this is over? I'm looking on the bright side and hoping we get out alive. You'll be a famous man – how do you fancy being on chat shows?' Her voice had lost its defensive, sniping quality, 'I guess you'll go back to Kathy.'

'Perhaps.' Grant went over to the door and stood examining the light-switch.

'We never did hit if off, really, did we?' Lisa said. She slipped off a shoe and ran her toes over the floor.

'I love you,' Grant said without looking at her.

'What's that got to do with it? It's a case of whether two people can live together.' She stopped. 'But thanks anyway – I guess that among all the failures and the compromises it's a sort of victory.' She felt at her dress and then said, 'You know, I don't have a damned handkerchief to wipe my eyes.'

Grant had returned to the bed where he stripped off the blankets and dragged a mattress over to the door.

'What are your night-eyes like?' he asked.

'Okay as far as I know.'

'And your fingernails?'

'Not exactly manicure standard but they'll do. Why?'

Grant turned the light off. Outside he heard the sound of an engine starting. 'Golubyev and Knights have agreed on a price,' he said. 'The car will be taking Golubyev to wherever he's going. Quick, come here!' He pulled Lisa towards him and they stood in a pool of moonlight by the door.

'Now what?'

'I want you to unscrew the cover-plate from the switch.'

Lisa felt for the screwheads. 'I can't. They're sunk.'

'Then bite your nail to shape.'

Grant left her to work at the screws and returned to the window. There was a spotlight throwing a beam on to the gravelled space and a driver standing by one of the cars; snow had been cleared from its windscreen. Somewhere on the ground floor a door opened and a patch of light like a carpet covered the snow. He could hear voices and there were shadows hovering in the doorway.

'How are you going?' he asked Lisa.

'I've got one out but I've broken a nail. I don't know if my nails are strong enough to unscrew the other.'

'Try it,' Grant said as he watched a figure in a heavy coat clutching a parcel get into the car. 'Golubyev is about to say goodbye,' he said. 'Once he goes then it's just a question of how slowly Harrison wants to cook us.'

'I . . . think . . . I've . . . done . . . it,' Lisa gasped and pulled the cover clear disclosing the internals of the switch. Grant was at her side as soon as she said it. He moved her aside and went to work to expose the wires, pulling the positive lead out prominently and folding the neutral back.

'Is that it?' Lisa asked.

'Make up the bed,' Grant said and stepped off the mattress.

'What exactly happens?' Lisa said as she replaced the sheets into a rough semblance of order.

'I'm trusting to human reflex to switch on the light when entering a room. After that it's anybody's guess – I'm no electrician.' As he spoke Grant went over to the washbasin, turned on the tap and scooped up a handful of water. He crossed back to the door and threw the water on the floor by the switch. He returned to the basin and repeated the process another couple of times.

'Now we say our prayers.'

The snow clouds obscured the moon and the room fell into complete darkness. Lisa and Grant sat on the bed where they could be seen plainly from the door. They didn't speak; there was nothing either of them felt could be said. From below came the music of a violin sonata; Knights was choosing the mood music for his fantasy.

A few minutes later the silence was broken from outside by an engine noise and the chopping of blades.

'A helicopter,' Grant said. He looked out of the window. The machine wasn't visible but something was stirring up the snow from the ground. 'They'd be crazy to fly in this weather,' he said, 'but they don't have much choice than to get out of here tonight. Golubyev will be back in the morning with some KGB hoods to clean this place out.'

'That means they have to take care of us tonight,' Lisa said.

'In about five seconds,' Grant said and watched the cover on the judas-hole slide back and a pencil of light shine into the room.

'Turn on the light and stand where I can see you,' Harrison said.

'The light doesn't work.' Grant stood in front of the judas-hole where he could be seen and held Lisa to him. 'We're both here with nothing up our sleeves.' He moved back towards the bed.

The door opened slowly. Harrison and one of the ageing guards were silhouetted in the doorway, guns in their hands. Grant thought suddenly, They're not going to come in! They're going to kill us from where they stand.

Harrison advanced a step and stood squarely only six feet away. One hand held a gun, the other remained at his side. He grinned. 'For what you are about to receive, may the Lord make you truly thankful,' he said and raised the gun. Behind him his companion raised a hand to switch on the light.

There was a flash and the guard let out a cry. The whole house was plunged suddenly into darkness. Grant pushed Lisa to the floor as Harrison loosed off three shots that shattered the window, then he dived for the other man's legs.

His eyes unadjusted to the darkness, Harrison was blind, but he was a professional and he was armed. He brought the gun down in a swipe at Grant as he keeled over backwards and retreated on his hands to block the door. Grant ducked the blow and threw himself at the other man who lashed out with his foot, catching Grant on the chest and sending him spinning against the wall. Harrison got to his feet.

Grant lay against the wall. His shoulder felt as though it was broken and he wanted to vomit from the pain in his chest. He was trying to get up as Harrison raised his gun. There was a shot and Grant was rained with blood and fragments of bone as the other man's brain exploded through his face. Lisa was standing by the body of the dead guard, holding his gun in her limp hands.

There was no time to register emotion. Grant grabbed the gun and dragged Lisa after him out of the room towards the stairs. There were voices everywhere and the hammering of feet.

The whole house was in darkness. They ran into two men on the stairs. Grant kicked the first at neck height before he could draw level, and the body careened into the second and sent them both flying backwards. A voice below was asking what had happened and bellowing for lights. They reached the second flight of stairs leading directly to the ground. Someone had found a paraffin lamp and was guarding the bottom step. He picked up the lamp and held it out as Grant and Lisa came running towards him. Grant fired at the light. There was a blast and the figure folded up in a surge of flame. Behind the blaze a door stood open.

They were out in the snow, running across the open expanse, the cold cutting into their lungs. Behind them there was a bedlam of cries and shots and the yelping of dogs trying to get loose.

'Head for the trees!' Grant shouted and let Lisa run ahead whilst he turned to hold off the pursuit. But there was no immediate pursuit.

Lights began to creep back on in the house as someone switched the supply back on and there appeared to be a fire catching hold in one of the downstairs rooms. Figures were running about outside and Grant could see Knights in the doorway shouting orders. What he didn't see was the dog.

The dobermann came flying at him out of the darkness, a black shape with its teeth bared. The impact of its rush bowled Grant over before it could fix its fangs into him and they tumbled backwards in the snow thrashing at each other as the dog tried to sink its teeth into Grant's windpipe. Grant curled up to protect his throat and pulled his knees up under the animal, all the time grabbing for its forelegs. The dog seemed to sense what he was doing and its mouth tore at Grant's left hand laying open a wound to the elbow, but Grant kept his grip and pulled the legs outward against the arc of movement of the joint until he heard the joint snap or the ribcage break. There was a crack, the dog let out a howl and loosed its grip.

Grant rolled from underneath and started running whilst the dobermann struggled, kicking up the snow with its back legs and then lay silent.

'I'm here!' Lisa shouted. She was at the edge of the trees. Grant sprinted towards her, clutching his arm. Blood spots sprinkled the snow.

They had covered six hundred yards. Lights were clustering round the house and there was a roar of engines being choked into life. The helicopter they had heard earlier was visible in a veil of snow driven by its own blades. It was hanging like a hoverfly at roof level.

'They've got some sort of snow-buggies,' Grant said. The words were choked by the bile rising from his stomach and the pounding of his heart. 'They'll use the helicopter to look for us on the ground.' He gave an ironic laugh. 'It's like the Americans chasing the Viet Cong!' As he spoke, a white spot on the helicopter drove a shaft of light on to the ground and Grant could see the outlines of the vehicles. 'Our only chance is the trees!' he shouted over the roar of the machines.

They pushed on into the wood. It was dark with pine trees, broken only by spots of moonlight. The ground was covered with fallen branches and forest litter half-hidden by the snow.

'Can they follow us in here in those things?' Lisa asked.

'I don't know,' Grant said. 'My guess is that they'll circle this wood with the buggies so we don't get out and the rest of them will come after us on foot.' He looked up as the helicopter made a pass over the trees. They heard the chop-chop-chop of its blades and the down-thrust dislodged snow from the branches. 'We'll just have to hope that these trees are too many for them.'

Grant took Lisa's hand and they pressed on through the trees. There was an eery stillness, an absence of movement, just the flicker of lights at the edge of the band of forest and the sound of motors being forced through their paces. They made another few hundred yards and then paused for breath. Behind them a loose spangle of torchlights followed their trail. There was a crackle of automatic fire.

'They've seen us!' Lisa whispered.

Grant shook his head. 'They're just trying to draw our fire so they can get a fix. Come on.'

They started again, running as fast as they could in the

darkness across the steep, broken ground with its treacherous blanket of snow. Under their thin clothes the sweat froze to their skins. Behind them the lights got closer.

Ahead the trees thinned out to a clearing two hundred yards wide to the next belt of trees. One of the buggies was there, waiting, two men in it, one manipulating a searchlight, the other following the arc of illumination with a machine-gun. The helicopter made a pass overhead, hovered over the clearing then beat its way back over the trees where Grant and Lisa were sheltering.

'I don't think I can make it any further,' Lisa said. The voice was calm and there was no need for any explanation: Grant could see the flimsy shoes, sodden and torn to bits by the undergrowth and her bare legs, red and freezing. Exposure or frostbite would get them if they remained on the mountain, even if their pursuers didn't. But there was no way across the clearing whilst the buggy was there.

Grant raised the gun. He didn't know how many shots it held, but he did know that the chances of hitting a human target at a hundred yards were negligible; but his brain was running out of ideas. He loosed off the clip of bullets.

The machine-gun returned his fire even as he was shooting, and a swathe of bullets tore through the trees. Then there was a blast as the fuel in the buggy's tank ignited from one of Grant's shots, a ball of incandescent flame and the vehicle erupted with a wave of heat and shock that swept across the clearing and subsided as quickly into a burning twisted carcass of metal that rattled with random shots from the machine-gun ammunition. Grant and Lisa ran half-blinded to the safety of the pines on the further side of the clearing.

The explosion drew the hunt like moths to a flame. Grant had time to catch a glimpse of Knights standing in one of the buggies giving directions and then the chase was on again.

Grant looked at Lisa. She was finished, her body exhausted and cold. He looked at his own arm where the dobermann had gouged out a furrow of flesh. The wound was still losing blood. Grant knew that without help they would not get off the mountain.

He remembered the building he had seen from the window – somewhere to their right, perhaps a little further down the slope, there was a hotel, or, at least, people. He prayed that it wasn't far.

Lisa needed to rest every hundred yards, but Grant drove her and himself on, downwards and towards the right. It was a move that took them away from their pursuers who hadn't covered this side of the wood. Grant wondered why but hadn't time to work out an answer.

The trees ended. There was an open expanse of snow and then, like a cuckoo clock decorated in fairy-lights, a building that was thumping with rock music and life. Grant looked for signs of the chase but there was nothing except a sparkle of light a mile away in the sky, the helicopter looking as though it had given up and was heading over the mountains, and, somewhere in the wood the dim echo of voices and the gunning of engines moving away from them and down the slope. Grant slipped his arm around Lisa's waist and they staggered across the snow towards the hotel, where the sign hung under the eaves said Zum Goldenen Adel.

In the lobby was a pair of après-skiers, wearing the best negligence that money can buy. As Grant and Lisa burst through the door they gave a look of distaste and disbelief, then decided it was a management problem and moved off to get a drink. Grant helped Lisa to a chair and then approached the desk.

'I want the manager,' Grant said to the desk clerk. She was neat and polished and looked as though she was used to throwing out the poor but uncertain in their case. She called the manager and then, as guests began to leak out of the bar and restaurant, she collected them and tried to clear the lobby.

The manager came out of his office, a small, fussy man who, when he saw them, tightened the knot on his tie to say something unpleasant. Grant didn't give him a chance.

'I want you to call Lucerne or wherever the nearest town is and get the police. But first I want your girl to give me some help with my friend. She's injured and so am I.'

The little man looked at Lisa then at Grant and murmured, 'The police from Lucerne – yes, of course. Please, will you come this way and I'll have someone take care of you.' He opened the gate and lifted the counter top to allow them behind and then began excitedly, 'You look as though you've had a terrible time! Has there been an accident – a car crash? Please, you must make yourselves comfortable in my office. I'm sure there must be some first-aid we can do. Hot water, yes? Do you want some hot water?' As he spoke he ushered them into a small room laid out as a comfortable office. There was a log fire burning in the hearth and two big chairs looked welcoming.

The girl came in with some large towels and draped one around Lisa's shoulders to keep her warm. Grant had tied a tourniquet around his arm and there was a bowl of hot water on the manager's desk from which he washed the wound. The girl asked if they would like something to drink.

The manager came back. 'I've called the police,' he said. 'They'll be here in a minute. Have you managed to recover a little?'

'A little – thanks,' Lisa said, which seemed to please the man and he fussed around with a tray of glasses until he could present each of them with some brandy. He toasted their health finally and then said he had to get back to his guests. Lisa smiled at him and curled up warmly on her chair.

'I guess he must be wondering what a couple of monsters like us are doing coming out of the cold,' she observed quietly to Grant when the other man was gone.

'I imagine so.'

'What do we do now? We've saved our skins, but Golubyev has the diaries.'

'We have the text and we know that it's genuine,' Grant said. 'Bart could publish and take his chances. He hasn't had to pay.'

'So everyone's happy after all,' Lisa said wistfully. She stretched her legs and her toes winked at the fire. 'And what will you do?'

'Go back to my other book, write it, hope that it gets published. And you?'

'Find a college and see if I can get my Masters – at least I've had some experience of research now.' She sipped her brandy and grimaced at the taste. 'Thanks for saying you love me.'

'My pleasure,' Grant said. He bent over and threw a log on the fire.

She smiled. 'You Englishmen kill me.'

There was a knock at the door.

'Come in.'

The hotel manager came in, looking nervous and anxious to please. 'There's someone here to see you,' he said.

'Thank God for that, bring them in.' Grant turned away from the fire.

The manager held the door open and a man came into the room. It was Simon Knights.

'These are the people you telephoned about, Herr Knights?' the little man said. He hung in the doorway wanting to go, wanting to stay. In his small, nervous way he was a voyeur of life, haunting the fringes and looking in.

'You have done very well,' Knights said and added, '*Die Spinne* will remember you.'

He sat on the desk, one foot hanging loosely, tapping the floor. His blue eyes had a preternatural, exhilarated look. For a while he didn't speak. He seemed to be drinking in the prospect. Then: 'My congratulations, Jonathan – and you too, Lisa. I completely underestimated you.'

'I've heard those lines before,' Grant said. 'Which film was it? Probably one with a nasty ending.' He stooped and slipped on his shoes. He sensed Knights' smugness and guessed the cause. 'You called the hotel from the house before you set the pack on us? I wondered why it was so slow on our trail.'

'I couldn't be sure of tracking you on the mountain so I set the hotel as a bait to lure you and made it easy for you to find it.'

'There was nobody patrolling this side of the trees,' Grant said and knew that they had been perfectly trapped.

'What happens now?' Lisa asked. 'Do you murder us here or outside?'

'It hardly matters,' Knights said. 'And it will scarcely be murder, will it, Jonathan? More a case of suicide.' Grant didn't answer; he finished the remains of his brandy and put the glass on the table. 'You can't leave things alone, can you?' Knights said in a voice touched with insincere reproach. 'You have to pursue your illusion of truth, never taking facts at their face value. That's a fatal illness, Jonathan.'

Grant didn't waste a reply because Knights was listening to nothing but his own posturings. Amongst all the jaded gangsters who had survived the war with the help of *Die Spinne*, Knights and others like him kept fresh the old grandiose images to eke out and give substance to their own insubstantial souls. The gloss and paper-thin suavity only underlined his dangerously pathetic nature.

Grant stood up and helped Lisa to her feet. Knights backed away and opened the door. Another of his henchmen was waiting outside, a gun gleaming dully by his side. Grant looked up into the elderly man's lined, parchment face and tried to imagine the young SS officer it had once belonged to.

'Out!' Knights said and pushed them through the door. The hotel lobby was empty. In one of the rooms a band was playing an anodyne melody. The outer door was opened and Grant and Lisa stepped again into the snow and cold.

The clouds had passed, the night was glittering with stars. Knights shoved Grant along with the point of his gun whilst his companion stood clear in case Grant tried any move. They crossed the snow-covered gravel towards the waiting cars.

Grant recognized the green BMW. It had been parked outside the house and visible from the window. Knights opened one of the rear doors and told them to get in. There was a man sitting in the back seat holding a gun fitted with a silencer. As Grant stooped to get in, the man raised the gun and pressed the trigger.

There was a dull 'whup' and the bullet hit Simon Knights in the forehead.

Max Weiss got out of the car. The place had suddenly filled with men standing in the shadows by the doors of the parked vehicles. Weiss wiped his forehead and examined the bodies of Knights and his companion, whose death Grant had not even heard. Then he spoke the words of the Hebrew prayer: '*Shema Yisroel. Adonai elohenu. Adonai echod.*' He looked at Grant and Lisa who was held close to him, her head buried in his shoulder, and said, 'Let's go, shall we?' He held open the door and helped Lisa into the car; then he slipped into the passenger seat. The car drove off silently down the mountain followed by three others.

In an effort at conversation Weiss turned around and asked, 'By the way, Jonathan, have you ever been to Berchtesgaden before?'

Thirty-seven

19 December 1980

They met in the bar of the Zurich Hilton – Grant, Lisa, Max Weiss and another, younger Jew who gave his name simply as David. He was a tall, bronzed type, like all young Israeli men seemed to be, as if in one generation they had managed to breed out every trace and recollection of the ghetto. Grant recognized him as one of Max's companions from the time Knights had been killed.

For two days Grant and Lisa had taken refuge in their hotel room. Max had stayed away, simply leaving a number at reception where he could be reached when they wanted to know the world again. For a while they didn't want to.

On the second day Grant placed a call to Barton Magruder. The normally gloomy publisher was almost cheerful: he was glad that Grant had pulled through; he was sorry that they didn't get the diaries; no, Magruder-Hirsch weren't going to publish what they had – on the evidence, the photocopy text would lack authenticity. In the end they had done a deal with the State Department and salvaged the penalties they were incurring on the Lockheed contract.

'You have the diaries?' Grant asked Max. The other man still had the damp, rumpled look of someone who lived out of suitcases.

'We stopped Golubyev on the road before he could get away with them.'

'Did he put up a fight?'

'He's a survivor. He knew when he was beat, and that he was a dead man if he went home empty-handed; so he came quietly.' Max took a handful of peanuts from the small bowl that sat on the table between them and slung the nuts one at a time into his mouth to join the mints he habitually sucked.

'How did you know where the hand-over of the diaries was taking place?'

'We took a gamble on Knights' vanity. To his way of

thinking it was a great historical occasion. We thought he wouldn't pass up the chance of hosting it at his own place. It was as simple – as stupid if you like – as that. So now we have the diaries and Helsingstrup. We rescued him in Paris from a pair of Knights' hatchetmen. In fact we have all the original evidence.'

Grant nodded. He had been an amateur fishing in water reserved for professionals. He couldn't complain if the pros took all the fish. Which particular agency Max Weiss belonged to – Mossad or, as Grant suspected, some unofficial Jewish anti-Nazi commando group – remained implicit and unexpressed.

'Were the diaries the whole object of the operation?'

Max shook his head. 'We knew they existed and we guessed that Xanten might have them, but primarily we wanted him: we wanted to break *Die Spinne* and cause all the Nazis to rise to the surface like scum as the source of their money dried up.'

'We'll trawl them in gradually over the next couple of years,' the man called David commented with a calculated relish that turned Grant cold.

'How did you know that the diaries existed?' Lisa asked. She looked at Grant. 'I mean, we didn't even suspect it before Knights offered to sell them.'

'When Knights first opened negotiations with the Russians we got a leak through an emigré Jew.'

'And what will you do with them now?'

'It isn't my decision,' Max said. He looked as if he felt sorry for Grant, cheated of the only final victory he wanted – publication. 'There are Jews who want to leave the Soviet Union. Knowing we have the diaries, maybe the Russians will see reason. What good would it do to publish them? Would it make the Poles any happier to know the truth about Warsaw?'

'I don't make decisions on the Poles' behalf.'

'Uh huh – well, maybe. Have you heard the latest news? Kosygin died last night.' He flicked a peanut on to his tongue. 'The Kremlin haven't made their minds up yet as to what he died of, so the news isn't official yet.'

'Are you trying to suggest something?'

'Months before your involvement, at about the time that discussions were opened to sell the diaries to the Russians,

Kosygin was retired. Now that the Russians have lost the diaries, Kosygin dies. Who can say what the coincidence means? He was an old, sick man.' Max put his hand on Grant's. 'There are limits to where you can chase the truth.'

Grant changed the subject. 'You persuaded Rama not to publish what they had?'

'We paid them off.'

'Not too much, I hope – they must have been glad to get out.'

'No, not too much.'

Grant gave a bitter smile. He suddenly didn't want to talk to Max or to anyone like him whose job was to hide the truth. Max seemed to sense it. He looked as though he was searching for something to make the way easier for Grant.

'There's a joke on everyone,' he said with the trace of a smile. 'You lost your chance of publishing the diaries, the Soviets lost the evidence they were trying to suppress – and we lost Xanten.' He took another handful of peanuts and tossed them back. 'I thought it might comfort you to know that you're not the only one holding the shitty end of the stick.'

Lisa looked at Max gratefully. 'How did you lose him?'

'Search me! He was too old and frail to be running about the mountain with Knights after your blood, and when we checked out what was left of the house after the fire you two started, we found nothing. You think that's funny, huh?'

Grant didn't answer. He was recalling a report he had heard on the radio. A helicopter had crashed into the mountains in bad weather sometime on the sixteenth or the seventeenth. All the occupants had been killed. If Grant was right, Xanten was one of them. In the chaos and poor visibility of that night, Max had probably never seen the machine hovering near the house.

'He could be in South America laughing at us,' Max said.

'You're probably right.'

'What will you do now, after all this?'

Grant looked at Lisa. He wondered if either of them knew how it would stand between them tomorrow or the day after. With people there were no easy solutions. It was sufficient that, tonight at least, they would make love.

'You'll go back to your other books?' Max asked.

Grant looked up from his thoughts. 'I've not given up on this one,' he said.

Thirty-eight

24-25 December 1980

'Lisa?'

'Jack.'

Jack Robarts gave a jaunty grin that was begging for the assurance of a smile in return. 'How's things? Okay, huh?' He put down his airline bag and, on impulse, gripped Lisa by the hands and kissed her on the cheek. His smile peeked out again. 'I'm acting like it's kiss-and-make-up time, but we never really quarrelled, did we?'

'I've got no complaints,' Lisa said neutrally and let Robarts put his arm around her waist and walk her along. Their footsteps echoed from the walls of the pedestrian subway.

'I came like I promised,' Robarts said, 'but what sort of place for a meeting is this, the subway outside Frankfurt main station? Where's Jonathan that he couldn't be here? Another attack of the old paranoia?' Lisa paused and stared at him. 'I didn't mean it,' Robarts retracted. 'Jonathan's a warm, lovable human being. Is that any better?' He held her waist more firmly with the same misplaced intimacy.

They emerged from the subway on the far side of the street from the station, where there was a cluster of shops and hotels. Other streets full of small clubs and cinemas ran off at right-angles. They took one then turned off again into a nondescript side-street of cheap hotels and sex shops.

Lisa removed Robarts' arm from around her waist. Its associations of past affections, before she had met Grant, were of a time so remote that for Robarts to revive them seemed faintly obscene. They were on the pavement where the light from the hallway of a *pension* leaked out of the doorway and she had an excuse in moving out of the way of two swarthy types in working clothes who brushed past them and started to quarrel on their way upstairs.

'Turks,' Lisa said. 'There's an illegal gambling joint on the third floor.'

'Whatever happened to the high life, Jonathan Grant the successful writer?'

'Whatever happened to Jack Robarts, the up-and-coming marketing man?'

Robarts nodded. 'The diaries, I guess.'

They reached the second floor, a corridor dimly illumined by a night-light. Lisa knocked at one of the doors. 'Come on in,' Grant's voice said.

'How did you know where to get in touch with me?' Grant asked when they had settled with a glass of whisky apiece. The room was cramped with cheap furniture and Robarts sat stiffly on an upright chair whilst Grant sat on the bed, their knees almost touching.

'Your friend, the cop McCluskey. I figured that someone had an address at which a message could be left. You took everyone by surprise when you left Zurich in such a hurry and just disappeared these last few days. What happened?'

'What happened to you?' Grant answered. He caught the edginess in Robarts' manner that had nothing to do with jet-lag on the transatlantic crossing.

'The day the deal collapsed – well, Bart threw me out.' He looked up from his drink and scrambled his features into an ingenuous expression, 'Some story about a deal I was supposed to have done behind Bart's back.' He finished the glass and came fighting back. 'What the hell, it's a risk business.'

'So now you're out on the street.'

'You got it.'

Grant watched the other man help himself to another Scotch. He remembered the dinner party at Magruder's house: Robarts loading himself with booze because he had no other way of relieving the tension of ambition that was tearing him apart. He wondered what the other man was at now.

'So,' Robarts began slowly, 'I find myself on my tush' – he waved the glass in his hand – 'you know, the bastard just locked me out of my room – not even a chance to clear my goddamn desk. And naturally no copy of the diaries, since mine is locked up snug in the safe.' And that was it.

'You have some deal for the diaries?'

'Come on, Jonathan, I wasn't born yesterday. I know your track record, all your screwball ideas about the truth. You cleared out and hid yourself because you still want to see the diaries published and you're scared that someone will try to stop you. I even know about Max Weiss. He may be one of the good guys for now, but, if you publish the diaries, then he'll lose the lever that he has against the Russians – the lever he needs to get some Jews out of the Soviet Union. In his shoes I'd start to turn tough.'

'You have a proposition?' Grant asked.

Robarts relaxed a little as though he had won a victory. 'With a string of disasters behind you, Jonathan, your credibility is all fucked. No publisher, no newspaper, is going to take the diaries on the strength of your word. What you need is a good marketing man.'

'Like you.'

'Like me. Remember that I'm the guy who pulled all the punters when Bart couldn't even tell them what the title of the book was.' Robarts bent over and said with an air of intimacy, 'I know this stringer for *Der Spiegel*. I've got him interested and he thinks he can sell the deal to his paper. What do you say?' He placed a hand on Grant's wrist, thought better of it and poured himself another drink. He looked around the room and out of the narrow window at the bleak buildings across the street. 'Jesus, what a way to spend Christmas!'

Grant watched the other man. He had just been offered the chance to sell the diaries to a German magazine and yet he resented it.

'Is that all the diaries are to you?' he asked. 'A commodity?'

Robarts laughed and then turned serious. 'This is morality time? Okay! What good is the truth going to do for the Poles except get a few more of the stupid bastards killed? They can't revenge themselves for what the Russians allowed at Warsaw. At least Max Weiss has a purpose for the diaries: to help a few persecuted Jews leave the Soviet Union. What will publishing the diaries achieve except screwing up a world that's already screwed up enough?'

'The world is screwed up because people prefer illusions to the truth. Hitler, the diaries, Xanten, Simon Knights – what do you think that was all about except the pursuit of illusions?' Grant spoke with a calm passion.

Robarts stared into his drink and shook his head. He seemed more sober and collected. 'Man, you are one arrogant, English bastard,' he said softly. 'Me, I don't know whether the diaries are real or fakes. In fact I don't know how anybody knows the truth about anything for sure.' He paused. 'But you – you got that *killing* certainty that Hitler and Knights and all those other crazies had. You have this image of yourself as the knight in shining armour chasing after the truth. But' – he breathed in and seemed to hold his breath till it hurt – 'if the diaries *are* fakes, then I don't see that there's all that much difference between you and Knights.'

They sat quietly for a moment and then Grant asked, 'What do you need?'

Robarts shook himself slightly, like a man waking up; the marketing man forced his way back on to the stage. 'This guy I mentioned, he needs to see a copy of the diaries. I know you have a copy, the one that Bart gave you to work on. Can you let me have it?'

'No.'

'Why not?'

Grant looked at the other man, seeing in his eyes the changes that had been worked on him since the diaries came to light. He wondered whether to tell him the truth.

'Because I don't trust you. How do I know you'll hand the diaries over for publication? There are people who will make you a better offer.'

Robarts showed no surprise. He stood up, straightened his tie and picked up his airline bag. 'Okay, Jonathan, I don't hold any grudge. But if you don't deal through me, my guess is that you'll have nothing but problems.'

'I'll live with them.'

'That's your decision.'

They shook hands in a curiously formal and final way; then Grant watched Robarts walk the length of the hallway and disappear at the head of the stairs. He returned to the room.

'We'd better pack,' he said to Lisa.

'What, now? Are we leaving the hotel?'

'Yes.'

She shook her head and then laughed. 'Hey,' she murmured quietly, 'it's Christmas and this is Frankfurt. Where are we going to find a stable?'

Grant helped her throw some things into a case and then went to the window and pulled back the edge of curtain. In the darkness of the street he saw Jack Robarts cross to a car that was parked in the glimmer of a pharmacist's shop.

'What can you see?' Lisa asked.

'Max Weiss,' Grant said. He had noticed the hand extend from the passenger side and offer a candy from a packet of mints to Robarts.

Lisa joined him. She saw Max's face through the wound-down window of the car and Robarts joining him on the rear seat.

'I don't understand,' she said. 'What was that about?'

'Remember,' Grant said. 'Max is our friend, one of the good guys. I think he just gave us our last chance. He wanted to find out whether I was serious about publishing the diaries, and he gave me an opportunity to hand them over to Jack.'

'And what now?'

'He'll probably try to kill us. He may even succeed.'

They turned from the window and picked up their bags. Then they went downstairs where Grant stuffed some bank-notes into the hand of a surprised night-clerk before they left by an alley at the rear of the building.

They walked by side-streets to the same pedestrian subway by the station where Lisa had earlier met Robarts.

'Where do we go?' Lisa asked. She looked down at her hand and realized that Grant was gripping it closely and tightly to him.

'We could walk about the streets until dawn.'

Lisa laughed. 'That sounds impossibly romantic.'

'Doesn't it?' Grant said. He looked at her and felt the tenderness and compassion that is the substantial part of love. Then their eyes turned away and regarded the sterile tiled expanse of the subway, where dawn seemed a long way off. A man of about twenty, with fair hair and a wispy beard, sat against one of the walls, peaceably smoking dope. His guitar was parked against the wall next to him. As they went past, Grant reached into his pocket and threw a few coins into the cap that lay at the musician's feet, and in returned received a smile that was uncannily innocent.

'*Fröhliche Weihnachten*,' the young man said.

'Merry Christmas,' Grant returned. He hugged Lisa to him for warmth as they walked on and, behind them, the musician picked up his guitar and plucked out a few bars of 'Silent Night' before putting it down again and resuming his cigarette.